T0248200

ALL I SEE IS VIOLENCE

ALL I SEE IS VIOLENCE

A NOVEL

ANGIE ELITA NEWELL

GREENLEAF
BOOK GROUP PRESS

This is a work of fiction. Although many of the characters, organizations, and events portrayed in the novel are based on actual historical counterparts, the dialogue and thoughts of these characters are products of the author's imagination.

Published by Greenleaf Book Group Press
Austin, Texas
www.gbgpress.com

Distributed by Greenleaf Book Group

For ordering information or special discounts for bulk purchases, please contact Greenleaf Book Group at PO Box 91869, Austin, TX 78709, 512.891.6100.

Design and composition by Greenleaf Book Group
Cover design by Greenleaf Book Group
Cover images used under license from
©Shutterstock.com/Bogdan Sonjachnyj; ©Adobe Stock/Videohotdogs;
©Adobe Stock/fotoslaz; ©Adobe Stock/alona_s

Publisher's Cataloging-in-Publication data is available.

Print ISBN: 979-8-88645-132-0

eBook ISBN: 979-8-88645-133-7

To offset the number of trees consumed in the printing of our books, Greenleaf donates a portion of the proceeds from each printing to the Arbor Day Foundation. Greenleaf Book Group has replaced over 50,000 trees since 2007.

Printed in the United States of America on acid-free paper

24 25 26 27 28 29 30 31   10 9 8 7 6 5 4 3 2 1

First Edition

-For Ross-

My ancestors, you've been asleep for far too long.

This world is in grave, grave danger,

and it is time for my people to awaken from this nightmare.

Now gather around, for I have a story to tell, and I remember everything.

CHAPTER 1

▲▲▲▲

I LEAN AGAINST THE KITCHEN COUNTER, the cold metal edge cutting into my lower back. I feel myself sigh; the color of the sick green linoleum is only slightly improved with the light off, I think, watching the light from the living room cast shadows all around me. The gurgling of the percolator fills the kitchen with noise. I hear the light clinking of metal and glance at the open doorway to the living room.

"Nancy? That you in there?"

I already know who it is from the scent of mineral spirits. Its sharp odor drowns out the aroma of coffee, making me crinkle up my nose.

"Yeah, Dad, it's me. Want some coffee?"

"It's not that mule one, is it?"

I smile. "No, Dad, I made sure to get the Folgers."

"I'll have a cup."

My smile stays on my face as I push off the counter and go to the cupboard, grabbing two mugs. I pause and look at our dishes. *No two are alike—years of just getting through the day*, I think. My thoughts stop as the fluorescent lights flicker on, casting their unnatural brightness over me. I close the cupboard and look at the pale green linoleum of the table, counter, and matching floor. *They look sicker than ever*, I think, my smile fading.

I look at Dad and find my smile return. He is fully dressed, his white hair slicked back. I look at his feet; his boots are on and laced neatly.

He looks me up and down. "Big day today?"

I look away and pour us each a cup, mine an overly cute baby chicken, and his a *Best Dad*. I try not to look at that one too long.

"The first day is always a big day," I say, handing Dad his mug. I watch as he takes his seat, the one closest to the door where you can watch the whole house, the chair's yellow linoleum seat squeaking under his trousers. I sit down across from him and bring the edge of the hot mug to my lips, letting it warm my nose.

"Are you wearing makeup?" Dad asks me as I brush some of my hair off my face and glance at the dark kitchen window. The sun wasn't even hinting at rising yet.

"I'm worried about Timothy," I say.

I glance over my mug at Dad, and he nods. We sip in silence.

"It's a strange thing, war," he says.

I look at Dad. He looks me straight in the eye, his lips pursed. I want to hear more, but at the same time I don't.

"They tell us violence is wrong," he says. "They tell us if we hurt one another we will be punished, then they tell us that they need us to kill another man, and that killing that man is not only good but necessary, necessary for us to survive in the way we know it."

Dad pauses now, looking through me to a place I don't think I'll ever see. He said he was there, the day they landed on the beach. He looks back at me, his hazel eyes bright. He's back.

"You never forget the men you killed. For some, it's not just the men, but the women and children too. They stay with you, and they don't know—the white man doesn't know—how to get rid of them so they don't come back with you into the next lifetime."

"Have you . . . have you talked to Timothy about this?" I ask carefully, quietly.

"He's not ready to listen."

Dad drains his coffee. I get up to get him another one.

"There was a time, Nancy, when we killed with god. In that time, the women were just as powerful warriors as the men—some would say the women were better, slower to forget."

I hear it before I see it, its long tail trailing behind it on the counter.

"Jesus fucking Christ!" I scream and throw the mug in my hand. The mug explodes, the shattering ceramic shooting off in a thousand directions. I watch as the rat disappears behind the radiator. I hear Teddy cry and his door open. Dad shoots from his chair into the living room, running in at the same time as Teddy.

"Dad, you might wanna put that down," I say, nodding at his Garland he has already cocked on his shoulder. Teddy, in his blue fuzzy sleeper, wails, waddling toward me. I scoop him up and take him back to his room.

"Mama, I had the dream."

I nod and put him back under the quilt.

"It's not morning yet," I say, brushing back his black, tear-soaked hair.

He nods as he shuts his eyes. I sit there staring down at him. He still has the brush of baby to him, a little too round. I stroke his hair one more time and make for the kitchen, closing Teddy's door softly behind me.

I pause in the kitchen's entry. A dark shadow came home with Dad from the war he fought and hasn't ever left.

"When did you get in?" I ask, glancing over at Dad sweeping up the bits of mug.

"Killing rats with Dad's mug?" Timothy asks me, holding up the piece that says Best. I make a noise that's the closest I can to a laugh.

Timothy grabs at where his right arm would have been.

"Are those disco waves?" Timothy asks looking at my hair. I try not to look at him as he helps Dad put the remnants of the mug in the trash.

"Dick Wilson wants to sell the Black Hills."

Dad and I both look at Timothy.

"I thought the government purchased that from us in 1876?" I say.

Timothy laughs a laugh I've only ever heard since he's been home.

"The government never bought shit, Mom; they *stole* it from us around that time before they forcibly relocated us to this shithole. Oh, and then they slaughtered us here for *dancing*."

I nod, saying nothing. I don't want to egg him on.

"Your mother knows that, Timmy. Watch your mouth when you speak to her."

Timothy looks at Dad.

"Or what, Grandpa? You'll take me out back and shoot me like them Nazis?"

Timothy looks at me, and I glance at the piece of mug he's cradling in his only hand. He shoots us a look that makes my heart stop. He doesn't look at either of us again as we watch him make his way to his room, still holding the fragment of *Best*. I hear his heavy feet thump up the stairs.

I glance at Dad; his gold eyes meet mine. I turn, looking behind me at the wall, 5:04. I've got six minutes before I have to go. I look out the window above the sink.

"We need to get out of this place," I find myself saying almost in a whisper. I watch as Dad gets out a new mug and pours one for me to go. I take it, the warmth seeping through to my hands. He pours himself a fresh one and looks at me before taking a sip.

"The trouble is, Nancy, there's nowhere for us to go. This is Oyate; this is home."

I feel tears coming to my eyes and blink, taking a deep sip of my coffee, and then look at the peeling linoleum floors. This is home.

CHAPTER 2

▲▲▲▲

I TRACE MY FINGERS OVER THE COLD, engraved wood. *Spencer Carbine*, those were the letters of the words that Sha Shunkawakhan had said were *English* words. It had cost us twenty deer hides. I'd spent the past fall shooting at anything I saw. It was like no rifle I'd ever shot—not that many young women even shoot guns. I think back to when I was a child, and I don't remember the women getting to hunt; it was something I learned—someone had to—and Sha picked me. It was fast, fast enough to kill a rabbit or squirrel running. I'd feel my fingers dig into the cold metal, waiting to see where our bullet landed.

My fingers drop from the letters and rest on the trigger. I sense it before I see it. It freezes, its white tail like a flag; without antlers, it looks naked. I smile as I cock the carbine and steady it against my shoulder.

God, give us food. I pull the trigger. It explodes, the deer collapses, folds in on itself before the noise can even shock it. I slowly rise to my feet and tiptoe through the snow, so quiet I hear the soft flakes drifting from the sky trickle through the spruce's branches.

I look down at it, its brown eye wide open. Its beautiful, still death is silent. I look around; all that greets me is the forest. I make my way back to the camp. I'll get Bloka and White Elk to help me bring the deer back.

I smell the smoke and see the tipis peeking through the bare branches. I smile, but I feel my smile fade at the silence that follows me. I crouch and blend into the trees as I near the camp.

I see Sha at the fire with a man I've never seen. I weave through the tipis to them. She glances up at me, her face tight. I look at the man dressed in worn buckskin. His skin is browner than bark, and he is thick as the tree he is colored as.

"Little Wolf, this is Standing Bear."

I want to smile; never did a man suit his name more. I nod, and he looks me up and down. It makes me shift in the snow, his eyes settling on the carbine on my shoulder.

"What have you got there?" he asks me, nodding at the rifle.

"A Spencer carbine," I say, the English words feeling strange in my mouth. He nods.

"What for?"

I frown and look at Sha.

"Little Wolf is our hunter."

I watch as Standing Bear hides his thoughts.

"All the Indians are to turn themselves in to the agency," he says to me, chewing on the inside of his full cheek. I look at Sha.

"What's that got to do with us?" I ask him. He laughs, a small laugh for a big man.

"You're an Indian, are you not?"

I look around our small camp.

"We can't travel that far in winter," I say.

"I told him the same," she says, not looking at him, her eyes forcing their way into my thoughts.

Standing Bear smiles a smile that is more of a showing of teeth. "That's what the White Chief wants."

"Our babies to die?" I know I shouldn't have said that to him, a man I don't know. I feel Sha's sharp eyes on me, blacker than night.

"Don't think the White Chief cares," the massive man says.

"What if we don't come?" I ask.

Standing Bear looks at my rifle. "They'll come and get you. They said once they do, they'll starve you," he says as he straightens his fully lined fringed jacket, a trading post jacket.

"What are you, Standing Bear?" I ask.

He grins at me. "A messenger. I'm seeking the last chiefs of the Black Hills. The White Chief found special rocks here, and he now says this land is his. You come in nice, and they'll give you bacon and sugar; you come in mean, and they'll give you blood."

I look at Sha; her face is pale.

"Where are you going now?"

He glances at the sky, then back at me.

"To find the Chief of Thunder and tell him the same thing I just told you."

I look at Sha, then back at the tipis. I hear the new baby start to cry.

"Standing Bear, I think it best if I came with you, before we move the camp."

I don't dare meet Sha's eyes. The giant man nods at me, and I pray that I am home by the next sunrise.

CHAPTER 3

▲▲▲▲

I SEE HER HOLDING HIM THERE. In the sunlight, his hair shines gold. He smiles at me, his cheeks round and full. I think I know what love is.

"Autie?" Libbie says.

My eyes open, not to a white canvas rooftop but a planked ceiling. The sunlight has yet to trickle in and make the dust dance.

"You were having dreams again?" Libbie asks me.

"Yes, Libbie," I say and try to smile. I feel her slide from the bed, leaving nothing but the hint of her warmth. I look to see her pulling a knitted shawl over her shoulders. It makes her look like a ghost in her starched white nightgown, like she's floating. Her shoulders are stooped more, fuller than when we met. I guess we all carry the weight of something.

She looks back at me and smiles, making her once youthful face crack. I sit up and reach for my breeches, hanging off the post next to me.

"Will you meet with the president today, Autie?"

This time I actually smile as I pull up my breeches. She brings me a glass of water. I take a deep sip. It helps to wash her and him from my memory. I pass the glass back and sit down on the edge of the bed to pull my boots on. I leave her in front of me, cradling the water.

"I really think it would be best, Autie, if you stayed out of the pages for the time being. You've become the headline of the nineteenth century."

I don't meet her eyes. I straighten up and take the water from her waist and drink the rest in several big gulps. Her eyes look me over, vacant, pretending to see nothing.

"I think it best, Libbie, if you make your way to Monroe. I'll send word where to meet me from there."

I hold out the glass for her and watch as she puts it gently on the dresser. It bangs awkwardly. She takes my lieutenant's coat from the hanger and carefully nods her head. She doesn't agree, yet she hands me my coat. I lean down and kiss her cold cheek, gently grabbing the side of her soft head. Barely pausing, I swing my coat on and make for the door, taking my hat and revolvers from the hook I'd hung them on the night before. I close the door softly behind me. I hear her voice as I make my way down the stairs, fastening the revolvers. I put my hat brim forward on my head.

"Lieutenant Colonel, I hope you're coming in here for a bite to eat?" the proprietress calls to me from the kitchen. I hear bacon sizzling.

"Thank you kindly, madam, but I must make my way to military headquarters."

The woman beams at me the way my wife would have. *No wonder they were fast friends*, I think, as I make my way out of the house. The air is damp and rank. I long for my horse and spurs. As I tip my hat at a passerby, mud splashes near our feet from the carriage of bread that is barreling down the street.

I see it, beaming white, my destiny. First I need to pay my respects to the commanding general, and I take a right, weaving my way through the filth of the city to General Sherman. I see the smaller white building looming before me and think of the simpler but violent years of my youth. The women, the battles—they dance in my head as I make my way up the stairs. It's strange what you remember: smoke, screams, blood.

I nod at the officer appointed to the door. He salutes and swings it open. *It's not any warmer inside*, I think, as I listen to the echoing of my boots against the wooden floorboards.

"Now, that is not what I am saying at all," a man says. "I am saying that he might be one of them. He surrounds himself with them, and some of the things he's said, General, it makes me and my men nervous. And we all know after Washita he shared his bed for too long."

I know that voice and smile. Sherman's door is wide open, making me grin even wider. My moustache tickles my lip.

"Surely, Captain, you have seen some of them? Only a man lacking manly urges would be able to resist. Some of them are like creatures from heaven itself."

I hear the other men laugh, and I am still grinning as I graze my knuckles gently against the open door.

Sherman stands, forcing the room to rise with him.

"General, just the man we were talking about. Your captain here has some concern with which beds you choose to lie in."

I look at Captain Benteen. His chin is tipped to the floor, his meaty face turning red.

"I assure you, General, it does nothing but improve my performance in the field."

The room roars, and I watch Benteen go a deeper shade of magenta.

"Captain, you are dismissed," Sherman says abruptly.

I watch as Captain Benteen is forced to salute both General Sherman and me before he can make his way to the door.

"Captain, close the door on your way out."

Captain Benteen glances at Sherman in a way that makes me uneasy as he goes to the door, closing it a little too loudly behind him.

"General Custer, please take a seat," Sherman says, gesturing to the one vacated by Captain Benteen.

I nod, glancing at Alphonso Taft and Rufus Ingalls. Both men nod, and we all watch Sherman collapse back into his massive desk chair. He snaps open a drawer and pulls out a cigar, pops it in his mouth, and the smell of sulfur from his match fills the cold room. We watch as he takes deep breaths of smoke. He looks at it, satisfied, and then looks up at me, his sharp, sloped eyes and nose reminiscent of a hawk.

"General, I am afraid we've got some bad news for you," General Sherman says, looking at Alphonso.

I follow his eyes. Alphonso looks at me sympathetically.

"The Secretary of War was unable to plea to Congress upon your behalf."

I look back at Alphonso. His lips part as though he is going to explain himself before General Sherman cuts him off.

"Seems the president is more cut up over this Belknap ordeal than any of us thought."

"This expedition should already be under way," I say, using all my might to not say the words I'd like.

General Sherman nods. "I wholeheartedly agree. The Plains will soon be ripe for the picking. Me and General Sheridan have decided to send General Terry in your place."

I swallow my anger; it goes down my throat like cold molasses. General Sherman watches me, then looks at the glowing ember of his lit cigar as he begins speaking again.

"General Terry is an incredibly competent leader and was present at the Fort Laramie Treaty negotiations, so he knows what we're up against. All this business with Crazy Monkey and Sitting Zebra or whatever the hell name the Indians have taken won't spook him."

General Sherman pauses, looking me in the eye before finishing. "I mean, we all saw the Civil War," he says. "We saw those Southern devils dance through the woods."

"He wasn't at Gettysburg, though, was he?" I say. I feel my right leg begin to shake uncontrollably. I put my hand on my thigh, trying to steady it. I watch Sherman's eyes glance at it.

"No, General, he was not."

"We think it best you try to speak to President Grant himself," Rufus says, interrupting us. I look at Rufus, old Ingalls, Quartermaster, that walrus. Always full of so many promises, just like every other man on this hill, especially President Grant. Promises they never intend to keep.

"Anyhow, we intend to launch a winter campaign in 1887. This will all be long sorted by then. And you, General, you will lead it."

Sherman's words hang dead in the air. I swallow, trying not to reply.

I slowly look at the general. He meets my gaze just as hard, almost willing me to speak. I feel my mouth open, even though I should keep it shut.

"You know as well as I that a winter campaign is nothing more than a sentence of death, if not for us, then for our horses. They know the land; they will easily evade us, especially in the dead of winter."

"Best you speak with the president, Armstrong."

I look at Alphonso. He didn't say it to provoke me, the Secretary of War I'd helped crown.

I rise to my feet. I hold Sherman's eyes as they cloud angrily. He hasn't dismissed me. I feel my hand fumble by my forehead in a weak salute and stalk from the room. I bang my hat on my head. I don't close the door behind me for fear I'll slam it.

I make my way with haste. The posted private has to move quickly to open the door to the street, which is just as dank as when I'd left, the brightening of the cloudy sky doing nothing to improve the smell of shit and lies.

I walk quickly back the way I came, making for the biggest lie of them all, the White House.

CHAPTER 4

▲▲▲▲

I FEEL MY JAW TIGHTEN WHEN THE SAILOR SONG—"Brandy"—comes on the radio. I fucking hate that song. It's 1972, and it's almost as though music in a lot of ways is getting worse, not better. I reach forward and snap the radio off. I roll down my window. The cold air rushes in, waking me up. I long for spring, which is a good distance away. I glance at the sign *Black Hills State University*. I look back at the road, streaked with the golden bright rays of fall sunshine. I roll my window back up.

The sunlight trickling through the trees makes me squint as I wind my way to staff parking. I steer, more like guide, the Savoy into my spot. I see him, the new professor, Joshua, a few stalls down. The lot isn't even half full yet. I look at him leaning against his black Chevy smoking a cigarette, and I feel embarrassed. He sees me and tips his chin. I look at my ignition and turn the engine off and focus on shuffling through my papers beside me. A clinking knock at the widow makes me jump. I look and see Joshua making a gesture for me to roll down my window. I roll it down, trying to smile.

"Nancy, are you coming out of there or what?"

Joshua has one of those easy smiles that engulfs his whole face.

"Just making sure I have my lecture notes," I say, looking at the papers in my lap.

"Well, if you haven't, you'll have to wing it. Surely you'll not be able to drive—what is it, three hours?—back to your place to grab them."

Three hours in good weather, I think. I feel myself nod. Looking away, I slowly put my papers back in my bag, hoping he'd make for the university. I've only met Joshua once, a month ago at a history staff department meeting. We weren't really on a walk-together-to-the-university stage in our professional relationship.

I hear my door open and see Joshua smile as he flicks his cigarette. He gestures for me to come out. I roll up the window and slide out, worried if my polyester suit pants are sticking to my ass in an unflattering way.

"How'd the rest of your summer go?" Joshua asks, shutting my door. He gestures for me to go in front of him. I do so, leading us to our department offices.

"It was fine."

"I kept on hoping to run into you in town." His sentence trails off.

I nod my head. I don't want to tell him we never come up this way. The wind blows through the fading oak trees.

"It's a nice time of year, isn't it?" Joshua says, holding the massive wooden department door open for me.

"I've always been more of a spring person," I say and try to smile.

He grins at me like I've just told him a secret. I realize my turtleneck is making me too hot, so I pull off my suit jacket.

"Nancy, let me help you," Joshua says as he takes my bag.

I try to say thanks, but nothing comes out other than my strange smile. He nods as I take my bag back and I make for the office kitchen. I want nothing more than a peaceful coffee after what had happened earlier. I try to shut it from my mind, but the same thing keeps on running through my head that had for the past four hours: *Our house is infested with rats. Timothy needs help.*

I put my bag and jacket on the office kitchen table. Joshua has followed me in. I feel strange. I want to tell him this is my time. I look at the coffee maker and I'm surprised to see the glass coffeepot black, full, and waiting.

"I got here early," Joshua says, "a little nervous, first day and all."

I force a smile as I take a mug out of the cupboard. I feel Joshua behind me and hand him one. We go to the coffeepot in a weird procession. I take the pot and hold it in the air like a hostage, offering to fill his mug; he smiles and steps closer to me, holding out his mug, making me step back into the counter. He looks at me, unsure, then takes a good step back, leaning against the counter. He looks at me again and asks, "What do you think of this AIM?"

"Alcatraz?" I say, frowning as I put the coffeepot back and hold my mug under my nose. I inhale its earthy goodness.

"Of the word that they're going to Washington."

"Washington?" Timothy comes to my mind, and I feel my stomach turning.

"I just thought you might know."

Joshua's sentence drops off again. I take a sip of my coffee; it's a little too hot and burning my mouth.

"Because I am an Indian?" I say looking at him sharply.

Joshua smiles and gives me a lopsided shrug. I let out something like a single note laugh.

"You probably know more about it," I say. "You're the expert? Are you not?" I'm still looking at him, and Joshua laughs a laugh that fills up the whole kitchen, and I hope none of the other professors are in yet.

"I look at colonization," he says, "nothing too centered on the Indians themselves, but I think we should add a course as such."

"Crazy Horse 101?" I suggest, my mouth on the edge of my mug.

Joshua smiles and does his lopsided shrug. "More like how colonization impacted them and their traditional way of life."

I watch him search my face for approval, but I keep it carefully neutral. I sip my coffee and gaze out the window behind him; everything is burnt from the summer.

"Nancy, why did you choose to study the French Revolution?"

I find myself smiling. People love to ask me this question. Usually I lie and say something like how inspirational the foundation of democracy and enlightenment is to me as a human being.

"I like that they cut off the aristocracy's heads."

I look back at Joshua to see his brows lift in surprise, and he lets out another one of his room-filling laughs. I find myself letting into a real smile, and a lightness fills me that I haven't felt in a long time. I glance at the clock.

"Nancy? Could I take you out for dinner or a drink sometime this weekend or next?"

I take my empty mug to the sink and turn back to look at Joshua. "I am married."

He nods and shrugs at me.

"I just thought . . . I'd heard."

"That my husband is in jail?"

Joshua gives me a good-natured nod. My husband has been in jail for the last four years and has ten more to go.

"I better get going. There's quite a bit I need to do before I get to my lecture," I say, more to myself than Joshua. I gather up my things and look at him. He's a good-sized man with a mop of dirty-blond hair. His face is covered in the same hair. *Nothing like George*, I think, and smile. "Thanks for the offer, Joshua, of dinner or a drink."

He smiles, and for the first time since I'd met him, I see what disappointment looks like on him, in his smile. It doesn't reach his eyes, and he stands stiffer, his mug slack in his hands. I make for the hallway and wonder if that is what I always look like—disappointed. As I make my way to my office, my steps sound as hollow as I feel. I wonder what George feels like, if he thinks of us, or if we made each other empty. I try to remember if I ever felt full.

CHAPTER 5

▲▲▲▲▲

THE SNOW CRUNCHES UNDER MY FEET.

"Little Wolf," Standing Bear says, "do you know what your jacket means?"

I glance down at the gray wool and shiny buttons. "That it is a white man's?" The trader I'd traded it for had tried to talk me out of it, but the moment I saw it, I loved it. It was as soft as moss, and the line of buttons were too much, ridiculously shiny. I'd never seen anything like it.

Standing Bear burst out laughing. "It definitely is a white man's jacket, the wrong kind of white man's jacket."

"Haven't met a good one yet," I find myself saying, my words cutting through the freezing air. I glance at Standing Bear.

His dark eyes study me curiously. "I'd be careful with words like that."

"Doesn't matter—none of them understand our words anyhow."

That makes Standing Bear laugh again. I look at him. He throws his head back with his mouth wide open, looking like the animal he was named after. My eyes wander to the horse he's riding. I watch the muscles in his hindquarters flex with each step. *So much power*, I think.

"Where are you from, Little Wolf?"

I feel myself frown, and I look to the branches in front of me. "Where are you from, Standing Bear? Your Brulé is odd, to say the very least."

He grins down at me.

"Fair enough, we'll keep our origins a secret."

He brings his horse to a standstill and puts his arm up at me like he's an army halting us. I stop.

He nods up at the sky. "Smoke."

I nod, following the streak of gray against the sky. We'd been walking most of the day, and the sun was taking a long time to disappear.

"This will be the Chief of Thunder's camp," Standing Bear says as he slides from his horse. I nod. My carbine is slung across my back in the rawhide-and-buckskin holster I had made for it. Standing Bear whispers in his horse's ear and pats it. He looks at me and gestures toward the camp. We weave our way through the spruces. I hear running water; they must have dug a creek out. I pause at the camp's edge. I see some of the biggest tipis I have ever seen, most of them painted, depicting mostly horses and buffaloes. At the center is the biggest tipi of them all. Standing Bear follows my eyes.

"That is where we are headed," he says, stepping into the camp. He stops and looks back at me, waving me to come. I rest my hand on my rifle and follow him through the camp. The Indians that we pass stop whatever they are doing to stare at us. A woman carrying wood with a baby strapped to her back looks at us with a coldness in her eyes, making us know we are not welcome.

I notice that most of them are made up, their hair tied back, braids woven with feathers. Most had blankets or furs across their shoulders, carrying baskets of tubers and roots or piles of wood. We stop at the tipi, the big one. Two men are waiting at the entrance. They look between the two of us. Both have on silver breastplates under the furs draped over their shoulders. One was wearing a coyote hide, the other a wolf. Their faces are very similar, though one of them is substantially taller.

"I thought Sitting Bull killed you?" the taller one says to Standing Bear, a grin spreading across his mouth. *His smile makes him handsome*, I think, turning my attention to Standing Bear, who is straightening up to his full height.

"That was just a misunderstanding."

"That you're two-timing for the White Chief?"

"No, not all of it," Standing Bear says, putting his hands up in surrender.

"Who's this?" the tall man says, nodding at me. I watch as Standing Bear looks at me thoughtfully.

"Little Wolf."

"Little Wolf who?" the tall man asks.

"Brulé, I guess," Standing Bear says. He looks back at the tall man. "We are here for the Thunder Chief."

"Both of you?" the tall man asks again, looking curiously at my coat.

"I told her camp this morning what I am about to tell this one, and she said she wanted to come with me."

The tall man looks at me again, more thoroughly.

"You know that's a Confederate soldier's jacket, right?"

I shrug. "Makes no difference to me."

The tall man smiles at my answer, then scowls, looking back at Standing Bear. He disappears into the tipi as though he had never been standing with us. I look at Standing Bear, who glances at me with a greasy dark eye. The tall man pops back out in a cloud of smoke.

"Crazy Horse will see you," he says, holding the flap for us to enter. Standing Bear glances at me, nodding for me to follow as he vanishes into the dark, smoky tipi. I crouch in after him. A strongly lit fire is in the center. The air is so hot it feels like you can't breathe.

My eyes adjust to the darkness and the brightness of the fire, and I look to see three men sitting cross-legged dangerously close to the fire, passing a long pipe. None of them have shirts on and sweat rolls down their torsos like rain. The one in the middle glances at us, then back at the fire. Like Sha, he has hair and eyes the color of gold.

Standing Bear plops down across from them on a red blanket. I hesitate. No one tells me what I should do, so I follow Standing Bear, kneeling carefully beside him.

"Is that your gun?" the man in the middle asks me quietly, not taking his eyes from the orange and yellow flames.

"Yes."

"Are you with Standing Bear?"

"I suppose right now I am."

The man to the far right of the middle man laughs a low laugh. I look at him, my eyes lingering. He is wearing a gray wolf pelt, the wolf's head upon his own so they look one and the same.

"I already told Swift Fox that I picked her up this morning," Standing Bear says.

The man in the middle looks at Standing Bear in a way that makes us both shift a little, causing the blanket under us to rustle.

"All Swift Fox told us was that the traitor Standing Bear was wanting to speak to us with a Confederate soldier," the man in the middle says, glancing at my gray coat. The fire makes the gold buttons look like they are on fire.

"Crazy Horse, all of that with Sitting Bull was a misunderstanding," Standing Bear answers, and I hear a twinge of desperation; it lingers in the thick air like sweat. The man in the middle's eyes flick from him to the flames, and he nods his head slightly.

"What do you want, Standing Bear?" the man in the middle,

Crazy Horse, asks quietly. I look at Standing Bear. He is shifting under his large fur-lined, trading post hide, large beads of sweat running down his forehead from under his black woolen hat, making his long black braids slick.

"The White Chief has summoned all the Indians to him at the agencies he has made."

"What does that mean?" Crazy Horse asks between deep breaths of smoke that escape his mouth with his words.

"That you all have till the end of this January, the year of 1876, to turn yourselves in. They want this land."

I watch as the man in the middle, Crazy Horse, again picks up the pipe that has been resting in his lap and takes a long drag. He blows out an enormous cloud of smoke, which sweetens the air and mixes with the harshness of the fire's smoke.

"I told you this was coming," the man in the wolf pelt says, not taking his eyes from Standing Bear.

"Why are you here?" the man in the middle asks in a puff of smoke, looking at me.

"Standing Bear brought us the same words. We can't make that journey now—the children, the babies . . ." I trail off.

The man in the middle nods knowingly. He looks back at Standing Bear, his hazel eyes piercing through him. "There, you have your answer."

Standing Bear looks from me back to the man in the middle. "Crazy Horse, I don't think you understand. The White Chief, he's different now; he needs this land for his people."

Crazy Horse laughs a laugh that cuts through the hot air and smoke and makes the hair on my arms raise. "He needs our land for his people," he says. "He needs our land for his people without our people."

Standing Bear begins to speak, then stops. I watch as he swallows hard and begins talking quickly.

"Crazy Horse, they're no longer fighting one another. They've united and will now fight us."

"Us?"

"You, all of you," Standing Bear says, glancing at me. Crazy Horse looks at me.

"Can you shoot that carbine?" he asks.

"As long as I can pull the trigger."

Crazy Horse nods and looks back at Standing Bear.

"This land was given to us before the white man. Before what we know as time even existed, before the buffalo, before the moon, before the stars, given to us by Wakan Tanka. You'll drag me through my own blood before I give this—this land, as you call it—this land is all we know, all we've ever known. This land is *thiyáta*, this land is home."

"They will all come for you," Standing Bear says, his voice breaking.

"Not until the snow melts. Tell them I'll look for them. Tell them I hope they find me first."

Standing Bear nods. He looks at me, and I watch him stand, sweat pouring from his face onto the blanket. I look at Crazy Horse, who doesn't take his eyes from Standing Bear.

"Little Wolf?" Standing Bear asks, looking down at me. I look at him standing at the tipi's flap.

"She is with us. I want you gone before the first star," Crazy Horse says, still looking at Standing Bear. His eyes, they mimic the fire's flames. Standing Bear looks at Crazy Horse, then back at me. I don't move. He gives me one last look before disappearing out of the heat. Cold air washes over me as Standing Bear disappears into the darkening sky.

I look at the men across from me.

"You are welcome at my camp," Crazy Horse says, passing the pipe to the man in the wolf pelt. I nod, looking at the other man, who has said nothing. He has a halo of black feathers woven into his dark hair. The man doesn't look at me but keeps his eyes focused on the fire in front of us.

"I brought nothing," I say, looking at Crazy Horse

"You're armed with a rifle nicer than mine. You brought me a fool whose location we need to keep track of."

I feel myself frowning.

"What should we do now?" I ask, looking at Crazy Horse.

His fire eyes meet mine. "We wait for the snow to melt."

CHAPTER 6

▲▲▲▲▲

I TRY NOT TO THINK OF WHERE I'M GOING. The trees fly by in a blur of autumn glory—greens turned to rich reds and all shades of gold. The yellow middle line telling me to stay in my lane is a blur. I feel my hands clutching the Savoy's worn leather steering wheel and force them to relax, my knuckles aching. My eyes flicker to the unnatural orange construction-paper pumpkin on the passenger seat, the black eyes and mouth all uneven. Teddy gave it to me to give to his papa. He knew where I was going without me telling him where I was headed.

I smile, thinking of Teddy. He wants to be Scooby-Doo for Halloween. I have no idea how I'm going to make a costume of that ridiculous dog. My smile fades as I see the sign for the turnoff, *South Dakota State Penitentiary*. I make my way up the short road to the guarded entrance and unroll my widow to the officer behind the mesh.

"Name?" the guard calls down to me. I'm stopped in front of the chain-link gate, where I look ahead of me. It looks just as ominous to those outside of this place as it does to those trapped inside.

"Nancy Swiftfox, visiting George Swiftfox," I say, struggling to look the guard in the eye.

The man nods and checks a clipboard. "Go ahead, Mrs. Swiftfox, park in 6F." He pushes a button that buzzes loudly, making me wince. I feel a headache coming on and wish I had some water, my mouth all of a sudden feeling too dry.

The gate uninvitingly jerks open. I force my foot on the gas and steer myself into the assigned parking spot. I grab my pumpkin and bag.

I will myself out of the car, throwing my bag over my shoulder, and push the heavy car door shut. I pull my purple-knit cardigan tighter around me. I should have worn a winter coat.

The penitentiary, like the university, is old. The red brick tells on it. I hurry for the entrance, the cold air biting at my face. I can feel my nose starting to run. A guard nods at me and opens the door with another buzz. I enter and encounter two more guards inside. The door behind me slams with a click—I'm trapped. I hand the guards my purse, and they immediately start fishing through it, and then I spread my arms and legs. The guard firmly grabs me, reaching down each limb and around my waist.

"She's good. Mrs. Swiftfox, you'll be seeing your husband in suspended visitation today—one door further down."

I frown as the other guard nods and hands me back my purse. I force my legs forward and make my way down a long hallway. I notice for the first time the prison is shrouded in the same sickly fluorescent green as our kitchen—*both of them government built*, I think with an audible snort. I pass the usual visitation room and look through the door's tiny rectangular mesh window. The visitors and inmates are all perched at the metal tables and chairs, like crows on a garbage can. I make for the next door, where a guard is waiting.

"He'll be out in a minute," the guard at the door says as he opens it for me.

I pause, my chest tightening. There are six seats opposite each other, separated by glass in a half-assed cubicle. You have to pick up a phone to talk through the glass, or maybe it's plastic. I walk to the only seat unoccupied; no one looks at me as I sit, and I don't look at them. Heat rises to my face; I feel embarrassed simply by being here. A red light beside the door on the glassed side lights up, and I try not to reach for the papers in my purse, buried under the pumpkin.

The door opens, and there he is. His hands and feet are cuffed. My heart sinks. I can make out his muscles through his beige uniform. George is bigger than when I saw him last. I notice his black hair is long now, hanging halfway down his back. His skin is tanned like a hide, his face hairless, with a full mouth and high cheekbones. He's still the most beautiful man I've ever seen. He smiles when he sees me. His teeth are a perfect white—they always look like they're glowing against his dark skin. I don't smile back, and he grins harder, shuffling toward me in his shackles.

He sits across from me and awkwardly grabs the phone. I slowly reach for mine.

"Nancy," he says, grinning.

"I want a divorce." I meant to wait to say it, I meant to ask him how he's doing, I meant to talk about the boys.

George chuckles. "Nancy, Nancy, Nancy, how have you been?"

He has a lazy, slow way of talking that is pissing me off right now because I like it.

"How do you think I've been, George?" I hiss into my phone.

His black eyes search my face. "You look tired." He studies my face—which I can feel is getting hot, but no longer out of embarrassment.

"Yeah, George, I'm fucking tired. I'm raising your four boys, supporting your dad, and driving six hours a day, every day. Yeah—I'm as tired as I must look."

"Have you heard from Timmy?" he asks, not listening to a word I'm saying.

"Of course, he lives at our fucking house."

"No need to swear so much, Nancy."

I feel my cheeks going redder.

"I haven't seen him in a while," George says, looking at the man beside him distractedly. I take a good look at George, the man I married, my eyes growing hard.

"He didn't come by," I say, "to tell you he made off with a band of Indians he doesn't know to march on the nation's capital to protest the broken treaties?"

I am unable to control the anger in my voice. I watch as George's eyebrows shoot up and he starts to laugh, his attention now fully on me. His laugh draws looks from the other inmates and fills up his whole face, making his black eyes dance mischievously.

"That's our boy," he says, his voice husky from laughing.

"Yeah, that's one of them."

The smile and laugh fade like the sun.

"You never bring Paul, Daniel, or Teddy to see me."

"Neither does your dad."

I know I said it too quick. George winces.

"I thought you might be too busy seeing Lola," I hiss at him. George looks at me, his large brown eyes sad. He shifts, making his shackles jangle.

"They keeping you pinned up for good behavior?" I ask, looking at the shackles.

George looks at me, his eyes soft. "Just a little misunderstanding with the boys out back. Who is the guy, Nancy?"

"Who's what, George?"

His face strains with whatever patience the glass wall is making him have, the veins in his neck becoming visible.

"Who's the guy you want to fuck? Jim?" he says to me through clenched teeth. I feel myself scowling, thinking of his best friend, and try to make myself stop because I know it makes me look old.

"George, I'm nothing like you." I can feel my tone is dead—I'm exhausted, exhausted of worrying, exhausted of caring, exhausted of being the only person trying to hold our ill-fated family together.

He smiles a fake smile that has always infuriated me. His lips curl, but his eyes home in on me, and they're mean. "No, Nancy, that's just the problem; you and I are exactly alike. We talk the same, we dance the same, and we fuck the same."

I fight everything in me not to hang up the phone and storm out of there. I want to break the glass and make him sign the forms I paid three hundred dollars for. I want to pretend we never met.

"Who is it?"

"No one you know," I say, my voice fading as my anger rises. He laughs a cruel laugh. A guard comes up behind him and taps him a little too hard with his baton.

"Problem here?" he asks, looking from me to George.

"No," George says, not taking his eyes from me. They're hot and black as coals.

"Timmy said there was a white guy sniffling around your pussy at the university."

I look away, the shame sweeping over me, sucking the wind further out of my sails. I wondered if I had been that obvious. I don't even remember mentioning Joshua, but I know the harder I had tried to not think about him, the more he had ensnared himself into my everyday thoughts.

"Five more minutes," the prison guard that just tapped George calls out, specifically looking at us.

"What does it matter, George? White, Indian, I am leaving you. I have papers here; you clearly won't be able to sign, but I am here to tell you I am done." I look at him, a man I wonder if I ever really loved. Our eyes hang on each other. I think of the time we had together that was good. It is short enough to sum up in my memory in the minutes we have left together.

"You move on then, Nancy, with your white man. See if he can raise my Indians, see if he can teach them to fight and hunt."

George begins to hang up.

"He'll do a better job than you!" I shout into the phone.

I watch George's full lips purse together. He nods and hangs up the phone hard despite the cuffs. I know he heard me, and it doesn't make me feel any better; my heart, I can feel it sinking, I can feel that it really is over, and I thought I would be happier.

"Inmate 37689 clear," one of the guards calls out, and another comes to escort George back to what I guess is his cell. All the guards—I notice for the first time in all the years I have been coming—look the same. I wonder why. The faceless men, that's what Timmy always said, they hide behind everyone, pretending to be no one. I sit there realizing I am still pressing the phone to my ear too hard. I can feel it ache. I watch George disappear through the metal door. *I forgot the pumpkin*, I think to myself, watching him vanish.

"Time's up," the guard calls out, too loud, on our side. I hang up the phone.

CHAPTER 7

▲▲▲▲

I STEP OUT INTO THE COLD AIR, the heat from the tipi making me lightheaded. Crazy Horse, the Chief of Thunder, his words dance in my head with all of what Standing Bear had said: Give up everything or die. *Why?* I wonder. *Why can't we stay in our home, why can't be stay beside these people, why do they have to take us prisoner and make us like them?*

I feel myself jump from hot air blowing on my cheek, and I turn my head to it. In the fading light is the tall man we'd seen on the way in, the one that did all the talking. My eyes search his face. He's standing a little too close to me and doesn't move. He is tall and strong, his long hair clubbed off his face. My eyes settle on his ears, which are lined with small silver hoops.

"Little Wolf, I've got to continue, but you're welcome to come with me back to the agency."

I am surprised to hear the voice of Standing Bear. He steps out of the shadows in front of me, and his boots crunch in the snow as he walks toward me. I can feel the tall man's eyes burning into the side of me; he still hasn't moved or said anything.

"I think it best I go back to Sha and tell her what we think, what I have learned."

I feel myself say it a little too quietly, wishing the big man was already gone. I look at the packed snow beneath his feet, then at his harsh face. Standing Bear is looking at me thoughtfully.

"Well, then, I hope to see you and your camp soon at Red Cloud's Agency," he says, glancing at the tall man next to me, who says nothing. Standing Bear nods, and I watch him walk away, continuously checking over his shoulder. I wonder if he is looking to see if I'm still here or if maybe I've decided to follow him. I hear the howling of a wolf pack, long and mournful in the distance, and I smile.

"Your namesake?" the tall man standing beside me asks. I watch his breath form white clouds, making my cheek warm.

"I suppose so," I say, looking at him.

"Are you a guard?" I ask, making the man laugh—his laugh, it's honest.

"I hardly think Crazy Horse needs me to stand watch over him."

"Why is he also called the Chief of Thunder?" I find myself more asking the young stars starting to craze the sky than the man next to me. I look at him, and he glances at the tipi right behind us. I follow his gaze, my eyes tracing the buffalo, lightning, and hail spots painted all over it.

"Do you want something to eat?" he asks, not answering me. I guess he knows I'm asking the stars as well. I'm so hungry, I would have eaten bark. It had been a long walk in the snow, and Standing Bear never offered anything to eat or to stop.

"I could eat," I find myself saying quietly, looking at the tall man who smiles down at me. He turns abruptly and I follow him, our soft soles crunching. I always like the sound—almost like rattles from a summer dance. We weave our way through the camp toward the tree line.

"Do you know Standing Bear well?" the man asks me, cutting into the silence of the settling night.

He doesn't look back at me; I'm a few steps behind him.

"No, I only met him this morning," I say, and the man looks back at me, surprised.

"What did he want?"

"I think you better ask your chief."

We stop at the entrance of a small tipi, alone at the further reaches of the camp. The hide is plain, no pictures; I can see in the dim light that it is well-tanned, even and smooth. I want to touch it.

"This is me," the tall man says, ducking in through the flap.

I look around. The people we saw earlier have all disappeared as the air grew icy. My stomach turns in hunger, and I follow him through the flap. The tall man is already crouching in front of the fire, rekindling it. It hisses awake from his flint, and he tucks it into the hide pouch tied to his leggings. They aren't decorated like the tipi; there are no fringes or beadwork, but I see whoever made them knew their way around an awl, just like the tipi.

"I'll be right back," the man says as the fire fully reawakens.

There's a heap of furs in one corner. I am kneeling on one of two trading blankets, the rough wool already feeling itchy through my hide leggings. I unbutton my jacket and slip it off. I am thinking of taking off my fur vest when the flap opens; the man is holding a cast-iron frying pan with four freshwater trout in it.

"The flesh is a little funny when it is cold like this, but still good," he says, smiling at me, plopping the pan into the middle of the fire. I watch as he goes over to a covered basket in the corner and pulls out a small wooden box.

"Bear fat," he says, scooping out a handful into the pan, making it sing.

"You have a soldier's tunic, too?" he asks, looking at my soft white sleeves.

"Came as a pair," I say with a shrug, making the tall man smile wider.

"I'm Swift Fox," he says, kneeling on the hide floor and using the blanket he was sitting on to shake the handle of the cast-iron skillet, making the fish hiss.

I watch as he grabs a stick and flips them quickly, the cooked side a perfect golden brown. I feel my mouth watering, wanting it.

"Has your camp been here long?" I ask as he nestles the pan of flipped fish back into the fire.

"A day or so."

A satisfied look settles on his face, and he pulls the pan out of the flames and places the skillet between us. I see sprigs of cedar swimming in the hot fat.

"We'll have to wait for it to cool," Swift Fox says, sitting back on his heels. I look down at the four fish, then back around the tipi.

"Is your family coming?"

Swift Fox laughs. "It is just me; I can eat two or three," he says as he pokes the fish. He rips off a piece and stuffs it in his mouth and gestures for me to do the same. I crawl off the blanket and onto the hide next to him and adjust my body to face him and the pan and rip off a piece from the fish he'd torn into. The skin is crispy and the flesh hot.

"Where did you come from?" Swift Fox asks between mouthfuls. I look at his face carefully. He has high cheekbones like me, but his face is squarer and his lips fuller. His long clubbed hair falls down his back loose; mine is woven into braids.

I swallow before I answer. "A little south; we'll move north when the weather becomes warmer. Green Leaves just had her first baby."

"Green Leaves?"

I smile. "She had another name, but after that, she didn't want to use it anymore."

Swift Fox nods at me carefully.

"You have any babies?" he asks me. I watch his face grow still. I chew, wondering why he is asking.

"I don't think I'd be here if I did," I say after swallowing my large mouthful of fish. The cedar adds something to it. I am going to try it with deer meat when I get back to camp. Silence settles between us as we watch each other eat.

"Tell me what Standing Bear wanted," he demands.

"Why do you say his name like that?" I ask, thinking of the strained meeting between Standing Bear and the three men in the tipi. What had they said of Standing Bear? Another Indian had tried to kill him, he was a traitor. I think about what Crazy Horse had said, that Standing Bear worked for the Great White Chief, the one that wanted the land and the special rocks.

"Tell me what he wanted, and I'll tell you," he says.

I meet Swift Fox's eyes; it's like there is burning coal behind them.

"You're not part of your chief's council," I say, thinking of the three men in the tipi I had met with, chiefs of thunder.

"You are of your chief's?" he says to me in a way I don't like.

I try not to glare as I am eating his fish.

"I guess," I say, looking at the fish as I tear off another piece.

I've never really thought about it till this very moment. I think back to my life, and I realize I am the council. Swift Fox is looking at me in the same quiet way he had when I first came in here with him.

"You wear a soldier's uniform, with a soldier's gun, and you are part of your camp's council. How old are you, sixteen, seventeen?" he demands. I watch him looking me up and down, sizing me up. I feel my eyes narrow, and I now know why Sha kept grown men limited at our camp.

"Eighteen," I say, letting my agitation slip into my voice.

"I am not part of the council because I am not from this nation. I am visiting from the Masikota, where there's trouble," he says with the same tone. He's looking at me but I don't want to look at him. What is it, anger? I wipe my hands on my leggings.

"There's always trouble," I say. We look at each other. I am thinking of reaching for my rifle I had put down beside me.

"You're a dog soldier," I say, looking at him, his piercings, and silver breastplate.

Swift Fox grins. "I don't think you are a Brulé."

I shrug. "Nobody's where they started anymore."

"Since the white man came," he says as though he is finishing my sentence. I shrug again, forcing myself not to look at my rifle.

"Always something, stolen horses, stolen women, stolen land. The white man's different, though; they steal and destroy."

I don't meet Swift Fox's eyes. I shift and try not to think about what he is saying to me. We all have to live in this world they are taking from us. Better to just breathe than dwell on what you can't control. I can feel him still looking at me as he continues his speech.

"They take the land and make it unusable; they rape it, then cast it aside; their great chief looks after no one, unless they're bringing him something. I saw Deadwood. Standing Bear says all of this is theirs now, and we're to go to Red Cloud's Agency. Then people like Crazy Horse can argue about where to march us to next. All the while, we all know they're actually marching us to our death. Dead, dead like them."

I look at Swift Fox.

"Dead like them?" I ask.

He smiles. "They kill with no god."

I frown at him. I know what he is; his weapons aren't just for hunting animals and fish.

"Are you like them, Little Wolf?" he says.

I meet his eyes. "Do I look like I am?"

I want out of this tent.

"You have no problem wearing their clothes."

"Clothes don't make a person; they only keep them warm."

Swift Fox laughs a laugh that rings through the air and makes me blush.

"Now, tell me of Standing Bear," I say, seeing he has settled down. He is still grinning at me.

"Frank Grouard is half black or a Sandwich Islander, depending on the day you ask him. He kills like a white man, without rules. Sitting Bull took him in, and I don't know what happened. Something. They cast him out, and he went to the white man's army telling stories, drumming up war, and they listened to him. He's going to bring Hi-es-tzie here, that's who we're looking for. If you follow Standing Bear, you find the Great White Chief's henchmen."

"Hi-es-tzie?" I ask, the word sounding stranger than *carbine*.

"Long Hair," Swift Fox says to me in a way that I should know what he's talking about.

"Long Hair?" I say more to myself than him.

"Lieutenant Colonel Custer."

"Oh," I say, recognizing the name now. Indian killer. A silence comes over us. I remember something I've spent my whole life trying to forget.

"Where to for you now, Little Wolf?" Swift Fox asks, breaking my thoughts.

"Back to my camp; I need to provide council," I say. I smile.

"That's the first time I've seen you smile," he says, looking at me over the cold fish. I shrug. No point in smiling unless you mean it.

"What will you say?" he says to me.

I look into the flames of the fire; they dance in the darkness.

"I don't know. I don't think we should move to Red Cloud's Agency."

Something sits heavy in my stomach thinking about it. I look at Swift Fox; he nods, he agrees with me.

"They'll come for us, that's what Standing Bear said," I say.

He nods again at me. "They'll come either way," he says in what I think is a reassuring tone. I nod, thinking of Green Leaves. None of our choices seem like good ones.

"We're going north this spring, for the Sun Dance this summer—your camp should come," he says, looking hard at me. It is more of a demand than an invitation. I feel myself frowning.

"I've never been to a Sun Dance," I say, looking back into the fire, trying to remember if my parents had taken me to one as a child. With Sha, we didn't hold celebrations in a formal sense; we just tried to stay invisible. No different than trees, she always said.

"Well, then you must come; this might be the last one."

I look at him, my brow pinched. Swift Fox shrugs at me. I shrug and feel myself smile.

"Your smile," he says trailing off. I pick up my coat and pull it on. I look at him and nod. I grab my rifle and stand. He stands with me.

"You can't go out there; it is too cold," Swift Fox says, looking at the tipi's flap. "You can stay here, if you want. Or I can find you a different lodge," he says in a mumble I haven't heard yet through his self-assured tone. I look at him.

"I won't be able to sleep," I say, pulling out the gloves I had tucked into my leggings. Sha embroidered them with glass beads we'd traded for last summer in Deadwood, dead like them. Swift Fox had said that it was like a hell, remembering back to the mud and the people, the smell. He's right. I would rather wait for them to find us than live in that.

"Take this," Swift Fox says, reaching into the pile of furs he probably sleeps in. He pulls a massive gray wolf hide out of the mess.

"For protection," he says, handing it to me. I run my hand through the soft fur.

"I have nothing to give you for it."

"You can bring it back to me this summer, at the Sun Dance."

I find myself smiling, thinking about him dancing.

"Thank you," I say, looking at him. He looks at me; his face is drawn, solemn.

"Safe travels," he says, reaching out and touching the fur next to my hands.

We stand staring at each other. I search his eyes as though they will tell me what to do next, but he says nothing. Finally I nod. He reaches behind me and pulls the tipi's flap open, and I take a big step out into the night. The cold air bites at my face. I pull the hide over my shoulders and around my body, the fur tickling my cheeks.

I weave through the camp and into the forest, nothing but the crunching of snow cutting through the silence of the night. I pause and look at the moon. He is full, making the trees almost as bright as though it were day. I look at him, round and full, and I think of Hi-es-tzie, Standing Bear, and the chiefs in the tipi, and I know what I must do. I know I can't live in a log house. I know I can't wear one of those dresses. I know it's wrong to work the land when she gives us what we need without asking. I know this summer I must see the Sun Dance. I know this is the only way to talk to god and truly be free. I know I can't live in the prison these people are trying to make for us. I know I'll have to fight.

CHAPTER 8

▲▲▲▲

THE GLASS IS COOL ON MY FOREHEAD, even though it feels thin, fragile. The train thuds, vibrating methodically, and lets out its mournful shrill whistle, like a war—a cry of expansion. My eyes watch the dead browns swirl past us, dizzying. The snow of the long winter had begun to sink back into the earth but was not yet showing the lushness of summer or even really a promise of spring. I hear them before I see them—heavy steps, boisterous voices. I feel the uneasiness of the past year fall down through my boots. I am grateful to have rid myself of the city and long for the comfort of my saddle.

"Autie!" shouts Boston. I see him making his way down the narrow aisle. His thin golden curls wisp round his face like his limbs. Clutched to Boston's chest is my real attire, and despite Boston's slight demeanor, he bumps into arms and petticoats hanging in the train's narrow aisle. I watch as the train folk shoot him annoyed glances, and I allow myself to smile.

"General," Tom says, following from behind him.

I hear my other brother Tom correct Boston, the middle child. He tips his gray captain's hat, looking out from behind him. I nod, and they both sit on the bench opposite me. I see James carefully making his way down the swaying aisle, unlike my two brothers, although he is not as neatly decorated as Tom. I still feel proud being with them. I watch James's face—his round cheeks are flushed, a newspaper tucked under his arm. He nods at me and sits down heavily next to me, making the wooden bench creak and moan.

"General, you will not believe what has been written within the *New York World* this morning," James says, holding out the paper from under his arm as though a rare specimen for us all to behold.

I grin, and Tom lets out a whoop and leans across and slaps me on the knee. The four of us grin at one another. The train sounds its shrill whistle and lurches forward to a stop. I look up to see one of the conductors strolling down the aisle toward us; he nods at me, and I nod back.

"Chicago! The train is headed for Chicago!" the conductor shouts, passing us and disappearing out of our car. I hear the wooden door leading to the next car shut with a slap, the train's steel wheels humming as they stop her tracks.

Boston reaches across and snatches the paper out of James's lap. James grins and leans back on our bench a little too hard, making it creak with even more concern than before. I watch Boston unfold the paper and clear his throat dramatically.

"President Grant has today performed an act which appears to be the most high-handed abuse of his official power he has perpetrated yet."

Boston pauses, looking at each one of us, grinning. I sit up straighter and nod for him to continue, and his grin widens to a smile as he continues reading.

"President Grant has removed General Custer from command in a summer campaign against the Indians in retaliation to his testimony in the impeachment trial concerning the Secretary of War, William W. Belknap. Both General Sherman and the new Secretary of War,

Alphonso Taft, have protested that Custer indeed was not only the best man, but the only man fit to lead the expedition now fitting out against the Indians. To all their entreaties, President Grant turned a deaf ear. General Custer himself believed he was merely doing his duty as an American citizen by testifying and that he himself had gone to see President Grant only to be sent away."

Boston tosses the paper back to James. I look at the three smiling faces fixed on me.

"General?" Tom asks me, leaning forward as though I have a secret. I had wired Tom, telling him we were ready for the campaign. I look at my little brother and wonder if I should have said anything else.

"I paid the president a visit, and he did not pay me the respect of his company," I say as my brothers and brother-in-law laugh to the point of drawing looks. I tip my hat at the glances; they can look the other way.

"He didn't pay you any mind?" James asks in disbelief.

"I left him a note."

Tom laughs till tears begin to stream down his face. I force a smile, thinking of the hours that man kept me waiting in the anteroom. I think of Alphonso finding me in the chair, waiting like a naughty child, and how he had said that he would see to the president himself. He returned with nothing more than a note, a note saying that President Grant could not be bothered to see me that day. So, I had in turn responded with a note.

"Autie?" Boston asks.

I look at him. "I am sorry, Boston, I missed that."

"What did the note say, General?"

Tom answers for our younger brother. I look at Tom, in his gray captain's suit. He'd follow me to hell and back. Those were long years, the war. Even with five years between us, Tom never seemed to be very far behind me.

"That I desired this opportunity for a matter of justice, and that it was with my deepest regrets I had not been permitted to meet with him."

"Humph," James says, grabbing at his moustache. My brothers shake their heads, still smiling.

"Where we off to then, Autie?"

I smile at my Boston; in his simple tweed suit, he sticks out among us yet is always wanting to be included.

"We must stop off in Chicago, as I've got to check in with General Sheridan, then onward to St. Paul's and finally Fort Abraham Lincoln, where Libbie, Maggie, and Little Autie will meet us."

My brothers look at me with something I've only seen now and again in my men: uncertainty. It makes something in my chest go cold. I knew that seeds that were planted like that always tended to be weeds. My eyes drift out the window at the rolling sea of dead land.

"Well, come autumn, the president will feel more than foolish once you've whipped those heathens off our land."

I feel myself wince. I don't look at James. He'd missed half the war, gallivanting with his brother through Europe. He'd not seen what Tom and I had seen. I knew he wrote to his wife, my sister, with tales of the Indians who fascinated and disgusted him. I think of my son.

"What do you know of the Sioux, First Lieutenant?" I hear myself ask in a low tone. I catch a glimpse of Tom looking at us with bright eyes, and I watch Boston sink into the bench as though it will cover him. My head turns sharply to look at James. I've seen that look, the look many men had wiped from their faces with an arrow to the heart or worse.

"They are no different than the rest of the Indians we've defeated—greasy hair, rank bodies, and it is more than difficult to tell the men from the women."

I feel myself nodding at his idiotic conviction. I'd seen them in the field for years now. The papers might make them out to be imbeciles, but no imbecile fought the way they fought. I feel myself speaking, even though he doesn't deserve to be spoken to.

"They know this land better than us, they fight in it better than us, and I think it would be fair to say there is more of them than us. They train their warriors from children, girls, boys, no matter. If their sun god says they are fighters, they are fighters. What have we got, James? Farmers, and then the rest of them are German and Irish immigrants who struggle to understand English, let alone fight in combat on a horse. We've been outsmarted by these 'heathens' and outfought on several occasions. But you know that, James, don't you? Because you were there."

I look at my brother-in-law, his round cheeks flushing various shades of red.

"Then what are we doing here, Autie?" comes the voice of Tom, the voice of my own soul.

"Doing the only thing we're good at, Tom."

"Killing Indians?" Boston, the civilian, asks in a childish sort of way. I don't take my eyes from Tom's.

"Fighting wars."

CHAPTER 9

▲▲▲▲

I SQUINT, LOOKING OUT THE DARK WINDOW above the sink. It's too dark out to see the world's tiniest flakes of snow. I smile to myself as I move my sponge around the last plate.

And in other news, the American Indian Movement has taken its protest even further and is occupying the Bureau of Indian Affairs in the nation's capital.

"Dad, turn that up!" I yell, tossing the sponge next to the sink. It lands in a soapy splat, and I make for the living room fast.

I pop through the entrance. I glance at Teddy in the corner with a plastic Scooby-Doo I picked up for him in Rapid City last Friday. I look at Paul and Daniel; at fourteen and eighteen, they are now squished together on the couch. *Teenagers always manage to take up more space than they need,* I think, glancing at Dad sitting in his chair, his rifle he is in the middle of oiling resting in his lap as he looks at the TV. I turn to face it, with its too-bright light sucking me in, showing me chaos; there are so many people crowded together they look like ants. I don't see Timmy. It would be impossible to pick him out in the ocean of darkness. I still feel sick to my stomach. We all watch in silence as the Bureau of Indian Affairs is being ripped apart.

"He'll be fine, Nancy."

I nod my head absentmindedly.

"We should have gone with him."

I look at Paul, his voice cracking. Somewhere between driving to the university and worrying about Timothy, he'd become a man.

"Could you imagine? All of us piling into Mom's Savoy?" Daniel says, making both him and Paul break into giggles.

"What's so funny about that?" Teddy asks, looking up at all of us as though he'd just seen us for the first time, Scooby-Doo clutched in his chubby hand.

"I don't think nothing," Dad says, giving my two older sons a stern look.

They both stop laughing, but you can see the giggles are just beneath the surface, and just like that they are children again, still a good ways from adulthood.

"You going soon, Nancy?"

I look back at the TV. The reporters had already moved on to President Nixon and the Vietnam War. I look at my children, all reflections of some aspect of me and their father. I think of the last time I saw George, and my blood runs a little cold.

"Yeah, Dad, I think I am," I say quietly.

"So, is he like your boyfriend?" Paul says, glancing at me.

A drink hardly makes a boyfriend, I think, saying nothing but feeling myself frown.

"That's enough, Paul," Dad says standing, putting his rifle carefully on the table beside him.

"I'll see you off, then," Dad says, making for the kitchen, leaving the kids to the TV. Paul was already at the dial trying to find something before Dad could get back and demand more news. I smile and go to the couch and kiss the tops of Paul and Daniel's black heads; both pretend I am not there, I go to Teddy, who springs up and gives me the biggest hug his small body can muster.

"Daniel says we're going to build a fort to keep out the ghosts like in *Scooby-Doo*."

I look back at Daniel, who shrugs at me.

"Is that right?"

"Uh-huh," Teddy says puckering his lips for a kiss. I smile at him, even though he reminds me so much of his father, and plant one on him.

"Thanks, Mom, see you in the morning!" Teddy says, sitting back on the ground heavily.

"You're welcome."

I look at my boys on the couch. I cringe as the *Hawaii Five-O* theme songs cries through the air from the TV; it will be stuck in my head for the entire drive.

"I love you all."

"Love you," returns the distracted half-man chorus.

Teddy is already fully engrossed in his toy dog, telling him about the ghosts.

I go back to the kitchen and the row of hooks next to the back door and grab the dark-green parka I've had a little too long. When I go to work, I leave it in the car and hurry freezing to the history corridor. I see Dad through the window outside smoking a cigarette. I smile and open the door.

"They'll be alright, won't they, Dad?"

"As good as any of us can be," Dad says, looking at the small snowflakes falling.

"If the weather becomes too thick, you should stay there, Nancy."

I feel the heat come to my face. I don't meet his eyes but busy myself with my zipper and snaps.

"My son."

I look at Dad; in all these years, I've never actually heard him speak of George.

"He's a real piece of shit."

I find myself laughing. Dad lets a small smile come to his lips, full lips exactly like George's.

"He can't help himself, been like how he is his whole life; you tell him no, and all he hears is yes. The trouble is, Nancy, the trouble with all of them is that they've got nothing, nothing but what's under our feet. The government, this government, took everything from us and told us we've got to be like them. The trouble is we're not them; they know it, and we know. We've been here since god created us; they come from somewhere else, like France."

We smile at each other.

"Joshua's white."

"Joshua," Dad speaks his name like foreign language. "I thought he'd be white; no Indian would want to go all the way to Rapid City for a drink."

"He lives there."

"Is that why you want to move us there?"

I feel it rising in me. Anger, anger I always somehow have managed to bury for the sake of my children, for the sake of my sanity.

"Dad, I want to move us there because this house is a rat-infested piece of shit. Timmy and Paul can't find jobs that are close, and there's something weird with Teddy." The cold cuts into my lungs just like the words.

I watch Dad, who looks at the sky while nodding his head, slowly and steadily.

"We can't run from this, Nancy. We can't run from being Indian; this is the cross we must bear. This is our penance for the Wampanoag helping the Pilgrims and how many other tribes since have helped these people, the Americans, in some way or another."

"So, seeing Joshua is a crime against being Indian?"

"No, but he won't understand. He won't understand why we're angry; he won't understand that we're trapped."

I look out into the night. It's only 4:00 p.m., but the clouds kissed the sun away a while ago.

"So, you're saying George is a piece of shit because of circumstance?"

Dad shrugs his shoulders in the same way Daniel does.

"We never really helped them, did we?" I ask, thinking of who we are. We belong to the Brulé, one of seven Sioux tribes, forcibly relocated, our land stolen, our children stolen. I wonder how my ancestors survived it, being marched in the snow and shot down in a field. I look at Dad; he shrugs again.

"I fought for them."

"Why?"

"Because it's in our blood; we're warriors. Nancy, I told you some of that, of Little Wolf. And I see that in you. After everything, you still haven't given up; you teach your white talk and raise your children."

I look at Dad hard. This is the first real conversation we've have since he came to live with us. He came when George was first locked away.

"You should run for Tribal Chairman," I say with a laugh, and walk for the forsaken Savoy's door. I heave the heavy thing open and pause, looking back at Dad, whose cigarette is almost done.

"And disappear only to be found dead?"

I watch as Dad flicks his cigarette into the snow. I think I see a smile as I climb into the Savoy and slam the door shut. I start the car and rub my hands together. Reaching over, I jam the button for the glove box, which had started sticking more than five years ago and seems to be getting worse. I hold my finger against it till it hurts; it finally pops open, and I grab my leather driving gloves. I pull them on quickly and put the Savoy in reverse; like the glove box, the gear shift drags and the engine roars heavily. I pause, my foot resting on the brake, and watch Dad disappear back inside. The door opens like a star in the night and then disappears; I'm surrounded by darkness. My thoughts jump around, and I wonder if I'm doing the right thing. I think of George and my three sons snug in the living room. I should be hunched over the ghastly kitchen table marking papers.

Despite that, I feel my foot lift for the gas. I want to make it stop, but I have the feeling that despite everything I have, I would like something for myself.

I think of what Dad said, and I think of my last visit with George, what he'd said to me, that we were one and the same; it has been bothering me ever since. I try not to think of Tim in the thick of those protests with one arm and something not quite right with his mind. I think back to who he was before; he was quick to laugh and always wanted to please. That's a problem, George had always said, but I thought the opposite—it was nice he wasn't a selfish piece of shit like him.

The snow trickles in front of the windshield hypnotically. I drive this road so much I could probably do it half-asleep. Did I blame the white people, the original immigrants, for all of our problems? I think about it for some time, my mind settling on the thought that blame doesn't sustain you. I feel like I'm always trying to move forward, but I'm stuck on some sort of reel, looping continuously back to where I started. I look at the white coating the road; it is getting thicker, and I wonder if that's what the American government's plan was for dealing with us, sticking us with a situation we couldn't seem to control, giving them, the government, the power to make every decision for us. Our food, our education, our children, our health, our homes—and in turn they could take our land and effectually our bodies, minds, and souls. Our soul was the land, that's what Dad always said, that's why we can't leave, that's why we can't seem to go forward; the land was a prisoner, and because we were one and the same, we'd become prisoners with her.

I wonder for the first time in my life why we are still confined to a reservation. I wonder why if we were to leave, we'd lose all benefits, which is essentially one of the few fragments left of our identity. I think of the warriors and wonder if things were easier for them. They didn't have to choose to be Indian or fight for who they were; they simply were.

I blink and am surprised to find myself in the city already. I pull into the bar parking lot, the bar Joshua said we should try. I'd driven by it many times, and it was one of those things you always saw but never really noticed.

I steer my car into one of the last spots, the wheels slipping a bit in the snow. A sweeping, sinking feeling runs through me, and I think I should drive home. Even though I've turned the car off, my fingers are still clutching the keys in the ignition. A knock at the window startles me. I look, and a small smile comes to my mouth, greeting the big one on Joshua's face, the snow sticking to his hair and beard. He pulls the door open for me.

"We should do something closer to you next time," he says, looking down at my face. I find myself smiling, thinking that he is already set on meeting again. I climb out, and he closes the door. I watch as he steps back and holds out his arm for me to take. I find myself smiling again and thread my arm through his and let him lead us to the door, the snow crunching under our shoes.

"I'm really happy you made it. I thought maybe with the snow you might not," he says in his perpetually cheerful manner. He's had a beard growing in since the autumn—I want to touch it; I wonder what it feels like. George can't grow facial hair.

"It makes me more like Abraham Lincoln," he says, touching where I'm looking. I find myself smiling wider.

"I guess I'd need a corset or something to get in touch with my area of history."

"Or a guillotine."

He laughs a little too loudly, drawing looks from the few people smoking in the parking lot, huddled in dark groups against the snow. I want to look at the ground but force my chin to stay upright as he pulls the bar's red door open for me. I let go of his arm and walk in. The bar is dimly lit with a few tables; the smell hits me in the face, and I wonder why people go out of their way to come here. Booths line the wall to our left, and in the center, there is a clearing for dancing. I feel Joshua take my hand. I'm surprised that his hands are so rough. Joshua pulls me through the dingy light, leading us to one of the last empty booths. Joshua guides me to the red vinyl booth bench; I slide across it, making it squeak under my jeans. I plop my gloves and bag on the table.

I find myself glancing around. People pause in their drinks and look at us; some whisper. Everyone is white. I look at Joshua; he doesn't seem to notice or is doing a very good job of pretending not to notice. Smiling, he lifts his eyebrows into some sort of question mark, despite my uneasiness. I smile and frown at the same time, letting a small laugh out under my breath. Joshua thumps his hand on the table, still grinning.

"What do you want to drink? I thought we'd grab something here, then find something to eat elsewhere," he says, looking around as though he would be very surprised to find food in such an establishment. I haven't had a drink in a long time and have actually never been in a bar. I am not sure if I want to tell him that.

"Whatever you're having," I say, like I always say that. He looks at me, and I watch as one of his eyebrows raise slightly.

"A Budweiser and a whisky it is, then?" he says, sliding out before I can answer. I watch him bounding to the bar; he jostles between the occupied bar stools, getting annoyed and annoying the people sitting in them, and I watch as people seem to accept his good-naturedness the same way I did. The bartender looks his way, and I can see Joshua nod and fish around his jeans pocket, pulling out a bill.

"I love this song!" Joshua exclaims over the music, putting the tray in front of me and sliding back into his seat.

"A big Simon and Garfunkel fan?" I ask.

"That was the biggest disappoint of Woodstock for me," Joshua says as he hands out our drinks, pushing the tray to the edge of the table.

"Cheers!" he says, holding up his whisky glass. I take mine and clink it against his. He smiles at me and downs it in one gulp. I raise mine to my mouth, the alcohol burning my nose. I take a small sip and try to fight my contorting face, making Joshua laugh.

"It's better if you take it all at once."

"I thought all Indians knew how to drink."

We both look at the table closest to us. Three men, all about our age, are staring at us. They wear flared jeans and baseball caps. The man in the middle was the one who said it; he turns his head and spits. I find myself looking at Joshua. I've never seen him look like that. With his jaw clenched, I notice for the first time how much definition there is under all the hair on his face. His forearms sticking out from his rolled-up flannel shirt are muscular.

"Woodstock?" I say to him, forcing him to look back at me. He looks at me, his face still clouded. I watch as it softens, and I feel myself relax, my spine pressing into the squeaky vinyl behind me.

"It was crazy," he says with his usual animation, that look disappearing as quickly as it had come. "The bill said they wouldn't be performing, Simon and Garfunkel. But you know, part of me hoped they'd just appear. I mean, what a crazy few years we've been having, with this war and everything. Did you work here during the protests?"

I feel myself growing still; I put my glass down.

"I've been on faculty since 1964."

"Was it crazy? I know it wasn't like Kent. Christ, the National Guard firing at those kids like it was fucking target practice."

I feel myself smiling, not at what he just said but what I had witnessed at the university.

"The veterans club, they flew over the protest and dropped pamphlets that said, *America, love it or leave it.*"

Joshua breaks into his loud laugh, and I feel myself laughing along.

"That funny to you two?" the same man barks at us. I take a sip of my beer and look at him. His blue eyes are rimmed red, and he looks like he hasn't bathed since Labor Day.

"My eldest son fought in the Vietnam War—did you three?"

I watch as the man makes a disgusted noise and takes a drink of his beer, tilting the glass bottle to the ceiling. He slams it in the middle with the rest of their empties and makes a motion to the bartender that they want another round.

"I didn't know, Nancy; I'm sorry."

I look at Joshua and try to smile.

"The conscription was barbaric," he says, his blue eyes large and sympathetic. I look at him, searching for some clue to who he really is.

"Timothy wasn't conscripted. He volunteered; every eligible man on the reserve did."

"Jesus," Joshua says, looking at me in shock; silence settles over us. The smoke and music feel like they are choking me. I look around, wondering how I can excuse myself and get back to my car, back to my kids, back to my home. Joshua catches my eyes. I look at him; he is studying my face, shifting on his bench. I wonder if I've made a mistake agreeing to come. He drinks his beer, careful not to finish it.

"Sorry, Nancy, I don't mean this as offensive, but why?"

"That's what we are, warriors," I find myself saying, thinking of what Dad had said to me before I left. Joshua nods his head politely; I think he is trying to understand who I am.

"Did you read *Custer Died for Your Sins*?" he asks, leaning toward me over the table.

"No, I've heard about it some; it's just that I haven't much time between work and my family."

Joshua nods his head again at me, taking a slow sip of his beer.

"I read it when it was published back in '69, and it changed my whole world. I mean, the whole way I structure my courses, everything. I heard it's the backbone to this movement, the American Indian Movement. What he, Vine, wrote about the similarity between your struggle and the African Americans . . . I mean, this whole county is formed on these fucked-up backward notions, and when someone tries to point it out, a bullet always makes it to their head."

I think of what Joshua is saying. I think of what is happening at Pine Ridge. It's the same thing. Somehow the US government has made its very own power movement—they call it "tribal council." I wonder if I should tell Joshua about it. I wonder if I should tell him about all the people gone missing and how the US government turns a blind eye. I think of what Tim said, that they still want the land they've been trying to take for ninety-six years. Christ, one hundred years, and we're still fighting the same bullshit. This time, though, the playing field isn't level, we don't have trained warriors, we don't have real chiefs, we're not on our own land, so I am not even sure Wakan Tanka can hear the *wasun*, the spirit caves, anymore that is in those hills—the hills they keep trying to take.

"Nancy?"

I look at Joshua.

"Are you feeling OK?"

I smile. "It's just that I am not used to drinking. My son, the same one that fought in Vietnam, he went with the AIM to Washington."

Joshua laughs and hits his hand on the table hard. I find myself smiling about it for the first time.

"That kid is going to have some stories to tell! Unbelievable!"

I feel my smile fading. I look at Joshua; his eyes are so wide open and believing. He is looking at me like I've just given him some sort of gift.

"I worry about him; he lost an arm."

"Oh, Nance, don't take this the wrong way, but I mean, he lost an arm, but he didn't come back in a fucking black bag. That kid's going to make it; he sounds like a fighter."

I smile, thinking of how strong Tim was when his father went away. I think about how he held me the day Lola turned up on our doorstep.

"I'd like to meet him, and your three other sons. You know, Nance, we should make a course, an American Indian course, at the university; it would help the kids, the non-Indian kids, to understand what is going on, why the Indians are so upset."

I feel myself looking at Joshua. I feel like I want to tell him that I don't think he actually understands. He doesn't understand that we're the losers to the Doctrine of Discovery, a false sense of entitlement, a language and culture barrier that found us excluded from the very nation that engulfed us.

"What would we say, Joshua? That we lost the war of industrialization, and the nation that swallowed us then told us we were to be governed by them through the Plenary Power Document, and if we sought any sort of redress, guess what? We are excluded from the protection of the Constitution, your Constitution, we are excluded from the great Civil War amendments, the Thirteenth, Fourteenth, and Fifteenth amendments. Why? Because then your country would have to admit that it stole something, and that maybe the grandiose lies it tells itself aren't true?"

I find myself shocked I let those words come out of my mouth. What George said to me slaps me in the face. What he and I are. I understand right then what I think he meant. We are both Indians. Joshua can go home at night with the sense that he has real freedom.

We, on the other hand, go to sleep every night with an ache and a longing in our soul for something we can't even remember if we ever had—freedom.

"Nancy, that is exactly what we should be saying," Joshua says quietly, reaching for my hand. I let him take it, my fingers unfurling. I hadn't realized I had clenched them into fists. I look at our fingers intertwined, my flesh dark against the white of his, and I feel tears coming to my eyes.

"I don't think the university would let us. I don't think they would let us say what would have to be said."

"Then we will fight them."

I don't look at Joshua. I let his words hang over us and blink the tears from my eyes, thinking about what he has said, wondering if change is actually possible. Led Zeppelin's "Thank You" cuts through my thoughts.

"Oh man, I love this song. Nancy, dance with me."

I look at Joshua, his plaid shirt, a deep red-checked with blue and black, and I look to the middle of the bar where two other couples are swaying under a string of Christmas lights. I take a big sip of my whisky; it burns my throat, and I smile at Joshua. He stands up and holds out his hand for me. I grab it; it engulfs mine, and his palms are tough like he works outdoors. I am careful not to meet the eyes of the three men as we weave past them; I can feel them looking at us. I notice Joshua doesn't look at them either as he leads us to the middle of the dance floor between the two other couples. They don't pay us any mind, and Joshua, still holding my hand, pulls me close to him, his other hand resting on my low back. I can't bring myself to look at him, even though I like the way his hands feel.

For the first time, I feel something wash over me, something I never felt with George, even when we made love. The song ends; I look at Joshua, thinking we should go back to the booth. He leans down and presses his lips to mine, and I feel myself pressing into him, the warmth of him filling my body, awakening something in me I didn't know existed. Joshua smells like pine trees.

"Well, that's about the most disgusting thing I ever did see."

I feel Joshua's back muscles tighten. I didn't realize my hands had traveled there. I pull away, looking at the same man who'd been after us the entire night, his faded eyes looking at us, picking his teeth with a toothpick. I look around at the other two couples who have stopped dancing. The few people at the other tables stare at us. I look at the bartender who is leaning forward into the bar, his eyes cocked on Joshua. I stand there, not sure what I should do. I pray someone selects another song from the jukebox.

"What the fuck is your problem?" Joshua shouts at him. He lets go of me and goes toward the man still sitting at the table. I feel my heart stop as the man slowly rises from his chair.

"Bad enough we got to share our schools and restaurants with the Negroes; I don't think we need to share our bars with the Indians."

I watch like the world has stood still as Joshua pulls his arm back. His fist cracks the man hard in the face. I feel confused. Blood is pouring from the man's nose and into his mouth. He straightens up quickly and swings at Joshua, who steps back fast. The other two men rise to their feet, one of them knocking over his wooden chair in his haste. I watch as one of them tries to grab Joshua as the other seizes one of the empty bottles from the middle of their mess and cracks it over his head. I see his face contort in pain, and he struggles to free himself from the man holding him. I feel my feet moving. I grab the fallen wooden chair. I feel myself raise it up high and bring it above my head and slam it into the man, the man who'd been taunting us all night. It lowers the man but doesn't knock him off his feet; he stands up and turns, looking at me, and slaps me hard across the face. I feel like my jaw is going to fly off my face.

I stumble backward and land hard on my side. I hear a rifle shot cut through the noise, and I notice the music still isn't playing.

Everyone stops and looks at the bar, all drawn to the noise of the shot. I feel a hand roughly grabbing my arm and look to see Joshua, who is pulling me to my feet.

"You best take your squaw, man, and get the fuck out of my bar," the bartender calls out, looking at me; his rifle is cocked and pointing at me. I look at Joshua. Blood is pouring over his face from his head, his blond hair drowning in a sea of red. I feel him pulling me to the booth that we were sitting at. He lets go of me, and I watch as he gathers our coats and my bag. I look over at the three men. They are in no better shape. We are all going to have some bruises. Joshua grabs my arm and pulls me toward the door.

"I don't want to ever see your type in here again!"

I look at Joshua, who has let go of me. He gives the barman the finger, slams the door open, pushes me through it, and in silence we march toward our vehicles in the deepening snow. We stop in front of the Savoy, and he hands me my parka.

"Nance, I'm really sorry," he says. I start to cry. I can feel myself shaking. I want to stop, but I'm trembling. I feel his arms around me, and I sob. I feel his hands on my head. I feel him kiss me.

"Where are your keys?"

"They're in my bag." My voice is shaky. I watch as he goes through my purse; he finds them and leads me to the passenger seat. He unlocks the door and guides me in. It feels strange; it has been a long time since I have sat there.

He starts the engine.

"Thank fucking god it has at least stopped snowing," he says, throwing the car in reverse. I look at him; his hair is matted to his head with blood. "That was un-fucking-believable." He says this more to himself than me. I want to tell him that this sort of thing is normal, that every time we leave the reservation, something like this happens, a comment from a shopkeeper, a comment from a customer.

"We can go back to my place. I'll call a buddy to take me to get my truck before those assholes fuck it up. We can have some coffee and get you cleaned up before you make the journey home."

I feel myself nod into the darkness. Joshua weaves through the empty streets toward a cluster of apartments.

"I would have liked a house, but with that flood they had back in June, real estate's at a premium."

I don't say anything as he pulls up to a building and shoves my old Savoy between two newer cars on the curb.

"Alright," he says, getting out. I hear him lock the door and watch as he makes his way over to my side. He swings the door open for me and holds out his hand. I take it and am surprised at how warm it is. Joshua shuts the door, a little too loudly, and locks it. I feel him take me gently by the arm and lead me to a redbrick building with a cherry wooden door.

"This is it," he says, fishing keys out of his jacket pocket; he opens the door and motions for me to go first. The lobby is more of a landing, with a row of metal mailboxes. He closes the door and motions for me to go up the stairs; there is no other way to go. I make my way up them, the carpet squishing under my feet.

"It's number four."

I wait at the door marked with a black metal four. Joshua comes up beside me and unlocks the door; he waits for me to go first. I enter as he flicks on a light. I hear the door close softly behind us. His entire apartment is covered in wood carvings. There is every animal you can imagine. The tables on either end of his faded orange couch are made of one solid piece of wood, with stems that look like vines blooming with flowers, toys, cars, blocks, wagons, people; the four chairs around his kitchen table he'd obviously made as well. Another one of the chairs is next to the TV. Tools are scattered on the floor in front of it, next to a small log.

"I would have tidied up, but I didn't think we'd be coming here,"

Joshua says, gesturing to everything. I notice amongst it all is a spider plant that has taken over most of the ceiling.

"Here, you can have a seat," Joshua says, stepping forward and gathering the papers covering the faded orange couch.

"Midterms."

I nod, thinking that I should make more time to be marking my own papers.

I feel him take my arm and guide me to the couch.

"I'll just put the coffee on," he says, disappearing; the hole in the wall separates us from the kitchen. I hear the buzz and flicker of the fluorescent lights being turned on. The kitchen is so small I wonder how you could cook a meal in there. I hear a cupboard open and bang close and the tap turn on. I hear the fridge door open as Joshua pops back into the living room holding a frozen bag of corn. His head is soaking wet, he has washed most the blood off in the kitchen sink, and his hair is still lightly tinged pink.

"Sorry, I don't like peas," he says, sitting next to me on the couch as he gently presses the bag into my jaw. I realize that I am hurt.

"I think it's going to be a pretty nasty bruise."

I don't say anything.

"Christ, your kids are going to kill me."

"I don't think they will think that you hit me."

Joshua laughs, and I look at him.

"Holy Christ, I don't think they'll believe that you hit that man with a chair!"

I feel myself smiling, making me wince with pain.

"Christ, I don't think any of us saw that coming; the look that man had—I wish you could have seen it."

I feel myself smiling wider. A honk sounds outside. We both turn to the one window that looks out onto the street behind us.

"That will be Rick."

"The medieval history professor?"

"Yeah," Joshua says a little sheepishly.

"I didn't think he had any friends," I say more to myself, pressing the corn into my face.

"I guess he's got one. I think he scares them off, with all his renaissance fair talk." Joshua looks at me, almost embarrassed.

"Tell me about it," I say as Joshua laughs, using his arms to push himself to standing, the couch sinking like a seesaw.

I watch him walking stiffly, and I think he is more hurt than he is letting on.

"I'll be fast, help yourself to some coffee," he says, going to the door; he pauses with his hand on the knob and looks back at me.

"I'm really glad you're here."

I smile, making him smile. There's another honk, and he disappears out of the door.

I'm glad I'm here, too.

CHAPTER 10

▲▲▲▲

"KEEP BOTH EYES OPEN," I WHISPER TO BLOKA.

We're on our stomachs; the dew from the grass is seeping through my shirt.

"Now?" he whispers back to me, his voice sounding strange; with age it has grown increasingly raspy.

"Almost."

I watch the pronghorn's peculiar little antlers twitch.

"Now!"

I watch the Springfield trapdoor rifle fire into his shoulder so hard it pushes him back on the wet grass, and I'm reminded how young he is. The antelope screams; it's not dead.

"What now?" Bloka asks.

I can see panic in his eyes. I smile, wondering if that is what I once looked like. His straight black hair reminds me of my little brother, and I feel my smile fade and a heaviness sink over me. Gunpowder is smeared across his right cheek. From watching Bloka, I see that when no one guides you, everything can take years longer to learn, if you ever learn it at all. I reach out and try to rub it off with my thumb, which does nothing more than rub it more across his face. I smile. Bloka's fear-filled eyes are fully absorbed on the mess he's made in front of us. I follow his gaze to the animal flopping around the forest floor.

"We have to kill it," I say, standing.

I pull out my knife from the spot I keep it in the waist of my leggings and nod at him. I watch as he scrambles to his feet and awkwardly tries to tuck his gun behind him in the holster we'd made together from deer hide. I help him holster it, admiring our handiwork; we had woven dyed porcupine quills around it to give it more substance. I finish, straightening it diagonally across his back, his soft hide tunic moist from sweat. It isn't that hot, so I know the sweat is from fear. Bloka is looking at my knife. I nod, and he slowly pulls out his own from his legging's waist. I nod again, and we make our way to the screaming animal.

"It isn't clean," Bloka says. I can hear the disappointment in his voice. I don't tell him, but I think the Springfield doesn't shoot straight.

"Nope, but you hit it," I say, smiling down at him. He smiles his shy smile back at me, and we both sink to our knees in front of the pronghorn; I watch as he nervously tucks his hair behind his ears. I place my knife gently on the forest's floor, spruce needles framing it—nothing is between us and the dying pronghorn; the animal flails, in too much pain to acknowledge us.

"Forgive me, creator, for I know not what I do, and thank you for the gift we are about to receive."

I scoop up some of the moist forest floor. It has that softness you can only get in early summer. I close my eyes.

"Thank you for this nourishment," I say, sprinkling the dirt over my knife. "Thank you for this abundance. Thank you for this life." I tilt my face to the sky; the sun rains down on my face, trickling through the tree branches like beams from heaven itself. I close my eyes and release the last of the dirt over me. I open my eyes and stand.

I don't have to look at Bloka to know he is doing the same. I feel my knife in my hand even though I don't remember grabbing it.

I look down at the antelope, foaming at the mouth. I come down to one knee and slit its throat, my knife dragging through its flesh. I shove my hand into the blood spilling from it; it's warm and sticky, and I press my hand to my face. I feel my fingers digging into the flesh on my forehead. I hear Bloka, whispering another prayer to the mother earth and to the father sky.

I look at him and nod; he has to do the rest. It is time for me to go. He nods back at me, his chin tipped up with uncertainty. I smile—you never know unless you try on your own—and with that, I turn and disappear through the trees; they rustle their goodbye. I hold out my hands and let my fingers gently touch their needles and leaves. *Be safe*, I think, *don't let too many people make you into cabins and clear you—what had Swift Fox called it? Raping you.* I see smoke swirling toward the sky and smile. I've always loved this time of year. We gather and hunt, gather and hunt, all for the snow, which brings to us its silence, the test of resilience; many didn't like those long, cold days, but I relished them. As a hunter, it meant some time to not think of the stillness engulfing you.

I had taken my tipi down early that morning. I see the fur on the same rock I had left it on before I'd gone with Bloka on our last hunt. I see Green Leaves, sitting in front of her tent, her daughter strapped to her back on a cradle board. I watch her awling with a determination of survival. We had told them, when I returned covered in snow, what was wanted of us, what would happen if we didn't comply— they would come for us, they would punish us for disobeying their theft, that's what Standing Bear had said. No one wanted to go; we all agreed it was better to die in the trees than die with nothing. I watch the baby grab two fistfuls of her mother's black hair, her yellow hair as bright as the sunshine. Green Leaves can feel me looking at her and pauses; she looks at me, fear, anger, worry all cloaking her face.

She touches her heart, then gestures to me. I do the same, my hand lingering in the air; I smile, letting the sadness touch my mouth. My arm drops, and I grab my fur bundle and army coat underneath it, my fingers finding the shiny buttons.

I weave my way through our small camp, ten tipis, and see Sha squatting in front of her tent, pounding dried corn with the same stone mortar and pestle that she has had us dragging around for years, ever since I had joined. I walk toward her; she pauses, hitting the corn with the same determination as Green Leaves when shoving her needle through the tiny hide moccasins. She glances up at me with her honey eyes and white hair and puts the pestle in the bowl.

"This is it, then?" she says, not with sadness like I had thought but almost with relief.

I smile at her. "I think we are only beginning."

She nods; her face is always almost straight. Never judge before you think, that is what she always said to me.

"I had a dream last night that you were surrounded by wolves. They screamed at the grandfather and a massive black bear stood before you. The ground was covered in snow, and to kill the bear meant you had to walk on a frozen river because the ice was thin."

I find myself frowning at her words; the vision doesn't sound promising.

"Did I kill the bear?"

"No, I woke before, but if you did, you would live, I know that."

"We all die," I say, thinking of everything I had learned in the past few months of the American people coming and everything I already knew of them. She looks at me with the same eyes as the Chief of Thunder's, spirit dreamers—there is a depth to them I cannot give a full thought to truly understanding.

"The white men are coming here soon," I say to her. We had had endless, unresolved conversations of what we should do with our camp—go north or turn ourselves in to the agency. Canada, we had heard, was no better—a different white man was taking over there.

"I know. The trader said they are already digging up this earth, ripping her apart. We are to be worried about it, for they will make us them—it is a strange thing, isn't it?"

Her words make me look into the forest. I feel a tear run down my cheek. I feel Sha brush it off; she always smells of the forest floor, earth, pine needles, and medicine.

Sha softly whispers to me, her hand on the side of my head. "I have always wished for a time, before they came, when the earth, she gave us everything we needed. When we gave our people everything they could want. I wished we could stay in the Black Hills and hear the wind call the trees and the trees answer with their song. And the magic of *wasun* called to us undisturbed."

"We killed a pronghorn," I say interrupting her; I see the surprise on Sha's face.

"We have not seen them in some time," she says to me, studying my face, weighing if it was good or bad for me.

"So much of what we know is disappearing. Where does it go, Sha? Will we go with them?"

I watch as Sha turns her head to a noise only she hears; the summer wind shakes the trees.

"No, what we know of us, *Indians*, lives, in broken fragments. They kill us, they cheat us, they will steal our children and rape our mother, but we live, we live hundreds of years—our souls carrying from one lifetime to the next. The secret of abundance, the secret of vitality, the secret of the god they try so hard to know or hide. We whisper these secrets to ourselves at night and forget in the morning, but we will whisper long enough till we remember while we are awake."

Her words . . . I feel them settle into my soul; I know they now live in me, and I will pass them on.

"Will I see you again?" I say, making Sha look at me hard, her hazel eyes seeing past what most of us can see; they dig into me. When I was small it used to make me uncomfortable, and now—now I find it reassuring, the knowing that everything is at once one and the same; we are all connected.

"Yes, I made these for you."

She takes a small pouch from around her neck and puts it over my head. It is a small hide satchel on a soft leather cord.

"A *wotawe?*" I say. No one in our camp has ever needed one. She smiles at me.

"Yes, and this," she says, handing me a larger pouch. It's not to be worn, and I take it. The hide conceals something that is soft and crunchy.

"Medicine?"

"Yes, if you don't want a child, you will take it."

"How?"

"You'll know when the time comes. I should get back to this maize," she says, gesturing back to her mess of corn. "We've more babies than I can ever remember us having."

That means we're done. I touch the pouch embroidered with small stones, turquoise and a gray one I'm not familiar with.

"For protection," she says, looking at my fingers on the stone.

"Thank you," I say. I don't just mean for the gifts—I mean for everything, for this life; she knows and steps forward to embrace me. Her arms are solid and strong.

"We will not be able to stay here, and we will reach the outskirts of Red Cloud's Agency."

I feel almost disappointed that she has decided to give up, surrender—that's what Standing Bear had said—I know this kind of surrender is not just about land. I tie my coat and fur bundle to my back over the top of my rifle.

"Today is a good day to die." I look at her. She's never said that to me; I feel myself smiling.

"What is that?" I say.

"Those are the Brulé words you will need to know now."

"Today is a good day to die," I repeat to her, letting them echo inside of me.

"Go with love, Little Wolf."

"Farewell, Sha," I say, our eyes lingering on each other. She gives me a sad smile, her eyes creasing, revealing their age. I watch her go back to her pile of ground corn and kneel back down in front of it. She grabs her pestle and begins banging the stone again, not missing a beat. I smile, trying to burn her like that into my memory, and turn my feet, making their way out of the camp, the song of her pestle beating. I feel myself pausing at the tree line, and I look back at all I've ever known.

I feel myself smiling. Most of the camp has gathered. They raise their hands at me, and I touch my heart and raise mine. I look at Sha, who doesn't look at me but is standing with them.

I nod and turn, making my way into the trees, my feet touching the pine needles through my moccasins. They poke and crunch familiarly. I pause; I hear one of the women from my camp letting out a trill, which makes its way to me as clear as if she had been standing next to me. I haven't heard a war cry since I was a child; the hair stands up on my arms. I hear the other women join in. I keep moving forward. I hear Sha scream above the others.

"It is a good day to die!"

The only males in our camp, barely adolescents, start whooping, their voices a little too high; they carry me forward. It makes my body shake. I force myself to keep moving north, toward the Little Bighorn Valley. Five or six days of walking, Sha had said, follow the trampled grass. I walk in silence; the trees have stopped talking, and the birds refuse to sing. My hand goes to the small pouch around my neck, and I whisper to god, "Forgive me for I know not what I do, guide me to help our mother, for she cries."

I hear an eagle scream. I close my eyes and let my feet guide the way.

CHAPTER 11

▲▲▲▲

"WHAT DO YOU THINK LITTLE PHIL IS GOING TO SAY?"

I look over at my brother Tom, wincing a bit in the sun's light. We had left Boston and James at the station to arrange our travel to St. Paul's; it was a welcome feeling to be away from the throng of civilians, rushing about like this world actually meant something for them, their purpose encompassed in the meaningless nothing of cosmopolitan life, petticoats, and the stench of shit—that's what our politics had been reduced to, swallowed up by the emerging industries, something that I could already see posed a much greater threat than the Indians.

These people pause and take notice of us. I feel myself stand a little straighter. The hide fringe lining the sleeves of my jacket and the outside of my trousers sways, moving like the dry grass of the prairie.

"I always wanted to ask you, General, why the buckskin?" my brother asks.

I don't have to look at my brother to know he genuinely wants to know; Tom, unlike Boston, always asks what is truly necessary.

"The one thing that has made me more fortunate than our contemporaries is that I accept that to win you must think like the men you are fighting," I say, still squinting.

"Or women," Tom says. The way he says it makes me glance at him.

We'd noticed since Washita that half the warriors have been women. It seemed to upset him more than most, who simply choose not to mention it. I'd been trying to pry information about them ever since. All Indians would rather die than give up their war secrets; even Monahsetah wouldn't speak of it to me in the dead of night in the safety of our sheets, or our scouts, and I trusted them with my life, so I never pressed the matter any further.

"Unfortunately, my own imaginings limit me to my own gender," I say, and Tom laughs. We both pause, the Department of the Missouri looming before us; these buildings are meant to give those who work within their walls the conveyance that they are small, and the men in charge of them are mighty. The Indians, even their chiefs, lived amongst their men as equals—they gave their strength, their wealth, willingly to those they led, and the men and women that followed them fought with a determination and bravery that was unparalleled to any man of our own nation. Deep down, although none of us said, we all knew that is what the real Indian problem was: If they aligned themselves with the tribes they opposed, they could halt our manifest destiny in its tracks.

I watched as our leaders did the opposite, choosing and making a point to glare down on those beneath them, making sure we were subjugated to their illusionary conquests, as they moved a pen and expected us whom they ruled to bring them all they thought they were entitled to, we the people soaked in blood while their fingers remained long and clean.

"This is it," Tom says, shaking me from thought. We make our way up the stone steps, our boots clicking. I push open one side of the heavy, double-sided doors, the brass lining letting us know where we are is something of importance. I nod at the private sitting on guard on the inside; he stands and salutes. I lead us to the right to General Sheridan's office, our boots echoing through the corridor and hallway. I pause at the massive oak door shut to the world and put my ear to it; silence rings back. I give a loud knock and push my way in. The general's small brown head pops up at us from a stack of papers; being tucked behind his massive black mahogany desk gives him the appearance of being even more demure in stature than he is. His thick eyebrows lift in surprise.

"General Custer! And to what might I owe this pleasure?"

"General," I say, saluting and removing my hat.

I stride toward one of two chairs in front of the huge desk and take a seat. I glance at Tom cuddling his captain's hat. He takes the empty seat to the left of me. I feel some warmth in my chest. I am glad to have let him join me in this endeavor.

"I've come here for the Spring Campaign orders, General," I say firmly, my moustache tickling my lip.

"Spring Campaign?" Sheridan says with an incredulity I don't appreciate; I ache to cut him off but keep my lips sealed shut, my fingers digging into the brim of my hat.

"I've got word from Sherman that you are locked in some sort of verbal quarrel with Ulysses, and that I am to incept you at all costs."

I feel myself nodding. The blood rushes from my feet to my head, making my heart thump with anger; my breath seems to catch in my chest, the same way it did in those first still moments before a pitched battle—the smoke, the metal tang of fear and blood, always seemed to disappear and for a moment the world was totally silent. Words begin to tumble out of my mouth, my mind taking over with my thinking.

"Given my history with the Sioux and the Black Hills, I think that it is more than fair to say no man is more suited for such a campaign then I am, General." I finish, leaning toward the small man fighting to destroy a people with a pen and paper. I talk as though I can make him say what I want him to by merely looking at him; I know my eyes are cold, like ice—all us Custer boys had them.

I think of the Indian campaigns I have led over the past few years to the great benefit of our fledgling unified nation. I watch as Sheridan leans back in his chair, bringing his hand to his chin; he strokes it as he looks at me.

"I fully agree with you, General Custer—in fact, you are my first choice in any of this. I had a hell of a time persuading President Grant to abandon his cowardly peace policy toward these savages. You and I know as long as they are out there roaming, they pose a threat not to just us, but to our country as a whole. It is my idea to put them all in one area, containing them in a reservation of sorts, with large military outposts stationed amongst them, reminding them that we own this land now. To do this, I've needed a bigger budget and more men. Your quarrel with Ulysses Grant could not have come at a worse time, for he has finally seen reason and granted me my wish."

I feel my eyes burning into General Sheridan. President Ulysses was a vain puppet pulled in any direction that benefitted him— Sheridan the Protector of the Plains under the Department of the Missouri. A feeling sinks heavily over me that I've never welcomed but always manages to find me, my fate tied up in someone else's decision about my character. General Sheridan looks at me, studying my face, weighing out the battles yet to come; I know he is wondering who is a worse enemy and what can win him the war, the war of land.

"Of course, I can do nothing of the sort if you are already on the train to St. Paul's, where you'll continue on to Fort Abraham Lincoln and be promoted to commander of the entire Seventh Cavalry. That is, you, General, will have all twelve companies of the regiment." Sheridan leans back in his chair, his mind decided about who will come out victorious.

I feel lighter than air and can feel Tom knowing we are victorious. I don't have to look at him to know that he's proud, perched on the edge of the seat as though he is a bird of flight.

"General, there is truly no way in which I can show my deep appreciation for your decision," I say, making Little Phil laugh.

"They don't understand you like I do, General. They don't understand the full extent of the task they have rewarded me in securing the land of the Plains all the way to the Rockies to be a part of this glorious nation. They don't understand that to do this, we have to kill those sneaky scoundrels and savages. Your task is not only defeating them but also breaking the power of the chiefs. We've done a good campaign against their buffalo; now we must work on the Indians themselves. They have straight up defied the call that they must come into the agencies, and they continue to roam at will. We will use the excuse that the Sioux are attacking the Arikaras and the Crow unprovoked as a means to breaking the Treaty of Fort Laramie. The president has already signed off on this."

I watch as Sheridan pauses his monologue and waves his hand dismissively in the air. I hadn't realized I had slid to the edge of my seat, my fingers still dug deep into brim of my hat. The small man searches my face, checking if I have truly heard everything he has said. I nod that I understand; we're about to fuck them—there will be no mercy, and if this nation has to be secured in blood, so be it.

"This will be by far the hardest fight we've had. General Terry will be aiding and leading you. He is a good man but prone to quiet bouts; I have never trusted a man who is too quiet—they don't tell you what is in their head in their correspondence—so I feel he will be in dire need of your aid."

He pauses for the laughter we have to give him, Tom and I both oblige him, our hollow chorus ringing through the coldness of the air.

"I have also assigned General Crook and Colonel Gibbon; you three always got on, didn't you?"

I nod, thinking of Gettysburg, hellfire, and smoke—if you had seen it, you were bonded in a blood oath.

"I've briefed both gentlemen; as this will prove to be difficult, I've provided you with more men than ever before. They've got a chief, Crazy Horse, who is supposedly fearless, sees a bullet and rides into it, can't be killed. He's allied with another man by the name of Sitting Bull, who I think they call a spirit dreaming, or some nonsense like that—you know that rubbish they like to go on and on about. Nevertheless, they are both different than the chiefs who have answered and shown up to the agencies; they are drawing different Indians to them, and agency Indians as well, who were already settled, are flocking to them. Something like five thousand warriors have made their way to them—men, women, and children. These women, they are not the Indian Princesses we have become accustomed to, either."

General Sheridan stops and grins at us, and I know that Tom is smiling enough for the both of us. "So, I think it would in our best interest if you wire Sherman and tell him your story, that we met and I told you to head back to Washington. He already knows what I have actually told you, as it was partly his idea. Also tell him what exactly happened with you and the president. He'll wire me, and I'll say that we spoke and told you to make your way back to Washington. You and you alone on your own account will wind up in Fort Abraham Lincoln, and we will all have a merry American Independence Day clearing this land for the glory and destiny of our people."

Sheridan was already somewhere else; I watched as he picked up the paper in front of him and began reading it, as though we'd never spoken.

"My gratitude is to you as always, General," I say, tipping my chin to him.

He looks up from his paper. "Ah, General Custer, you are like a son to me. Remember that the only good Indian is a dead Indian, and I look forward to your field reports." He looks back down at his paper, and I watch him scan the black type.

"Thank you, sir," I say, standing and saluting. Tom mirrors me.

"Good luck to you, gentlemen, and I'll see you in the autumn," he says, not looking up from his reading. I make for the door. I can hear Tom behind me. We step into the hallway, and I close the door firmly behind us; it shuts heavily, protecting what is behind it.

"Where to now, General?" Tom asks, putting his small cap on his long curls, looking at both sides of the empty hallway. I follow his eyes, adjusting my own black brim on my head.

"We'll use the wire here to contact General Sherman and Libbie, then make for the fort," I say, leading us down the hallway toward the wire housed on the second floor with the rest of correspondence. We walk past all the black doors set against the white walls, the wood floors shined and gleaming, our boots thundering. The Chief of Thunder enters my mind, something stirs—the excitement of hunting such a worthy adversary. We were almost the same age, mid-thirties, and we were leaders of men.

"What do you really think of Gibbon, Crook, and Terry?" Tom says in a hushed voice, disrupting my thoughts. I think of the embarrassing defeat Crook had had recently against the Indians we were just talking about. Having been outsmarted by them myself, I felt that I couldn't judge the man too harshly.

"Gibbon's a solid fighter. Terry thinks too long, long enough to get us all killed, and Crook, I think we've all heard whispers of his horse-meat marches." I feel myself trailing off. Tom lets out a half laugh.

"Was it not General Sheridan who wanted Monahsetah?" Tom whispers to me.

I think back to Washita and the pleasant months after.

"He had asked for her, but there were so many for the taking that he didn't put up too much of fight when I took her. I let him have one night with her as an appeasement."

"What was she? A chief's daughter or something?" Tom asks. I can sense that he is frowning. I remember what her face looked like as she nursed our son.

"That she was, Tom."

"Libbie made you give her up?"

"Libbie doesn't make me do anything."

"Where is she now, Monahsetah?"

I feel irritation sinking over me like a stone thrown in a pond.

"I don't know, Tom, where have we put all the Indians? On some forgotten parcel of land that no one else wants?" I say, not preventing my agitation from entering my voice. I've moved on; in these short moments, I need to start mapping out my fate, our fate for the battles to come.

Tom makes another half laugh as we reach the top of the stairs. We pass two privates hurrying out of the office, clutching papers. I pause at the closed black door and look at my brother, who looks at me with a bored look. Tom is restless.

"Enough of the past, Tom, let us do what we came here for—let's finish this last war for independence."

"Here, here," Tom replies, and I push the door open.

Now is the time for me to choose my words wisely. Now is the time to think of nothing more but where I am. Now is the time to be the only thing I know: winning wars.

CHAPTER 12

▲▲▲▲

I CLOSE MY EYES AND LISTEN, a *guledisgonihi*, cooing cry, cuts through the trees. I think of my mother, my heart pangs—she always said the mourning doves made that song for the acorns, and I know, hearing them so close, that I made the right decision. I call back; the dove coos, confused, and I smile. My breathing is heavy, and my back is soaked in sweat from the fur I've been dragging along for days, the only respite that it had provided me with a bed for the past few nights. I had taken to holding my carbine; when I had it holstered on my back with the fur, it dug too deep into my flesh. A stick snaps, and my eyes open as I step silently behind a low bush and crouch, raising my rifle to my shoulder. The trigger clicks as I cock it.

"What are you waiting for?" a tall man with a very short man asks me, stepping out of the forest and directly into range. I aim at his narrow face; his accent is strong, and it does something to me, pulls at something I don't like, the way I'd felt bartering with the traders at Deadwood.

"A man named Swift Fox," says the tall man, answering for me, making the little man grin. He is wearing a painted loincloth over his hide leggings. My eyes linger on his leggings, a color I've never seen before. I wonder what animal they are made from.

"Swift Fox? You don't need to find him if it is a man you are after," the little man says, looking at me through the brush.

"You are warriors?" I ask, looking both of them over.

"Do we look like warriors to you?" the tall man asks. He is wearing a feather bonnet, which looks to be mostly eagle feathers. The little one just has a painted face, his hair woven into simple braids.

"Maybe," I say. That makes both men laugh, their laughter booming through the trees.

"Lower your gun and come with us; we'll take you to the dog man," the little one says, cocking his head behind him; they both turn, not waiting for me, and make their way up the small hill behind them. I lower my rifle and have to run to catch up with them, the fur pounding against my back, sweat beading down my face.

"Did Swift Fox give you a baby?" the little one asks, glancing at me as I catch up to them. We roll over the hill and are making our way down the other side. I look at the man, surprised; the taller one is looking at me, interested.

"I don't think that is it," the tall one says, making the little one look at him.

"Does Swift Fox have many women show up with his children?" I ask, making both men laugh.

"No, they're usually just madder than thunder," the tall one says, making them both laugh even harder, cutting through any sounds left of the forest.

"We were just on a hunt, and a crier said there was a strange-looking Indian in the forest, so we were sent to find them, which I guess is you," the little one says. I see he is beginning to sweat as, even with no shirt on, his bare chest is gleaming in the sun.

"What did you kill?" I ask, making both men grin at me.

"You are the Indian Confederate soldier, aren't you?" the little one asks, ignoring my question. I feel my brow scrunch together.

"I've never met so many people interested in my coat," I say, making both of them laugh again.

"Swift Fox said you were funny."

"He spoke of me?" I ask, feeling heat run to my face.

"He has really only spoken of you since the winter when I guess you met him. He has been harassing our Wicasa Wakan so many times about whether or not you were going to show up that when he now sees Swift Fox, he pretends to be fast asleep."

"This is true," the taller man says, and both men once again break into a fit of giggles.

"We can be in the middle of a lodge and Swift Fox comes in and Horn Chips drops like he's dead."

Both men start laughing again.

"Well, I suppose if he needed to find me that bad, he could have come and found me," I say, thinking how long this winter seemed to have dragged on—every time the snow began to melt, another storm seemed to rush in. God was telling us to think, Sha had said.

This makes both men laugh so hard that we have to stop walking. I pause, getting my first good look at them, their cheeks bright red.

"We said that much to him in the spring, and he said he forgot to ask where your camp was," the little man says, gasping between laughs, tears streaming down his face. I feel myself smiling with them.

"I am Little Big Man, and this is American Horse," the small man says, waving his hand in the direction of the taller man, who nods at me.

"Chiefs?" I ask.

Little Big Man grins at me and begins to walk again; we follow him. I smell roasted meat, unlike any meat I've ever smelled. I see the first tipis peeking through the trees like the first stars in a night sky.

"The camp is bigger than it has ever been. We ran into Crazy Horse, who'd already run into the Dog Warriors, and then we all ran into Lone Horn, Gall, Sitting Bull, and Black Moon."

"Not to mention the agency Indians," American Horse says. I look up at him, and he glances down at me.

"Those are the Indians who have touched the pen," he says, nodding.

"Swift Fox says your camp won't."

I take a deep breath. Sha, she said she was going to make for the camp, touch the pen.

"I don't think it is the right thing to do; you can't take what is ours because you've already stolen what is someone else's," I find myself saying. The more I had walked, the more I had felt upset with her decision.

"I think Swift Fox was right about this one," Little Big Man says, grinning at American Horse. American Horse looks at me again.

There must be at least one hundred tipis, all standing like a colorful forest and all different sizes. Children are running through them like playful coyotes, making me smile. I see women carrying baskets brimming with chokeberries and timpsila. We pass a massive fire.

"Buffalo?" I ask.

"You are a Brulé, and you have never seen a buffalo?"

I can see that Little Big Man is smiling, even though what he had said wasn't kind. I pause, looking at the beast's massive head propped up next to the flames of the fire. Apart from the missing eyes, it is fully intact. Massive slabs of meat and ribs are skewered on sticks balanced between stripped birch logs. I watch fat drop into the flames, causing it to hiss.

"My wives are overseeing the drying of the rest."

I look to see another small man standing with us, a new man. He looks different again from the other two, older, his face scarred, from battle I suppose—they look like they had once been knife cuts. He is shirtless as well and reminds me of the oaken barrels from Deadwood; he is the same color, a deep, rich tan.

"Is this the soldier?" the new little man asks.

"Yay," American Horse exclaims, his voice a mixture of disappointment and amusement.

"They were hoping you were Pehin Hanska," says the new man. I look at him.

"Custer," he says, answering my silent question. I still feel like they are all speaking a different tongue from me. With their accent and all the words they use, which are familiar but not quite the same, with many I have never heard before, I feel out of place. I feel a sinking feeling, my certainty drifting from me. I shift in my moccasins, feeling wary, tired, and hot.

"She is looking for Swift Fox," American Horse says.

"Ah, I think we all knew that," the new little man says knowingly. I look at him and he looks back at me seriously. My wariness lifts a little.

"He is still with the others," he says, looking at me and glancing at the two other men. His eyes, they were like ravens, taking in everything, measuring, thinking of what he has to do next.

My eyes are drawn back to the massive head by the fire. I find myself walking up to it, glad to leave these men behind me. Crouching in front of it, I gently put my fingers to its thick brown fur; its holes for eyes stare into the vast emptiness of the afterlife. The fur, it is coarser than I would have thought, all shades of brown like the grass is yellow at this time of year. My fingers trace along the horns that adorn the top of its skull, and I wonder what it would be like to hunt something of this size.

"You have never seen a buffalo?" the new small man asks me. I look to see only he has silently joined my observations.

"No," I reply, looking up at him; his face, despite the scars, is kind.

"I am my camp's only hunter; I think we would need more than me to take down one of these."

"And some horses." He studies my face with his raven eyes. I nod, thinking about it, trying to imagine it.

"Your camp doesn't have any horses, does it?"

"No."

The silence is awkward. I look back at the head.

"We have some dogs," I say, making the man laugh. It is a low laugh, a laugh only meant from him.

"Pehin Hanska, one of his chiefs, Sheridan, is killing them all, the buffalo." He nods at the head. I listen to his voice; it quivers with anger, and he takes a deep swallow before he can continue. "With Indians they have corrupted with venomous, empty promises from their honeyed tongues. He thinks, the White Chief, that if the buffalo are all dead, so are we. What do you think, Little Wolf, do you think we can survive without them?"

The little man, his question rings through my ears. I walk back through my life, my fingers still on the beast's horns, and I think of my mother, my father, my brother, Sha, the people she had found and gathered.

"We will just find something else to eat," I say, looking up at the small man, and he smiles a smile that reminds me of my father, a smile that says he knows many things.

"I will take you to Swift Fox. You two, you should go to Crazy Horse and Sitting Bull. They're both still in the lodge, praying for the white men to reveal themselves."

I feel unsure; things had already started to come back to me that I would have rather left buried.

"Come, Little Wolf, I'll take you to what you seek," the little man says gently, reading my mind. I slowly stand, the sun hot on the top of my head. The little man nods and makes for the left through the forest of hide.

"Many mouths to feed," the small man says, leading us deeper into the camp.

"You enjoyed hunting it," I say to him.

"How do you know it was me?"

"By the way you looked at it," I say, knowing that feeling well—that what you killed, you somehow bonded with.

"Are you Wicasa Wakan?" The small man asks.

I look at the small chief, surprised. "No," I answer. I think my mom was; I remember the smell of plants and roots dried in a basket she always had—she slept with it next to her head. I remember those nights—the breath of my parents was so reassuring; people would come to our tipi, at all hours, and she would slip from the furs, grabbing her basket like it was a part of her arm.

"Then I will tell you this because I am a father to women. I would keep my distance from Little Big Man. He is not an *ongloge un*, a shirt wearer."

"Is Swift Fox a shirt wearer?" I ask. That makes the small man burst into laughter.

"No, he is a Dog Soldier. They answer to no one but god; he will keep you safe," he says, glancing at me. "Or maybe you will keep him safe," the little man says, more to himself.

We leave the tipis and start to weave through the narrow pines, reaching a clearing in the forest. I am halted by what I see. Close to one hundred men and women dressed for war are mock fighting, drums are being pounded, guiding their dance and leading them. It is a swirl of feathers and colors; silver, shields, gunstock clubs, and war clubs bang against one another. Part of the music, part of the dance.

"We are getting ready for the Sun Dance. Your Swift Fox is somewhere in there, talking to god. I am Chief Gall of the Hunkpapa; I am sure I will see you again."

I look at Gall, but before I can nod and tell him any thanks, I see him stalking back into the tipi forest, and I watch as he barrels through the trees, rustling the brush. The noise pounds away my uncertainly; it as though it is the beat, the rhythm of the earth's heart.

"Did you just arrive?" I hear a gentle voice shake me from my thoughts and look to see a slight woman; like me, she has on some clothes of the white people, her white blouse tucked into a calico skirt made with many shades of summer blue that seems to engulf her. She is studying me just as curiously, her dark eyes darting from my rifle to the fur I am still trudging with. I notice in her arms, under her long hair, is a baby she is holding to her breast. I watch the baby's small dark head, so intently focused on eating, totally oblivious to the beautiful chaos around him.

"Yes," I say, my voice drowned out by the drums.

"I am Shadows Fall. My wife is in there, somewhere. Red Hawk," Shadows Fall says loudly, nodding at the beating circle. We stand together, watching the warriors swirl.

"Have you come for the Sun Dance?" she calls out to me. Not taking her eyes off the warriors, we watch as one man takes a deathly blow at another man who ducks back, meeting his club with a hide shield.

"It seems as though I have," I say.

I look over at Shadows Fall, who gives me a small grin. Her baby finishes eating, and I watch her close her blouse and rewrap his dark-red woolen blanket around him. He has the most beautiful face I have ever seen on an infant.

"He is beautiful."

"She. Would you like to hold her?"

I hold out my arms, and Shadows Fall passes me her child. I watch the baby pinch its face from being separated from its mother. She squirms, settling into my arms.

"She is our third, our first girl; I am relieved."

I look at Shadows Fall, who smiles at me.

"Our sons have joined the other children; they've all turned into wolves."

I laugh.

"I thought they were all more like coyotes." I look at the tiny baby, her body as warm as the fur on my back. Shadows Fall laughs with me.

"If you want a camp to join, you can join us. We're all *winkte*, easy to find even in this mix," she says, glancing at the blur of movement in front of us.

"Thank you," I say, feeling genuinely grateful.

The drums and the dancing stop. I get my first good look at the warriors. They are all gleaming with sweat; you can see their spirits have been made very high.

My eyes are drawn to a woman who is stalking, the same way Chief Gall moved through the mess of warriors toward us; the sides of her head are shaved, showing nothing of a black shadow where her hair would have been, and what she left on top is braided in a thick braid falling halfway down her back. Small feathers dyed red are woven into the braid making a mohawk down the center of her skull. It is beautiful. In comparison, I am feeling pretty simple. Her dark eyes show through the color on her face, painted half white and half red. She is looking at the slight woman next to me, and I can see that even through the face paint, she is beaming at her. My eyes rest on the gunstock club and rawhide shield she is clutching in either hand. The shield has a red hawk painted in the middle of it.

"Who's this?" the woman says to Shadows Fall, stopping in front of her, her chest heaving, her speech coming out between the deep inhales. Both the women look at me.

"I am Little Wolf. I'm looking for Swift Fox," I say, looking between the both of them.

"You Cheyenne?" the warrior demands.

"No."

"Humph," the woman says, looking me up and down.

"Your daughter is beautiful," I say looking down at the small baby making the warrior smile.

"Like her mother," she says, handing her gunstock club and

shield to Shadows Fall, who takes it carefully, and the sweaty woman gently takes the now sleeping infant from me. My eyes linger on the sleeping baby for a moment, and then I feel something like the air stirring, and I look up to see him. He is wearing nothing but hide leggings and a silver breastplate. His hair is done similar to Red Hawk's in a large braid down the center of his head. Black feathers are woven into his braid.

"I didn't think you'd you come," he says, stopping in front of me and trying to catch his breath. I watch his chest heave, beads of sweat rolling down his face.

"We will see you," comes the small voice of Shadows Fall. I glance at them as they disappear among the warriors and tents. I feel a pang in my heart to be left alone; I never knew you could feel so alone surrounded by so many people.

"Swift Fox! Is this it? What we have all been waiting for? I bet that is what you danced in there for!" a man dressed just like him calls, looking at us and grinning. Like Swift Fox and Red Hawk, he is breathing heavily; I recognize him—he was the one with Swift Fox from Crazy Horse's camp back in the snow. I notice there are several of them, all in silver, all carrying clubs that are slender, and shields with more elaborate designs—animals, people—swirl flecked with silver, glittering in the sun against the rawhide.

"Come, I want my fur back," Swift Fox says to me, ignoring what I think are his friends, his people, his tribe. He walks past me, and I hesitate, looking at the silver men, all starring at us, before I warily turn and follow in the sure footsteps of Swift Fox, weaving his way easily between the trees back to the camp, where his friends whoop and cry, their voices chasing us through the forest.

"I've just about had it with them. If the army we have been promised doesn't show up, I'm going to leave for Canada."

I look at him. His face is painted black with a red zigzag down the center, and through the black paint, I can't read his face, only hear his voice, and I can't tell if he is serious or not. We burst through the trees and into the camp—it looks like a beehive, with people shooting off in different directions with great certainty and focus. Women hurry along with woven birch-bark baskets and armfuls of hides and moccasins in need of mending; children run screaming and chasing on another, dogs trailing after them. We both step aside as a dozen small people charge past us, totally oblivious to us walking through them.

"I always like the edges in camps like this," Swift Fox says, weaving us between the tipis. My eyes are drawn to the paintings adorning them. Battles are depicted, animals, landscapes, stars, fire. Slowly the tipis become more scattered, revealing a floor of grass, then they disappear, and we are back in the narrow spruces, their sharp pines filling my heart. I see his tent, the same simple one, just like in the winter, standing all alone.

"We are lucky the American army didn't come upon you; I am guessing you were the soldier the crier sounded about?" Swift Fox says, stopping at the entrance to his tipi. I don't answer, thinking about the soldiers, the American army. I know what they do, the army—they kill most everyone and burn everything else. The buffalo now, too—nothing escapes their death march, their need for more. I wonder what it would be like for them, the American army, to come upon a camp such as this.

"I can take your pack," he says, nodding at my back, breaking me from my thoughts. I look at him, the man I had crossed a valley of danger for. He searches my eyes, then ducks into the tipi, disappearing through the flap, and comes back out without his shield or gunstock club. I smile and undo the rawhide strap I've been using to keep the pack tied to me. I can feel the dent it has left in my skin. I gladly hand him the bundle; my shirt is stuck on me. I watch as he tosses it in the tipi carelessly, making me smile. A mourning dove calls out through the trees, also making me smile. I feel the same way as he does, I realize—I'd rather hear the earth than the noise of other tents. Swift Fox holds his hands out to take my carbine. I give it to him, pausing as he grabs it, not letting go. He smiles and gives me a reassuring nod, and I release my fingers. He disappears again; I hear rustling in the tent before he pops back out into the sunlight.

"Do you want to come with me to the stream?"

There is nothing I would love more after five long hot days walking with the pack. Just the word *stream* makes me long for the cool water on my face. I smile, and he nods, disappearing through the hide flap of his tipi again. I hear clanking, and Swift Fox reemerges without his breastplate. My eyes travel to the marks on his shoulders where the breastplate must have been cutting into his flesh. His ribs have several large red marks that look like they are going to bruise badly.

"Don't worry. I gave as good as I got—this way," he says, stalking off into the woods. I have to take quick steps to keep up. I hear the water and feel myself smiling. I close my eyes and feel the hot breeze try to stir the hair stuck to my head. I open my eyes to see Swift Fox looking at me. I smile at him. He stops walking; I stop with him. I see the water, the sun dancing off the top of it, calling to me.

"Marry me."

"What?" I say, the smile fading from my face. I forget how dry my mouth is.

"Marry me tonight."

I feel the hair stand up on my arms.

"Let's drink, and then we can talk about weddings," I say, looking at the stream again. I can't bring myself to meet his eyes. I feel his hand touch my shoulder; I look at his moccasins.

"Water first," I say as I feel his hand drop from my shoulder, and I make for the stream. I feel hot, I feel like I'm floating, I feel like I am in a dream. I kneel by the water and scoop it into my mouth; the water cools my body. I scoop up handfuls of it, rinsing my face. The water travels down my back, and then I let my fingers get lost in the stream's current. I give thanks. I look at Swift Fox, kneeling next to me and looking at me intently. I look back into the water, feel my cheeks growing hot.

"Marry me," he says again, quietly, almost like a prayer. I feel elated and empty at the same time, the same look I have seen on a woman's face after she has birthed a child.

"I don't know if it is a good idea," I say, forcing the words out, not looking at him, my eyes fixed on the water rushing by us.

"Why not? Have you married someone else?"

"No." I answer quieter than I would have liked.

"Do you not like me?" His voice is demanding.

"No, I like you," I find myself replying without even having to think about it.

"Then there is no reason not to. I will go back with you to your camp if you are worried about your camp's babies still."

I watch as his fingers find mine in the stream. He gently touches them. When I don't pull away, he interlaces his fingers with mine. I think about my life. I think about how long I've been running from the white people taking my home, chipping away at every place we come to that we think is finally safe. I think of Frank Grouard and what he said in the winter.

"I think it would make all of this harder," I finally say, meeting his eyes. I am taken aback from their intensity; it is almost as though they are on fire. With his face painted, his eyes are all I can see. They are black and burning into me, as though they alone can make out my thoughts without me speaking any words.

"All of what?" he says—his mouth, it is almost angry but something else, too, determination maybe. That's how you survive, Sha had once said, with hope and determination to keep breathing.

"This," I say, looking into the forest, her trees, her birds, her deer, her buffalo; it isn't just us they are trying to kill.

"What Frank Grouard said, that this isn't ours anymore but theirs, and we have to move to these agencies, these prisons, their prisons, our prisons," I say, feeling the tears run down my face. I hear the truth I have shoved deep down inside of me start to bubble out. I had not said any of this to Sha; she had asked what we should do, and neither of us knew, so we just stared at each other across her tipi's flames, our faces getting hot. And god didn't answer.

"When we are finally forced onto those and have to no longer be what we are, I think it would be harder to have a family," I say, the tears now freely flowing. I feel them, like the water I had splashed on my face, running tiny rivers down my neck. I feel his fingers clutch mine more firmly.

"No, you are wrong; it will make it easier. I will stand there and fight with you. When they force us onto land and make us stay in a mud-baked shithole of a cabin, I will slip out under the moonlight with you, and we will hunt and gather and store things where they would never think to look. Out there, we will dance and sing to our children the songs of a past they are trying to kill. You will not go to sleep full of sorrow for I will share it with you. When we grow old, we will then whisper the truth to our children's children and die old and content, knowing we never gave up; we never truly became what they wanted us to be. We will go into their towns and hold our heads high, for their win will be full of shame and deceit, and god only ever smiles upon those who love. So, no, Little Wolf, I think you are wrong. It won't make it harder but half easier, for I will take half of your burden and gladly carry it with mine."

I feel the tears still running down my face and look at the fingers clutching mine. I meet the eyes of a man that loves me. Silence dances around us, and I think of everything he has said to me. The mourning doves call out, and the stream continues to babble. I glance at the blue sky, a decision entering my heart.

"I will marry you, Swift Fox; I will marry you tonight."

I watch his tears smear the black and red paint together on his face and laugh through my own tears. He smiles at me; he takes our hands from the water and puts them over his heart, pressing my fingers to his bare chest.

"You are the only person ever meant for me, and I will love you till I die," he says to me. It is done, we are bound to one another, through this life and into the next. I smile, my tears running into my mouth. He lets go of my hand and grabs the back of my head, pulling my mouth to his. It is warm and soft. I close my eyes, letting the warmth wash over me. I hear the mourning dove sing its bastard song, and I wonder what it would feel like to actually believe that everything will be OK.

CHAPTER 13

▲▲▲▲

THE WARMTH OF THE SUN PRESSES THROUGH my hide tunic, warming the black hat on my head. I close my eyes, taking a deep breath of the scent of dry grass, the summer air warming my lungs. I taste promise on the tip of my tongue, the promise of victory, the promise of finishing what I had started long ago—there is nothing more satisfying than knowing that you are coming into one of the final battles before winning the war.

"General, I have the strong inclination that they must be waiting on you."

I smile, her voice ringing in my ears like the first chirps of the birds at springtime; my eyes slowly open, taking in the tall grass swaying in the stirring breeze.

"And I reckon it is the thought of my little wife that I ought not to make them wait for my appearance?"

Her giggles ripple through the air, reminding me of the girl I married.

"Tomorrow will come too soon," she says, leaning against the wooden fence rail, her small shoulder pressing into my arm. I look at the small bluebells adorning the white dress sleeves, how she favored flowers. My eyes drift to her face, and I slide the arm she is leaning on up her back to the back of her head, cradling her head in my hand; she is so small, so fragile; I often wondered if that was the reasoning for her inability to bear a child. Her pinned hair presses into my palm, reminding me that she needs protecting, and despite this, she always insisted on coming with me on my calls of duty. Deep down, I had the inclination that she was willing to risk her life to prevent me from taking another Indian into my bed. She disguised this fear in tales of undying love for me and that she couldn't bear to be apart for so long, and we both accepted the lie silently, the hallmark of a successful union of marriage, knowing that togetherness more oft than not is an illusion.

"Do you ever wish that things might have turned out differently, Autie?"

I know she is speaking of the children she has longed to bear, meaning our thoughts have been upon the same currents.

"I'm proud of the man I've become and the family we have made. When this war is finished, we will take some time off and enjoy singing, books, and maybe take in some theater, go to New York and Monroe. Just how things were for a while, before all this," I say, watching her smile. I believe those truths more than she does. I look away and out into the vast nothingness. The void beckons to me in the same distinction that I know frightens her.

"Do you ever hear any word of General Crook turning up yet?" I ask, watching the bugs lazily float through the air, above the grass, mimicking the same lazy sway; everything is one, that was what Monahsetah had said—her words, they had so much power and conviction that they often came back to me, and I wonder if she was right, we are all connected.

"I heard from Maggie that he has been summoned to speak with General Terry."

Libbie answers in a way that can't help but spread a grin upon my face. "Now, Autie, you know that that is none too kind." Libbie chastises me in a way in which she would have spoken to the children we never had, and I feel my grin growing wider, my moustache grazing my cheeks.

"I reckon General Sheridan sent him here to teach him a lesson," I say, more joyously than necessary.

"Well, we cannot all be the respected General's favorite now, can we?"

My grin returns, pressing my moustache into my lip.

"General!" Tom's holler silences my moment with Libbie, cutting through time. Something always comes between us, always just under the surface, calling me away from her.

Tom comes into our view, and I watch my brother hurrying through the grass toward us, his boots taking exaggerated steps through the thigh-high sea of grass. I glance at Libbie; she knows it, too. I pull a single strand of golden straw from my hide trousers pocket. I place the long grass blade in between my teeth and begin grinding at it, chewing it, thinking, dreaming of what lies before my brother and me, watching him make a steady pace. Tom, he'd not quite been right this expedition, something I'd never felt in him before—*anxious*.

"That brother of mine, he has been more like Boston this trip than himself," I find myself saying softly, not wanting Tom to hear a hint of my words. Libbie doesn't answer straightaway. I glance at her; her dark brows are knit tight together, her mouth set, thinking, something she seemed to always be doing. When I see her with that look, I always wondered what thoughts dance through her small head.

"I think I know what you are saying, Autie. I've noticed it, too, in all the men actually. There is something in the air with this campaign, like a charge before a thunder and lightning storm."

I look down at my tiny wife, her face pinched, her black eyes searching the grass for something that isn't there. I wonder how it feels to live like that, to be in a perpetual state of worry; it was not worry that plagued my men—something close to it, though.

"We will all be just fine, Libbie," I say hollowly, the same words I have said through the entire Civil War. I lean over into her, pressing my lips against the top of her brown head amongst the hairpins pressing into my face. I release her and look at my brother.

"I best make my way to them before the generals come looking for me. Or else I run the risk of being court-martialed yet again." I look at the tight smile that comes to her lips.

"Till this evening, I bid you adieu," I say, pushing off the fence and giving Libbie a small bow. She smiles and nods at me, the sun against her face showing her age. I hop over the wooden rails and make for Tom, who at least had the good sense to stand a few yards from us. I look him up and down; he is leaning lazily to one side, his fingers stroking the long grass, his captain's hat cocked to the front of his sweat-soaked brow.

"General," he says to me, barely opening his mouth. The heat did that to my men—it made them slow. I nod at my brother.

"Captain, is General Crook settling in nicely?" I ask, making Tom laugh.

I make haste for the general's tent. Tom falls in instinctively beside me, and we walk as though we are one person. As we near the camp, the cluttering of tents and men, we pass some of our men, who stop to salute. I nod hastily at them.

"He is already in there with Colonel Gibbon and General Terry."

"Well, then, here is hoping they have a parley of good news for us," I say, approaching the massive tent that General Terry erected right in the middle of the fort. The private manning the entrance holds the canvas flap open for us, saluting. Tom and I duck through without pausing.

My eyes focus in the dim light on the men sitting around a very weathered square wooden camp table with a massive buffalo fur for a tablecloth. I look at the varying lengths of fur that had once covered the massive animal's body and smile, thinking of the one time I had the chance to bring such a creature down. The rush of wind on your horse, the booming force of a satisfactory kill shot on something that was so big and powerful—it had been my best hunting experience to date.

"General, Captain, nice of the two of you to finally join us," General Terry says, nodding at the aged wooden camp chairs waiting for us. We salute in unison and settle on the old things, creaking and giving in a way that they threatened to fold in on us. I look at the paper map set on the buffalo's fur in the middle of the table and a smile settles upon my face, for it had been me who had set out on the conquest of the Black Hills, opening them up like a pot of gold for the nation, surveying the very land we now had claim to; with blood and the stroke of a pen, we conquered like empires of the past.

"Both General Sheridan and General Sherman want us to get these hostiles under control. The main problem lies with the claim to the Black Hills. We are actually in violation of the Fort Laramie Treaty, which was settled upon in 1868. But President Ulysses S. Grant has been so gracious as to review Indian policy with the new ministers and Congress. So we now sit upon a great moment in time, gentlemen, a precedent. We are here, and we are going to make history."

General Terry pauses, sucking the very air out of the tent, looking into the eyes of each and every one of us, implanting his words upon our thoughts.

"We have somehow managed to wiggle General Custer among us, praise be to the almighty god, as the great general here has had some great difficulty in joining us in this campaign."

I feel myself grinning as Terry eyes General Crook hard. I feel my smile widening as I watch the poor man turn red.

"Before we proceed, I think it is in our best interest to consult with the Indians themselves," General Terry says, and I smile, knowing that was my guidance.

General Terry leans forward, barking at the closed canvas flap, "Private Smith, send in the scouts!" We could all hear the private's boots moving fast on the prairie's ground, giving us a glimpse at how Terry managed to get such a high-ranking post.

I don't have enough time to size up Crook before the massive frame of Frank Grouard ducks into the tent. In his bastardized Indian apparel, it makes even the dark man look incredulous. I look at the slight figure of Bloody Knife who appears from behind the small giant; Bloody Knife glances at me and nods, and I dip the brim of my hat, an ease settling over me like a cool drink for the first time in months. We wait for the three scouts—the half-breed Billy Garnett, his employer Baptiste Pourier, and his brother-in-law Louis Richard—to crouch through the flap, the sun flooding in with them, seeming too bright.

"Have a seat, gentleman," Terry demands of them in his calm manner, nodding at the pile of folded camp chairs in the corner. The men shuffle the chairs out as General Terry watches them. Producing a pipe from his uniform's pocket, he knocks it loudly on the table, then methodically stuffs it with tobacco he has hidden in the same decorated pocket. I watch as he strikes a match, filling the tent with the sharp scent of sulfur. He holds it to the pipe, sucking on it and letting out fragrant clouds of smoke, filling the tent with more hot air.

"Tell me what you all know," Terry says between puffs of smoke, eyeing the interpreters and scouts; he'd aged from the war, gray streaking his faded brown hair and neatly designed beard—separated from the rest of his hair and isolated to the middle of his face, it had always reminded me of an icicle.

I watch Frank look at the other men, who give him some dark glances, then swallow and clear his throat before words start to tumble from his thick lips. I notice that none of his contemporaries look at him. Frank is focused solely on General Terry, his voice wavering with uncertainty.

"I sent word out in the winter that the Sioux were to make for Red Cloud's Agency for relocation, but for the most part I was met with hostilities." Frank pauses, clearing his throat again.

"But they were not congregating?" Terry says, his strong voice cutting through Frank's quiver.

"No, scattered."

"Why are they congregating now?" General Terry shouts through mouths of smoke.

"The Sun Dance," Frank says, annoyance slipping over his face like a whore's silk.

"Were these Indians together at Powder River?" General Terry asks.

I realize they must have been through all of this a few times before, proclaiming it in front of us, from the look Frank shoots at General Crook.

"No," Frank says, the agitation replacing the uncertainty, his dark eyes darting between all of us—a weasel, that was one of the things the other Indians called him.

"But I would guess they would be by now," Billy quietly replies, softly gazing at the map on the table. I look at the half-breed—he is handsome, a strong face mirrored by a strong body, and I wonder what my son would look like now.

"Why is that?" General Terry asks.

"Because General Crook burned their supplies," Billy says, looking the general in the eye. I find myself trying not to grin. I dare not look at Tom, instead keeping my gaze on General Terry, who has a darkness growing over him.

"Because General Crook burned their supplies," Terry repeats, looking hard at Crook.

"Do you think they know we are coming?" General Terry asks, looking back at Billy.

"To my knowledge, they've got a pretty good idea and are

scouring the forest and plains looking for you," Billy says, still looking only at the general.

"How many?" Terry demands.

"Tough to say. With the rations being limited by you, it drove many from the agencies, meaning they would carry word of any and all preparations they'd seen. I'd say many." Billy's eyes fall back to the map; I'm wondering why he is so interested in it.

"Tell me of the chief, Crazy Horse," Terry says to Billy.

Billy doesn't take his eyes from the map and quietly folds his hands in his lap. I watch as the other scouts go silent; none of them meet our eyes, not even Bloody Knife, as though to even speak of him would bring them harm. Terry looks around the table, impatiently puffing his pipe aggressively.

"He is in the same fashion as Chief Sitting Bull, is he not?" Terry asks, staring at Billy. Billy looks at him and spreads his palms as though he is defeated.

"In that they are shirt wearers," Billy answers carefully.

"What is the difference between these chiefs and others we have conquered?"

The scouts shift in their chairs, and we are greeted with nothing more than the perpetuate creaking of silence.

"Well, then, come on, out with it. We have all got a supper waiting for us, gentlemen," Terry says in a way that I know means his patience is waning.

Silence settles over the tent, and the only noise now cutting through it is the deep huffs from Terry as he fills his mouth with smoke. Terry's sharp eyes—hawks' eyes, we all said—narrow in on the handsome Billy.

"He is touched by lighting," Billy offers up, not looking at him.

"What does that mean?" Terry demands, pressing them further, making Billy's lips press together as though he'd already damned himself by revealing that.

"He is a thunder dreamer, blessed," Frank says in his deep voice, looking at the general with dark, angry eyes.

"Bullets, they find everything but him," Baptiste finally pipes up, looking at all of us uncomfortably.

"So, they think this chief is special, blessed?" Terry asks.

The men, the scouts, they just look at Terry. Terry's eyes shoot between all of them; I am starting to feel his frustration.

"He is looking for General Custer," Frank says, nodding in my direction. I watch as Billy shoots Frank a look. I take special note of that.

"Well, some would say General Custer is blessed with the same blessing," Terry says, bringing chuckles from Gibbon and Tom. I look at Bloody Knife, whose stoic face is solemn, his two black braids framing his high, tanned cheekbones, draining anything funny about it for myself.

"So, what are we to do then? With this dreamer?" Terry asks, leaning back in his chair.

The scouts shift in their seats, and I hear Billy take a deep breath.

"I guess the thing about lightning and thunder is that neither seem to last very long. Storms strike hard and swift, then float away," Baptiste says, glancing around the table.

"The exact thing I was thinking," Terry says quietly, looking at the man through half-closed lids, finishing his pipe. "That will be all," he says, dismissing our lifeline to the world we must conquer.

The men look at the general as though they don't believe him. Bloody Knife glances at me, and I nod; he is the first to rise. He makes a small bow, then I watch him disappear through the tent's flap, letting in a much-needed breeze. The other three mixed-race men and the white man rise, nodding at us and following Bloody Knife. That leaves Frank, who slowly rises; his height is so great that he has to crouch lest his greasy black head graze the top of the tent.

Frank looks at the tent's flap and then back at us, wet marks of sweat soaking through his cloth shirt where his braids rest upon it.

"Sometimes the power of belief is stronger than actual force," the big man says to us carefully, his eyes looking at each one of us to see if we understand.

I find myself looking at him intently. "How is it, Frank, that you always wind up on the side you think is going to win?" I demand, and Frank meets my eyes unflinchingly.

"Guess I've got a little thunder in me, too," he says, glancing at us one more time before making for the flap. My eyes settle on Crook; Frank is his man. No one seemed to have taught Crook that choosing a scout is like choosing a whore or a mistress—choose wrong, and you could end up dead.

"Well, gentlemen, what do you think of that?" General Terry asks after we know the Indians and scouts are out of earshot. He is looking at the four of us left: Crook, Gibbon, Tom, and myself.

I look around at the other men—Crook is slumped over like a child who has been told he has been naughty, Gibbon's blue eyes stare lifelessly at nothing, and Tom is clearly thinking of other things, his foot twitching annoyingly on the flattened brown grass beneath his polished boots.

"I would say that the Sioux and the other hostile nations that have joined with them are a formidable enemy. I think it will take a certain amount of discipline and stealth to round them up, as we discussed on the steamship *Far West*," I say. General Terry looks at me with a hint of a smile hidden by his moustache.

"I think General Custer here is right, and we will stay with our combat design, which I have previously discussed with General Sherman and General Sheridan. We will go through it once more now as we are to set out at sunup," General Terry says, restocking his pipe. He smacks the tobacco out of it on the table, all over the great fur. It holds my eyes, ashes on a buffalo. I look to see him doing the same methodical ritual of filling it. I feel an anxiousness sweep over me, like thousands of crawling ants. I feel my booted foot start to tap, aching for my stirrup and the saddle. I need to be in the saddle. I need to breathe the great nothingness, the expansiveness of promise, of freedom. Smoke fills the tent again, bringing me back into my body, back to the tent.

"As I have already stated and have outlined, we are going to take a classic hammer and anvil operation, no different than what we used against those Johnny Red bastards when they went guerrilla on us. General Custer, you are to march south with your Seventh Cavalry up the Rosebud Valley on the trail of the Sioux and Cheyenne. You will then follow where we think they have gone, west toward the Little Bighorn. You will attack any and all villages, driving the inhabitants north to myself and General Crook. Colonel Gibbon will come up with his foot soldiers hot on your trail, killing any of the Indians who have managed to escape your wrath. General Crook and I will be proceeding at an easy pace," Terry says, pausing between a drag of smoke, his eyes settling on Crook. "This summer's heat has been all but punishing, and I don't want any of my men to be strung along starving or dying."

"Yes, sir," we all answer in an uneven choir. I glance at General Crook, whose solemn face is tight, looking at no one but the general.

"The president has graciously gifted us more resources than we have ever had for fighting Indians. It is paramount that we make this a success, being we have given General Custer the entire cavalry, all twelve companies. And he is to charge in like thunder and lightning, for the best way to beat a foe is with the same tactic."

I don't have to look at my brother to know he is beaming; I feel it bubble up in myself as well, a lightness grounding me from my longing for the field.

"General Custer has been given orders from General Sheridan to attack any and all Indian villages he comes across. We are not taking prisoners; our mission is to clear them off this land, break the power of the chiefs, and get them all neatly settled on the land the president has generously allocated them. This we extend to any and all of those savages who live to see the end of this summer. Any questions?" Terry asks, looking between all of us.

"Are we to take the women and children we come across back to the agencies?" Colonel Gibbon asks.

I look at the colonel and remember the dark-haired man I fought with at Gettysburg. He is now faded like Terry, soft-spoken and graying, a bushy beard joining his moustache.

"I think it is in our best interest to shoot anything that moves; we all know the women fight as hard as the men," General Terry says, looking at all of us.

"Yes, sir," we answer back. We understand: We are to shoot to kill.

"Lastly, General Crook and General Custer, you are to keep your newspapermen in line, is that understood?" General Terry says, his voice rising slightly.

"Yes, sir," we answer at the same time in the automated fashion West Point had imparted upon us.

I find myself looking at Crook. It used to be me alone that sought to document my expeditions. I was none too pleased to have someone copying me, in particular a man whose defeats had become front-page news.

"That will be all, then, gentlemen," General Terry says, rising, making us all stand with him and salute.

We file out according to rank. Tom makes for the door, followed by me, then Colonel Gibbon, and lastly General Crook. I step out into a dusky sunset; dust fills my nose. I look at the setting sun, making the world look as though it is on fire, and I think how I must have been blessed by thunder as well. A thunder dreamer, a chief in my own right.

I nod good evening to the other two men, on whom I am going to have to depend to give Sheridan his victory, and I find myself straightening my aching back. I look at Tom, who nods, and we make for Libbie, our family. Nothing but the song of crickets accompanies us as we make our way through the long grass that caresses my knuckles. *Like the earth's hair*, I think.

"That was something, that yours and Elizabeth's house burned down," Tom says, cutting through my thoughts.

"That it certainly was, Tom," I respond, wondering why he is not himself.

I force us back into silence. I think of all the things Terry and the scouts told us, their uncertainty. I think of what I will tell my reporters, my newspapermen—certainly not what they had said, that the Indian chief was special. Couldn't be struck by a bullet is what they had said.

"I am glad, General, that we are all here. I mean, I think this is the first time we have fought as a family, outside of our Civil War family," Tom says as though I had demanded something of him.

I don't say anything. I think I know what Tom is trying to say. There is a certain comfort in having men you are close to, fighting with, as opposed to the men that usually have filled out my ranks since the war, white immigrants and farmers.

"Do you think that Maggie and Libbie will have finished the supper?"

"Well, Tom, I hope for both our sakes that Libbie has had very little to do with any of the cooking," I say, smiling.

"She still can't cook?" Tom asks, startled.

"She has a supreme talent for burning anything she puts in the fire," I say into the fading light, smiling. Tom laughs as we come upon the small cabin we resurrected from the burned one. I hear the sound of many voices speaking as one dancing from its walls. The light trickles out of the cabin's windows, shooting off in every direction like the sun's rays in water, or the first stars in a clear night sky. I finally understand what Tom was trying to say. For the first time in a long time, it feels like we are home.

CHAPTER 14

▲▲▲▲

CLINK, SNAP-THE SOUND OF A KEY TURNING in a lock forces my eyes open. I blink several times, the light stinging my eyes, the smell of wood hitting me in the face, and I remember where I am. Blood rushes to my stomach, a sinking feeling overtaking my chest as the night starts to replay in my mind.

"Sorry it took so long, Nance; it's really coming down out there."

I slowly sit up, the pain rushing to my face. I look at Joshua, locking the door he had just opened, snow falling off his shoulders and head. I blink at him, hoping I am dreaming; an ache is settling in my head, knowing that the blow I took was a nasty one. I try to wish it away—the bar, the fight, those men—but the throbbing in my jaw doesn't let me.

"The snow," he says taking a soft step toward me, his eyes narrowing, looking at me with a look a doctor gives you, measuring how much you understand of what they are telling you, sizing up my pain. I twist around to look out the window behind me, wincing in pain. The snow is coming down so hard it has blurred the street into an eerie, orange-tinged white, the streetlights lost somewhere in the blizzard.

"Did you get a coffee yet?" Joshua asks, hanging up his coat. He comes over to me and sits on the edge of his wooden log table, his eyes looking my face over. I notice that he has long blond lashes that brush his cheeks—like his hair, wet from the snow. If he were a woman, it would be considered pretty.

"No, I think I fell asleep," I say, looking at him. He stands, and I watch him stride to the closet of a kitchen. I wonder what it would be like to live in such a tiny space on top of and surrounded by so many other people. I don't think I would like it; even in the silence of the night, it seemed loud. I hear mugs clinking. I look for the bag of corn he had given me and see it in a mushy pile on his green shag carpet, beads of condensation dripping off of it and forming a large wet ring around it. It must have fallen off while I was sleeping. I lean forward, wincing, and pick it up as Joshua comes back, holding two steaming mugs of coffee. Like our mugs at home and at school, they are mismatched. One has an overly jolly Santa and the other a palm tree and an overly sexy hula dancer that says *Maui, the friendly island.*

"I better get rid of that," he says, nodding at the thawed corn in my hands. He hands me the hula dancer mug and takes the corn. I watch as he goes back to the kitchen. I hear the bag thunk as he drops it in the garbage. He reappears, smiling, but he doesn't meet my eyes, instead glancing around at the mess we are sitting in. I sip my coffee, strong and black.

"This is good coffee."

"I should hope so. I picked it up at this Italian cafe a few blocks from here, and it was almost the same price as a month's salary."

I look at him, wondering if he is serious; his eyes are scanning my jaw.

"I'm really sorry, Nance, about the whole thing. I didn't think anything like this could ever have happened."

I let out a scoff, which I meant to be more of a nonchalant laugh.

"Didn't you hear of Raymond Yellow Thunder?" I say, looking at the blank TV in front of me.

"Yah, I mean, fuck," Joshua says.

I feel him shift uncomfortably beside me on the couch. Silence hangs between us; a sinking feeling fills my stomach as I think of the last time I saw George. He had said we were alike. I try to bury my memory of him, all of them, and look around the apartment.

"Did you make all of these?" I ask, nodding toward the wooden creations. Joshua laughs.

"When I've got some spare time, I guess."

I feel myself smile, thinking of him alone, whittling away on a piece of wood with a knife. I wonder if he works in silence or with music or the TV on. I wonder what it is like to be alone in a quiet, content way. I had spent my whole life surrounded by the noise and chaos of a family, but every night for the past twenty-one years, I've truly known what the emptiness of being alone felt like. I try not to remember the fights with George, him not coming home, him not taking the boys out, him not working.

"It was something my father taught us growing up. I grew up on a real working farm in Idaho. We couldn't afford a TV or nothing. I think he taught us to whittle more for his sake than ours."

I smile again and look at Joshua, who is staring at the coffee cup resting on his knee. I watch as he puts his coffee down on the carpet and walks over to the small round table that I guess is supposed to be used for dinning. It is covered with wooden figures and carving tools. Joshua picks up a van and a dog, a big dog, the dog I've heard about incessantly for months. I watch his eyelashes flutter, looking at them in his hands. He finally comes back to the couch and sits down heavily, making the springs squeal under the multicolor polyester tweed.

"I made these for Teddy. This is the van from that show he likes, the mystery machine, and the dog himself, Scooby."

I feel like I am going to cry. I put my coffee on the table and reach for the two toys Joshua is holding in front of him. I take them. My fingers trace them; they are smooth, all the details are etched into them. Scooby's collar and spots, the goofy look he always has on his face.

"Teddy is going to love these," I say. I want to say more, but nothing else comes out, and I don't know what else I am supposed to say. No one has ever done something so thoughtful for me.

"I don't know how to thank you," I finally say, still looking at the van and dog in my lap.

"Let me take you out again."

I look at Joshua. He is looking at me with an earnestness I have only experienced with Teddy, and I can see he wants me to say yes. I feel a fluttering in my stomach, like I am a girl who is going out with a boy for the first time. George is the only other person I ever dated, and he had never really asked me out; he had just assumed I would— that was the problem with us, he always thought of us as the same person, like somehow he had absorbed me right into him. Back then, I knew exactly what he meant; we were one and the same. It is almost a relief being able to see George as he truly is, and also devastating the amount of time I had wasted with him.

"I think I'd like that," I hear myself saying, my feelings of doubt slipping away from me like melting snow.

Joshua leans toward me, and I meet his lips. I feel him gently take the van and dog from my hands. I hear the soft thud of them hitting the shag carpet. Joshua's hands are on my back, his tongue in my mouth. I let out a moan. I feel him make his way down my neck; he pauses and grabs the bottom of my sweater. I let him pull it off.

"Should we go to the bed?" he says to me.

I feel myself smile; I'd forgotten about my swollen face. He stands and holds his hand out for me. I take it, and he pulls me to my feet. He leads me down a small hallway to the bedroom, with the only bathroom opposite that. He lets go of my hand and turns on a small lamp on the bedside table. I notice the homemade quilt and wonder if he made it. He walks back over to me and pulls me down to the edge of the bed. Our mouths meet again. He makes his way back down my neck and stops. I watch as he pulls off his own shirt. I try to keep a neutral face, even though I am horrified by the amount of hair on his body. It is lighter, but I can see it is coarse and covers his entire body. I wonder if that's normal for all white people. He smiles at me and kneels on the bed in front of me and undoes my pants. He kisses my stomach, tugging my pants off. He begins kissing me through my underwear. I let my head fall back and moan. I feel my hair against my naked back and wonder when the last time I had sex was. Five years ago—no, now closer to six. Joshua stops and kisses my thighs.

He pulls off my underwear and stands, unbuttoning his jeans. He pulls them off with his briefs, and I feel embarrassed. He lifts me gently, moving me to the middle of the bed. I lie down, looking at the white ceiling cast in a rosy glow from the lamp. I feel him undo my bra and then start sucking on my breast. My hands go the back of his head; his hair is thick and coarse, unlike George, who has hair like silk.

"Joshua, I am not on anything."

I feel him pause, balanced on top of me with his forearms on either side on my body, his coarse body hair rough against my skin.

"I don't have anything, protection—should we stop?" His voice is soft, his breath warm against my neck.

I grab the back of his head, pulling his mouth to mine. I can feel him smiling, and I find myself smiling back. He enters me softly; his mouth pulls away from mine and makes its way back to my neck. I find myself meeting him in a way George never let me. I discover a pleasure I didn't know existed. I feel him finish, my body filled with his warmth. His head hangs heavy next to mine, his sweaty, hairy torso pressed against me. I feel myself smiling with the same enthusi-asm he usually has. Joshua slides off of me and eases himself onto the bed. I feel him reaching for my hand, then he intertwines his fingers with mine.

"Nance, I've been married before."

I turn my head to look at him; he is looking at me seriously.

"Well, Josh, I am still married."

He smiles a sad smile at me.

"She couldn't have children, and it tore her apart. I told her it didn't matter. That I didn't need to have children to fulfill our life."

I look at him and think how Timothy was an accident that altered the course of my life. An accident that I wouldn't take back for the world. I feel myself smiling.

"Did you choose me because I seemed fertile?"

"No, I chose you because you're beautiful."

I look away. In all my years with George, he never once said that to me.

"I became pregnant with Timothy when I was seventeen."

"I figured as much; did you and your husband marry straightaway?"

"No," I say, looking at the ceiling and remembering back to that time. I was like a different person, the uncertainty, the worry.

"I don't think George wanted to. I don't think I wanted to. But I think we both knew that it was probably the right thing to do, and we made a go of it. And we had more children, none of them planned," I say, glancing at Joshua.

He is smiling a smile that doesn't reach his eyes. I can see he is sad thinking of the lives we both have had. The one blessing of being so busy, I think, is that there isn't much time to dwell on your failures.

"The next thing you know, the years have flown by. You are so distracted, always just trying to get through one day to the next, and you realize the person you are with is a total stranger," I say, feeling a tear slip from my eye.

I feel Joshua reach over and gently wipe it away. I look at him again, and he is looking at me in a way I didn't think anyone could ever look at somebody else.

"We can't live here," I say, looking back at the ceiling.

"In this apartment? I don't think it is even meant for two people, let alone six."

"No, I mean off the reserve."

I can feel Joshua looking at me. My eyes dance among the shadows on the ceiling, thinking of everything that seemed to be crashing in around me. Tribal corruption, government corruption, greed, war.

"I would gladly come to you."

"We have rats," I blurt out, not meaning to. I hear him laugh and look over at him. He is looking at the ceiling, still laughing. I watch his hairy chest heavy up and down, matted from sweat.

"I grew up on a farm. They are pretty hard to get rid of but not impossible. Did you get a mouser yet?"

"What?"

"A cat," he says looking at me.

"No," I say, staring at the ceiling. I am embarrassed I hadn't thought of that. I hear Joshua laugh again.

"I can help you."

I wonder why no one else in my house had thought of that.

"If I lived with you, you'd have company on the drive."

I smile and look at him again; he has thought about us living together.

"I don't like to talk in the morning," I find myself saying. The car ride was something I had come to look forward to. Silence, no one demanding anything of me, my mind could turn to an expansive nothingness. Driving through trees, the prairie, the farms.

"That's OK. I'd rather sing anyway," Joshua says, sitting up. He pulls the quilt out from under us and covers us with it. It's warm and soft. I feel sleep washing over me; it feels too good not to close my eyes. I feel him roll on his side, and his heavy arm drapes over my torso.

"Nancy, I'm glad I met you," he says softly.

"I'm glad I met you, too," I say, already half asleep, my eyes refusing to stay open.

Smiling, I feel as though I am in a dream. I feel Joshua sit up, and I hear the click of the lamp being turned off as total darkness descends in this windowless room. I feel him lie back down next to me. He moves closer to me and puts his arm over me again. I feel the heaving of his chest, and I hear his breathing grow slow and deep. I smile as I drift off to my dreams, wondering what my family will think of my decision to bring someone like Joshua into our life. And for the first time since I was a child, I feel like I'm not alone.

CHAPTER 15

▲▲▲▲▲

SWIFT FOX LEADS ME BY THE HAND THROUGH THE CAMP, drawing glances.

"Do you know all of these people?" I ask, catching the gawkers' eyes.

He glances around. "No," he says, leading us with a determination that forces people to get out of our way.

The tipi I had journeyed to with Standing Bear rises before me, the lodge of Crazy Horse; no one guards the flap. Swift Fox pulls us straight to it and ducks in, never letting go of my hand, our fingers intertwined as one. I look around; the hide is glowing from the growing night and the tent's lit fire. I count ten men sitting cross-legged around the hot fire.

"Swift Fox, Little Wolf," Crazy Horse says, nodding to us, his blond hair hanging loosely around his shoulders. Crazy Horse gestures to the blanket beneath our feet, and Swift Fox kneels, tugging me to the ground with him.

"I'm going to take Little Wolf as my wife, and she is going to take me as her husband."

Crazy Horse glances at me and nods solemnly. I see the same two men that were with him in the winter. I watch as they pass around a pipe, the same as when I met the chief the first time. The only difference is that this time their dark eyes are glinting with amusement. I make out the round, dark figure of Gall, who gives me a wide smile. I smile back at him.

"So, share a tent," Crazy Horse says, taking the pipe from the man who had worn the wolf hide. Tonight he wears nothing but a loincloth. I find myself staring, for I've never seen someone so heavily tattooed. A massive hawk makes its way across his ribs and chest wrapping around to his back, and a pattern of lines run down half of his face.

"Little Wolf needs to be made a warrior," Swift Fox says to Crazy Horse, who looks at me, his gold eyes blinking through me.

"You ever kill anybody?" he asks as though I am not there.

"No," I answer quietly.

Crazy Horse's eyes flicker back to Swift Fox.

"Maybe this is the wrong girl," he says.

I feel Swift Fox's fingers tighten around mine.

"No, this is her," he says with the same determination he had walked with.

I look at the strong face of the man who wants to call me his wife. Swift Fox's eyes are boring into the tattooed man.

"Is it not?" he demands.

The man with the tattoos looks me over carefully.

"Who was your father?" the tattooed man asks me in a tongue I have not heard for a long time. I feel myself grow cold, and the hair on my arms stand on end.

"My father's name is dead," I answer in the same language.

I hear Swift Fox laugh, a laugh of triumph. The tattooed man is still looking at me, searching for something most people's eyes can't see.

"It is her," Crazy Horse says more to the group of men than to me, although they are all focused on me now.

"There is only one way to find out," the tattooed man declares in the same language we had just spoken in.

"Little Wolf, do you want to be a warrior?" the tattooed man asks me, again in the tongue of my childhood.

Nobody had ever asked me what I wanted. I've always done what I've had to do to keep on breathing, to stay on this earth. I look at the fire before me, its flames rippling like blood, and I think of the edge of the river, of how Swift Fox had promised to always stay with me. Did I want to be like Shadows Fall and wait by the side with the children? Did I want him to hunt game while I wait to dry the meat? No, I wanted to stand next to someone, not behind.

"Yes."

I watch the tattooed man take a medicine pouch from around his neck and grab a hollowed gourd. He dumps the bag into the gourd and starts to chant, his words making the fire's flames dance. The man on the other side of him, wearing a full-feathered headdress, starts to chant along with him, and the rest of the men join in. I close my eyes as I hear someone begin to softly beat on a drum. I open my eyes to see the man with the gourd; the tattooed man looks at me and I look only at him.

"You are to leave here with nothing but your soul when I give this to you—you are to drink it all."

"Yes," I say.

I feel Swift Fox's fingers slip from mine. Our eyes lock; I feel their strength; I feel a nervous smile come to my lips.

"I am Horn Chips, Wicasa Wakan, and I will guide you. I am Horn Chips, Wicasa Wakan, and I will guide you. I am Horn Chips, Wicasa Wakan, and I will guide you!" he shouts, echoing around the tent. I watch as he takes a mouthful of the liquid and spits it into my face over the fire. It doesn't make it to me and sears in the fire, making the flames turn blue.

"Now, drink," he says, shoving the gourd at me. Through the blue flames, I take it. I take a pinch of the earth and drop it in my mouth.

"For protection," I say, making him smile, and I drink the gourd.

It tastes sour and too hot, then too sweet and salty. It tastes of every regret I've ever had and every life I've mourned. It tastes like home. I am gone; I am not in the tent. The men are gone. I am in a field. The field is so full of wildflowers you can taste them in the air. The grass is taller than me and my brother.

"Gray Wolf!" I call out.

We are playing hide-and-seek. The sun is hot on my face. He is three years younger than me; at five, he can play this game all day. I am growing bored and know that our mother needs my help with the awling. We spend half our days punching moccasins back together.

"Gray Wolf! It is time to go back!" I shout into the green all around us. I hear gun shots.

"Gray Wolf!"

I'm shrieking till nothing comes out of my mouth. I hear screaming. I smell smoke. I'm running for the camp.

"Little Wolf, stop!" I hear my dad scream at me.

There are men I have never seen before, many of them. They are on horses. There is one that stands out among them all. I stop. He has long golden curls covered by a black hat, black as night. He jerks his horse around and looks at my father. My father, his chest is a wolf, his headdress is on, black-and-white feathers run down his back. They point their rifles at one another and shoot. I watch my dad fall to the ground, and the man in the black hat starts picking out my people from the crowd; his rifle cuts through them like our awls through hide. They drop like animals. I hear war cries, and I see the women and children streaming into the woods; more men gather around them, chasing them on their horses, rounding them up. I run for our tipi. I stop.

"Gray Wolf!" I scream, falling to the ground on top of my baby brother.

He is clutching a small tomahawk. I feel myself weeping. Someone says something to me, and I look up. It is one of the men on a horse. They feel safe on their horses. I duck between the animal's legs, causing it to rear up, and make for my mother. Why do I know she is there? I can feel her. They are burning the tents; they are burning everything. The air is thick with black smoke and ash. I see it, I see the painting of the pack of gray and black wolves. I run to it and slide under the back side on my stomach, dirt and rocks snapping at my body. I wince in pain. I see my mother; she turns and looks at me. She is always glowing; she is so beautiful—her hair braided in two thick black braids. She smiles sadly.

"Dad and Gray Wolf . . ." I don't get to finish. She nods. She is a Wicasa Wakan. She is powerful. She hands me something, a bear's claw.

"What is this?"

She folds my fingers around it.

"Run, Little Wolf, run the way no one else will go."

"I am afraid—I don't want to be alone," I say through my tears.

"To lead is to be alone."

I feel her kiss my face; she always smells of sage and hope.

"Now, go."

She points to where I came from.

"What have we got here? I knew there was someone in there," a deep voice says in English.

"Go," she mouths at me.

I crawl under the tipi's thick hide, and I pause. I look back. I know I should go, but I need to see what is coming next.

"Holy Christ, this one is as beautiful or more so than the chief's daughter."

He looks like the man that shot my father, except this man's eyes are dead.

"Tom, you know what your brother said—we gotta go."

"I'm fucking her first."

My mother looks back at me, and I disappear. I run the opposite way that my people are being herded. I jump over my friends' fathers, tears blind me. I run faster and farther than I ever thought it possible. I run till I collapse. I sob; the sobs rack my body. I can't breathe. I think of my brother; he was so small.

"Little Wolf."

I look up and see myself being picked up by Sha. I remember that day in the woods. I pushed the day so far back in my memory that I had begun to think I had dreamt it. I watch us disappear into the pines; she cradles me like an infant.

"You will not find what you need in the trees."

I feel like I am going to be sick. I look. He is not far from me; his flesh seems to be melting off of him. He is white.

"I am sorry. I should have found you. I should have found you in the grasses."

My tears are blinding me; he is holding the tomahawk he died with.

"It was hide-and-seek, and I heard the screaming," he says, looking around childishly.

"You fought?"

"No, I died."

"What do I need to find?"

"The grass."

I feel myself sobbing. Gray Wolf holds out the tomahawk for me. I don't take it.

"You need to take this."

I cry harder.

"I should have died, too," I say. I had often wished I had died, too.

"No, no, Little Wolf, no one really dies."

I close my eyes, then open them. He is gone. I see the axe, the axe of my father. Its handle is smooth and bound in rawhide that is dyed red—three feathers, eagles' feathers, dance, hanging from the bottom. I feel myself stand. I walk to the axe and look down at it.

"I should have died, too!" I scream at it, thinking of the *Tom* with my mother. My father's head . . . it had been partially blown off. I remember now, and I don't remember forgetting.

"I want to die!" I scream, closing my eyes.

I open them. I am standing in the plains, the same ones I had grown up on. They go on and on like the sky. I feel raindrops falling, and I look up. It is night. Clouds are rolling across the twilight so fast that I feel dizzy watching them. There is the roll of thunder and a flash of lightning, and the whole world lights up for just one second.

I see the man that shot my father standing on a raised wooden ground, surrounded by dark red fabric. I look down at my feet. The ground is red and soft; there are people everywhere I look, all seated in rows. White people, their clothes glitter and are of no use. I wonder how they even walk dressed like that. I walk closer to the man; everyone is laughing. The man is totally naked, he is holding a black hat over his manhood, and I see in the other hand he is holding a severed penis. The people are looking at him and laughing harder, pointing. I look at the people and back at the man. I feel sorry for him. A flash of lightning lights up the room. The people laughing, their faces look evil. Their flesh is black, and you can see their bones. I know I should feel frightened, but I am not. I look at my feet, and relief floods though me as I feel the stiff blades of grass under the soles of my feet.

I see what my brother wanted me to find. He is beautiful. It isn't a pony but one of *their* horses, an American horse. He is gray like my brother and has a white mane; his massive hindquarters are covered in white hail spots. The thunder rolls again. *I am thunder dreaming*, I think to myself. The lightning flashes, and the horse is walking toward me.

"I don't want to make you a slave!" I shout through the blowing wind. The horse shakes his mane; he has chosen me. I walk to him, tucking the axe into my leggings. I have to leap, my hands grabbing fistfuls of his coarse mane. I pull myself onto his back; he cranes his head back at me. I touch his nose; he shakes his head and starts to run as fast as the clouds. I feel myself laughing. I hear the thunder and lightning but don't feel it. We are it. I lie back; our backs are together as one. My legs squeeze him hard. The sky shows me things I've never seen, I've never known. We are in an existence where for a single moment I am one. I am complete. I am whole.

My horse, Gray Wolf, comes to a halt. We are in the woods; the land is not level but rolling. There is the smell of smoke and gunpowder in the air. I reach for my carbine and touch my own flesh. Nothing is there.

"This is your stop."

I look at the forest floor to my right. I blink away my tears.

"You are still here," I say barely above a whisper.

"I never went anywhere," the small voice replies.

I smile and look down at him. So small in his buckskin shirt and pants my mother and I had made him; he was always clever like that, too clever, irritating.

"*Yonks!*"

"What was that?" I ask, startled.

"That is where I live now. I have to go soon; you should kill the bear," Gray Wolf says, nodding toward the top of the hill. I look, and at the top of the hill is a massive black bear fighting an entire pack of wolves. They keep charging him, nipping him, drawing blood, but none of them even come close to really wounding him.

"I don't have a gun."

"Sometimes your mind is more powerful than a weapon," my brother says.

"I miss you," I say, looking at the small boy I had loved so much.

"We'll be together again; no one really dies, Little Wolf. Now you must choose—kill the bear or die."

I watch the rolling body of wolves, and I watch the bear growling, showing his deathly sharp teeth.

"Will the bear kill me?"

"Only if you want it to."

"Why can't the wolves kill it?"

"They are trying to; have you ever seen a pack of wolves take down a kill like that?"

"No."

"They need help. Now you must choose."

I look down at my brother and slide from the horse. I go to take his hand, but he is gone. I find myself walking toward the chaos. The wolves charge the bear, and he swats them off like flies. I touch the axe at my hip and the *wotawe* around my neck.

"He wants his claw back."

"Sha?" I ask, looking around.

"I am right here," she says clearly.

She stands to my right, watching the dance of death.

"Is that what you gave me?"

"That is what your mother gave you. I kept it safe, then gave it back to you when she wanted me to."

Sha looks at me with her golden eyes dancing in the violence; the wolves snap, the bear roars.

"If I give it to him, will he leave us alone?"

"No, he'll just come back looking for more claws."

I feel the tears running down my face.

"I don't know if it is right to kill him," I say through trembling lips.

"These times are unlike any we have ever lived to know. We are in a mist; they have separated us from god as they are separated from him. You have to look deep, deeper than you ever should have—find that voice and listen to it; it will guide you."

I look to Sha, her words echo in my ears, she is gone. I am holding my axe. I collapse on the ground; I can't stop crying. I pick up a hand-ful of dirt and sprinkle it on my head.

"Forgive me, I know not what I do. Forgive as I take this life not in your image but mine."

I pour the rest of the dirt in my mouth, filling myself with earth as I stand. I hear a voice call out, "Today is a good day to die!"

I run toward the bear; he is swatting off the rolling attacks from the wolves with his massive paws. I see the one with the missing claw—the paw seems less powerful than the other. The bear pauses; he looks me, his eyes blacker than night. I run toward him. I can feel myself screaming. I leap at him, and my axe comes down between his eyes. The bear raises his huge paws into the air and lets out a roar, a roar louder than thunder. He smells putrid, like death. The bear tosses me to the ground just as he had the wolves, like I was nothing, like I was the wind. The bear is screaming, grabbing at his face. I can see the silhouettes of the wolves; they stand around the edges dancing like shadows, watching, waiting for me to kill it.

I spit out dirt and stand back up. I feel the claw in my wotawe. I look at the sky; the fast-moving clouds part, and the sky is alight with stars. They light up the sky and the ground like the sun. The bear is looking at the sky just as I am. The stars—there seems to be more of them, and they are brighter. I move fast and strike the bear hard in the chest.

I feel the cut pierce deep into his chest, the whole tomahawk's head is buried in his flesh. I jump back as the bear staggers and col-lapses on its side, screaming in pain.

"Today is a good day to die!" I scream into the too-bright light of the night. I kneel next to the bear, next to the bear I've killed. His head is heavy on the ground and at an awkward angle. His black eyes are wide open, lifeless. I pull out my axe. It takes me three tries; blood has soaked his fur. I tuck the axe back into my leggings and put my hand on his chest. The blood is already cooling, and I put my hand on my face, pressing the sticky, metallic red into my flesh.

"I remember who I am; you cannot kill what you remember," I say to myself in the night. I hear the pack howl. I stand and look back into the shadows; there are hundreds of them.

"It is yours!" I scream at them in front of the massive mass of black fur.

The wolves approach with caution. I make for my horse. Glancing back, I see them hungrily tearing at the bear's flesh. I smile. I hear a howl; I howl back, and I am echoed in return by a chorus. I weave between the pines under the bright stars back down the hill. My horse is waiting for me. He shakes his mane at the sight of me. I go to him, and he doesn't back down from the smell of blood. I take the hand I used to mark my face, and I press it to his, on the white star between his eyes.

"We are the hunters of death," I tell him. He shakes his head. He knows he sought me. I go to his side and pull myself up on his massive back.

"Take me to the light," I tell him. He turns around and breaks into a run for the grasslands we came from. Take me to the sun, take me to the man that loves me, take me to my home.

CHAPTER 16

▲▲▲▲

"HEY, NANCE, WHERE SHOULD I PUT THIS?"

I slowly stand up from the box I'm crouched over and wince, stretching my back. I look at Joshua waving a worn-looking spatula in the air. I'm wondering why he bothered to bring it.

"Second drawer on the left," I say, using my chin to guide him, my hands still pressed firmly into my spine. He smiles, and I find myself watching him trying to cram it into the drawer. It's so full he has to push my utensils aside to make room. I think to myself, *I should have gone through my stuff before we brought in his stuff*—to be honest, his apartment was so small I had been utterly astonished how many things he actually had, like those clowns getting out of the car, Paul had said.

"Josh, you coming?" I hear Daniel bellow from the living room.

"Yup," Joshua bellows back, bringing back my wince.

"Are we all done here?" Joshua asks me, looking around the kitchen. I follow his eyes; it's somehow even more of a fucking mess.

"I think so," I say, unable to keep the skepticism from my voice. Everything is as tidy as it is ever going to be.

"You should have a rest."

I can hear the concern in Joshua's voice, and a small smile comes to my lips.

"Maybe later," I say, glancing out the window at the sunlit, freshly fallen snow. The storm had finally cleared to reveal a sun we hadn't seen in at least a week.

"Do you need help with your essays?" he asks, lingering in the kitchen and looking at me. I can see he is struggling to balance his own time with my time, with the kids' time. I felt a bit sorry for him—when you have your own kids, the adjustment is gradual. I had seen him on several occasions standing in the middle of everything just looking around, stunned, his bushy eyebrows raised.

"Oh no, I can practically do those while I'm driving," I say, thinking that in September I was going to have to update all the courses I am leading as the predictability was even getting to me.

Joshua grins at me and steps over the box I had been unloading and kisses me long on the lips. I feel myself smiling as I kiss him back.

"Joshua!" cuts through the impatient voice of Daniel.

"You guys, I hope you are having fun in there!" Paul says in the doorway, tapping his fingers on the wall.

Joshua pulls away from me and smiles in their direction. He looks back at me, and I raise my eyebrows and shrug. They have never been that interested in having my company, with the exception of Teddy, and I think that was solely by default as I was the only parent he had ever known. Joshua gives me a smile, squeezes my shoulder, and then disappears into the living room, which now happens to look like his apartment. There is wood everywhere, complete with the spider plant taking over our ceiling. I feel the small body of Mittens pressing up against my legs. I look down, and she digs her small black-and-white head into my shin, purring and meowing.

"Joshua says we can't feed you anymore today or else you'll stop doing your job," I tell her, scratching her under her chin. She squeezes her eyes shut in bliss.

"Mom! Who you talking to?" Teddy's small voice rings out.

"Mittens," I call back.

"Mittens!" he exclaims.

I hear a chair being shoved away from the new woodworking table, which was Joshua's kitchen table, now in our living room, and the heavy steps of my last baby.

"There you are!" Teddy says to Mittens, his hands on his hips. I smile. Teddy, who is almost always wearing the *Yellow Jackets* football T-shirt Joshua had given him. That was something else that had come with Joshua, the love of football, something I knew nothing about—and from what I'd seen and learned, I still felt the same way about it. To the boys and even Dad, on the other hand, it was becoming a weekend religion.

The cat looks at me apologetically and goes to Teddy, who I'm pretty sure is feeding her extra to what Joshua said we could give her. Make her want the rats, he had said.

"Mom, I made a mouse for Mittens, come see!" He's squatted next to the cat, who is purring so loudly even I can hear it, and rolling all over his tiny feet. Teddy's small black eyes dance looking up at me. I smile; there is so much enthusiasm at this age. It disappears somewhere with their high-pitched voice and making a disgusted face when I kiss them.

"Honey, I think I'm going outside for a few minutes. Can I see it when I come back?" I say, feeling like I've been spinning. I had never had this feeling when I was pregnant with the boys.

"Are you still feeling sick?" the little voice demands, concerned.

"A little," I say wearily—even I was fed up with myself and my new bodily functions.

"Oh, OK," he says, scooping up the cat, who melts into his arms.

He steps his heavy steps toward me and puckers up for a kiss. I lean down to him and kiss him, getting a good amount of fluffy cat fur in my face. *He'd never met George*, I think, watching him disappear back into the living room. Maybe that's why he is so different from Timothy, Paul, and Daniel—sweeter.

"Hey, buddy! Should we make Mittens a house?" I hear Joshua call to Teddy; our walls are so thin it's as though I'm in the living room with them.

Well, maybe not every man's enthusiasm disappears with puberty, I think, smiling at Joshua's voice. I look down at the half-empty box and sigh in defeat. I pull on my winter boots; I'm ready to be done with them, and I know I've still got a ways to go. I stand back up and pull on my parka and mitts and step out into the biting cold. I shiver as I pull my hood up.

I see Dad out by the new hunting shed he and Joshua made. I see the carcass of a buck strung up from the tree next to the shed. I make my way through the deep snow; it crunches singingly beneath my feet. As I near, I see the throat of the deer has been slit, and his blood is being drained into a bucket.

"Nancy," Dad says, smiling. I haven't seen him smile like that in a long time, a smile that seems to light up his whole body.

"Dad," I say, a bit out of breath, sitting on the stump they've been using to split wood.

"What do you think?" Dad asks, nodding toward the buck.

"It's beautiful."

The lifeless black eyes look out into nothingness. I don't have to touch the fur to know it's as soft as silk.

"Joshua thinks we should make a smoking shed this spring," I say, nodding at the deer.

"Instead of doing it outside?" Dad says and smiles at me.

"I think he just likes building stuff," I say, and Dad laughs.

"You know what I said, Nancy, about the white people."

"That night?"

I remember; his words often hit me in the chest when we are all together at dinner and weekend suppers.

"I'm sorry," he says. I smile and feel myself tearing up.

"Do the boys know?" he asks.

"No," I answer, unable to keep the dread from making my tone heavy.

"I don't think they'll mind," Dad says, looking at me carefully.

"I wish me and Joshua—" I'm not able to say it out loud; it's one of those truths you don't want to face, and no matter how hard you try to bury it, it always seems to eat at you, whether you're honest or not.

Dad nods.

"You were always traditional like that; brought you some shame, didn't it? Timmy, that is."

I think back to the day I found out and told my mother. She just looked at me and said, "Well, I guess you'll have to marry him."

"I wish it didn't," I say, feeling a deep pain in my chest; me and my parents, we haven't been right since George was convicted.

"We all are who we are, nothing to be ashamed of. I'm glad, or else what would I have? Lola Littlehawk?" Dad says, making my stomach sink. I wonder if this will pain George the way Lola had pained me.

"Should I tell George?" I ask, looking at Dad.

Dad stops sharpening the knife he's going to use to skin the deer and looks at me, still like stone as he glances at my stomach.

"I've been thinking I should go speak with my son. It's not right what he's doing; he needs to let you go."

I feel the tears run down my face, hot in the cold air.

"Don't worry about it, Nancy; we will all be fine. This will all get sorted out. I'll help you the best I can."

I let out a small sob. This is the one thing I've always hated about being pregnant. It's like my emotions control me in ways I can't even understand.

"Teddy, he is calling Joshua 'Dad,'" I say, trying to get control of my voice. Dad looks at me. I can see he is uncomfortable. His knife hangs awkwardly at his side.

"Are you happy or upset about it?" he asks, looking at me like I'm nuts.

"I'm just so happy," I say between sobs.

I can hear Dad laugh even though I can't see him through my tear-blurred eyes. I take deep breaths, trying to stop the tears from running down my face. Dad looks sharply past me, and I bend around to the sound of a truck. I see a beat-up blue Ford making its way up our snowy lane. I see only one person in the cab. I wipe away my tears. As the truck plows through the snow toward us, I can see Timothy's head. I look at his one hand trying to shift and steer through the snowdrift all at once.

"Dad, did you know Timothy was coming home?" I ask, not taking my eyes away from my first son.

"No, Nancy, I did not."

I look at Dad; his tone makes my chest tight.

"We should go meet him at the door," Dad says.

I was thinking the same thing. I watch as Dad doesn't put the knife away but tucks it into his belt. He walks toward me and holds out a hand, not taking his eyes off the truck. I take it, letting him pull me to my feet. We make our way quickly to the truck door as it squeals open.

His hair is longer than before and seems to be blacker. He looks just like his father. He nods at us, lighting a cigarette with his one hand.

"I didn't think you were coming back," I say to him, looking him up and down, searching for the child I used to know.

"Didn't know if I would," he answers, blowing out puffs of smoke through the corner of his mouth.

"How was Washington?" I ask.

He looks at me, smoking. His eyes since he'd come back from Vietnam, they've been dull.

"Don't know what we've achieved," he says, still not bothering to take the cigarette from his mouth.

I nod.

"We need to talk to you before you go inside," Dad says.

"Can I get out of the truck first?" Timothy asks. My son slides out of the cab, and Dad steps forward and slams the truck's rusted-out door shut. I look at Dad, surprised. I never would have described him as aggressive.

"What's this?" Timothy says, nodding and pointing his smoking cigarette at the shed and deer.

"A hunting shed," I say, more carefully than I had intended.

"You got a band permit to build that?" Timothy asks sarcastically.

No, I think, looking at my son.

"What's going on?" Timothy says, looking from me to Dad.

"My partner has moved in with us," I say wondering why I would use a word like *partner*. Timothy smiles the same mocking smile that his father has, making me wince.

"A guy you're fucking," Timothy says. I feel like I've been slapped, and I'm even more hurt knowing that he wants me to feel like that.

"Don't you talk to her like that," Dad says with genuine anger in his voice.

"Joshua's been here for us when you've been who knows where," Dad says, almost shouting.

I look at Timothy, who is as surprised as I am.

"Dad says he thought you were fucking a white man," Timothy says, looking at me and blowing out smoke. He flicks his cigarette violently into the snow.

"It's more than that," I find myself saying, admitting it even to myself for the first time.

"You are welcome to stay with us as long as you earn your keep and are polite to all of us," Dad says, interrupting us.

"Or what? You'll kick me out?" Timothy says with the same sarcastic sneer I had been privileged to.

"Yes," Dad says, answering for me.

We all look at the back door opening. Joshua fills the open space. He looks like Paul Bunyan with his mop of blond hair, beard, and red-flannel shirt tucked into his jeans.

"You must be Timothy," he says with an easy smile. I look at Dad. We're both watching Timothy the same way you would a dog that might bite.

"Yeah, who are you?" Timothy spits.

"I'm Joshua, Nancy's boyfriend."

"You living here?" Timothy asks even though we'd just told him that. I glance at Dad, whose eyes snap in his direction.

"I am. It's nice to finally meet you and have you home," Joshua says, looking over at me carefully. "You should come in. I'm making spears with your brothers."

Timothy makes the same grunting noise his father does.

"Dad!" Teddy yells. I watch as he pops out from behind Joshua.

"Hey there, buddy. I'm coming back; your brother is home," Joshua says, nodding in Timothy's direction. I look at him in the snow wearing nothing but a thin green army jacket, his hair loose around him. I wonder when he became so much like George.

"Timmy's always too busy," Teddy says, tugging at Joshua's sleeve.

"Alright then, let's go. Nice meeting you, Timothy," Joshua says, disappearing with Teddy. I look at Timothy as he awkwardly gets out a cigarette from his top jacket pocket. I look at Dad, who looks at Timothy in a way you'd look at a poorly behaved child, waiting to reprimand him.

"What the fuck was that?" Timothy asks, looking at me with his hard black eyes. "'Dad'? Teddy's got a fucking dad, and that is not him," he says, pointing angrily at me with his cigarette.

I've had enough. "Teddy's never had a dad—you barely had one yourself. You can stay here, Timothy, until you get your shit together, but it is time you became a man. You need to go out on your own if you think you can talk to me like that. And you can smoke out here—Joshua and I are going to have a baby."

I glance at Dad, who nods at me, and I make for the back door. I leave my sullen son puffing next to the truck he got who knows where. I step inside, greeted by warmth and Led Zeppelin being played softly and the sound of my three other sons laughing.

"I swear to god that's how you kill a fish," I hear Joshua saying to more laughter.

I pull off my coat and look out the window. I look at Timothy, who looks at me; the anger in his eyes makes me flinch. I watch as he gets back in the truck and starts it so hard it stalls. He throws it in gear and reverses, tearing through the snow back toward the road. I look at Dad, who has already made his way back to the shed and is starting to skin the deer. Dad glances at me and then holds up his hand to Timothy, saying goodbye the old way.

I wonder if I'll ever see my son again, and I feel sick as part of me hopes he'll stay away for a while.

CHAPTER 17

▲▲▲▲

MY FINGERS ARE A WARM BLUR IN the chipped enamel basin revealing the dark cast-iron beneath its fragile exterior; the white had long faded to a dirty cream. The water is still like the air, and warmer than it ought to be. I scoop some up and splash it on my face. It does nothing more than mix with the sweat upon my brow, making my skin feel even more clammy.

"I certainly hope this is not the hour of your departure; is it, Autie?"

My eyes are drawn back to the bed, where my wife is all but engulfed by the sheets, a shadowy mass of starched white. I can make out the silhouette of her bare body, and I feel myself stir.

"I am afraid it is all but that, Ms. Libbie." My remorse of leaving her is tinged with the knowing of the fulfillment of the saddle, the pistol, and the hunt.

"Autie," she says to me.

Her voice hangs in the warmth of our timber-laid cabin. The sun is peeking through the small, square windows, enormous over the plains, rising above the grass like the god the Indians loved to keep secret from us. The sun I can feel from the weak early morning rays is going to be punishing.

"I certainly hope, Ms. Libbie, that you are still engaged with the plan to ride out with us and spend the night with me in our tent," I say, glancing in the mirror that tops her dresser, a dresser stuffed with more clothes than she would ever need here. My eyes sink to the tops of her breasts, heaving with every breath her small body takes.

"I most certainly am, General," she says to me, looking at me in the mirror. I watch as she raises her arms seductively over her head.

"Well, then, that is one thing I am surely glad of," I say, smiling. I stride to the door, where I had hung up my buckskin leggings and tunic. I take the leggings, my fingers entwining in their soft fringes that make their way up and down each leg. I remember making the switch to skin. The relief of not having wool stick to you, making your skin crawl on a ten-hour march in the middle of summer, sometimes still gave me pause as I watch my men suffer in their blue standard issues. The skins protected you in both summer and winter, adjusting to the weather not unlike they would have on the animal they were taken from.

"I have heard some of the men talking—talking amongst themselves, Autie—that this campaign is different," Libbie says. Nothing dreamlike hangs on her demeanor anymore.

Fully dressed, I turn to face my wife and smile. All these years and all these battles, and she still worried as though we were still courting, and the Civil War was still raging.

"It is our great hope that this will be the last of these hostiles' belligerence. Now, get dressed, Libbie. I cannot be late for my own march," I say to her with mocking belligerence tingeing my voice.

I don't wait for her reply as I make my way from the small log cabin. It is barely more than the room we sleep in and a foyer for entertaining. I don't pause as I push open the simple wooden-plank door. The sun greets me, caressing my face, the memory of Washington growing ever more distant as I look to the rolling fields ahead of me, contrasted with the sea of dust, of yelling men rushing about readying horses, mules, pack wagons, and weapons in front of me. I'm forced to give a small pause as I finally am where I am supposed to be; it was worth barreling through the corruption and bravado to get here.

I make for my men, entering through the chaos, my hat firmly upon my head and my pistols heavy upon my hips. I feel my knife courageously tucked into my boot. Soldiers sparkling in new issues salute me as I pass. I barely give them pause, for I see who I am looking for: Bloody Knife. His dark eyes sense me, and he instinctively glances in my direction—raven eyes, that is what the other Indians say. Bloody Knife is readying his massive dark horse, such a rich brown it is almost black. He sees me making my way to him and stops preparing his mount and makes his way toward me. Bloody Knife, he always wears the same mask, the same expression, no matter what is going on around us, a solemness that makes him look like a statue of antiquity in a wealthy person's garden, a strong nose and chin with high cheekbones. I have yet to see him cheerful or distressed, but rather a man in charge of his fate.

"Your Indian men, they are at the ready," Bloody Knife says to me in his broken way, approaching my side. The sun, the heat, or really any of the elements—they never seem to bother the Indians as they do the rest of us. I nod and keep on walking, forcing him to fall in next to me. The men we pass move like a current around a rock, letting us through.

"What did you think of what Billy Garnett said last night?" I ask softly from under the brim of my hat. I need to find my officers, and this was something I did not want them to get word of, the thunder dreamers. I knew that almost all privates had already heard some horrifying tales of what could befall them on this march should it turn disastrous; stories had come back of dismemberment and torture.

"I think the Sioux have always caused trouble. It is only now they are causing you trouble," Bloody Knife says, not paying my discreet tone any mind.

"Are they too powerful for us to successfully deter?" I ask, stopping to look at the man with whom I have trusted my life all these years. Bloody Knife doesn't face me; his eyes scan what is ahead of us, as though there is a play being enacted from a theater that only he can see.

"I think they will always be dangerous, even when we think them defeated. Billy was right, they dream of thunder, their medicine. It is strong; it is what you would call rich." Bloody Knife only ever bothers to say what was of the utmost importance, and his words sink into my soul.

"Rich," I say, more to myself.

"They have plenty," he says, meaning they would not have to take what Uncle Sam had to offer.

I nod to that as I see Tom weaving his way excitedly toward us.

"General!" he calls to me, all but shoving the other soldiers from his path. He stops in front of me, his cheeks flushed red, his eyes bright, his uniform already causing sweat to bead down his face from beneath his small captain's hat.

"We have almost all 150 wagons loaded, as well as the three Gatling guns being dragged by mules. You angering the president may have been the best thing to ever happen to us. We've never been granted resources like this, not since the war," my brother says, bursting with enthusiasm.

I nod at that, already articulating in my mind what sort of damage I can enable with that much artillery.

"Did you find Captain Keogh?" I ask, wondering how my stoic Irishman has been faring. There had been word that he returned to Ireland; he was a man one could not help but admire. Like myself, he had made a life of battles; where we differed was that he had made his warmongering a transcontinental affair.

"Yes, sir, he is waiting with the others by the horses."

"Captain Benteen?"

"Yes, sir, the captain is present and waiting as well," Tom replies. I glance over and grin at Tom, who grins back at me.

"Boston and Little Autie?" I ask, wondering of our kin as they were not military men.

"Attending to their civilian duties, gathering up their prospecting equipment so we can tame this wild land," Tom says. My smile grows bigger, making Tom's grin widen as well.

"Nothing can tame you, though, Tom, can it?" I say, looking over at my brother. We are both dashing in our own right, with our height, our spiral golden locks, and our ability to mount and conquer any horse or gun.

"Some things are untamable," he says. I catch sight of my six officers on the far edge of the chaos, next to the fort's logged defenses, gathered by the horses and merrily chatting amongst themselves just as Tom had said they were. My officers see us making our way to them, and I watch as they cease their chatter, place their hats on their heads, and straighten their spines. Most of these men I've been fighting with for the better part of fifteen years, and they are almost closer to me than family. They know me better than my own wife; that is how we had all lived to grace the earth another day. Fighting was intuitive—you had to be able to predict not only your enemy's next move but also your leader's.

"General," they call in unison as I stop in front of them. I hear a murmuring of "Lieutenant-Colonel" from none other than Captain Benteen. I ignore him, my eyes finding and settling upon Major Reno. I try to burn into him, wondering if he has been off the liquor long enough to see this mission through without getting himself and his men killed.

"Captain Keogh, did you enjoy your visit to Ireland?" I say, looking away from Reno to the handsome Irishman. He stands a little taller than the other officers, and his hat falls to the front of his head in a proud and enduring sort of fashion, almost like an actor. I feel envy as green as Keogh's eyes slipping into my thoughts.

"I always welcome a trip to the place of my birth, General, but I fear this is now my home," Keogh says, in his voice always a tinge of the continent.

I smile at Keogh, a brave man nonetheless, wandering around the world, fighting fights that weren't his. I nod, taking a deep breath of the dust that has been stirred up around us.

"This is the first time in my career with the United States Army in which I have been given full control of the cavalry. We are splitting from General Crook's infantry, which will head south in lieu of General Terry, and it will be us who drive the hostiles toward them and Colonel Gibbon."

My speech is interrupted.

"General, are we to round up the Indians and bring them back here or to Red Cloud's Agency?" asks Yates. I glance at Captain Yates. He's put on some weight, making his blond moustache look disproportionate to his face.

"We've been instructed to take no prisoners," I say firmly to all six officers.

Yates nods at me, his eyes clouded with a seriousness, knowing we will be killing.

"I fear that after the blunder of Powder River, President Grant and General Sheridan have it in their right mind that we finish this dutiful task and tame this wild land once and for all. Part of this mission is to put an end to their wandering and seize the title to the Black Hills. Now, let us ride out to 'Garryowen' and show this fort what a true cavalry looks like."

"Yes, sir," sounds back to me as Captain Yates steps forward with the reins to my horse, Vic. He comes to me eagerly, shaking his massive head. I take the reins, nodding at Yates, and give my horse a solid inspection before mounting, patting his neck and hindquarters. I make certain my stirrups and saddle are secure. Vic's coat is a rich chestnut, gleaming in the sunlight from being well brushed out. I pat his nose, and he huffs his hot air into my hand. I think of all the battles I've fought mounted—most. We are to be one and the same, myself and the horse. Every horse I'd ever lost has been like losing a piece of myself; something died with every mount lost, something that was never to fully return to me.

My eyes close; the morning sun has warmed the air in a way only summer is able to. I think of what my life has been—marching, fighting, killing—and I step into the saddle in one easy stride, my boots resting upon the iron and leather stirrups. I open my eyes and find myself smiling as I steer my horse toward the fort's entrance—a blur of fallen logs, every fort taking the same appearance, an empty vessel upon the wilderness's landscape. I hear the men's mounts' hooves fall in behind me, louder than crashing waves. I look in the distance at our simple cabin, and I see my wife and sister on horses, their straw bonnets that shade their faces from the sun and dust making them look as though they don't have heads.

I wave at them, and they trot their mares over to us. Their massive skirts heaving up and down, their yellow, cream, and lace looking grossly out of place. I look back at my officers, all signaling to their companies who are mounting. There are hundreds of us. I smile from the pit of my stomach; my wife and sister pull up alongside me. I look at Boston, Tom, Little Autie, and James, who hurry their horses toward us, and I pull out my saber. A bugle sounds, and the brass of the band rings out and quickly harmonizes into the melody of "Garryowen." Holding my saber high, I tap my horse, and he surges forward. It is me and me alone at the front. I hear the men begin to sing—a booming, boisterous choir of hundreds of voices blending into one, more powerful than lightning and thunder.

> *"Let Bacchus's son not be dismayed,*
> *but join with me each jovial blade,*
> *come booze and sing and lend your aid,*

to help me with the chorus,
chorus!
Instead of spa we'll drink brown ale,
and pay the reckoning on the nail,
for debt no man shall go to jail,
from Garryowen in glory.
We are the boys who take delight
in smashing Limerick lamps at night,
and through the street like a spotter's fight,
tearing us all before us!
We'll break windows, we'll break doors,
the watch knock down by threes and fours,
then let doctors work their cures,
and tinker up our bruises!
We'll beat the bailiffs out of fun,
we'll make the mayor and sheriff run,
we are the boys no man dare dun,
if he regards a whole skin!
Our hearts so stout have got us fame,
for soon 'tis known from whence we came,
where're we go they dread the name,
of Garryowen in glory!"

I lead Vic up the hill leading us away from the fort and the brass of the band. The voices slowly trickle to a stop, and I sheath my saber. An odd man still calls out, trying to get the song going again. I look at my wife, now beside me. She beams up at me from under her bonnet, all dark eyes and lashes. I find myself glancing back at the fort, which is buried in a cloud of dust, and look ahead of me at the vast wilderness greeting us, grass and trees painting a picture of expansion.

"Will we settle out here when the fighting's done?" Libbie's voice rings in my ears.

I look at my little wife, her face pinched from the sun. Her bonnet is tied in a massive sea-green bow under her chin, making her look like a present.

"Do you like it out here?" I ask, wondering what she would do with herself with no ladies to have to tea or play bridge with, no attending or hosting dinners in my honor.

"I think it has a peacefulness to it, as opposed to the fort and, of course, the city. Once this land is settled and safe for inhabitants, it might be very favorable to be tucked out here near a stream," she says in a way that lets me know she is more telling me than asking.

I smile, thinking that next I will most likely be sent to settle the Nez Perce, and there also has been word that an Indian called Geronimo—more cunning, ruthless, and wild than any other—could evade both the American and Mexican armies in the south. I could not foresee any quaint cottages in the forest with a stream out in the middle of the new territory; it would take many years before it could be declared totally free of any remaining savages.

"But who will be around to do the cooking?" Tom asks, interrupting my thoughts, making us all ripple with laughter. My little wife looks over at my brother with her small chin pointed in a dignified fashion to the sky, the smile on her face contradicting the chastisement of her body. I hear the sound of fast hooves and see Captain Keogh pulling up next to me. I tip my hat to the captain, who steers his gelding, Comanche, between me and Tom.

"I know what we are doing, General, but I am a bit curious . . . where are we going?"

I smile at the soft Irishness in his voice that Captain Keogh hasn't been able to shake, even after all these years.

"My ladies," Captain Keogh says to my wife and sister, making my little wife look up at him demurely from her bonnet, her eyes twinkling. I smirk and look ahead.

"General Crook is making for the Rosebud, so we'll make for the Little Bighorn Valley."

"That will take us to about a month from now, then, General?" Captain Keogh asks. I can feel him and his reconnaissance and how it would be retold to his men.

"I reckon that it should," I say, chewing on the inside of my cheek, my saddle rhythmically swaying me to the tune of the land.

"And what about you, ladies?" Captain Keogh asks, looking across me at my wife and sister, making them giggle as though they were unmarried and a decade younger.

"I am afraid this is but the end of our journey, but we will eagerly await your safe return," my wife says in a soft voice I don't recognize. I glance at her; she is still batting her eyelashes at the captain. I find myself smirking again.

"Captain, have you found yourself a sweetheart to pine for you in your absence yet?" my wife asks nonchalantly. I look to see my sister perk up and glance at him, interested. *A house by a stream in the middle of nothing, indeed!* I think to myself.

"I've not found such a lady as you or Ms. Maggie that would be so accepting of a soldier's life, so, alas, no sweetheart will pine for me in my absence."

"General," Captain Keogh says to me, tipping his hat; he disappears as fast as he had appeared, having dismissed himself. Before I get annoyed with my wife's flirting, I smile. We've been together a long time, these men and me. They know me better than I know myself; Captain Keogh knew better than to linger.

"Are you going to be near Powder River, Autie?" Libbie asks with overly feigned concern. I feel myself trying to fight off an annoyed look on my face, hoping my brim is doing a good enough job to conceal it.

"I don't suppose we will be unless we are led there," I say to Libbie without looking at her, still chewing on the inside of my cheek.

The day wears on, and the sun grows high into the sky. I urge Vic slightly ahead of the charge into a gallop and let the breeze take my worries. I close my eyes for a moment, the wind rushing around my face and body, cooling me from the hot air, and I thank god for giving me this extraordinary opportunity, for giving me the gift of an entire cavalry, for giving me the gift of showing this president how to win a war.

CHAPTER 18

▲▲▲▲

"LITTLE WOLF?" SWIFT FOX'S VOICE SINGS IN MY EARS. I slowly blink.
I remember the sky, the clouds, the blood.

"Little Wolf?" his voice says a little louder. I force my eyes fully
open. The sun warms my face. I am safe inside a glowing hide; I am
in a tipi.

"When did I get back?" I ask, closing my eyes, enjoying the
warmth of the sun traveling through my body.

"A few hours ago, around sunup."

I remember the stars, the moon brighter than the sun. I wince; my
head pounds with each beat of my heart in a way I didn't think was
possible. I feel too heavy to sit up, and I long to go back where I came
from—my heart aches with a pain worse than my head. Gray Wolf. I
long to see my baby brother again, even just for a moment.

"They told me to give you this," Swift Fox says, cutting through
my thoughts. I feel his strong fingers pulling me up from under my
arms to a sitting position. I open my eyes, feeling irritated he would
take me from such a sweet surrender. The sun's light makes my head
pound even harder. He is pushing a horn cup to my lips; he tips it,
and the liquid gushes into my mouth and what doesn't runs down

my chest and makes my mouth feel like it is on fire. I force myself to swallow it; it tastes like earth, roots, and fire. The fire goes to my belly, and I try not to vomit. I feel Swift Fox gently brushing my matted hair from my face.

"We should go to them," he says to me.

I look at him. His black eyes pierce mine, and he hoists me to my feet. I wince at the pain shooting up my body from my toes to my scalp.

"It looks like you were attacked by a bear," he says, looking me over with dark, serious eyes, eyes trained to look for wounds.

I touch my ribs lightly; they are where the most pain is, and they are bound.

"I made a dressing," Swift Fox says, letting go of me. He throws open the hide flap. I see him, the horse from my dream. He stands between the thin trees, waiting. He looks at me and lets out a neigh, stomping his white hooves.

"Gray Wolf," I say as he shakes his mane.

"He brought you back," Swift Fox says. I look at the man I will marry; he is glowing with pride—he is proud of me.

"I thought I only dreamt him," I say; my voice is hoarse, raspy from the fever dreams.

"You had a thunder dream," Swift Fox says, his way of explaining.

"How do you know?" I choke out.

"Very few have come back with a beast," Swift Fox says, taking my fingers in his, pulling me along in the direction of Crazy Horse's tent and away from my beautiful horse. I glance behind me to see if he is real. Gray Wolf the horse looks up at me from his meal of prairie grass, and the hair on my arms stands up—if the horse is real, what else is real? The camp is fully awake even at this early hour, people rushing with baskets of food and mending, children run screaming and chasing one another. Things are just as they had been, except this time everyone we pass pauses to look at us. I glance behind us; the horse is following us.

"An American horse!" I hear the voice of Gall call out, making me smile.

The short, stocky man tumbles toward us from the other side of a tipi.

"We need you back here by sundown!" a woman shouts at him, coming out from behind the same tipi with two small children at her side. The children are undeniably his; they are the spitting image of their father, short and solid. They carry a courageousness that could be mistaken for arrogance. It's as though they don't even have a mother. I wonder which of my parents I look like. Their faces fade more and more with each passing year, even from the dream; how they looked and sounded is already beginning to disappear from my heart, making it ache even more.

"My wife," Gall says to us, taking me from my dreams. We all look at the fair woman scowling at him; her face makes Gall smile as she pushes past us. The children shyly look at me, and the three of them disappear into the throng of people.

"This Sun Dance has got everybody worked up," Gall says to me, glancing at both of us. Swift Fox tugs at my fingers, pulling us forward, and Gall falls in beside me, letting out a whistle and looking at my face.

"The scratching and the bruising are worse on your face than I thought," he says, making my free fingers flutter to my cheek. I touch it lightly; the drink Swift Fox gave me seems to have numbed any feeling from my skin.

"It doesn't bother me as much as the ribs," I say, pain shooting into parts of my body I have never even thought about. I wished the drink had numbed those as well.

"I didn't know it got you on your body as well," Gall says, surprise making his words loud. I glance at Swift Fox, who is looking at Gall, nodding, and I feel my numb mouth try to smile, as Swift Fox is beaming at me with even more with pride.

"And this guy?" Gall says, pointing with his thumb back at my horse still following us.

"You need to show him where the real grass is," Gall says.

I smile a full smile, feeling the true rawness of my face for the first time. The three of us fall into silence, walking a slow and steady pace to the tipi that looms before us. Even in the morning sun, I know there is a fire lit in there, though somehow from the outside the tipi always manages to look dark and empty.

"They are waiting for us," Gall says, disappearing through the tipi's flap. I feel my legs grow heavy, my feet hesitant. I look at Swift Fox—he nods at me, reassuring; we can speak without speaking. I had only ever been able to do that with one other person, Sha. I look over my shoulder at Gray Wolf; he looks at us lazily, his tail swishing away the flies trying to land on his back. I can see that he is gray and speckled in brown hail spots, a white star on his forehead, "a horse with the power of thunder," I had once heard my father say of such markings. My eyes go to the bloody handprint on top of the star; I touch my own face and feel the sticky blood on myself to match.

"What should we do with him?" I ask.

Swift Fox follows my gaze. "Just leave him."

I nod, and I feel Swift Fox let go of my fingers and gently nudge me through the entrance. I will my feet forward and am greeted by a soothing, dim light that eases the pounding behind my eyes. Six men are sitting around the strong fire, five of them I now recognize as Crazy Horse, Sitting Bull, Horn Chips, Gall, and American Horse. "Shirt Wearers," Gall had said of them.

"Sit," Crazy Horse says, gesturing to the blanket on the ground, the same dark-red one that was always out, waiting for guests. I feel Swift Fox's fingers gently tug me, helping me gently to the ground.

I settle on my bottom, my knees too raw from my bear fight to crouch on.

"Tell us what you dreamt of, and we will tell you if you can fight as a warrior," Horn Chips says, looking at me with his dark eyes— *thunder eyes*, I think. I feel myself nod; my fingers lightly touch my face, my fingers back in the blood. I look into the flames, trying to remember, and it comes back to me bubbling in the flickering light.

"I woke up in the grass of my home. I was the person I used to be, a person I wish I still was."

The tears sting my wounds. I taste salt, and the metallic scent of blood mixed with pain runs into my mouth.

"I walked in the grass, people were screaming, they were cries of war. The others, their war cries were the happy sound of music. I was trying to get to my mother and brother, my father."

I let out a sob and know I need to tell them everything; for the first time I want someone to hear everything, I want them to know my pain.

"He would have had his axe and bow. He would have told my mother to get us and run for the woods. We were playing farther than we were supposed to—I always had to go to the grass."

I let out another sob, remembering what I saw, remembering what I lived through. Everything was taken from me in a single morning, and I was helpless to do anything but watch, trying always to forget all of it when it came back in my dreams.

"It called me like fresh grass would to a deer in the dead of winter. I always went where I knew they couldn't find me, and my brother, he always followed."

I stop, letting the sobs take from my ribs any comfort left in them. I don't see anyone in the tent. I see the field, the flowers, I smell the scent of the earth.

"I am running, looking for my brother. I become who I am now. The grass disappears from under my feet. The ground becomes hard.

I look at it, it is made from trees. All around me are white people. There is a massive red tent; it hangs from the top. The women wear the most ridiculous clothing I have ever seen. They swim in it. The men look like dark soldiers. The red tent lifts, and a man that looks like a man I once saw is standing in the middle. There are all these torches illuminating him; he wears no clothing and is holding his penis. It has an arrow in it, and his people start laughing. They laugh until their faces turn red and they start to vomit, the flesh melting from their bones. They are evil. I hear my mother screaming for us. I can't take my eyes from the man. He looks at me and a single tear falls down his face. My mother screams, and I am back in the grass, I am running. I feel like I can't go fast enough. I leap over the body of my father. I don't stop because I hear my mother. I then see my baby brother; there is a bullet in his head."

I stop talking because I can't stop sobbing. I remember everything I've tried all these years to forget. I feel myself screaming my brother's name, and I hear my horse scream, answering my call.

"Where were you?"

I look at the medicine man, the vision of the dreams fading from the flames.

"You know," I manage to bark at him. He nods his head.

"We need to hear it from you."

"Washita," I whisper into the flames.

I feel the silence of the dead. The men look at me, and I look back at the men.

"They took the women and children that remained, they took them and made them their prisoners. Black Kettle's daughter, Monahsetah, was forced to be George Custer's wife, and she bore him children. After that, he let his men have their way with her and others before they cast them aside. Those women were left with diseases we've never heard of or seen, a certain kind of hell we didn't even know existed. We don't have medicine to heal them. They forced them go to these reservations to die of starvation and sickness so they can take what is left of our land, our homes, our souls. And they now give us the same offer, the offer you have lived through." It is the first time I have heard Sitting Bull speak. I start to gag. I feel like I am going to be sick. I edge myself off the blanket and vomit on my hands and knees into the earth what little I have in my stomach. My own bile burns my throat and nostrils.

"His brother Tom raped my mother while I was in the tent. She told me to go, to run. I ran." I shout out to them through sobs, still hunched over my vomit. I vomit again. I feel myself begin to hit the earth with a strength, an anger I have pushed down for a long time.

"I should have stayed," I say, sitting back up, forgetting the pain from my knees. I look at the men. I look into their eyes. The fire lets out a loud pop, and sparks are released all around us.

"We all have a path. It is important when we look back that we have no regrets for the path we choose. It was chosen by us before we were us, and it is our mission here to finish the journey," Horn Chips says to me.

I look at him. I blink, my eyes raw; for a moment his eyes were that of the fire's flames and the shape of wolves.

"What happened when you ran from the tent?" he asks me.

I watch the ten-year-old version of me go with the woman that took me in.

"A Brulé, *phejúta wichasha*?" Sitting Bull says over the fire. I look at Sitting Bull; he is like a cross between Crazy Horse and Horn Chips.

"Yes," I say to the chief, his skin like gold.

"You don't go with them? Your family?" Horn Chips asks; my eyes go to him.

"No, but then my dead little brother calls me back to the grass," I say, my heart longing for my small brother.

"And you go?" Sitting Bull asks.

"Yes," I say, looking into the fire. I feel all the men looking at me. I can't take my eyes from the flames.

"There was a storm, and my horse came to me. I got on his back, and he took me to the bear." I remember the taste of the night, when I had mounted my horse and for a single moment, the pain in my heart had disappeared, the first time since I lost my family that I had been able to lose that pain.

"The bear?" Crazy Horse asks.

I touch my face.

"There was a hill in the trees. My pack was trying to kill it, but they bounced off of it like we swat away flies. I had nothing but the axe my brother gave me; it was my father's," I say into the fire, the flames soothing me. I am starting to feel very exhausted.

I touch where I had tucked it into my leggings; my hand freezes on the bone handle. I slowly pull it out, as though it might disappear. The bone handle is carved and painted with wolves. The rawhide strips that dangle out of the bottom still have the rock beads and hawk feathers my mother had tied on, "for protection," she said. I put the axe between me and the fire. I touch the medicine bag under my soldier's shirt; my own is soiled beyond repair. Blood, vomit, and dirt hide what was once white. The medicine bag, the one Sha had given to me, the one she had said she was safekeeping for me, is still around my neck. I pull it out, proving to myself that it is real, and I open it— the bear claw. I put them side by side on the blanket in front of me.

"Did you kill the bear?" Crazy Horse asks.

I don't take my eyes from the things I collected while I was dreaming.

"You know I did," I say, still looking at the claw.

"We need to hear you say it," Crazy Horse says.

I look at Crazy Horse. "I drove my axe into his chest and between his eyes. You are preparing the hide and fur for me."

Gall lets out a war call, and the four other chiefs join him. I watch as Horn Chips gets up, scoops up a handful of dirt, and mixes it with something from his pouch. He sprinkles it on my head, then sits next to me. I turn my body to face him. I see he is holding a rattle with a bear painted on it.

"Little Wolf, you dreamt of thunder. Your ancestors gave you a horse stronger and faster than a white man's. You were once the daughter of a great war chief. You now walk on your own. I give you strength," he says, shaking his rattle over the top of my head. I see myself, different, in a thick fog, holding the axe in one hand and a small pistol in my other, ducking beneath the forest's brush.

"I give you power," he says, shaking the rattle over my heart. I see myself walking barefoot in the snow, a vast emptiness before me. "I give you courage." He shakes the rattle over my hands, over the axe of my father's.

I see myself killing men.

CHAPTER 19

▲▲▲▲

SWEAT TRICKLES DOWN MY BROW LIKE HONEY, slow, thick, and sticky with dust, adding to my irritation. I wipe at it with a kerchief I tied to my saddle's horn, which seems to do little more than smear it about. I shake my kerchief and retie it, looking around. The sun seems to have baked anything that it touched, the brush a ripe yellow and brown. Vic could not be persuaded to move much faster than a meander, the heat stifling even the great beast.

"General, do you not think we should have happened upon them by now?"

Tom's voice has a tone I don't like, not quite worry but too darn close to that. I glance over at my brother swaying in his saddle. His cheeks apple red from the sun, his golden curls matted to his head in a dark sticky mass, he slaps haphazardly at a horsefly trying to take a chunk out of his neck.

"I think it would be quite certain we would have happened upon them by now," I say, chewing at my cheek. The stillness of the air is suffocating. I look back at my men, a sea of them, all swaying on their mounts. We'd been marching slowly, as though we were stalled in a sleepless slumber. I wince from the brightness of the sun and search the horizon ahead of us for Bloody Knife. I bring Vic to a halt. In the expansive openness, I finally see Bloody Knife in the distance, running his horse toward us, his black hair waving behind him like a flag. Five of his men trail behind him, kicking up a massive dust cloud, their haste sucking even more life out of the dead air. As Bloody Knife draws his mount to a stop before me, I see that he is bone straight in his saddle, his black hair a wild mess.

I hear Captain Keogh's horse let out a shrill sound and look to my right to see it stomping its hooves. I glance at the Irishman who is yanking hard on the reins, trying to steady her. I nod at the half Humpapa, half Arikara man I've come to know so well. The look on Bloody Knife's face unsettles me more. I raise my arm to officially halt the march. I hear my officers yelling my command. I shift in my saddle, making Vic shift with me.

"What did you find?" I ask, looking into the noble dark eyes of my savage.

"They have already had their Sun Dance. Looks like there would have been hundreds, if not thousands, of them."

I fight the urge not to glance backward at my outnumbered infantry.

"Any sight of Colonel Gibbon, General Crook, or General Terry?" I ask, forcing my face and voice to remain neutral. The Indian shakes his head no; I see he is sweating, too, something I hadn't seen too often. The elements didn't seem to affect the Indians the way they affect us.

"What makes you think so many?" the voice of my brother-in-law interrupts. I glance at James, annoyed; he is leaning forward in his saddle nervously.

"The grasses have been stomped out, and the game scarce. The land has been flattened from many tents, and it looks as though they were all in one spot for the Sun Dance, then moved up the river," Bloody Knife answers tonelessly, implying that he thought it was as dumb of a question as I did.

One of Bloody Knife's men, Yellow Face, starts talking to him rapidly in Arikara. Bloody Knife looks at him sternly and answers the man. Yellow Face starts gesturing at me.

"What is this about?" I ask, looking at Yellow Face.

"We saw some things we may want to talk to you about privately," Bloody Knife says to me, glancing at all my officers. I look at them.

"Tom, Captain Keogh and First Lieutenant Calhoun, Major Reno, Captain Yates, and Captain Benteen, with me. Captain Moylan, attend the halted men, break for food, and water the horses."

Moylan nods, raises his arm, and screams, "Dismount!"

I look back at the soldiers. I can see they are happy, smiling and joking as they dismount. I watch as they pass around canteens; I feel doubtful their contents are full of water. I see many of my men have unbuttoned their shirts or taken them right off, as well as their caps. As the weeks passed, it had grown insufferably hot. More and more men had begun undressing. My inclination had been to chastise and punish them, but I knew standard-issue army uniforms did not take this sort of heat into account and had decided to let it go.

I steer Vic away from the clambering men. My officers follow me as I lead us into the sparse forest, the shade giving us some respite from the sun. I see the small river we've been following. I walk Vic to the water's edge and slide from the saddle. I loosen his reins, and he shakes his head and dives his nose straight into the water, drinking noisily. I pat his hindquarters, and going to the water, I crouch down beside him, scooping some of the river and splashing it on my face. I take off my hat and splash it over my head and scoop more into my mouth; it tastes sweeter than molasses at Christmastime. I watch my men as they do the same. Their horses drink noisily as we wash. I stand, putting my hat back on my head, and turn to the trees. I see that the Indians have dismounted and are standing a few feet back in the shade of the narrow pines observing us; some crouch to the ground. Bloody Knife is standing straighter than straight—agitated, I think. I make my way to them, amazed at how their dress can make them disappear into the flora and fauna of this wild land; in the brown of their hides, they all but disappear as bark and brush. I hear the boots of my men following, snapping twigs and stomping grass. That is where we differ once more from the savages—they could walk in the roughest terrain silent as a ghost, and if you were tracking one, they could suddenly disappear as though they were a ghost as well. Bloody Knife nods at me, and I take my water flask from around my body and take a long swig. I spit out some of my mouthful, trying to get the taste of the river from my mouth.

"It looks like there was a battle," Bloody Knife says, not waiting for me to finish drinking. You could never get an Indian scout to quite fall in line like an American soldier; that was why we all hold a certain distrust for most of them. My officers settle in next to me, us across from them, smelling of horse and of unwashed humans.

"A battle between whom?" I demand.

"The Sioux and the American Army," Bloody Knife says. His eyes don't flinch, meaning that what he saw terrified him. I look at Bloody Knife's men, who don't meet my eyes. They shift in their moccasins. I've seen that in soldiers many times before, trying to unsee what they saw.

"What? And when?" I ask, putting my canteen back around my torso.

"Less than a fortnight ago, there had been a dance of death," Bloody Knife answers.

"What do you mean?" I ask, studying Bloody Knife, watching his every twitch, but he remains totally still.

"They used their gunstock clubs, axes, and knives to dismember the bodies and string them up into the trees; they left some in tipis so they will be able to find them in the land of Neshanu Natchitak," Yellow Face replies.

I look down at the man's face, covered in shadows. Yellow Face is crouching in a squatted position I have only ever seen Indians rest in, his smooth brown fingers softly playing in the dirt under our feet. I watch as the Indians make a sign with their hands and whisper words I've never cared to learn.

"What is this?" I ask, looking back at Bloody Knife.

"On the Rosebud, the dead were beyond recognizing, stripped bare. But I could still see the white of their flesh, and the Indians, their parts were mixed with others I would guess were their guides," Bloody Knife says, the color draining from his tanned face.

I take a deep, silent breath and look at my officers. They are still, weary in their dark boots, their eyes transfixed on Yellow Face and Bloody Knife as though they would enact it and it would appear less grave.

"How far are we from there?" I ask.

"With the whole army? Two days," Bloody Knife says.

"If we strip the column?" I demand, anger flooding my voice.

"One," comes Bloody Knife's apprehensive reply.

I nod, trying to work out which one of us has come under attack. I could guess that it was least likely to be General Terry—too seasoned and methodical to waltz into a rich stew pot of Indian warriors.

"You think the Indians had a victory?" I ask, weighing out which of us should go survey further to see if there were any survivors.

"They were able to dance for the dead and string up all their enemies, so they were not running from there," Bloody Knife explains.

I nod, looking off into the shadows of the trees.

"Who do you think it was, Autie?" comes the voice of Tom. I say the first man that comes to mind, the one hungry enough to try to force a win.

"General Crook."

"Any sight of where the remaining army might have made for?" Captain Keogh asks softly.

"Looked like a retreat," Yellow Face replies.

I nod, confirming my suspicion.

"Take us to the lodges of the dead. The next day, we will ride with the hope to catch sight of the other two columns. If none are seen, we will then send a runner. Either way, our mission as the cavalry was to drive the Indians to the foot soldiers," I say, looking back at my men. Their somber faces make me think of the war. I look at Bloody Knife, and he nods at me.

"Let's put an end to the Indian's blatant and flagrant disobedience," I say, looking back at Vic. He and the other mounts have made their way to a grassy knoll. They eat lazily in the sun; their tails swing in rhythm, swatting the flies. I look over at my brother.

"Tom, you will tell them to sound the bugle to continue the march, and that the column is to be stripped," I say, looking at my brother, and he nods at me. I can see his blue eyes twinkling at the promise of a fight. I have often wondered if that was born into us, the need to destroy to make way for something better.

"How do you plan on catching them with this lot?" comes the bumbling voice of Benteen. I look at the captain; his fat cheeks are so full they're taut. I see something in him I had yet to see, or at least I suspected: fear tinged with the usual disdain.

"You can go and tell the men that we are stripping the column to make up for lost time," I tell him.

"Have you lost your mind?" Benteen says to me, his cheeks flushed and jiggling. I step toward the captain, so close we are almost nose to nose. I didn't want this man to be any part of my cadre of officers, but given my standing with the president, I was in no position to rid myself of him.

"If you question my judgment or orders again, I'll put a bullet between your eyes. You are dismissed," I say, spit flying from my lips into his face.

I feel the hot breath of the captain on my face, like a deer before you killed it, frozen. My hand on the butt of one of my revolvers, Captain Benteen takes a cautious step back. I watch him slowly turn, doing what he is supposed to be doing, gathering his men. I watch him disappear into the pines.

"I understand what the captain might be saying, General; we should at least take the Gatling guns," comes the soft voice of Keogh.

My eyes study Captain Keogh; his captain's hat is cocked to the side, making him look even more dashing despite the hellish heat ravishing the rest of us. There is that part of me again that was jealous. He had something you had to be born with, not something that could be taught or mimicked.

"You cannot shoot with your rifle, Captain?" I ask, looking at the man I'd fought with so many times.

"I can, General, but if there are as many hostiles as Bloody Knife says, it may be in our favor to come with heavy ammunition." He replies with an evenness and dignity he has always managed to maintain.

I look at the Irishman, thinking of how many hours we would lose to the three massive Gatling guns; they were loaded on their own special wagons that had to be dragged by mule. It would take three, more like four, days to get there. I think of General Crook being grossly outnumbered and potentially chased, and I would hope if the situation were to be reversed, my fellow commanders would be brave and courageous enough to enter the mouth of hell for their fellow soldiers.

"Have you fought against a gunstock club, Captain?" I ask Keogh.

"Aye, that I have, General, and I know that when you are looking for them, they are as slippery as fish and that even with a stripped column, they'll most likely spot us like gold in a pile of shit."

I smile at that.

"You're a good man, Captain," I say, stepping forward and slapping him on the back a little too hard. "But we must capitalize on this skirmish—look around you. Most these men are green. Most are immigrants, and they are really frightened of what you just spoke of. I hear them asking each other of the gunstock clubs and the insane notion that these people can shoot pennies thrown in the air. We need to season them if this is to be our last campaign against these people. I know that you yourself long for a more civilized post."

"Aye, General," Keogh answers, leading us back to our horses. I look at him; he has a sadness that settled over him at Gettysburg that has never lifted. He and my brother often found themselves lost to drink, but not so much so like that bastard Reno.

I look around for the major as I hoist myself into Vic's saddle. I see him, his nose bright red in the sun. I watch my brothers and kin making their way to us—Tom, Boston, Little Autie, James, and Myles. I smile at the sight. Never in my career did I ever think we'd be all together under my command.

"Ready then, gentlemen?" I call out.

Tom grins at me, and I feel my own smile fade from my lips as I settle into the saddle.

I raise my arm through the suffocating heat and dig my spurs into Vic, nudging us all forward, leading us to where no American has yet to tread. Into the heart of the land of the thunder dreamers and the wild unknown, the land that will now be our home.

CHAPTER 20

▲▲▲▲

"TOMORROW IS THE START OF THE SUN DANCE." His breath is warm on my ear.

I blink my eyes open. It is dark. I let out a groan, rubbing my ribs a little too roughly with my palms, making me wince and shut my eyes; my ribs have settled into a dull throb. Horn Chips gave me two different root teas that seemed to dull the pain, but it didn't take it all away.

"I don't even want to think about dancing right now," I say, rolling onto my side. It doesn't make the pain any better, and I flop back onto my back. I hear Swift Fox laugh and feel myself smiling with my eyes closed. I had liked right away knowing he was next to me, even if it was the first time I had slept next to someone since my family.

"Do you want help to sit?" he asks me, meaning it was time to get up.

I shake my head no. I blink myself awake and inch myself up, my ribs aching as they arch into a sitting position.

"Did you get this beat up from your dreams?" I ask, expecting him to laugh. He has moved from our fur bed to the other side of the tent and is readying some water for me to drink. I watch his back move; despite it being hard, his body seems to move and con-tort like a stream running through a valley. He drains his hide water sack into a tin cup.

I hear nothing but a hiss from the fire; its embers are mostly smothered. He looks across at me, his black eyes catching the last of the fire's glow. I glance down at my blood-soaked tunic—once a pretty white, it had turned to the rusty brown shade of dried blood. Swift Fox moves like the animal he's named after. He comes to me in a crouched position and, sitting softly on his heels, hands me the cup. I take it, tracing my fingers over the dented metal.

"Ever seen one before?" he asks.

I sip the cool water, wrapping my fingers around the cup. It's cold, too.

"No," I say, frowning, wondering why we had never acquired such a useful object.

"It is actually pretty good, travels well," he says, and I nod, think-ing that it must.

"That's what I thought of this shirt," I say, glancing at the mess I've become.

Swift Fox laughs.

"Chief Gall's wives have offered to help you dress for the dance."

I look at his face; he is looking into the fire, not meeting my eyes. He has a strong profile. His face, big nose, big lips, square jaw seem to balance everything out. Without his shirt on, I can see bruises on top of his shoulder and arm muscles from the dance the day I came to this camp.

"Will you still marry me?" he asks for the first time. He looks up at me briefly, shyly. I smile into my water cup.

"I think I probably should," I say over the cup's rim.

I watch as his solemn face turns into a smile. His smile, when he finally gives one, lights up his whole face; his dark eyes twinkle like stars. I smile wider, looking at him, perched on his knees as though he might run. I watch his chest heave. He seems to be breathing again. He eases himself into a cross-legged position with effortless silence, not even unsettling the dust beneath him.

"They do a lot of mending, quill work, and beading with the woman you were talking to, Shadows Fall. She should be there, too; they are making crowns for everyone."

I feel my brow furrowing.

"Crowns?"

He smiled at me. "A ring of flowers and leaves for your head."

I smile, nodding and raising my eyebrows. I know what a crown is, just not why they are making them for everyone.

"Why?" I ask, frowning.

"To connect us to the mother and protect us from those who mean her harm," he answers in a way hinting that I should already know that.

"How do Shadows Fall and Red Hawk have children?" I blurt out, remembering them from that first day.

"Same way everyone does, I suppose," Swift Fox says. I look at him; he is trying not to laugh at me.

"No, it is that . . ." I find myself trailing off, feeling like I've already said too much.

"They are both women?" he finishes for me.

"Yes," I say.

"They are *winkte*; they have magic they are born with."

I nod, thinking about it, looking at the tin cup.

"Have you heard of them?" he asks me.

"A little," I say, remembering the camp I grew up in.

"They are usually medicine healers or warriors. We are very lucky that they have joined us—they have two spirits."

"Are they all women?"

"This group."

I nod again.

"Are there many women warriors?" I ask. That day, they all moved as one; I couldn't tell.

"The call seems to be pretty even. You were called, but you missed it," he says to me, any laughter that had been in his voice now gone.

"How do you know?" I demand, thinking if I had been called, I would have known.

"I could tell the first time when you came to the tent—your gun, it is a part of you."

I think of all the animals I've killed over the years, and I know he is right; my rifle moved with my arm from my heart. I never had to fire twice to kill something.

"Why haven't you married yet?" I ask, looking at the man that loves me.

Swift Fox grins at me.

"I've been waiting for you," he says, reaching out and yanking softly at my hair. I smile at him, placing my empty cup on the fur I am half-covered by.

"What did you dream of, when you were called to dream?" I ask, watching Swift Fox study my face. He meets my eyes and takes a wooden bowl out of a basket and passes it to me.

"They told me to feed you this."

I look at the creamed corn and smile. You only get this if you are sick or a baby. I scoop some into my mouth and force myself to swallow it; it tastes sweet, but my jaw is so swollen it is difficult to swallow.

"I saw a fox; he took me to my father." He settles back into his position of quick flight, on his knees.

"Is your father dead?" I ask, thinking I haven't asked him anything about himself. I feel like I have known him my whole life.

"No," he says, looking into the dying fire.

"What did he say, or show you, the fox?" I ask, thinking of the wolves; I watched them and knew what I must do.

"Nothing. I was given the choice to kill him."

"The fox or the father?" I ask, hoping he is talking about the fox.

"My father," Swift Fox says quietly. I watch his eyes scan the fire; it was the same thing I did when Horn Chips asked me to remember what I saw. My mind struggled to differentiate between it being real or a dream.

"Why?" I find myself asking, even though I think it would be better if I didn't know. Swift Fox shrugs and looks at me.

"He did some terrible things," he says, taking a deep breath.

"Why didn't his band kill him?" I ask, more to myself.

"They didn't get the chance. He left me with my mother in the dead of night."

"Did you kill him?" I ask, making him look at me.

Swift Fox looks deep into my eyes. I want to look away but don't.

"What do you think I did?" he asks softly but firmly.

"Left him to be," I say, hopeful.

The fire pops; neither one of us moves.

"I killed him," he says, looking deep into me.

I can feel his anger, and I feel myself grow cold. Swift Fox nods at himself.

"He had a new wife and some children," he says, sounding like he is going to say more but stops. A silence settles over us. I try to make sense of everything he is telling me.

"Still want to marry me?" he asks, looking at me.

I look at the fire, the smoldering coals. I think of this man I barely know killing the man that gave him life. I think of what happened to my family, and I think of what Gall said to me.

"I think I will," I find myself saying. I know for the first time in my life I don't want to be alone, and to survive, I need someone to stand with me.

A sad smile spreads across Swift Fox's face, making my heart grow cold.

"Then let me take you to the lodge of the chiefs," he says.

I put down the bowl and let him help me to my feet. I look around for my moccasins. I see them at the door and go to them. Swift Fox crouches down to help me, wiggling them onto my feet.

"How is Gray Wolf? Still eating grass?" I ask, a picture of my beautiful horse popping into my head.

Swift Fox smiles and stands.

"He has taken to the other horses and ponies and fancies himself their leader." I smile, thinking of how tall he is.

Swift Fox reaches out and lightly grabs my fingers. I let him lead us out of his tent and into the night. I am surprised at how bright the camp is. Lit with torches and lodge fires and a full moon, it is almost as bright as day. Very few seem to be asleep. Women are gathered in groups with young children, sitting around fires in front of the lodges, mending clothing and weaving crowns, some of them softly singing as my mother would have. As we wind through the camp, I can hear the gentle sound of drumming, its low vibration echoing through the people, forcing you to match their beat. No one so much as glances at us as we thread our way through, engrossed with their own work and the rhythm of the night.

"Is there always drumming at this time?" I ask, wondering how you could sleep through it; I suppose that was why everyone was up.

"No, Good Weasel chose the pole earlier, and they are blessing it. Horn Chips has chosen me as one of the men who will give a sacrifice." Swift Fox is determined to get to our destination, but I am exhausted from the short walk and wish we could take a break and just watch everyone moving through the night, their illuminated silhouettes giving off dreamlike shadows and forms.

"What does that mean?" I ask, thinking of the pole.

"You should tie something to the upper branches," he says to me, knowing exactly what I mean without me having to say it. I think of the bear claw.

"Not your wotawe," he says, glancing down at me.

"How did you know I was thinking that?" I ask, amused and surprised.

"Your hand went to it." He smiles in the darkness, his fingers squeezing mine.

I look and see my free hand lightly resting on it.

"You'll need that if you ever have to fight," he says into the night ahead of us. His words linger in my ears, and I think of what I saw or maybe did, my axe piercing flesh. I stop walking, forcing Swift Fox's determined steps to halt.

"Swift Fox, have you killed many men?"

Swift Fox glances at a large lodge we are headed toward. His dark eyes look back to me, and he lets go of my fingers and steps close to me. I can feel his breath in my hair, and he puts his hands on my shoulders.

"I've done what I've had to do; ask anyone here, and they will tell you that. We have been forced to become murderers, for there is nowhere left for us to go. We kill them or they kill us—you know this maybe better than me." He says this in a way that is strong but not forceful. I feel a tear slip down my face. He gently brushes it away with the back of his hand.

"I will now take half your pain with my own as I promised, but even if it wasn't the Sun Dance and you didn't want to marry me, you would still need something new to wear," he says with seriousness.

I look down at my shirt and let out a half-cry, half-laugh. He smiles, a smile that cuts into me, and lets go of my shoulders; his hand slides down my arm, and his fingers find mine. He interlaces them, letting go of one of my hands, then gently tugs me forward to where we were going, to the big lodge.

"I am here with Little Wolf," Swift Fox calls into the tent.

"Thank goodness."

It's the woman we saw scolding Gall that morning—I recognize her voice, soft and pretty like her. We are greeted by her opening up the tent's flap, light pouring over us. Swift Fox tugs me inside, and Gall's wife nestles back into her spot in the circle of women on the floor. The tent is big; you could easily fit ten people standing inside. A tidy bed of furs is on the far side. I see two small children snuggled in them, fast asleep, their small faces serene. I wonder after all the horrors I have lived through if I still look like them when I am asleep.

I find myself examining every corner of the tipi, my mind trying to commit it all to memory, as I had never seen a tent like this. I count seven women in the tent, all sitting on the floor on a thick, rich-looking woven blanket; this wasn't a trading post blanket, something better. They were doing the last of the puncturing and beading, their awls piercing into hides with a blind persuasion, and stringing glass seed beads into shirts, leggings, and moccasins. Each woman had their own patterns they were working on—shapes, flowers, leaves, animals, animals' prints.

I see Shadows Fall tucked away quietly in the shadows on the outskirts of the women; she feels me looking at her and glances up at me shyly from her beadwork. I smile at her, noticing once again my aching jaw.

"We will get her back to you when the sun rises," Gall's wife says to Swift Fox, whose fingers are still intertwined with mine.

"Before they raise the pole," another woman adds. Next to her is a baby, neatly fastened to a cradle board, looking like nothing more than a tiny head fastened to a hide. I find myself looking at Swift Fox; our eyes hold for a long moment. He finally nods, slowly letting go of my fingers, and disappears back into the night, letting the tipi's flap fall, shutting out the rest of the camp—my hand already aching for his.

"You dreamt of thunder?" asks Gall's wife, glancing at me.

"Yes," I say, frowning; wouldn't their husbands have told them?

All the women pause from their work and look me over, searching for how I am to them. I notice two of them have eyes the color of smoke. Sha had said people with eyes like that could control the rain.

"I am White Horse, one of Chief Gall's wives," says the woman I had seen earlier that day. I nod, making the woman smile.

"I am Little Wolf; I have come for clothes," I say, looking down at my bloody tunic. The lodge fills with laughter.

"And you are getting married," Shadows Fall says to me, glancing back at the children sleeping in the fur.

"Come in," one of the women says, gesturing to a fur laid in front of the fire. I hear a baby start to cry. I see the cradle board being lifted as I slowly lower myself to the fur.

"Do you want me to get it?" one of the women asks, looking up from the beaded red prairie rose on the bottom of the moccasin she is working on.

"No," the woman says, pulling the infant free from the cradle. She puts it to her breast.

"If his brother rises, you take him," the woman feeding the baby says. The other woman nods at the woman nursing and goes back to her rose, her single hand just as skilled as when it worked as a pair. I look around and see that most of them are beading the bottoms, the soles of the moccasins.

"Why the bottoms?" I say, looking at the flowers the woman is working on, small blue cornflowers. She looks at me with her startling gray eyes.

"Because we are chief's wives; we don't walk." She says this in a way that I know I have almost offended her.

I feel my brow furrow.

"We only ride," the woman nursing the baby says softly.

I look at her and the tiny infant, and I know what I am going to tie to the Sun Dance pole.

"Horses?" I ask, making the women laugh again.

"The men were right, you are funny," Chief Gall's wife says to me.

"We will give you clothes, but I think you have to wash first," the nursing mother says, looking me over. I don't argue; I know I am starting to stink, my own blood with the blood of the bear caked into my skin and my hair.

"Black Dog, will you take her to the river? And try to round up our children?"

A woman looks up from the tunic she is tying elk teeth onto in tidy rows. They will clatter when the wearer walks.

"Yes, will you finish this?" the woman says, gesturing to the tunic and the woven basket of teeth.

"Of course," the woman replies.

The other woman nods, putting her mending aside. I watch her stand from cross-legged. She unfolds like a flower blooming, making quickly for the other side of the tent. She picks up a small rawhide box.

"Come with me," she says, grabbing a folded red wool blanket from a stack of them. Without waiting to see if I am going to follow, she steps through the tent's flap like a deer going through the forest, as though her feet don't hit the earth. I try to hurry; my feet are as sore as my aching body. I can feel myself staggering, and I try to make myself walk normally, making myself stagger worse. My pain is deep. I follow her into the night, where the quiet fills my ears and calls my heart. In the short time I had been in the tent, the noise had died down considerably.

"I am Black Dog, Gall's other wife. We will go to the stream on the far end," she says, still moving fast, leading us off into the trees I had yet to venture through. We both move silently, not making a sound; not even a stick breaks beneath our feet, something we are all taught to do as children. I hear the voice of the mother, *Quiet or you'll wake an angry spirit.* The sound of water takes me from my thoughts.

"My husband, he doesn't tell us too much, but he told us of you, of your mother," the woman says, glancing back at me.

I feel my throat tighten; my heart feels as though it has stopped beating, bringing me great pain.

"That is the one fate any of us actually fear—Monahsetah," she says with her voice dropping off.

I think of the women who were stolen. I try to remember what Monahsetah looked like. The memory of her is like a shadow to me, the chief's daughter. I just remember everyone saying how beautiful she was, more beautiful than a summer's sunrise.

"Do you know what happened to her, to Monahsetah?" I ask, thinking of what they had said, that they'd left her to die far from our home.

"The same thing that will happen to all of us," Black Dog says, leading us to the edge of the creek.

"They will round us up and kill us," Black Dog says, her toes on the edge of the water. I stagger next to her and look at the black water shining and trickling with moonlight. I feel the hair on my arms stand up. A wolf howls in the distance; it isn't fear that enters my heart but a hollowness, an emptiness that can never truly be filled if you've lost someone you loved.

"Here," Black Dog says, opening the box. She passes me soap and a cloth. Crouching down, I place them gently on the edge of the stream. I begin to try to take my tunic off with my one good arm. I feel her hands behind me; grabbing the edge of my soft tunic, she hoists it over my head.

"We have three children; I am used to helping," Black Dog says to me.

"Do you need help with the leggings?" she asks.

"No," I say, kicking off my moccasins and peeling my deer leggings off.

I pick up the soap and cloth and walk into the water—the water only comes to just above my knees. I lower myself into the stream;

the rocks are smooth, and the water rushes around me undeterred from its journey. I close my eyes and give thanks to god for everything. For letting me live. My eyes blink open, and I slowly begin to wash the blood and dirt from my body and hair, lathering the soap in the cloth. The soap has been scented with white buffalo sage.

"You came from a camp run by a woman?" Black Dog asks. I look to see her perched on a rock, like a raven, cloaked in darkness.

I think of Sha and feel a pang in my heart.

"Yes," I reply.

"Why not a man?" she asks me.

I now know that Sha's camp isn't usual.

"Because of Monahsetah, because of my mother, father, and brother," I find myself replying. Silence hangs between us as I finish. I rinse my hair in the stream, then make sure all the blood is gone from my hands. I keep my hands in the stream's water; with my fingers spread out, I can feel the current move through my fingertips. Like the mother's heartbeat, my heart is filled with sadness.

"Because all the men are dying," I find myself saying in the night's sky.

"Huhn," Black Dog says.

"Huhn," I reply, the Hunkpapa accent sounding strange to me.

"Take this blanket; as for your clothes, I don't think there is any saving them," Black Dog says, knowing I am done.

I look over at her; she is eyeing my pile of clothing like they have fleas. She sees me, and I smile. She comes to the edge of the water, and I hand her the soap and cloth. She crouches down to take them and places them back into their box. I watch as she takes the folded blanket and stands, shaking it out.

I force myself to stand; as I do, the night air runs a chill through me. Black Dog opens the blanket for me, and I step out of the water into her, wrapping myself in the blanket. It is a soft wool of thick yarn, softer than any trading blankets I had ever felt.

"We traded for it with some Navaho."

I nod, feeling it. It is different from American wool. Black Dog doesn't wait for me and is already walking back toward the tipi. I force my legs to follow her.

"We will go to my lodge. White Horse would have put the clothes we prepared for you there," she says, barely glancing back to see if I am still following her.

We are greeted with silence; the camp has settled into stillness, the night finally taking over. I hear the hooting of an owl, and I feel my face pinch, not a good sign on the night you are to marry. I watch Black Dog touch her heart, then throw the energy away; she glances back at me.

"You should, too, they bring messages of death," she says, the night eating her words.

Many had told me that before, too, but I had never been instructed to ward off the message. That seemed pointless to me; death comes when it comes. I follow Black Dog, who leads us to a tent next to the massive painted chief's tents we had been in earlier. I notice that there are three tipis grouped together, all of them painted in the same style.

"That one is ours, too," she says, nodding to the colorful tent I am looking at beside the one we are going into and behind the one we had been in.

"Gall is most likely in there with god knows who," Black Dog says, nodding at the tent I am looking at. I look at her, and she leads me into her tent. The fire has burned down low. The tent is messier than the one we had been in with the other wives. Black Dog throws my bundle of dirty clothes directly onto the flames and crouches down, placing the box with the soap on the floor next to several others. She grabs another small box, throwing the contents of it into the fire as well.

"To protect you," she says looking up at me. She puts the box back, and as she is doing so, my clothes catch fire, lighting up the whole tent. I look at the hide walls; they are painted inside as well as out.

"I've never seen painting on the inside," I say to her.

"I guess we like a bit of color. Here are your new clothes," she says, distracted. I watch her fish out a bundle of clothing as she stands and shoves them at me.

"Thank you," I say, taking the bundle through the blanket, my hair still dripping wet. "I don't know how I'll repay you," I say, meeting Black Dog's eyes. She smiles a tired smile that barely manages to reach her black eyes.

"I hear you can shoot. The biggest repayment would be keeping my husband alive," she says wearily.

I nod. Kneeling, I place the bundle on the floor. I pick up the tunic, which is on the top. It is the most spectacular piece of clothing I have ever possessed. Sleeveless and made of very soft hide, *doe*, I think, rubbing my fingers on it. It is covered in elaborate embroidered flowers, pink prairies on green vines and leaves, glass beads, as the fringes make a "v" in the middle of the tunic's front and back.

"Shadows Fall made it for her wife, but they wanted to give it to you."

I look at Black Dog.

"Red Hawk and Swift Fox go back years; they have fought together many times."

"Is she a Dog Warrior?"

"No, but she is Cheyenne like you and him. They are your people."

I pull the tunic on. I notice Black Dog smiling sweetly at me, the first time since we had been together. I think she might like me.

"She made the leggings, too," she says.

I hold up the leggings. They are made of the same soft, light hide and also have fringes that run down the sides of each leg with a strip of beaded flowers, pink prairie roses running along them. There are loops on either side. I touch them.

"For your club and knife," she says, answering my silent question.

I nod and pull my leggings on. They are snugger than my old ones, which were so worn they had become part of my body.

"They need to be tight for when you are fighting on your horse." She watches my face, then grabs something from the top of the sleeping furs.

"These are from us," she says, smiling. When she smiles, something lights up inside of her, making her very pleasant to look at.

I take the mukluks she is holding out for me.

"The same as the leggings, you will need boots for riding," she says, again answering the question I had thought in my mind.

"Thank you," I whisper, blinking away tears.

"Try them," she says, softly nodding at them. I take them, smiling through my tears, and I pull them on my feet. This hide is stiffer, the soles thick; they lace in the front and have several flowers sewn on them, and pink prairie roses as well, but in a different style, they look flatter.

"They were going to be for our eldest daughter," Black Dog says softly.

"Thank you so much; they are beautiful—all of it is." I look down at my legs and feet, and they look strange to me.

"Well, it is not every day we get a new warrior at the Sun Dance. Let me take you back to your husband," she says, holding out her hand for me.

I take it, exhaustion settling over me. I feel like I could sleep for days, but know I only have a few hours. She pulls us into the night. I glance at the night sky; the full moon is making its descent to the sun and the new day. I hear hushed voices and a baby crying softly in the distance. We weave our way back to the northern edge of the camp. I see his lodge, a glow among the trees.

"He always liked to be alone, Swift Fox. We were all surprised when he showed up and announced he was waiting for his wife," Black Dog says, her fingers warm in mine.

I smile, thinking of how sure he is when he comes to a decision on something.

"You are odd like him. It is rare to become a warrior at your age. If you remember, you are usually chosen when little more than a baby and train your whole life."

I think of my camp. I remember being in the trees with my father, and I think I remember hitting things with a stick and him laughing.

"Sometimes the fight isn't with other people but yourself. Sometimes to bring good to others, you must first conquer yourself," I say, looking at the sky. It is tinged in the purple pink of a new day's promise. We stop in front of Swift Fox's lodge.

"Remember what I said of Gall—watch for him in the battle, shoot," she says.

I nod, and Black Dog hugs me. I am surprised. My body is stiff and I feel myself slowly relax into her embrace, my chin resting awkwardly on the top of her head.

"I will see you at the dance," she says, letting go of me. I nod and watch as she hurries away, disappearing into the forest of tipis.

"Thank you," I whisper into the air behind her. I look up at the night sky. The stars are slowly disappearing, and I wonder about the person I could have been if my camp had lived. Would I have been her? I duck into the tent. Would I have become a chief's wife, not carrying a gunstock club but balancing babies on a board? I smile. For the first time in a long time, I am grateful for the person I have become and look forward to becoming the person I am meant to be.

CHAPTER 21

▲▲▲▲

MY EYES TRACE OUR TENT'S POLES, SANDED DOWN TO SLIVERS. All three are even in thickness and shape, bound with precision, perfectly even strips of rawhide meeting in the middle like an explosion of togetherness. I stretch my arms above my head, the softness of our bed's furs cradling them. My whole body still aches, and I wince in pain as my ribs spread apart, but something swells in my chest, something I have not felt in a long time and I try to think if ever—hope.

My eyes, even though open, drift into a nothingness before me; our tent's ceiling becomes like the night sky, a blank canvas, and things flutter back to me, memories of everything I have come across in this life. I see Custer, his hair shining from underneath his black-rimmed hat, my family, crushed together in our tent in the dead of winter, my mom sings, my dad smiles, and my baby brother sleeps. Swift Fox, the first time I ever saw him. Snow blanketing the earth, and Sha always with her basket of herbs. I blink, and I am back in our tent, looking at the poles, thinking of Swift Fox and how much time it must have taken to get the poles so thin and fine.

The people of this camp seem to respect and like him—same as the first time I met him, no one spoke ill of him. My mind wanders to him telling me he killed his father. I think of my own father, the fragments of what I remember of him. I remember him trying to teach Gray Wolf to shoot a rifle, while my mother and I awled together whatever needed fixing, which with a family always seemed like everything.

"No one told me you were back." Swift Fox's voice cuts into my dream, one so real I feel confused about where I am. My eyes snap open. I didn't realize they had shut, and I didn't hear the tent's flap open.

"I didn't hear you," I say, not sitting up or looking at him.

"They didn't name me Swift Fox for nothing," he says, and I can feel his weight on the furs and know he is crouching next to me.

I feel his hand on my forehead, cool like the stream.

"How are you feeling? Should I let you sleep?" he asks. I can tell he wants me to rise but knows he should let me rest. I want to go back to my family; a longing is left in the place where the hope had been.

I slowly bring myself to a sitting position. I face him, and we are almost nose to nose. I watch drops of water slide down his slick black hair and drip onto his bare shoulders; he had been in the stream, which is why he is so cool. The air is hotter than our bodies.

"Your shirt, it is beautiful," he says, reaching out and touching the fringe. I touch his fingers and look at him. He pulls my hand to his mouth, kissing my fingers. His lips are warm even though his hands are cool.

"Come, I made us a surprise," he says, pulling me to my feet.

He tugs me out of the tent. I look at the sky; the moon is gone, and the stars are slowly disappearing. I hear the trickling of the stream. Swift Fox leads us across it. We step on stones to the other side and weave through the trees to the open grass. It is the grass I remember from my dream. It sways gently in the breeze. I see ponies and some horses sleeping with their heads resting on each other's backs.

Swift Fox makes a clicking noise, and I see Gray Wolf, the white spots on his hindquarters bright in the stars' light. He shakes his white mane, looks at me, and comes over to me. He presses his nose to my head, making me laugh. I nuzzle him back, our noses together.

"Come," Swift Fox says, hopping on his back.

Gray Wolf looks back at him as Swift Fox adjusts himself on his back and reaches his hand out for me. I take it and he pulls me onto my horse in front of him. He puts his bare arms on either side of me. I feel his legs squeeze Gray Wolf's massive rib cage, and the horse takes off, so fast it is as though his hooves don't touch the ground. I feel Swift Fox squeeze Gray Wolf again, and he breaks into a run. I feel myself let out a laugh as the grass swirls by us. We go for some distance before Gray Wolf slows to a fast walk. We cross through sparse forest as the sky turns into a blaze of pink and orange. Coming out on the other side of the trees, I feel my breath catch in my mouth. There are hundreds of buffalo grazing. One looks at us, then looks past us, then looks back at us—challenging, his black eyes are fire, his nostrils flare, and he shakes his massive horns.

"Have you seen them before?" Swift Fox asks me quietly.

"No, not for a long time," I say, my words catching in my throat.

I remember, a long time ago, my father and the other men, the chief, the hunts, the dances, the feasts.

"Not since I was a child," I find myself whispering.

"They are killing them. The Great White Chief and the Indians he has tricked into working for him, they know they are important to us; they run them off cliffs just to watch them die," Swift Fox says into my ear. I watch the buffalo meander through grass, as something in my heart beats with them.

"What will happen when they are all dead?" I ask, as a sinking feeling takes over my body—thinking of them being led to their death for no other reason than to watch them die.

"Things only die if you forget them," Swift Fox says into my ear.

His words ring through my soul. I let my family, my ancestors, die because I had lost the courage to remember them.

We watch them in silence, neither of us or my horse moving; it's as though we are frozen in time. I can feel the sun growing higher in the sky and the day grow hotter. I wanted to stay in this moment forever, a moment where nothing matters, a moment where some chief from a faraway place wasn't trying to steal our home, where the men he led but never actually truly led weren't trying to murder us, a time where almost everything I loved was dead or fading fast right before my eyes. I try to burn the buffalo into my memory through my tear-soaked eyes.

"After the Sun Dance, before we find a home with Sha, we will come back here and hunt one. We will bring her the hide so she'll never forget," Swift Fox says gently into my ear, urging me to come back. I feel my heart swell in my throat. I have nothing to say. I feel Swift Fox urge Gray Wolf across the field, away from the buffalo. The field slopes to a valley. I see a large stream as we weave down the rocky terrain.

"This is the Greasy Grass River."

I smile at the name as he leads my horse to the edge of the water.

"The Greasy Grass?" I say, looking at the dusty ground.

"More south, it is very grassy," he says to me.

I smile as Swift Fox slides from my horse. He lands softly on his feet. I notice his feet are bare, and he holds out his hands for me. I take them, sliding gently from Gray Wolf's back.

"Did the drink help with your pain?" he asks. I touch my face. It feels normal, and the ache in my ribs is steadily disappearing but still there if I move too fast. My eyes go to Gray Wolf as he trots to the river, shaking his head in anticipation of a drink.

"He likes water," Swift Fox says as we watch the horse walk right into the stream, his hooves making a noisy mess in the river's bed.

Gray Wolf doesn't look back at us as Swift Fox tugs me by the hand. I let him lead me away, and we walk in silence. I look down at our hands intertwined as one. I see where he is taking us: Along the river on a flat bank is a bed of furs.

"We won't get any rest back at the camp; they'll start singing and drumming by first light, deep in it by now," Swift Fox says, glancing at the sky. "Even though they won't raise the pole for some time," he adds more to himself than me. I smile; he often speaks to himself, and I am always happy to just listen. He doesn't look at me as we stop at the edge of the furs. I look across the river, and the hair stands up on my arms.

"I've been here before," I whisper. Swift Fox follows my eyes.

"Up that hill they found the bear," he says.

"How did they know where to look?" I ask.

"Horn Chips went with you." He says this like I should have known it.

"What?" I ask, feeling confused. I never once caught a glimpse of him—maybe he had hidden from me. I feel Swift Fox looking at me. I don't look at him, an uneasiness settling over me.

"Horn Chips can go places without going. He sits there in his lodge with his eyes shut lightly beating a drum and can see people, places, animals," Swift Fox says to me.

I feel a chill run through me.

"That is how they know about the army and Custer?" I ask, pieces of information starting to make sense to me.

"He can only see what they let him see," Swift Fox says. I don't have to look at him to know he is shrugging.

"Who are they?" I ask.

"*Ma'heo'o*, god, the creator," Swift Fox says.

I find myself nodding, even though I'm not sure I understand, and I look at Swift Fox, who turns to look at me, pulling my hand so I can face him squarely.

"This site, this place, I think it is sacred to you. I dreamt of you some time ago. I saw Crazy Horse in the dream, so I thought if I found him, I'd find you—and I was right. I am blessed that I can call you my wife, and I mean to take you and you only and hope that you feel the same way about me."

I look at this man I barely know and don't even have to think of my words. I touch his face. He leans his mouth to mine, pressing hard into me. I feel his hands grab the edge of my shirt, and he pulls it over my head, tossing it to the ground. I watch as he takes off his leggings and kneels down. He pulls off my mukluks and unlaces my leggings. He lays me on the fur and kisses me softly. I tip my mouth up, wanting more. He balances himself on top of me, not taking his mouth from mine. I feel myself pressing into him, aching for him. He slides into me, making me stop. He stops moving and looks at me.

"Stop?" he says.

"No," I say. He nods and begins to slowly press into me. It hurts and aches in a way I can't describe. I look up at the sky. I feel him finishing; his body shudders, and he gently pulls out of me and slides to the side of me. His fingers trace my face, my mouth, my nose, my cheeks.

"We will have children."

"How will I fight if I am heavy with a child?"

For the first time I see sadness in his eyes.

"What's that?" I ask him, searching his face.

"Maybe it won't be you that will fight, but them."

I feel myself smiling, thinking that's a foolish answer. The sadness . . . I watch it weigh over him, and I feel the smile slipping from my face.

"What do you know?"

"That everything happens for a reason."

I hear the early call of the birds and the sun start to trickle in through the branches shading us.

"I love you," Swift Fox says to me, his voice barely a whisper. I look at this man, his bronze skin, his muscled torso, covered in scars, his full mouth and smart eyes. I roll on my side to see him better.

"I love you."

He kisses me; I feel his tears in my mouth.

There is a wailing that reaches us. I sit up, looking around.

"They are announcing the Sun Dance; we should go," Swift Fox says, pulling on his leggings. I watch him, he smiles back at me shyly and hands me my shirt. I pull it on, looking down at the flowers, and grab my leggings, having to stand up to pull them on.

"Do you want me to braid your hair?" he asks.

I look at the long waves almost reaching my waist.

"Maybe," I say, thinking of this dance that everyone has gathered for. Swift Fox pats the fur he is still kneeling on. I sit back down with my back to him.

"Maybe, one big one," he says softly to himself.

I feel him gathering up my mass of clean hair and starting at the front. He is going to make a war braid. I smile to myself and close my eyes, letting the morning sunshine wash me of any pain left from facing my past. I hear the birds singing and the trees rustling, the water slowly swirling over and around the river's rocks.

"There," he says. I reach for the top of my head and smile.

"I think it is beautiful."

He laughs his rough laugh, and I feel him kiss my neck.

"Well, my bride, let us go," he says, standing.

He reaches his hand out for me to take. I take it, and he pulls me to my feet. He doesn't let go as we walk back to where we left Gray Wolf. I see him among the trees, rooting for grass. He sees us and slowly walks toward us. Swift Fox touches his nose; they seem to agree on something as he lets go of my hand and hops on his back. He holds his hand out for me and I take it, glad I don't have to make too much use of my upper body, and he pulls me in front of him again. I feel him nudge the horse, and Gray Wolf takes off at a brisk walk up the slope, back to the grassland. We ride in silence. I feel Swift Fox's arms around me. They don't feel strange; they feel like they should have always been there. I see the edge of the camp. I hear the drums and singing. It's louder than any I have ever heard. I smell roasting meat, buffalo; it has a grassy smell I've never smelled in the game I hunt.

"We'll leave him here, by the grass."

As Swift Fox urges Gray Wolf to a stop, the horse halts, and I feel Swift Fox slide from the horse, leaving me alone and with an empty feeling.

"We need to make for the pole," Swift Fox says, helping me off. I land on my feet and pat my horse. He noses for my hand; I give him a pat goodbye and watch him trot off.

"I need to go back to our lodge to get my offering," I say.

Swift Fox nods at me, taking my hand as we make our way through the deserted tents.

"Everyone will be at the dance grounds," he says to me.

Urgency has slipped into his voice, and he walks a bit faster, dragging my sleepy feet forward. The drumming grows louder as we come to our tent. He lets go of my hand, and I look at him, half clothed, his hair loose, and I notice for the first time that he looks tired too.

"Are you getting dressed?" I ask, looking at his bare chest.

He smiles at me.

"There is no point," he says.

I nod, even though I don't understand what he means, and duck into our tent. I see he has piled all my things neatly on top of a blanket next to the sleeping furs, my medicine bag on top of everything, my carbine next to it. I grab the medicine bag Sha had given me and hurry from the tent.

Swift Fox sees me, and his tired face smiles; he grabs my hand and leads me over the small creek and into the woods. We weave through the skinny pines that seem a little too close together, their long needles grabbing at Swift Fox's loose hair. He pulls his hair from the branches, a little distracted. I want to reach out and protect him from the snagging branches but worry that will only slow us down.

We come to a clearing where I can see that there are thousands of us. A sea of people has formed a circle around the pole—the pole with its empty space gives it the assertion of being honored. The drumming is so loud that it sounds like thunder, lodges scattered throughout the camp didn't give a good view of how many of us are actually camped together.

"Is it always like this?" I yell into Swift Fox's ear.

"No," he shouts back.

I see him mouth the words that disappear with the chanting and drumming. He pulls us through the mass of people, making for the middle, the sacred clearing. We eventually arrive, pushing against the crush of bodies, singing to the opening in the center, and I catch my breath. There is a massive cottonwood tree lying on the ground. It has to be seventy years old and has been stripped of all its leaves, but its branches have been left intact. Pieces of colored cloth and hide medicine bags are tied to it as though they are leaves. There are nine medicine men and one medicine woman standing in a circle around the branches, drumming and singing. I watch as a little girl fastens her offering to what will be one of the highest branches, and the medicine men and woman all start to chant the same song, beating their medicine drums. I recognize Horn Chips as one of the nine.

"You should go now. I think we are some of the last," Swift Fox yells into my ear.

"Do you have something too?" I yell back.

Swift Fox smiles at me.

"Not for the branches," he says, urging me forward. I nod and walk toward the tree, the sound of all the different drumbeats making me feel lightheaded. I see the branch I want, silver like lightning. It is thick on the bottom. I feel the medicine bag and find the herbs that will stop a baby from growing inside of me. I think of what Swift Fox said, that our children's children will have to fight the real fight. I tie the rawhide strips to the branch. I hear as the medicine men and woman all fall into the same song and pray to god to bless us with strong children, healthy children, and I pray to god that they never forget where they came from and what it is like to hear the forest speak. I pray to god that they don't forget him, the creator, and the love he has bestowed upon us, making and meeting our every need. I pray that they are strong enough to resist the Great White Chief and his evil thieving. I pray to god that I can spend the rest of my life with Swift Fox, the man so sure of his love for me. I raise my hands in thanks, and the medicine men and woman stop and call out.

"*Tunkasila!*"

Tunkasila, I say silently in my head. I make my way back to Swift Fox's side. He nods at me and takes my hand. The medicine men and woman swell outward, and several men step forward. I recognize the chiefs among the men I probably will never get to know. The drumming changes to a slow and steady rhythm, and the medicine men and woman are now burning sweetgrass and sage, using their medicine fans to purify the tree. The men begin to hoist it upright, bringing trills and cries from the crowd.

I feel chills run through my body. The tree looks like a ghost, a foretelling of what the future holds for us. They bring it upright, then four of the men let go and, using woven rawhide, they begin to stake it to the forest's floor. This balancing dance is done quickly. When the men are done, they return to the crowd, and the medicine men and woman begin to chant and smoke the tree. They stop and pick up a garland of sage and sweetgrass and weave it around the trunk.

I watch as the medicine men and woman step back and the crowd parts. I see all the elder women dressed in their best hides and blankets, crowns of clematis upon their heads. They circle the tree and begin to sing a song.

"Tuka 'sila
ho'uwa 'yin ate
nama 'hon ye
maka 'sito 'mniyan
ho uwa 'yin te
nama 'hon ye
tunka 'sila
wani 'ktelo '
epe 'lo."

They are calling to all the brave men.

"I'll be right back," Swift Fox says to me, making his way for the tree, his bare feet marking carefully upon the earth's floor. The tree's colorful branches sway to the prayers. Swift Fox pulls a hunting knife from the loop in his pants. Many other men have joined him, and the chiefs are all wearing headdresses, except for Crazy Horse. His golden hair hangs loose around his shoulders, two hawk's feathers woven into it. I watch as they all strike the tree with their axes and knives. There is a tension in the air, and their blades rip into the tree's flesh, like a buzzing before a storm.

The drumming switches pace and is slow and steady, like a sleeping heartbeat, while the sun is rising high in the sky, trickling through the forest and giving us its blessing. I watch the last man finish striking the tree, then they all disappear back in the circular sea of people. Swift Fox makes his way back to my side, and the elders begin to sing again, their voices wise and rich, rising over the drums.

"Eca ozu 'ye wan he,
ukte 'se celo
wana 'hiyelo
waka 'sota he."

Well, a war party, which was supposed to come now, is here—I have obliterated every trace of them.

The elder's song makes the circle part. I watch the chiefs' wives emerge, leading all the young women who will not be warriors to the tree, all dressed in their finest hides like the elders, with beads and elk teeth clattering, becoming a part of the drumming and chanting. The sunlight catches the glimmer of their blades, as they are all holding knives or small axes, their faces painted and their hair braided. This is the most beautiful procession of death I have ever seen. *Without death you cannot have life*, the words of Sha come back to me. The women make their way to the tree, each one of them striking it hard; they strike the tree harder with a deeper furiousness than the men, as if they want god to hear their pain.

The tree's silver flesh is now torn, shredded. The last woman finishes. She is the fairest of them all, tall and slender with a face so fine I am certain she has made men weep. Her hair, like a stream, ripples down her back. She strikes the tree the hardest, trills ring out through the sea of people, and I find myself joining the chorus. I watch Sitting Bull step forward; though he faces pain, I can see he is grinning.

"Let the Sun Dance begin!" Sitting Bull bellows, his voice somehow carrying above the drums. At this everyone starts to leave; children are scooped up. I watch in amazement at what it looks like—thousands of people in the forest, it reminds me of the buffalo amongst the plains. The only people remaining are the elders and men and women dressed for war. I see Red Hawk pushing her way to us, her hair braided into a mohawk with many hawk feathers sticking out of it, all of them painted red. She smiles at us, her bare arms showing the deep black ink of her tattoos. She is holding three shields, all of which are made of hard rawhide, with another one tucked under her right arm.

"What is happening?" I ask Swift Fox. He glances at me as Red Hawk shoves a shield at me. It is blank. She then hands one painted with a fox to Swift Fox, who nods and takes it, and hers is painted with a hawk.

"What is this for?" I ask, looking at the rawhide shield in my hand, the back of which has a thick braided piece of hide to hold on to.

"Protection," Red Hawk says, looking at me with her eyes wide in disbelief.

"Swift Fox, you didn't tell her what we are doing now?" she asks him.

Swift Fox looks between the two of us.

"I thought she knew," he says.

"She clearly doesn't," Red Hawk says, handing Swift Fox a war club. I look at the solid rock tied on the end, unable to take my eyes from it. It is stained dark, stained with blood.

"Here, I brought you a gunstock club. I personally find them easier to use," she declares, shoving it at me. I take it, touching the smooth wood. I look at the end that is supposed to look as though it fires bullets. The top of the wooden rifle above where the trigger would be has the sharpest double-sided blade I have ever seen.

"You can use one of these in a variety of ways, all very practical when fighting," she says, watching me look at the weapon she has handed me.

Her words echo in my head. I feel weightless and unsure. I hear the drumming start again.

"Oh, here we go!" Red Hawk says, the excitement trembling out of her voice. I look at her, wishing I felt the same way.

"What is going to happen?" I ask, looking at my husband. His eyes are distant, scanning the people who are surrounding the pole. Everyone is dressed and painted for war.

"Swift Fox, where is your medicine?" a man calls out, his face painted half red, half black. He is wearing a silver breastplate like the one Swift Fox had had on the day I came to the camp. I recognize him, both from the other day when I arrived and as the man standing with Swift Fox outside Crazy Horse's tipi on the day we met.

"Today I stand before god a humble man, born anew with a wife," Swift Fox says to the man, making the man's grin disappear. He glances at me, then back at Swift Fox.

"Many blessings to you, brother," he says.

"*Néá'ese*," Swift Fox says, looking at me.

"Little Wolf, this is my cousin and brother, Coyote Run."

The man who looks like a shorter, harsher version of my husband looks at me. His eyes are black, and I cannot tell what they are saying.

"We are going to reenact our greatest victories," my husband says, looking at me.

"In battle," Red Hawk adds, almost gleefully.

I look at her; she is hopping lightly from foot to foot, making her vest and pants jangle. Someone lets out a whoop, and all the warriors begin to dance. It looks like only dancing until I hear the bang of clubs hitting clubs and clubs hitting shields. Red Hawk lets out a piercing whoop and runs into the mass of fighting.

I look at Swift Fox, who's still looking off into the distance.

"It is a mock fight," he calls to me, glancing at me. Uneasiness spreads though my whole body, making my stomach sink.

"I've never fought another person before," I find myself calling out. Coyote Run makes an odd sound, making both me and my husband glance at him. My husband looks back at me and grabs me by the shoulders, still holding his club and shield in each hand. They dig into my flesh.

"You can do this. You are stronger than you think, and when we really have to fight, this will make you ready."

He looks away into the mass of people. I follow his eyes. It is a blur of flesh and feathers. His voice cuts through the chaos.

"Think of anytime in your life when you rode the back of victory.

Think of when you were so elated and sure of yourself that it was all you ever thought you could be. Hold that in your heart and no club, knife, arrow, or bullet can hurt you."

I nod, not believing what he has just said to me. I feel one of his hands let go of my shoulder, and he lightly touches my chin, forcing me to look at him. I look into his eyes; he nods at me. I can see he believes in me. Swift Fox leans forward, pressing his lips against mine. The drumming gets louder, his fingers slowly let go of my shoulder, and he steps back, nodding again.

"Creator, watch over us!" he screams, and with that I watch him disappear. I see Coyote Run is still standing behind me. I look at him. He looks at me up and down and then follows the trail my husband has left. I watch him dance into the middle, hitting shields and meeting clubs.

I look on helplessly. I notice that no one has stayed to watch. I see the massive, feathered headdresses of the chiefs dancing among the warriors. A woman in a silver breastplate, like Swift Fox's, is walking toward the war dance from the trees, and she looks over at me. She glances at my shield and smiles, nodding. I watch as she moves toward me fast, never missing a drumbeat, and raises her stone war club. She brings it down in one swift moment toward my head. I raise my shield and absorb the blow awkwardly. She hits me so hard it slams my teeth together. She dances backward and brings her club toward my side, making me shift heavily to the side. I absorb the blow; it makes me kilter to one side, losing my balance. I stumble backward, almost falling.

"Dance!" she screams at me. I look at her face. It is painted all white, her lips and mouth blood-red like she has been eating raw flesh. Her ears are lined in silver hoops. She raises her club again, and I move to the beat of the drum. She swings, missing me as I spin away.

I think of my mother and change my gunstock grip. I think of Swift Fox and lower my shield. I think of the bear and I turn, moving in light, quick steps. I take a swipe at her like a snake. She jumps back, surprised, breaking into laughter. She goes to hit me again, and I meet this blow with my own club. I hear her let out a trill. I hear nothing but the drums; my mind goes into a place of nothingness, a place I've never gone before, as the woman and I dance for some time. Then I lose sight of her and swing at whatever comes toward me, spinning and dancing to the beat of my own heart. Nothing can hurt me, for I am already dead—I was born to be who I have become, and today is a good day to die.

CHAPTER 22

▲▲▲▲▲

"TODAY IS THE DAY."

I pull the fur over my head and hear Swift Fox's deep laugh that sounds like heavy breathing. I feel him gently pulling the fur back. I open my eyes and roll on my back. Our tent's hide is filtering out the rays of early morning sunshine, making everything look like it is glowing, as though we were the sun itself.

"I don't even hear the birds yet," I say, rubbing my eyes. I feel his lips graze my neck, and I smile, then I feel him getting up.

"Maybe being a wife is making you lazy."

I come up to my elbows to see my husband pulling on his leggings; his hide is well worn, the color faded compared to the newness of mine.

"I was lazy long before I became your wife. Why do you think I became so good at killing things? It's easier than anything else," I say. His dark eyes look at me, and he laughs. I watch as he stands upright near the middle of our tent and laces up the front of his leggings.

"What will I do while you are tied to the pole?" I ask earnestly. Swift Fox's dark eyes find me.

"Pray for me. Watch me. So get dressed; it is time for you to help me," he says, the smile leaving his face. I have found that no one really speaks of anything that is to come; everyone just lives, today is the day of ripped flesh. The day of blood shedding, an offering to what we cannot see with our eyes but only feel in our hearts, that is what Swift Fox said last night when I asked.

"Maybe you should get silver in your ears," he says to me. I can hear the teasing in his voice and smile at him; his ears are lined in silver rings, piercings that you usually only get as a child. Feeling in the furs for my vest, I find it and pull it on, then I find my leggings and slide them on quickly. I see my mukluks by our flap; they are already looking a little worse for the wear, some of my beads lost to the dance the other day.

"Tomorrow I should pound them out," I say more to myself, trying to rub some of the stained blood off my left thigh.

"We'll leave tomorrow, just us. We go for the buffalo to take back to Sha, as I am eager to meet her," my husband says, smiling more to himself, but I smile with him anyway.

His dark eyes look at me, and he holds his hand out for me. I take it, and he leads us into the morning. The air is teasingly cool. I close my eyes for a second, letting it wash over me. I look behind us to see that the rest of the camp is rising in the distance. Women rush through the pathways with baskets full of roasted corn and wild greens and armfuls of wood.

Swift Fox tugs at my hand. I can feel that he has grown anxious, his hand stiff; he pulls us toward the low, steady beat of the drums in the woods. We weave through the pines, the paths now fully entrenched from the opening ceremonies and the crush of people that had walked through them.

I find myself pausing, my eyes narrowing; there has to be close to a hundred people gathered around the Sun Pole, in a circle like they had been the day before. Swift Fox leads us directly in front of the pole, which is just as amazing as the day they raised it, the colorful offerings swaying like leaves in its branches in the early morning breeze. The chiefs are gathered with the medicine men and the one woman in the front; they look at the pole, each appearing to be deep in their own thought.

I see what they are looking at: an effigy has been tied to the pole. A stuffed version of a person is bound to the tree, and although he is made of straw, I know who he is, and he looks totally void of life. The hair on my arms stands up, and a chill runs down my spine. It looks like the man they call long hair—I know him. I remember what they called him from the day I lost my family: Custer. He is complete with his fringed shirt and yellow straw hair sticking out from under his black hat, painted black shining boots sticking out from his hide trousers, also lined in fringe. I look beneath the effigy's feet; a cross has been painted on the ground in blood.

I feel Swift Fox tug on my hand, and I look at him; he nods toward what I am looking at.

"They put Hi-es-tzie on there. I thought it a waste of time; he is already cursed," he says to me.

"How's that?" I ask, watching the medicine men and woman purify the area where the sacrifices are to be made. They chant softly, sprinkling medicine and burying different herbs in the soil. The smell of sweetgrass and sage fills the forest. I see a hide on the ground with hundreds of small, strong wooden sticks and long strips of rawhide. I look back at the medicine men and woman and notice their hands are all colored red. My eyes go to the top of the hide on the floor, where four long-bladed knives are laid out, the kind we use for peeling the hide off of our kills. Next to the knives are two awls used to mend hides; I look at Swift Fox, feeling my brow knit together.

"Custer. He took smoke with Medicine Arrow some time ago, who told him that if he took arms against any of us, he and his men would perish. They are trying to live in the Black Hills; that is where the wasuns are," Swift Fox says to me, and I feel myself nodding.

I knew about the caves because we went there every two years to gather stronger medicine for Sha. I think about what Swift Fox is saying to me.

"Can we not go to the Black Hills if they take them?" I ask my husband, his eyes examining the knives laid out on the hide.

"Are we welcome in any of the land they have stolen? Have you visited Boston recently?" he asks, not looking at me, yet I can feel the anger in his palm, where it burns into mine.

I don't know what Boston is, but I do know that in the couple of American towns I have visited, I definitely did not feel welcome. I remember the people crossing the street and saying things to me I didn't understand. I could tell from the tone and gestures that they were not kind.

The drumming stops. I look over and see Horn Chips, his face painted half white and half red, wearing his massive gray wolf's hide, the wolf's head balanced upon his own as though they are one. He makes his way to the hide on the floor and perches in front of it, looking over the collection of knives, sticks, and rawhide strips.

"Today is the day we give the mother our blood. She gives us everything we could ever ask for and never asks for anything in return except that we don't abuse her. We now see she is being abused, her flesh raped and her breath enslaved. Give your blood to her now, replenish what has been taken from her!" Horn Chips calls out, his fingers scraping into the soil on either side of him, digging into the flesh of the mother.

The sunlight fades into gray. I feel the warm summer air grow cold. I look to the sky, and daylight has disappeared, yet it is not as dark as night. My eyes catch the sight of one of the chiefs stepping forward, the one that is more often than not taking smoke with Crazy Horse. Sitting Bull, they had called him; his wives had been in the tent the night the women had sent me off to marry. Sitting Bull's hair is long and loose down his back. Dark like my

husband, he is wearing nothing but hide leggings, his torso showing the wounds of war, the scars of many battles fought. He falls to
his knees in front of the bloody cross, his eyes fixed on the effigy
of Custer. I watch as Sitting Bull scoops up a handful of earth and
washes both of his hands with it, the soil cleaning his fingers, then
slips it back to the earth. I cannot take my eyes from him, even
though I feel as though no one should be watching, Sitting Bull
tilts his head to the sky, his hair looking like a wave of darkness,
and raises his arms to the sky, his palms to the creator. I watch him
turn on his knees and lie on his back with his head near the base of
the pole.

"He is going to give a great *tunkasila* to her, to the earth, for his
heart weeps at what they are doing," Swift Fox whispers into my ear
as a medicine man makes his way to the reclining chief.

"That is Little Abissan; he has strong medicine and is going to
pierce Sitting Bull's flesh to make an offering to Wakan Tanka, god,"
Swift Fox says to me, his voice growing even quieter—barely above a
whisper, his breath hot on my ear.

Little Abissan's hands are painted red and his face half-black, half-
white; his hair is in tight braids, eagle feathers woven into them. He
dances as he walks, goes to the hide, and crouches. I watch as he picks
an awl and a knife, the peeling knife, then he kneels next to Sitting
Bull's chest. I watch his mouth move in prayer; I cannot hear what
he says. Little Abissan digs his knife into the flesh of Sitting Bull's
chest, making a cut a couple of inches deep. He pulls the chief's skin
away without tearing it. I look to see Horn Chips hand Little Abissan
one of the skinny wooden sticks. Little Abissan places the awl in his
lap and the knife in his mouth, then takes the stick and skewers the
chief's flesh. I try not to wince or look away. The man then makes
another cut; the chief's mouth is firm and no sound leaves his lips; his
body does not rack in the pain it must be feeling.

"How many will they make?" I whisper to my husband, my eyes

unable to turn from what I am seeing before me, as blood streams from Sitting Bull, making long red lines into the earth beneath him.

"He said last night he'd take no less than fifty," Swift Fox whispers to me.

"Wakan," I say.

"Wakan," my husband says back to me.

Silence takes over. Not even the forest breathes; there's nothing but the sound of the drums and low chanting, as all of us are transfixed on the chief being skewered. The awl and knife rip his flesh with the same noise as when I mend a hide or peel the skin off an animal; the sound of ripping flesh cuts through the drumming. Little Abissan has made two rows of sticks down Sitting Bull's chest and when there is no more room on his torso, I watch Little Abissan begins to pierce Sitting Bull's arms, making his way from Sitting Bull's shoulder to his wrist.

Sitting Bull's entire torso is now deep red in his own blood. I watch in horror as the flies start to descend on the smell of wounded flesh, and the medicine woman comes to Sitting Bull, holding a hawk feather fan and a burning bundle of silvery white buffalo sage. She crouches and fans him in smoke, making the flies jump off of him.

With nowhere else to pierce, Little Abissan stands and takes the knife and awl back to the hide and places it back alongside the others. He holds his hands out, and Horn Chips scoops up a handful of the rawhide stripes and places them firmly in his hands. Little Abissan takes them and turns back, making for Sitting Bull. I watch as he quickly fastens the strips of rawhide to the wood sticks skewered in the flesh of Sitting Bull's body. Once every stick is fastened with a strip of rawhide, Little Abissan rises, holding all the strips secured to the chief's flesh. Then he goes to the trunk of the Sun Pole and fastens all the strips tightly around it. Someone lets out a trill, startling me from what I am seeing, and the drumming gets louder, drowning out any of my own thoughts.

"Now what?" I find myself asking, barely under my breath, glancing at my husband and back at the blood-drenched chief. The medicine woman closes her eyes and begins to sing as she waves the smoke.

"We wait for the vision, and his guides will break him free," Swift Fox replies to me.

"Swift Fox," Horn Chips calls out to my husband from the hides holding the knives and sticks. I look at my husband. He nods at Horn Chips, then looks back at me.

"I've been called," he says, kissing me lightly on my mouth, grabbing the back of my head. Swift Fox lets go of me and turns fast, silent, just like a fox. I watch him walk to Horn Chips, who has chosen an awl and knife and is crouched on the opposite side of the Sun Pole to Sitting Bull.

"You should go near him."

I am surprised to hear a familiar voice and am happy to see the little chief Gall standing next to me.

"I thought this was just a man thing," I say, watching my husband and Horn Chips. I look to see Gall giving me a small smile.

"Only men will be called for sacrifice. This is the first time Swift Fox has been called. You should go in case he says anything."

I frown at the chief, then look back at my husband, who is lying flat on his back, looking up at the sky. I feel a breeze blow through my loose braid, and I walk toward them. Horn Chips feels me coming and glances up at me. He is kneeling close to the top of Swift Fox's head. I crouch down at my husband's feet and my eyes wander behind me to Sitting Bull. The chief's eyes are closed and his chest is heaving in quick breaths.

"I give you two cuts," Horn Chips says loud and clear. "One for your wife and one for your son. May they both be blessed."

I watch as Horn Chips brings the long knife quickly to my husband's chest. He makes an incision about three inches deep, and the knife slices through his skin like a needle. I look at my husband's face. His eyes are shut. The color drains from him as the medicine man makes the second cut. No sound escapes my husband's lips, but I can tell from his tight jaw, it is a fight.

Horn Chips pulls out two wooden sticks from somewhere in his fur and shoves them under Swift Fox's flesh. I watch as he grabs some of the rawhide rope, ties it to the sticks, and then walks with it in his hand to the pole. He takes his rattle from his belt and shakes it, his mouth moving in a prayer. The drumming is too loud for me to make out the words. He then fastens the hide strips to the pole, and now Swift Fox is tied to it just as Sitting Bull is. I look at my husband and back at Sitting Bull and wonder how long they will lie there. Horn Chips is already bringing over another man to give a sacrifice. I look at my husband, once more willing him some of my own strength, and then I make for the outskirts of the circle on the far side where no one has chosen to stand. I sit under the first pine tree I come across and watch as more and more men are skewered, some only with one and some with many, but none with as many as Sitting Bull.

The sun reappears, rippling its rays through the branches, and the light dances on my face. I feel my eyes growing heavy as I see people who had been watching start to disappear. There is to be a feast tonight to celebrate the last day of the Sun Dance, and I am looking forward to trying all the different foods I have never thought of preparing in the ways they are being prepared. My mind drifts to tomorrow and what it will feel like to hunt on the back of Gray Wolf with Swift Fox at my side, what it will feel like to take down a buffalo, my carbine pressed into my shoulder over the thundering of Gray Wolf's hooves. I wonder what Sha and the rest of my camp will think of my horse; I think of Bloka, and I feel a smile reaching my lips.

"It makes you glad you are a woman, doesn't it?"

I look up at Red Hawk, standing next to me, looking at the blood bath before us and dressed for war.

"Thank you for the boots," I say, smiling up at her.

Red Hawk smiles down at me mischievously, her black eyes glinting like a raven's. She sits down next to me cross-legged.

"That was Shadow's idea; she made them," she says, looking at the men.

"I am grateful," I say, making her glance at me.

"I thought you would be. You did good in the circle," she says, nodding at me.

I think back to that first day and feel something in my stomach stir. Not pride but an uneasiness settles over me like a rock smashing through ice.

"Where will your camp go tomorrow?" I ask, looking at Red Hawk; her arms are bare, and my eyes are able to trace her tattoos. They are like waves of water all interconnecting but never touching. I notice for the first time her ears are lined in silver rings.

"I think north, have you heard?" she asks me.

"About what?" I ask distractedly, watching her silver earrings reflecting the sunlight. I hear the drumming get louder, and my eyes go to the Sun Pole, where one of the men who is skewered at the base of the Sun Pole is standing up. I watch as the wooden sticks rip the skin from his arms where they were pierced through. Blood streams down his arms to his hands. He is in nothing but a loincloth, his face is painted back, and he is laughing as the medicine men and woman make for him.

"Long Hair is near us," he yells.

I feel myself grow heavy. I remember everything clearly now, and I feel like I am going to vomit.

"Rounding us up like the cattle, they are trying to make us dependent on them. They are going to educate us, make us like them. So I think it best we put some distance between us and them. Shadows Fall, she is wanting me to ask if you two will join us," Red Hawk says to me, and her words ring in my ears.

I think of Sha. I think of my vision, my eyes settling on my husband. He lies as though asleep. I shudder. Sleep wasn't the first thought that came to me. He lies as though he is dead.

"We need to find my camp. I need to make sure they are all right, but then I would be honored to join you," I say, looking at Red Hawk, who gives me a small smile, a tired smile.

"We will be easy to find. Go north, and just when you think you've gone far enough, go a little further," she says, standing. "I've got to go. They are doing the piercing soon, and one of my sons has earned a new earring." Her eyes linger on mine, and I nod, smiling up at her.

"Thank you," I say as she begins to walk away.

Red Hawk pauses and holds so still she looks as though she is one of the trees; then she looks back at me and smiles, giving me a wink at the same time. I smile back, then look at the pole. The sun is now high up in the sky, and more men are standing, the wood ripping from their flesh, the blood-soaked stick dangling against the Sun Pole like fishing lines. The medicine men and woman attend to them, and then their family comes to lead them away. My eyes wander to Sitting Bull, who is still lying on the ground. His blood has now dried on him. I look at my husband who is blinking his eyes before he shuts them tight again. The crowd has mostly disappeared as the afternoon grows hotter; I feel beads of sweat running down my back. The men left by the pole are fully exposed to the hot sun, and their bodies glisten with sweat; the medicine men and woman keep smoke burning strong to deter the flies.

I feel myself looking up at the sky. It is a clear blue, and I wonder why we are here. I wonder why we have to prove that we are worthy of our life to these people who have come from so far away. I wonder why they want our home so badly. I wonder why they don't take their big boats and sail back to where they came from. I feel a chill growing over me, the hair standing up on my arms. The sun is growing weaker. I look up to see my husband standing. I watch the two skewers rip out of him. I watch as he puts his right palm to his blood and then puts it on his face, just as I do when I make a kill. The medicine men rush to him and fan him with smoke. He turns with his face covered in his own blood. He is looking for me. Our eyes meet, and I stand and walk to him. Horn Chips looks at me, and I nod.

"Take me to your tree," Swift Fox says, his voice hoarse. I nod and lead him to where I have spent the afternoon sitting. I guide him to the base of the pine. He sits down carefully and leans his back to the bark, unbothered that it is on his bare flesh.

"We have to see what is going to happen to Sitting Bull. No one has ever taken that many cuts that I know of," he says to me.

I follow his eyes to the chief and carefully sit down next to him, nestling in the fallen pine needles. We sit in silence for some time.

"I saw all the buffalo dead. I saw all of us in white, and I saw you dead in the snow, beneath frozen water," Swift Fox says hoarsely, not taking his eyes from Sitting Bull.

I look at Swift Fox, surprised. The drumming grows as loud as thunder. I look to the drummers and understand why. Sitting Bull is starting to get up. I feel my jaw clench as he slowly lifts his arms. The skewers peel his flesh just as we would a loose a hide from a kill. Once both of his arms are free, we watch as he slowly walks backward while the skewers rip the flesh from his torso. The chief is soaked in blood. He takes his time. The sun dips low in the sky as the chief loosens the last skewer. The medicine men and woman rush to him. I feel myself standing as he silences the drummers and gives the motion for the medicine men and woman to back away from him.

The air is silent; even the trees know not to talk. The chief looks around at everything and nothing. He looks crazed, like a bear who has awoken too early from hibernation.

"I give you these because they have no ears! The white man, long hair, hundreds of them fell from the sky, dying!"

I hear these words. I think of what my husband said to me. I think of our dreams and feel them fading. I feel them blowing off from my soul like the wind. I remember what led me here, and I know what Sitting Bull has said. We are about to enter a war that sought us; we are about to enter a war not just for our bodies but a war for our souls.

CHAPTER 23

▲▲▲▲

I TAKE A DEEP BREATH OF THE STEAM from the coffee maker and pour myself a cup in my favorite school mug, an ugly blue-green home-made ceramic creation that is really too big to be classified as a mug; it is really more of a bowl with a handle. I put it down and reach for the sugar. As the pregnancy has progressed, I have been craving sugar—it is relentless. Teddy made a comment the other night that he thought there must be a hummingbird in there, then Paul and Daniel laughed way too long and hard about it. I feel fingers pressing gently into my back through my sweater, which is already soon to be too tight, as it hugs my belly, revealing purple pills in its yarn. I wonder why I hadn't noticed before . . .

I reach for a teaspoon that sits in a metal cylinder on the counter with all the other teaspoons—like the mugs, they are an odd collection, all different shapes and styles, like each professor had been obligated to bring one from home and leave it in the kitchen.

"Do you think that's OK for the baby?" Joshua says, sounding tired.

I feel myself smiling. Ever since the bump started showing, Joshua has become very vocal about her well-being. I think of George, who never really seemed to think about it one way or another; I can't remember if there was ever a time when George actually looked at me before our prison visitations, when he was actually *forced* to look at me.

"Better than breathing in your smoke," I say, putting my spoon in the sink, where it makes a soft clink. I turn, smiling at him, and sip my hot, slightly too-sweet coffee. It is March, and I've had enough of being constantly cold.

Joshua kisses me and then reaches around me to grab a mug for himself, and I slide down the counter, watching him—his face looks as tired as his voice, shadows below his eyes above his beard.

"Did you finish early?" I ask, looking at the clock. I'd left my watch in my office; the battery in it died during my morning lecture.

"Nope, just got out of there before I could get bombarded with questions."

I feel myself grow a little still. I'd seen two different women— girls—hanging around Joshua's classroom and office, always full of redundant questions. I'd catch glimpses of them and force myself to not stare and to keep walking.

He dumps some sugar in his mug, steps toward me, and plants a warm kiss on the top of my head before leaning against the counter with me. I sip my coffee and watch him take a deep breath, exhale, and slump over his mug, his mouth—usually so happy and animated— drawing itself into a line. I know that what is going on at Wounded Knee disturbs him deeply. The AIM, whom I think Timmy might have led here, took over the site of the 1890 massacre, bringing their fight for American Indian justice to our doorstep. I think back to Timmy in the truck, and I should have known right then and there that we were all about to be knee-deep in shit.

Joshua tries not to say anything, but what comes out of his mouth seemed to always draw sharp looks from me and Dad, who had cornered me in the kitchen alone the other night. I try not to laugh, remembering what he had said in a deep, hushed tone: "Nancy, Nancy," he had hissed at me. "I think Joshua is one of those hippies." I bite my lower lip, stifling the giggles, and remember how I had tried to explain to Dad that Joshua hadn't dealt with the American government in the ways we had, and no amount of peaceful protesting was going to bring about a resolution to two hundred years of getting fucked over, as you had to speak their language—blood and force.

For myself, the whole Wounded Knee debacle oddly has been a relief. I know that Timmy is involved in it, even though he hasn't confirmed it, and when we are at home, we are inundated with the distant sound of guns firing, but for the first time I know where I stand on everything: I am a traditional. I believe that the United States government has to answer for every treaty broken, which happens to be all 371 of them, and I know that our tribal government has been compromised for a long time and needs to be dismantled if my children are to ever stand a chance. I remember fighting with George about it when the mining had started, when something bad had happened to the water that we drank and bathed in, and I felt in my heart that that was where Teddy's problems had been born, as my hand instinctively goes to my belly.

"I've been thinking," I say to Joshua, looking into my mug. I feel him looking at me and turn my head to see his raised eyebrows. "About what you said about changing the colonial curriculum to something that reflects the Indians—us—more accurately. I think I'd like to help you." I feel my voice trail off, wondering if it is a good idea, or if I have been swept up in the Indian uprising twenty miles from our home.

I watch Joshua's big blue eyes search my face. We hadn't spoken much of it since the fall, our winter being occupied with our children and with learning how to be with each other.

"Nancy, I would be honored to work on this together. I mean, we can start now, but I don't think we can give it the time it needs until this summer. We'll have nothing better to do if you're going to get as big as Paul and Daniel say you're going to get."

I smile at Joshua. Our daughter is due in August.

"Dad, Eugene, he told me about our ancestors," I say. "They fought at Little Bighorn, and more notably, he spoke of a woman, Little Wolf, who was a warrior," I say almost like a question, like I need someone other than Dad to verify that it was indeed true. For me it had sounded almost too good to be real. I think of the story he told me about Little Wolf and how I had yearned to be her relation instead of George's, and how I had grown somewhat content knowing that she at least flowed through the veins of my children. I watch Joshua rub his whiskers on his cheeks and jaw, something he did when he was really excited.

"We should go to the band office this weekend and see if they have any records of her," he says, his face visibly brightening.

"What's this you two lovebirds are talking about?" Dr. Jeremy Williams asks, swooping into the staff kitchen from the hallway. I try to smile but am unsuccessful, my mouth falling into a grimace.

"Just about Nancy's heritage," Joshua says. I feel myself sliding a little further away from Joshua down the counter, stopping as I reach the edge, my shoulder softly grazing the wall, letting me know I am trapped.

Jeremy glances at me and my burgeoning purple bump. I can feel myself flush, and I shift on my feet; I feel Joshua's eyes burn into me. I don't dare meet them. The doctor opens the door to the fridge, pulling out a brown bag. I watch as he opens it and makes a face.

"It's always the same bloody thing with my wife, ham and cheese. She doesn't even work like Nancy here. You'd think she'd get a little more creative. How are the boys, Nancy?" Jeremy asks. No one has ever even offered to make me lunch—or dinner or breakfast.

"They are doing well, thank you, Dr. Williams," I say, wishing he would just rush back to wherever he had come from.

His eyes linger on my bump before he disappears from the kitchen. I listen to his footsteps disappear down the hall.

"When do you think we should tell them?" I ask, staring into my coffee cup.

"Probably pretty soon," Joshua says. I can feel him looking at me, and I don't bother looking at him.

Silence hangs between us.

"Nancy, I would marry you in a second."

I close my eyes.

"I know."

"Did Eugene ever have a chance to speak with him?" Joshua asks. Dad had told me he was going to speak to George; I think of the last time I had spoken with George, and it makes me think of Timothy. My heart grows heavy. We hadn't heard from him since he had come tearing home. I wish I had spoken more gently to him.

"I've been thinking that maybe I should go with you to speak to George," Joshua says, snapping me out of the fog I've been in since I began carrying his child, as though I had been slapped awake.

"I think that would be awful for both of us," I say without hesitating.

"I mentioned it to Eugene, and he thought it might be better if he saw us and could see that you have moved on," Joshua says to me, his mind made up. I feel myself frowning with anger that they had come to such a drastic conclusion without consulting me.

I close my eyes and try to shove the memory of Lola from my mind. Things had been done between me and George long before then; looking back I don't think he had ever truly been faithful to me, and instead of dealing with it, I had buried myself in my work and looking after the kids. I hear myself sigh heavily.

"Would it be better for you?" I ask, meeting Joshua's eyes. I see something I hadn't seen there before, pain.

"I think it would be better for everyone," he says.

I nod.

"Let me call Dad, then," I say, looking at the white plastic phone that had turned a dirty cream hanging on the wall across from me.

"What are you thinking, Nancy?" Joshua asks me.

I don't answer. Joshua puts my mug/bowl down, and I pick up the phone to call the house.

"Hello?" I am relieved to hear the deep voice of Dad.

"Dad," I say, my voice hanging in the air.

"Nancy?" He sounds bewildered; I don't think I have ever called him from school—if there was a problem, what was I going to do three hours away?

"Joshua thinks we should go see George," I say accusingly, staring daggers at Joshua, who shifts uncomfortably on his feet, his black boots squeaking on the kitchen tiles. This is their poorly thought-out idea; thus, it is their fault for whatever reaction we trigger out of George.

Silence holds us both to the phone, and I know Dad is weighing the responsibility of going there.

"Should you call the prison or should I?" Dad finally answers.

"Maybe you should and put all three of us down. You know how to get there?" I ask, as it has been a long time since Dad has visited George there, and I had driven all of us there. It had only taken one family trip for me to figure out it wasn't a place I wanted to bring my children back to.

"I'll figure it out," Dad says, then I hear a loud click, and the line goes dead. I hang up the phone and look at Joshua, whose tired face is now also anxious.

"Dad's calling us in as visitors. It's eleven now," I say, looking at the clock.

"It will take us about six hours to get there. Visiting starts at six, and we get one hour. If George stays that long, that is. I personally have never seen him for much longer than fifteen minutes."

Joshua glances at the window; the sun is shining down on the last of the winter snow.

"The boys," he says.

"Dad will make sure things are straight with them," I say, thinking they'll probably get dumped at their grandma's, with whom they've been more often than not with the occupation of Wounded Knee, as my mom lived further north in the Badlands.

Joshua nods, his eyebrows knit together, thinking.

"I have to cancel two meetings for this afternoon. I'll just leave a note on my door," Joshua says, more to himself, as he washes both of our mugs and puts them in the sink. He grabs the tea towel from the hooks on the side of the cupboards and dries them, turning to look back at me.

"I'll be right back," he says, and I nod, watching him put everything away. I let Joshua leave the kitchen before I make for my own office. I stand there in the silence wondering what will happen to our relationship after Joshua meets George. I find myself taking a deep breath and leave the kitchen, relieved not to see anyone lurking about as I make my way through the hallways to my door. I push my way in and find myself smiling at my small room. It has been like a sanctuary for me all these years. I come here, shut the door, and forget about everything. *Until you, that is*, I think, rubbing my baby growing inside of me. *You brought the outside in.*

I see three notes for me stuck to the top of my desk. Student questions. I tuck them into my leather briefcase as sadness sweeps over me. It had been a gift from George when I graduated from Kent State in 1963. I pull on my jacket and scarf and take the three books about the Enlightenment I planned on reading over the weekend and make for Joshua's office. I am surprised to see him standing outside my door.

"You should have come in," I say to him, locking the door behind me.

"I thought you might need space," he says to me.

I nod, feeling my sadness mixed with his anxiousness. *We'll have six hours to wallow in our feelings*, I think to myself, following him silently out of our building. His boots and my loafers sound like they are peeling off the floor. I look at Joshua; his denim jacket always looks so out of place over his tucked-in shirt and black trousers. His hair is a little longer than when he first moved in. I've noticed that the boys have all started growing their hair to his length. Joshua pushes open one side of the university's double door for me, and I'm greeted with a gush of cold air; I find myself frowning, my eyes tearing from the icy bite of it.

We walk silently to Joshua's truck, and Joshua walks me to the passenger side and yanks open the door for me. "Thanks," I say, hoisting myself into the passenger seat, flopping my leather bag and purse between us.

"I should have helped you," Joshua says, climbing in and looking at me. I give him a smile.

"What are you smiling about?" He tucks in his briefcase and paper folders next to mine.

"Just your hair," I say, glancing at him as I fasten the seatbelt under our baby.

"I am sorry, Nance, I'm just nervous," Joshua says, putting the key into the ignition. The truck roars to life, and he throws it in reverse, driving us away from the school. I look out the window as the bare trees swirl by.

"It is probably better to do it this way, then none of us have much time to think about it," I say in the silence. Joshua doesn't say anything in return. He drives us from the city to the forest, to the plains, my home.

I let my mind wander. I think of the boys and the child we're going to bring into the world. Half-white, I think, and it makes me want to laugh. I look at Joshua; his jaw is tight. I study him intently. I guess you would consider him a handsome man in his own way.

"I meant to tell you, I heard from my mother. She would like to come up this summer to help us," Joshua says to me. I have actually yet to meet any of his family.

I smile. I think of all the babies I have had and raised on my own. The most help I ever got was when George got locked up and Eugene moved in.

"I think we'll be fine, but I would love for her to come and meet us all," I say, thinking that to have some woman I've never met trying to tell me what do with my fifth child sounds like some kind of weird punishment.

Joshua smiles and glances over at me.

"I think she thinks because it's my first, it's yours, too," he says, reading my thoughts.

I smile. "It's easy to think like that unless you live with Paul, Daniel, and Teddy," I say.

Joshua smiles. "What should we name her?" He looks at the bare road, lined with snowbanks; it looks like a maze, or a trap.

I find myself smiling again. He has asked this question at least twice a day for the past month. The boys loved to pipe in with their opinion, but so far nothing has stuck. A light snow begins to fall. *We're almost there*, I think, my stomach tightening.

"What did Teddy want to name her?" Joshua asks, his brow furrowing; he could never remember any of the cartoon characters' names.

"Shaggy," I answer, and we both laugh. I feel Joshua's hand reach for mine, and I let him hold my clay fingers.

"We're doing the right thing," he says to me, reassuring himself.

"Fucking over George?" I say, looking at the man I have begun to make a home with. I watch as he winces.

"I think it's better that I meet him now," Joshua says, his voice trailing off.

I suddenly feel the need to pee and shift in my seat, gauging whether or not I can make it to the prison.

"My wife, my ex-wife, I told you she couldn't have children," he says, letting go of my hand. I look at the man I feel like I am only starting to get to know. I wonder what is wrong with me. It seems like I can only start a relationship with someone if I am bringing a life into this world.

"She—we—went to a few specialists. We used all our savings. She used to blame me for her unhappiness about it, telling me I wanted to leave her because she was barren."

Joshua glances at me. I watch him. I feel myself growing very still, wishing he would stop telling me what he is telling me. One of the few lessons I learned well with George was that it is almost always better to keep some things to yourself.

"I never would have left her, not for that, and I never told her that I wanted children. And because she couldn't, it was something that we just couldn't talk about." I watch as Joshua pauses, and I squeeze my eyes shut, trying to will him from talking any further about it. I hear him clear his throat, and I know my wish is definitely not granted.

"But I did want children badly, and we both knew it. When her younger sister became pregnant and had her first child, she knew it, knew that that was what I wanted, and without me saying a word, she left me."

I look at Joshua, waiting for it, the other part of the story, something like he has children with another woman somewhere. He glances over at me and smiles.

"I've wanted this for a long time, a family. I'm sorry that George is in the middle of it, but I'm grateful to him for his sons. Your sons, they are good boys, Nancy, and we're going to be alright." Joshua looks at me, wanting me to reassure him.

"Why are you telling me this, Joshua?" I ask, looking out the passenger-side window. We're close now; I know this road well, every bend and barren tree.

"Because that was a mistake I made with Carole. I should have told her how I felt. I kept things in, even from the very beginning. I want things to be open with us. I want to be with you for the rest of my life, even if George makes us fight for the divorce and we marry when our daughter is eighteen." Joshua's words hang in the cab of the truck. I feel tears coming to my eyes. I was once so sure that I was going to grow old with someone else and had accepted that I was going to be alone before Joshua had come along.

"What makes you so sure?" I say, trying to hide my face, wiping my tears with the back of my hand. My voice breaks, giving me away. I feel his rough hand reaching for mine.

"I've never felt this way before. You're different—or maybe we're different together, I don't know," Joshua says, more to himself. He has a way of doing that. I once heard one of his lectures at the university, and it was like a schizophrenic arguing with himself.

"Or maybe it's Paul's cooking," he says, glancing at me and making me laugh. Paul's food was truly awful; Dad said that army rations tasted better.

"Anyway, I just want you to know that no matter what happens in there, I am sure."

Joshua's words hang in the truck's cab—like armor.

"George, he cheated on me when I was pregnant with Teddy," I hear myself say. I feel the tears running down my face. The truth burns something straight into my soul; I couldn't even say out loud to this honest man that I think George was never truly faithful to me.

"Jesus," Joshua says, and I can hear anger in his voice.

"She came to the house after George was put away. She wanted money for her and her baby. I told George, and he wanted me to give her money. He told her to go to me." I should have been angry, but it had always brought me more shame than anything.

I can feel Joshua looking at me. I close my eyes. I want to disappear.

"What did you say?" he asks.

I hadn't said anything. I remember going into a screaming tirade and being escorted from the prison by a guard.

"I said we were done and that if I had to support his sons on my own, she could do the same." I didn't add that was on my next visit, when I had been only slightly calmer.

"Timothy was there?" Joshua asks. I don't open my eyes but nod my head. Timmy had been there; I never would have brought him if I had thought it was going to turn out like that.

"Two years later, he went to Vietnam," I say, remembering when he had come home in fatigues, so proud of himself for enlisting.

I hear Joshua lighting a cigarette. I open my eyes and see the sign: *South Dakota State Penitentiary*. A cold gush of air reaches my face as Joshua opens his window. I wipe my tears on my jacket.

"You said it wasn't good for the baby, the smoke," Joshua says pulling up to the guarded gate, unrolling his window all the way.

"Visitors for George Swiftfox," Joshua calls out before the guard can say anything. The guard looks at the both of us.

"You are Nancy Swiftfox?" the guard, no older than Timothy, asks me.

"Yes, sir," I say, trying to gain control of my voice.

"Go right ahead; park in Section 4B," he says, nodding and pressing the button to raise the bright-yellow parking lot gate arm and roll open the barbwire-lined chain-link gate, which screeches as it activates.

"Thanks," Joshua says, rolling up the window halfway, as though that will shut out what we're about to enter.

"Nancy, what is George in here for?" Joshua asks with concern, driving the truck though the entrance to hell.

"Second-degree murder," I answer; I had been hoping he would never ask.

"Christ," Joshua says following the signs to Section 4B.

"He's lucky it was another Indian or else the sentencing would have been more severe," I say in a hollow voice, trying to forget everything I've just told Joshua. I see the Savoy and Dad's silhouette in the driver's seat. I smile. He didn't want to go in there without us.

"I see Eugene," Joshua says, parking across from him. I see Dad getting out of the car. He looks odd here, out of place. I actually don't think I've ever seen him off the reserve. Dad nods at us, lighting a cigarette of his own. Joshua turns off the truck and looks at me; I look back at him.

"I love you," he says, reaching over and squeezing my fingers.

I nod. I am shaky. I don't want to get out of the truck but force myself. Joshua is already out and coming over to help me. Dad lingers behind him, looking me over. I slide awkwardly from the truck and glance at Dad.

"I told him about Lola," I say.

He nods through his cigarette smoke.

"My son, he's been mixed-up his whole life," Dad says almost apologetically, looking at Joshua. Looking at the prison, he says, "Let's try to make this right."

"I just have to use the restroom before we go in," I say as Joshua takes my hand and we make for the prison. We get to the main entrance and the first security check; Joshua pushes open the door and holds it for me and Dad. We are greeted by a guard sitting lazily in a black folding chair; in their beige uniforms and beige guard hats, the guards always remind me of bastardized cops.

"We're here for George Swiftfox," Joshua says in a way that sounds more like a question. The guard looks at the three of us.

"I'll need to search her purse and pat you fellas down," he replies abruptly, standing up and looking at Joshua.

"You Swiftfox's attorney?" the guard says, nodding at Joshua.

"Me?" Joshua says, surprised. "No, no just visiting."

"Huh," the guard grunts rudely, patting him down. He goes to Eugene next and me last.

"Expecting?"

"Yes."

"It says here you are George's wife?" the guard asks, looking at a clipboard.

I feel my face growing hot. The guard looks at me, Dad, then back at Joshua. I watch the guard's face break into a grin.

"I see," he says, going through my purse. "Looks like George is in for quite the weekend," he adds, giving me back my purse.

"I'd be careful in there," the guard says, looking at Joshua. "That red man has got quite a bit of the devil in him and some force behind his punches. You'll be safe in there, but he moves fast, and he has just recently been allowed back in communal visiting room 1F for good behavior."

I look at Joshua; his jaw is set. I can see the anger in his blue eyes that cloud over like a storm. George's eyes would glint with fire when he was angry. The guard waves us through, and we make our way down the hallway, which is totally vacant except for the sound of slamming metal. I see the restroom.

"I am just going to go in here for a second," I say, thankful to have a moment to think.

"Good idea," Joshua says.

I watch both of them making for the men's room, and I make my way into the small, very brightly lit women's washroom. I head for the first stall, and relief floods me as I finally get to pee. I finish and wash my hands. I take one of the small paper cups from the dispenser between the soaps and drink several tiny cups of water, trying to calm myself down. I look at myself in the mirror. I cringe a little and fish around in my purse looking for some lipstick. I finally find it and put some on my mouth. *Maybe the pinker lips will make me look better*, I think, tossing it back into the abyss I got it from and heading for the hallway. Both Joshua and Dad are waiting for me, looking as anxious as I feel—like if I said "Run," we'd all make for the nearest exit.

"Ready?" Joshua asks, taking my hand. I nod and we head for 1F. The guard posted at the door looks at us.

"We're here for George Swiftfox," Joshua informs him.

"Go on through," he says, opening the door for us.

There are ten metal tables with four chairs attached to them, all bolted to the floor. Three of them are full; the rest are empty.

"They are here for Swiftfox," the guard from the door calls out to the guard posted inside. The guard looks at us and smiles.

"Take a seat there, and I'll get him," the guard says, pointing to the table furthest from the door. We nod and walk toward it; taking seats, we settle in, clinking, the metal underneath me cold and unwelcoming. The three of us sit perched in silence. I watch as the guard goes through a metal door on the far side of the room, and I look around and see that there are three other guards in the room, each of them looking bored. The other prisoners with their visitors talk in hushed tones. I hear the door open; my eyes go to it, and I feel my heart flutter. I see him, his black hair even longer. His skin looks darker to me after being with Joshua, his cheekbones higher. He's leaner, even more muscled than my last visit a few months ago. He looks like he belongs on the cover of a romance novel. George looks at the three of us. I can see that he is surprised but tries to hide it. The guard walks him to the table.

"No funny stuff," the guard says menacingly to George.

"No, sir, I'll mind my manners," George replies, making the guard grin.

The guard taps him on the shoulder with his baton and goes back to the door, leaving us alone with him.

"Dad, Nancy, is this the guy you're fucking?" George says, his eyes like coal. He has a tone I didn't expect.

"Are you jealous, George?" I say with a meanness I didn't mean to have. I see Joshua looking at me, surprised.

"That this honkey is trying to raise my children? Yeah, Nance, I am," George responds, looking at Joshua. I can see that both men are angry.

"Swiftfox, language!" one of the guards calls out; the other two look at us. I can see by their eyes under their caps that they are amused. George glances back at the guard in a way that makes me cringe. There's going to be a fight later.

"Timmy came out a while back, told me everything—you, him, the baby," George says, pulling out a cigarette from his prison uniform's shirt pocket and nodding at my stomach. My hand reaches for my belly protectively.

"I should have come here a while back," Dad says, his voice quiet. It makes us all look at him.

"I'm not signing those papers," George says suddenly, looking at me. I feel so angry. Tears fall down my cheeks, and George looks at me.

"You always get like this when you're knocked up; everything is such a big deal," he says, waving his cigarette in the air, dismissing me.

"What would you know of it, George?" I hiss at him through my tears. He looks at me coldly, colder than he ever had before.

"What would I know, Nance?" he says, his eyes fluttering to Joshua. "I hope she's going to stay around with you longer than she did with me; always the books were more important than any of us. I raised Timmy, Paul, and Daniel. Bet you left that out of your fairy tale, hey, Nance?"

"I put food on the table," I say through clenched teeth.

George laughs, smoke shooting out of his nose and mouth.

"Sure, Nance, you could have done that ringing up groceries, and then we would have seen you."

"Is that why Lola?" Joshua asks him.

I look at him, bewildered that he has asked with genuine curiosity, like everything now made sense to him. George's head snaps in his direction.

"She told you about that, of course she did. I never saw Nance.

Lola was there; we used to just talk. Nance didn't give us a chance, did you, Nancy? She blames me for her life, never thinking that maybe she deserved me and I her. I am not leaving you, Nancy, you're the mother of my sons. Now you're just as bad as me. So we're even." George looks at Joshua, blowing smoke in his direction.

"What the fuck is wrong with you?" Joshua says. I can see that his hands are trembling. "She can force the divorce, you stupid mother-fucker, and I am going to happily foot the bill. You know she'll get custody of Daniel and Teddy," Joshua continues with as much calm as he can muster. My eyes flutter to the guard nervously. I don't want us to be escorted out.

George stubs out his cigarette and looks at me. He looks me over like he did when we first met, sizing me up.

"I don't think she will," he says victoriously.

"George," Eugene says quietly, his red flannel making him look like a fireball under the fluorescent lights. We all look at him, his white hair is clipped close to his head, making his eyes even blacker and his skin appear more golden. "Leave her be with some dignity. Enough is enough. You are hurting; we can see that. But she's already Joshua's wife in the old way. She's already left you."

George's eyes are burning into me, and I force myself to meet them. I feel sadness wash over me.

"It's true, George. I love Joshua. We're having a daughter," I say, my other hand going across my belly. "Joshua's a good man. A good father. The boys are better with him and me than with just me." I put one of my hands on the table for him to take, as if this is our goodbye. George looks at my hand, he looks at me, and I can see he is going to cry. I've seen him look that way once before, the night that Timothy was born. George stands abruptly.

"Swiftfox!" the guard calls out. The other three tables turn to look at us. George stalks away toward the door he came from. We watch as one of the guards grabs him roughly by his shoulder. George is saying something to him. The guard glances back at us, then opens the door for him.

"The visit is over," another guard calls out. I feel the tears running down my cheeks, falling on the table with a splatter. I watch a life I had disappear with him through the metal door. I wonder if the person I was has also gone with him, too.

CHAPTER 24

▲▲▲▲▲

I REACH ACROSS THE FUR, MY FINGERS searching for Swift Fox, as a flash of light illuminates the darkness. I pause, holding my breath, and wait for it; it growls before the thunder rolls across me, causing my whole body to shudder. My fingers find Swift Fox's clammy bare back; we've been asleep for some time. He is already sitting up.

"Storm splitters," he says to me in the darkness.

I don't know what that is, but the hair on my arms rises. Another strike of lightning lights up our tent, making the hide look like it's on fire. I feel Swift Fox shoot up into a perched position, ready to move fast.

"What did Sitting Bull say?" I ask as the thunder rolls, drowning out my words.

"That they would fall from the sky," my husband answers, standing at the same time. He goes to our flap and opens it up, not bothering to put his leggings on.

"The chief said we are not to attack!" a man screams through the storm, running past our tent.

"What was that?" I ask my husband, pulling the fur we were sleeping under to cover my chest.

"An *eyapaha*."

"What's that?" I ask in a quiet voice, barely above a whisper. I want to hide, even though I am not too sure what from.

"A crier," my husband says, his voice far away and lost to me. I study his silhouette; his chin is tipped to the sky. The storm is sweeping over rapidly; it has an urgency that is making my heart beat fast.

"I think we need to dress," he says, closing the flap. He cracks flint onto our fire and it swooshes alight. I watch as he pulls on his leggings. He takes his rawhide medicine chest and pulls out a small bowl. He adds water to it from his water hide and begins mixing it with his fingers.

"You need to dress," he says, looking at me. "Quickly."

I feel like a deer before it is struck. I want to move—I know I am in danger—but I feel weighted to my spot.

I watch Swift Fox as he pulls his hair back into a mohawk, tucking hawk feathers into it. He scoops up the white paste he made in the bowl, and I watch as he smears it into his skin, covering his entire face quickly.

"He said we are not to attack," I say weakly as my husband pulls on his mukluks and laces them around his calves, over his leggings. I watch him open up his medicine chest again and pull out another sachet of powder, turning the white paste red.

"I know what he said, but we don't know if they are leaving, or whether something is coming."

I nod, my stomach sinking. I force myself to move, pulling on my vest and reaching for my leggings. I slide into them; they have already become a part of me like my old ones. My hair is still in the single braid Swift Fox wove it into the day before. I look at the flesh on his chest, which has crusted over in a dark red. He glances at me, covers half his face in red, and passes me the bowl. I lace up my own boots and pick up the bowl. Looking at the contents, it looks like blood. I know what I need to do. I push my hand into the red paste and press my palm firmly to my face. I look over at my husband; he is grinning at me as he fastens his silver breastplate to his chest.

"Today is a good day to die," he says to me, still smiling. I think of the child growing inside me. Swift Fox passes me the wotawe with my bear claw inside. I put it around my torso, the same as he is doing with his. He nods at me and passes me the gunstock club from Red Hawk and then my carbine. I put the gunstock club down as I fasten my rifle to my back. My husband is tying two hunting knives to his calves, and he fixes his own rifle against his back before shoving two revolvers into his leggings belt. I had never seen a small gun up close until he showed me his. He grins at me as he picks up his war club. My eyes go to the color of it—even through the black paint, I can make out the stain of dried blood.

"May the creator bless us with his mercy. May in this death we meet the creator's love and, in our pain, feel the creator's mercy," Swift Fox says, looking at me. I look at my husband, his words echoing over me as he goes to the tent flap. He holds it open for me to go through. I force myself to stand and duck out into the night. I feel him, already silently by my side. I feel his fingers reach for mine, and I gladly take them.

"Whatever happens, stay near me," he whispers quietly. I squeeze his hand so he knows I heard him, and we hurry in the direction everyone else is running. I look around; I am in a sea of paint and feathers, guns and shields. Everyone is dressed for war. A man, really no more than a boy, bolts past us.

"Today is a good day to die!" he screams. My husband lets out a trill that is echoed through the darkness. We weave our way through the tents and the sparse trees to the grass. Everyone is mounting their horses and ponies. A woman with so many feathers in her hair that she looks like an eagle comes out of the trees next to us.

"What is going on?" Swift Fox calls out to her. She looks at him; her eyes flicker to me, then back to him.

"Red Hawk was hunting and came across the Great Father's warriors."

She glances at me, then her eyes settle back on my husband, her thick lips breaking into a grin.

"Pehin Hanska."

"Custer?" my husband asks, the English word rolling weirdly off of his tongue.

"Yeah, Custer and his army," the woman says, grinning thickly.

"No," my husband says in disbelief.

"Yes. The chiefs gave a smoke and decided we shouldn't attack, but Red Hawk already told too many, and look," she says, nodding toward the rising sun, the kiss of dawn lining the horizon. In the middle of the chaos, I see six men on their horses, their headdresses massive, shining red in the rising sunlight. I see all but one has a headdress and no more than one feather woven in his long, golden hair—Crazy Horse.

"Better find your horses," the woman says to us before disappearing into the crowd of people and horses; dust is being kicked up in every direction. The chiefs look out at the chaos, and I hear Gall shout out from his horse.

"HOKA HEY!"

War cries and trills are screamed back, making the blood rush through my body. I see him, my horse. I let go of my husband's fingers. I look back at him, and he smiles at me. I nod and hurry to Gray Wolf.

I pat him, and he shakes out his mane. I grab a handful of his hair and pull myself onto his back. I see my husband making his way toward me already mounted on his tan pony. He looks at me, then lets out a trill. The trill spreads through the men and women ready to fight. The chiefs are running their horses northwest away from the rising sun, and the warriors are following, running through the grass like rolling thunder. I pause, frozen. Something feels like it did when I found my brother's dead body.

"Little Wolf, we need to stay with them," Swift Fox calls out to me. I look at my husband. Horses are swirling by us. I think of the vision of my dead brother. The flesh was rotting off of his body.

"They are going the wrong way," I say.

My husband looks in the direction of the warriors, dust rising up into the air, like smoke from a fire.

"Sometimes you have to go backward to move forward," my husband calls to me.

I nod, his words not calming the feeling in my soul.

"We need to go," he says to me again.

I hear the urgency in my husband's voice. I feel myself nodding as I gently squeeze Gray Wolf's sides. He starts forward anxious to join, just like my husband's voice. I look, and Swift Fox is riding beside me. The sun is climbing into the sky. I glance at a man wearing his silver breast-plate making his way through the rush and coming straight for us.

"My cousin," Swift Fox shouts at me, glancing at the man steering his white-and-black pony with ease through the thick of riders.

"Swift Fox!" Coyote Run yells.

My husband yips like a coyote, making everyone around us break into trills.

"Little Wolf!" Coyote Run shouts at me across my husband.

I nod my head. He's yelling something at Swift Fox, but I can't quite make out what it is. I hear the word *grabber*. I watch Coyote Run nod at my husband and disappear back into the thick of it.

"The Grabber is leading them!" my husband yells at me. I feel my brow knit in confusion.

"Standing Bear?" I ask, thinking of the big man standing in the snow.

"Yeah, Frank Grouard. I told you he was shifty," Swift Fox calls out.

"A shape shifter, more like it," I say, thinking of the giant man and making my husband laugh. A thicket of trees rises before us; a glint of light catches my eye.

"That is Crazy Horse signaling. Five means get on your horse, four means dismount, three means scatter, two means rush, and one means kill," Swift Fox calls out to me as we all slow to a stop.

Some of the warriors are dismounting. I see four flicks of light, and everyone begins climbing from their horses. I slide from Gray Wolf's side. My husband is waiting for me. He puts his hand lightly on my shoulder, looking me in the eye.

"Shoot to kill, Little Wolf," he murmurs in a hushed voice. I don't say anything. I can feel my brows knit together, my stomach sinking, my legs feeling like they are weighted.

Warriors couched over, some slithering on their bellies, trickle into the trees. Someone makes a bird call, and my husband answers it with his coyote yip.

"This way," my husband whispers to me, leading us away from the mass of people crouching low. The bird call rings out again, and my husband answers it, leading us down a slope. Near the bottom, I see a small river, and in the brush, I see Sitting Bull, Gall, Crazy Horse, two chiefs I don't know, and about ten other warriors. We make our way silently toward them, dancing over sticks, needles, and brush. I see Swift Fox's cousin Coyote Run squatting. He glances back at us and smiles. They look similar enough to be brothers.

We wiggle in next to him to see what they are looking at: an empty bank of a slow river.

"The Rosebud," my husband says to me in a voice quieter than a whisper. Swift Fox's cousin looks over at me, then at Swift Fox.

"The Grabber is on the other side of the water with some Crows. They know we are here. They're hiding like the white men they fight for," Coyote Run says, his eyes, like a raven's, glinting with mischief. His whisper is loud. He looks at the nothingness on the other side and makes a loud kissing sound at it.

"Come out, come out, wherever you are!" Coyote Run calls out in English.

"What did you say, Coyote Run?" one of the chiefs I don't recognize hisses at him, making everyone look at us.

"I left my white wife to join you. She reads this book called *Little Red-Cap* to our children. That is what the wolf says that eats the grandma," Coyote Run says, grinning at his own joke.

I look at my husband in surprise. He doesn't look at me but stares at his cousin with hard eyes.

"I have an Indian wife, too," Coyote Run says, looking at me.

An arrow shoots out from the brush on the other side and lands on the empty riverbank in front of us, making the men break into laughter; I don't get it and try not to look about bewildered. Everyone falls into silence as a man comes running across the river from the other side wearing a headdress of white eagle feathers.

I recognize him from the first day I found the camp—American Horse. Bullets crack through the air and bush toward him. From the Crow, I guess. We watch as he smiles and leaps through the water. He spots us in the brush and flies through it, collapsing to the ground and gasping for air. Someone passes him a water skin. He takes a deep drink from it and passes it back, still taking deep breaths. He looks at Crazy Horse, his war paint streaking from the water he has just run through.

"There has to be close to a thousand of them. A few Shoshoni and more Crow," American Horse says, his breathing growing steady.

Crazy Horse nods, not looking at him, his eyes lost to the river ahead of us. Sitting Bull leans close to Crazy Horse and whispers something in his ear. I watch as Crazy Horse pulls out the small mirror and tilts it to the sun, creating the flicker of light. One. Kill. The men make to stand, but Crazy Horse holds out his arm, signaling us to stop. I watch as he scoops up some earth, whispering something to it. He pulls out his mirror again. I watch him flick it, one, two, three, four, five times. Kill, on our horses. The men rise without hesitating, and it creates a whirlwind as they begin running back to where we had come from. I feel stuck to the ground and feel my husband's hand on my shoulder. I look at him, his eyes black as night. He's crouched close to me.

"What happened to your mother?" he asks me softly. I feel a tear run down my cheek, and I force myself to stand. I feel my legs move as though they can control themselves, and we make it to the top of the bank where we see everyone who had dismounted scrambling back onto their mounts, charging into the woods toward the river. It sounds like thunder, the sound of that many hooves hitting the ground. It makes the earth shake beneath my feet.

I see Gray Wolf standing still as though nothing is going on around him. Swift Fox breaks into a run, and I follow him. He runs straight for his pony, hopping on his back. I grab Gray Wolf's hair less gracefully and pull myself on. Swift Fox is looking back at me. He nods his head and takes off in the direction of everyone else, toward the Grabber. I urge Gray Wolf forward. He willingly obliges, flying over the ground as if his hooves aren't touching the earth.

Our horses race through the river; water splashes up, soaking my feet and leggings as we charge up the bank on the other side. Gunfire cracks through the air as we reach the top of the ridge. Dust has been kicked up like a thick fog, blinding us to anything short of what is right in front of us. It is just like the dance of the warriors from the Sun Dance but filled with blood and screams. The Crow wear mostly black and are dressed for war. The Shoshoni glint silver like the Cheyenne.

"Little Wolf!" I hear my husband's voice call out to me.

I look around, searching for him, and instead see a man with a thick headdress made of black crow feathers and a white painted face charging at me with a rifle aimed between my eyes. I lay my back against Gray Wolf's and see a bullet fly above me.

"Little Wolf!" I hear my husband screaming.

I sit back up, my hands trembling and my fingers struggling to grab on to Gray Wolf's coarse mane.

"Little Wolf!" my husband screams again. I look around as though I am in a dream, a nightmare. I see him to my far right.

"Like this!"

He screams at me, holding on to his horse's neck with one arm while the other has his cocked rifle. He slides to the side of his horse, shooting under his horse's neck, and I watch his bullet find the man that had just tried to kill me, missing him but getting his horse. Our warriors start whooping as the horse collapses, throwing the man from his back.

I watch as my husband slides back upright on his pony's back and tucks his rifle into his back holster and pulls out his war club. He raises the massive rock tied to a stick above his head and races for the fallen Crow chief. I watch in horror as he brings the club down with a graceful sweep on the man's head so quickly all I really see is the headdress and bits of skull fly into the air. It is like time has stopped. I look around in the dust storm; the metallic smell of blood fills the air even though it doesn't look like many men have fallen.

My hands don't reach for my gun or club. I am alone with my horse, standing still in the middle of what we are supposed to be fighting for. I am lost. I don't remember why I am here; I don't know if this will win us anything. I don't see Custer—I only see other Indians and I wonder why they aren't fighting for this land that is supposed to be ours.

"Little Wolf!"

I hear my husband's voice; my eyes find his face; it is covered in blood.

"We've been called back," he says to me.

I nod, looking at the few Crows lying dead on the ground. Our warriors have dismounted and are stabbing them with their knives. I watch their blades plunge into the lifeless bodies on the earth's floor.

"Let's go!" he calls out to me. I look at the man I married—there is something in his eyes I no longer recognize.

"Now!" he says, turning his horse away. My horse follows him even though I don't think I urged him to do anything. We race back down the slope and through the water toward the trees and grass on the other side. Out of the dust and in the sunshine, it is as if nothing has happened, as if no one lay bleeding to death on the earth's floor. My husband leads us to the group of mounted chiefs, who nod at him. His cousin is already there, looking at us.

"Brother!" he says to Swift Fox, grinning.

"I was just saying this isn't Pehin Hanska but one like him; they call him General Crook. Standing Bear hides behind him. The Indians that they have tricked into fighting their fight think they can wait us out, protect them," Coyote Run says, and I can hear the victory in his voice.

I look at my husband. He's nodding his head, his eyes darting back the way we came. I can feel he's thinking what he should do next.

"Where there is Crook, there is Custer," Crazy Horse says. He always looks the same, still, his voice always calm and soft.

"What should we do then? I don't know if we should waste men if Custer is coming," Gall says, looking around at all the warriors trickling out into the grass. Gall's bare chest is covered in sweat and blood, smeared like grotesque paint over him.

"Our men are even in number with the Great White Chief's soldiers. I think we should cut through the Crow and Shoshoni and get to the white men," American Horse says. Like Gall, he is covered in blood, his eagle feathers splattered red. I watch as Crazy Horse backs his horse up and looks the way we had just come from. The wind kicks up, blowing the one dark feather in his golden hair.

"This is about moving us, moving us from our souls. This is our home. We fight Crook how he fights, surge for surge, and then we watch and wait for Custer," Crazy Horse says, sliding from his horse.

We all watch as he goes to the dirt of a mole hill. He couches down, scooping up a handful of it, the dirt trickling through his fingers. He takes it to his pony and sprinkles it over him. Looking satisfied, he hops back on his back. Crazy Horse looks around at the circle of chiefs— some have joined that I never saw or noticed at the camp.

"We pitch, they will come to us, then retreat, then we will go to them, and they will leave us be. Each chief is to lead but not scatter," Crazy Horse says, making sure to look into everyone's eyes. Crazy Horse looks in the direction of Crook's army, then back at us.

"Hoka hey!" he shouts. The chiefs echo his call, and trills ring through the air as the men lead their horses to the warriors, looking for their lodges. I can feel Swift Fox looking at me.

"Can you come?" he asks me. I don't want to meet his eyes, but I do. I can see there is something in them close to anger. He turns his horse, and I follow him as he leads us further into the grass away from everyone.

"There is no shame in leaving," he says to me, the wind stirring over us, rustling the prairie grass together and making me shiver.

"You can go back to the camp. We always need warriors posted in the camps in case the white soldiers attack them," he says to me, as though there is no shame in my cowardice.

I feel my heart sink. I look at Coyote Run trotting his horse toward us. I can see he is looking at me differently than before. His eyes are hot, like two burning coals. The three of us are alone in the grass.

"I will come with you," I say to my husband quietly, but his cousin can hear us.

"Then try to shoot that rifle before you get one of us killed," Coyote Run says. I feel my eyes closing.

"Stop," my husband says sharply to his cousin. Coyote Run doesn't look at me.

"You know it is true, Swift Fox, we have seen it happen before," Coyote Run says to him, even though he is looking at me.

"You are so busy looking at her, you're going to take a bullet to the face."

"That is enough, follow me," my husband says, turning his horse. I can feel Coyote Run looking at me, but I don't meet his eyes. I urge my horse to follow my husband, trotting across the grass. I close my eyes, and when I open them again, it is to the glinting of silver. There are about twenty men and women all dressed like my husband and his cousin—dog warriors. They whoop when they see him coming, and his horse breaks into a run. Gray Wolf follows eagerly.

"Brother!" they yell at my husband.

Grinning, several of them call out to me. "Bless you with sons and daughters!" they call to us.

"We are to pitch!" my husband yells back. Those with rawhide shields bang them with their war clubs, letting out trills and whoops. My husband looks back where the other chiefs are off in the distance; there has to be close to a thousand warriors, mounted. The glinting of Crazy Horse's mirror in the distance catches my eyes: two, rush, then one, kill, rush them, then kill them.

"Let us fight for this earth. Let us fight through these Indians to the thieves! General Crook! Let us fight to kill Custer! Today is a good day to die!" my husband screams, and the warriors, the dog soldiers, scream back, "Today is a good day to die!"

My husband rushes his horse back into the trees. We all follow him, Gray Wolf doing a better job of participating than I am. Everyone is mounted, racing to the stream, I see the whirling feathers of the chiefs in the front. I feel myself slowing Gray Wolf, stopping, watching. I wonder if this is what my father felt like the day he died. I urge my horse forward toward the hell we had just escaped from.

I cross the river, and Gray Wolf races up the other side to the same mess we had just retreated from; bodies still litter the ground. The Crow and Shoshoni are matching our warriors as equals—the fighting is not easy; it is vicious. I see my husband and ride toward him; he has joined Crazy Horse's group. They are creating an opening through the Crow and Shoshoni with their war clubs. They swing them with such a force from the backs of their horses that it would definitely be a much kinder fate to meet a bullet.

I watch Crazy Horse pull his mirror from his belt, his war club balanced in his other hand. He flicks his hand—one, two, three, scatter. Everyone that sees the signal does just that, and those that didn't follow those that did. They race their mounts to the sides of the ridge. They don't fire their guns; they go backward and sideways.

The Crow and the Shoshoni look on, confused but not surprised. I see one man, in a headdress made of Crow feathers similar to the man my husband killed, yelling something at his men. Some are sliding from their mounts. I look at my husband; he is smiling at what the man said. He makes a bird call to Crazy Horse, who flicks his mirror, one, two, rush. Seeing the signal, everyone charges forward, killing anything that moves. I do nothing but hold on to Gray Wolf's mane and force my eyes to stay open. There it is, a clear opening through the line of Crow and Shoshoni. I watch as my husband and Crazy Horse charge for it with their men behind them; silver and feathers fly past me. I force Gray Wolf forward.

We charge into the trees, and the forest snaps at my hair and face. We break through the trees, and there they are, the men I remember from my dreams. Their uniforms are blue lined in yellow. They see us and begin forming a line; they clutch their rifles, fire guns. I see the glint of the mirror—one, kill.

Any warrior that saw the mirror is now charging toward them. A tall white man in blue, his face covered in dark hair, is screaming orders. Our warriors dismount like my husband did, firing under their horses' necks. Screaming rings out on either side. Some of our Indians fall. I see two white men fall, causing whooping to break out. I get close to the white men; their faces show that they are no older than children. They are sheet-white except for the hairy man who I think is their leader. They feel how I feel.

Next to him, the tall white man screaming, I see the massive frame of Standing Bear; he is yelling something at the hairy man. The hairy man screams out something again; the white men's line breaks, and they run. I watch as they retreat like a rabbit caught out by a rifle in the middle of winter. I search through the blur of feathers and horses for my husband, and I see him and his men charging at the retreating men. Crazy Horse lets out two bird calls through the hawk feather in his hair, making my husband stop. He pulls his mirror back out— one, two, three, scatter. The warriors, my husband's warriors, begin whooping, trills ringing through the air like an eagle screaming.

"Little Wolf."

I hear Red Hawk's voice to the left of me. She sees my face and laughs. She is on her horse, and behind her are her warriors, all women. She is splattered in blood and breathing heavy.

"It is always like that your first time, like fucking. The more you do it, the better it gets!" she yells to me.

The women close enough to hear laugh.

"You'll bring us all a great honor if you choose to shoot your gun," she says, pulling her horse closer to mine.

"Crazy Horse is pitching the battle; you can see that all the American army is confused. We are safe, Little Wolf; this is an easy fight compared to others we have fought." She talks to me like I think my mother would have.

I look around. Our wounded men are being gathered up, laid across the backs of horses, and taken back the way we came. Two of our horses that were shot are being shot again to make sure they are dead.

"What if I don't shoot?" I ask her, thinking of Coyote Run.

"Doesn't matter, we will still love you. Maybe you weren't meant to shoot here; maybe you're only meant to learn. Men are so narrow-sighted they only see the now—like death, it is a blessing and a curse," she says to me.

I feel a small smile come to my lips as I see my husband. The smile slides from my face as I watch him heave the heavy corpse of an

American soldier onto the back of his horse. I see Coyote Run taking another. I feel someone looking at me. I turn my head to Red Hawk, and her eyes search mine.

"I don't like him either, Coyote Run. He is taking those men to a lodge they will make for them, for their death dance. To show our enemies we were here, and we didn't die," she says, looking back at my husband's trophy.

"They will pay in their next life, those American men," a woman behind her says.

"Not until the battle is done, though," Red Hawk says distractedly, looking away.

I follow her eyes to Crazy Horse. Tall and golden like the autumn sun mounted on his horse, I see the mirror he uses for signaling resting loosely in his palm in his lap. I watch as he talks with Chief Sitting Bull, who is dressed in his massive war bonnet of red-dipped feathers, and the small Chief Gall, his black hair hanging down his back, looking even smaller on his pony next to their American horses.

"I am going to see what is going on," Red Hawk says, nudging her horse forward.

I watch as she trots quickly in their direction. The chiefs glance at her as she joins their circle. I watch my husband make his way toward me with Coyote Run at his side.

"Little Wolf," he says, stopping in front of me, his chest working hard to slow his breath. I frown, looking at the dead strewn in front of him on his pony. "Ready to go back?"

I look at the sparse trees ahead of us.

"Did you see the Grabber?" my husband asks me. I look at him; his voice is excited, his eyes bright.

"Why didn't you kill him when we came to the camp in the winter?" I ask.

I feel the words slip from my mouth. I can't look at him; my eyes focus instead on the trees swaying in the wind.

"Every man has a chance to prove himself. The Grabber unfortunately has proven himself in the wrong way every time. Next time he comes to a camp, we will kill him," my husband says.

I watch as Crazy Horse flicks his mirror in the early afternoon sun—one, two, rush. My husband glances at me, then charges the way the army had retreated. His men follow him. I don't move, watching the warriors swirl by me. I think of what it is I am supposed to be learning. I think of the day my family died. I wait there, still, under the hot sun, unable to move forward or backward. It is a long time before they come back through the thin tree line. I can see from the smiles on their faces they have done well. I see my husband; his silver breastplate is covered in blood, as well as his face. He looks at me on my horse and urges his pony into a trot, making straight for me.

"They are on the run; they think we are camped nearby," he says a little too loudly. I can see he is very excited.

"They think if they kill our women and children, we will bend to their will, so they will look for them, and we will watch them, waiting," he says to me, explaining his plan. I look at this man, the man I married. His eyes are bright and far away, and the hair stands up on my arms.

"Come now, we need to celebrate," he says, disappearing into the trees we had come from. I force myself to urge Gray Wolf to follow my husband. I am at the back watching his men, who are following close behind. Coyote Run is at his side.

"Get our two kills," my husband calls to Coyote Run. Coyote Run and another man nod and take off at a trot. I see Red Hawk pass us with her warriors. A dead Indian, a Crow, is slung over the back of her horse, and his massive black crow feather headdress bobs lifelessly to the beat of her horse's hooves.

"Where is the lodge?" Red Hawk calls to my husband.

"Up near the Little Bighorn. We go there to dress them, then we are to go back and move our camp there," he says to her.

She nods. I watch her make across the grass, heading northwest, riding in the pink and orange blaze of the setting sun. I see Coyote Run and the other Dog Soldier appear with their two dead white men.

"Let's go!" my husband calls out, kicking his horse in the direction of Red Hawk. I feel frozen in one place. I don't know what direction I should go—my heart tugs me two ways. I close my eyes to the last of the sun rays and pray to my family for guidance. I hear them, I see them, I feel them. I open my eyes and gently squeeze Gray Wolf's side. He shakes his mane and takes us forward, riding in the direction of my husband and the setting sun.

CHAPTER 25

▲▲▲▲

I PEEL MY HAT FROM ATOP MY HEAD, stuck to my head like molasses in January, my hair a wet mess against my scalp. I pull out a handkerchief from my breast pocket and wipe my brow. The sunlight blinds me. I look to my left at Tom and Captain Keogh, where they sway in their saddles. Their faces show the strain of the treacherous heat, turning their cheeks bright pink. Like me, their skin glistens, drenched with sweat; they both have removed their caps, placing them loosely on their saddle horns. My eyes are pulled forward to the horizon. I squint my eyes and see Major Marcus Reno and the three Indian scouts I sent with him running their horses toward us, kicking dirt up behind them like locusts in a crop.

"Looks like they found something," Tom says, his voice thick from the heat.

"Is that not what we're out here sweating for, Captain?" comes the soft voice of Keogh, bringing a small smile to my lips.

I see the faces of the Indians I sent ahead: Bloody Knife, White Man Runs Him, and the interpreter Mitch Bouyer. I don't like what I see. Their mouths are set in a way that suggests they want to contain what they found. I signal a halt.

"Tell the men to water their horses," I call to Yates, glancing behind me.

He nods, and I watch him make for the bugler. The poor soul looks at Yates; he is not just pink but has turned a sickly shade of red. We have been trailing along the Rosebud and just passed a generous pool of water. I could almost hear my soldiers' relief as the bugle's brass cuts through the march, telling them to stop.

"General," Major Reno says to me, tipping his hat in a weak salute, steadying his horse in front of mine, Vic.

I watch Major Reno's red cheeks puffing in and out of his face like a whore faking fucking. I look at Bloody Knife, who nods. I nod back so he can tell me what they found.

"There is a lodge, a tipi up ahead," the interpreter blurts out, speaking for my Indian, as Mitch's eyes dart between me and my captains nervously.

"How far?" I ask, wondering why Major Reno didn't open his mouth first. I narrow my eyes and look straight at the drunkard.

"Less than an hour's ride," Major Reno mumbles, looking back in the direction they had arrived from, his double chin quivering.

"They got their dead strung up," Bloody Knife says under his breath, stealing my attention. I look at the man I trust as much as my brothers.

"Dismembered?" I say to my Indian.

"Yes," Mitch answers for him.

"What kind of Indians?" I ask, looking at Bloody Knife.

He looks at me. His black eyes have clearly glimpsed something they didn't like.

"Not just Indians," Mitch answers yet again.

I look at him, feeling annoyed. A frontier man exists in a strange space somewhere between being American and being Indian, making him almost nothing.

"Settlers?" I ask, feeling doubtful that any immigrant would brave a journey this far from civilization.

"American Army," Bloody Knife finishes for Mitch.

My eyes drift to the horizon they came from, as though the land would give me the truth I wanted.

"We also saw a camp, General," Major Reno says, still struggling to catch his breath, puffing out air that stinks of a whisky casket gone putrid.

"Big," Bloody Knife says. I catch the glint in his eyes.

"Sioux?"

"Sioux, Cheyenne, Agency Indians, Sun Dancers," Bloody Knife says to me in his even tone. I nod, trying to make sense of what they are telling me. The dead men must be General Crook or his men.

"Officers?" I ask, putting my hat back on, as its sweat cools my brow.

"No, General, from what we can tell from what has been left of them. Just ordinary privates," Major Reno chimes in.

I nod.

"And some Crow and Shoshoni," Bloody Knife says, looking at me. I look at him.

"General Crook's scouts," I say, looking at the expansiveness ahead of us.

I think of all my time out here. There is a feeling this expedition has had, right from the onset, a sensation of being boxed in. Elizabeth, Libbie, had felt it too—like hot air before a storm, she had said.

"How many Indians?" I ask, thinking of what may have happened to Crook.

"Hundreds of lodges, many chiefs. I could make out the lodges of Crazy Horse, Gall, American Horse, and Sitting Bull, as well as the Cheyenne Dog Soldiers," Bloody Knife says, his voice still low and even; my Indian wanted a fight.

I bury the urge to curse or scream for joy. We have spent years looking for these hostiles, and I finally have the luck of finding them all in one place.

"Tom, we need to send a runner to tell both General Terry and Colonel Gibbon that we have located the Northern Indians, with the two chiefs that President Grant, General Sherman, and General Sheridan wanted in particular. Include that we are going to advance upon them, and we think that General Crook has been attacked and is in possible need of immediate reinforcements. Call all the captains for eleven this morning," I say, looking at my brother.

He is grinning, his eyes bright with the thought of a good fight. He nods and salutes, turning his horse in the direction of the men. I see that they have gathered by the river, in the shade of the skinny pines.

"Is there a lookout?" I ask, looking at Major Reno.

"Yes, General, upon a ridge that is situated almost above their camp," Major Reno says, nodding west.

"Gather the men. Captain Keogh, we are going to be approaching the Indians that we have been sent out here to kill. Tell the men we are taking no prisoners," I say, looking at Keogh; his eyes are cold. Captain Keogh nods at me, turning his horse. I watch as he trots briskly to the men my brother has gathered, and I can tell by the straightness of their backs that they are listening to my captains intently, ready in formation.

"Major Reno, we will ride ahead and see the death lodge and the bluff before making any advancements," I say.

I nod at Bloody Knife, who turns his pony in the direction they had just come from. The scout White Man Runs Him and Mitch do the same, and I nudge my mount forward. She goes willingly, making me smile. I feel Major Reno next to me, and I touch the hilt of my revolver. The wind tickles the air, cooling me some. The silence is a welcome change from the singing of my men. As the sun climbs into the sky, I see the silhouette of the tipi in the distance, all by itself along the stream. I can smell the men before I see them—the smell of rotten corpses cuts through the air, making me want to jerk in the opposite direction.

Bloody Knife stops his horse and slides from the saddle. I dismount along with him. I hear the other three men dismounting behind us. I stride toward the lodge of death. The tipi's flap is open, revealing three naked soldiers; slashes mark them up like a filleted fish. Their skin has already begun turning an unnatural color, a pallor of white tinged with green. One of the men's skulls has been knocked in, and they are all missing their manhood. I fight the urge to cover my nose and mouth from the smell accosting me.

"Where are the limbs?" I ask.

"Above us, in the trees," Bloody Knife calls out. He is standing some distance back with the rest of them; I am viewing the horror show alone.

I take a big step backward and look up. Hanging from strips of rawhide are blackened arms, legs, feet, hands, heads, all swarming with black flies. My eyes fall on one head, wearing a black headdress made of crow feathers.

"We should make for the bluff." The anxiety in Major Reno's voice makes me want to slap him.

"Do you think they are watching us?" I ask, glancing back at Bloody Knife, the sound of the swarming flies buzz drowning out any noise that may have been in the trees or in the water.

"Might have been for some time," he says.

I look around, wishing to spot one of them. Unlike the southern guerrillas from the Civil War, most of the Indians I'd fought against had an uncanny ability to disappear amongst the brush and trees. They walked quieter than ghosts.

"General," Major Reno says to me again, coming up to me and standing a little too close to me, enabling me to smell last night's whiskey. The stale, sour smell was almost more offensive than that of the rotting flesh.

"Take us there, then," I say to the major, not letting the annoyance slip from my voice.

His round cheeks are flushed not just from the sun but from his drinking habit, sweat pouring down his face as though it were raining. I catch a glimpse of Bloody Knife starting toward the river. I let my eyes fall from Reno and follow my Indian across the stream. He leads us up a hill that is deceptively long as we reach the top. I pause to catch my breath and then crouch down. Approaching the rock Bloody Knife is already perched behind, I see his back is straight as an arrow, and he's looking to the valley below.

"See?" the Indian says, pointing northeast.

I peak from behind the boulder. I feel my breath catch in my throat.

"They will know we are close. We should strike them now before they have a chance to organize," Bloody Knife says in his choppy English. I touch the hilt of my revolver and stare. I'd never seen such a large encampment.

"I don't think we have as many soldiers as we would need," I say, chewing on my cheek, weighing my options.

This was not a sleeping village. This was a group of warriors that had recently won. I knew from battles what that did to morale—it made men fight harder and braver.

"General, we have forty-five officers and 718 cavalry." It's the deluded voice of Major Reno, echoing through my brain and draining out thoughts of more importance. I glance back at him and wonder how he'd managed to stay in the army for this long. The man was in a semi-crouched position, to what his round belly would enable, and his hands were gripping his knees. Hunched over and still puffing, he didn't look like he could kill a baby, let alone lead a cavalry of men.

Major Reno isn't even looking at the death ahead of us. Camped along the Little Bighorn, but staring at me, I can see his eyes are blurred from drink. I want him far from me in this rising battle.

"We have no choice but to engage them. If we retreat, we will give them the advantage of stalking us," I say, thinking of the gunstock clubs that would be cracking my regiment's skulls open while they sleep and knowing that it was better to die facing your enemy than to be set upon like a hunted animal. "We need to get back to the other men now."

The last time I felt this sensation was the morning of Gettysburg. I remember the mist and the bugles. This enemy was different, though, always changing, unlike the Southern Army. What had they called them? Thunder Dreamers and Storm Splitters? They were dangerous because they fought for themselves. No man ruled them, and they didn't go to a church on Sunday to proclaim their spirituality. I'd seen it firsthand—their spirits, their gods, that lived in them wherever they went, whether it was bathing or stringing up limbs.

I lead us quickly back to our horses, running down the hill and across the river.

"General?"

I look at Reno as I hoist myself into my saddle, Vic adjusting to my weight.

"Major, do you recall what was said by General Sherman, what he wrote of these Indians? These warriors?" I find myself asking this fat, sorry excuse of a man.

"No, General, I am sorry; I do not recall what you are speaking of," Major Reno says, still huffing as he heaves himself into his own saddle.

With the Indians already mounted, I turn Vic and hurry us back to the men. Major Reno has to almost run his mount to keep up with me. I glance at him bobbing up and down in the saddle like a cork.

"General Sherman knows that fifty hostile Indians will checkmate three thousand soldiers. Think about that as you are leading your men today," I say.

I don't wait for a reply and urge Vic into a canter. The faster we strike, the better chance of a victory. I see them in the distance. I can feel the tension of the men before I get a good look at them. I see the dirt kicked up into the air and know that my brother and Captain Keogh have got them mounted. I smile, thanking god for small mercies as I urge Vic into a gallop to brief my captains. I see most of my forty-five officers lined up in the front, dressed and ready for battle. They look on—ready, stiff with tension, faces grim.

I pull Vic up to a halt, feeling the heavy breathing of my horse's ribs between my thighs as my men come toward me. I dismount, forcing them to do the same. The men approach me, and they know what I am about to say. I wait for Major Reno to clumsily dismount and watch him drag his boots over to us. I watch the Indians trickle away, back to our other scouts. I'm certain they will tell them in every detail what we just witnessed. With Major Reno finally in formation, I swallow and begin.

"We have come across what we have been sent here to fight. It looks as though there has already been a pitched battle with what I guess was General Crook and his men. We are going to perform the classic hammer-and-anvil strike."

"How many Indians are there?" interrupts the pinched voice of Captain Benteen.

"About three hundred of them," I say, giving him a cold stare. The man could be more useful than Reno, but he is the sort of fellow that refuses to live up to his potential. I deliberately underestimate the count. I need my officers to believe we can win.

"We are to drive this village to the south, toward Colonel Gibbon, who's traveling with General Terry. We will kill as necessary—that is part of General Sheridan's greater plan to drive them to the reservations we've generously given and allocated to them. Major Reno, I am giving you three companies; you are to cross the river and attack the south end of the village. Captain Benteen, you'll take three companies as well. You'll trail Major Reno in search of villages that I may not have yet spotted," I say, taking a deep breath.

I pause, looking through my men.

"Where is Captain McDougall?" I call out, not seeing whom I am looking for.

"We had to wake him from his slumber, General."

I look at Captain Yates angrily and see the wide girth of Captain McDougall hurrying toward us.

"Glad you decided to make the call, Captain," I yell, watching his round cheeks blaze red.

"My apologies, General Custer," he says, giving me a sharp salute.

"Captain McDougall, you are to take your company and flank the pack train, bringing them to us," I say to the stout man.

I can see the disappointment on the captain's face, and a small smile reaches my lips as I imagine the reaction of his company when they discover they have been barred from our first parley into any real action.

"Yes, General," Captain McDougall says, saluting me again. I look at Major Reno and Captain Benteen. I don't want them with me, but I am wondering if they can be trusted without me. I see Bloody Knife to the far right lingering in the shadows and wave him over to me; he nods and slides from his horse and runs in my direction.

"Bloody Knife," I say, looking at my Arikara Indian. He is tall and noble with long black hair; two feathers are tied into his mane, blowing in the light, hot wind.

"You will go with Major Reno here and help steer the Indians toward me," I say. Bloody Knife nods, his face revealing none of his true feelings. I look at the rest of my men.

"I will take the remaining five companies, and it will be us who will meet the Indians head-on. Captain McDougall, Major Reno, and Captain Benteen, you are dismissed," I say, not looking at them. I glance up to see their salutes and watch as they make for their companies, their officers trailing behind them. Lastly, Bloody Knife stalks toward Major Reno, whose men are making their way for him. I pray that my Indian will prevent Major Reno from doing anything foolish or cowardly.

I look at the captains I will be taking with me. My brother Tom, Captain Yates, Captain Keogh, my brother-in-law Captain Calhoun, and Captain Moylan—these are good, strong, seasoned fighters.

"Let's get the companies underway; I want to strike fast," I say. My captains salute and hurry toward their men, who are already mounted. I watch the privates smiling and joking; some break into the ballads from "Garryowen." For a lot of them this will be their first battle. The bugler rings out the shrill call to mount for those still filling their canteens in the river. I find myself grinning as I go to Vic.

"General."

I pause with my foot in the stirrup at the sound of Tom's voice. He has yet to mount his horse. I hoist myself up.

"Yes, Tom," I say, looking down at the baby-blue eyes of my brother.

"We should bring Little Autie and Boston with us. If there are as many Indians as you have said, they would most likely be safer with us than McDougall."

I turn, looking toward where we are going, and think of the bluff showing what I never even imagined was possible on this campaign. I think of what Tom is saying to me. I feel it in my bones that there is more to that camp, but I couldn't see it from the lookout; the rest of the village could be anywhere.

"Gather them up, then, Tom," I say, making my brother smile up at me. Despite the odd undertone of this campaign, it had been joyous with all of us Custers in one spot.

I watch him run off toward the men. I think of all the battles Tom and I have fought, and something warms in me knowing that our little brother would now be alongside us as well. I walk Vic to the edge of the chaos. I watch Major Reno gathering his companies, and Captain Benteen is already leading his men south. The sun is promising to be hotter than the day before, which had almost been unbearable. I take a drink from my skin, the tepid water wetting my dry lips.

"General Custer, we are at the ready when you are," comes the soft voice of Captain Keogh.

I look at the handsome man and nod. He nods back and raises his arm to signal the bugle. There is a pause, and then the shrill brass horn cuts through the hot summer morning. I urge Vic forward, and he leads us back in the direction we had just come from. I glance to the left and see my family as a smile reaches my lips. I feel something. I feel that there is a promise lingering, like a miner panning for gold. I look up to the sky. I dig the heel of my boot into Vic's side, and we take off in a run.

CHAPTER 26

▲▲▲▲

"NANCE? YOU ALL RIGHT?"

I blink, looking out of the window into the swirling darkness. A late spring snow had started to come down hard, blurring white in the headlights.

"That sandwich we stopped for isn't sitting right," I say, trying not to think of George.

"Do you think we should stop?" Joshua is glancing at me with genuine concern. The three of us had stopped to eat, and Dad and Joshua had put on a good show of trying to pretend nothing had happened, that George wasn't cold and alone and in the pain we had caused him.

I blink, looking back into the cold nothingness of my passenger-side window.

"No, we need to get back to the boys," I find myself saying. A fluttering in my stomach makes me put my hand there instinctively, and our baby moves reassuringly.

"Is the baby OK?" Joshua's voice trails off. I glance at him; his eyes are looking straight ahead. I don't envy him—to drive in a dark snowdrift was a challenge at the best of times.

"She's fine," I say, my voice husky from all the emotion we had lived through, and I close my eyes, leaning my head into the truck's seat, its coolness a relief. That's the thing about dressing for winter: Bits of you are always too hot, and other parts of you can never quite get warm enough. I want nothing more than some hot tea and the warmth of our bed.

"Nance, I never should have pushed. I mean, maybe it would have been better just to leave it." Joshua's voice trails off again.

I squeeze my eyes shut tighter to stop the tears from running down my face. I feel their wetness smashing into my eyelashes. I don't say anything, trying to burn the look George had on his face from my thoughts.

"It was better it came from us," I say, breaking our long silence. I feel Joshua looking over at me.

"I just wanted things to be OK, you know, for the summer," Joshua says to me, almost pleading his reason.

"I guess they'll be how they're meant to be," I say, trying to keep the annoyance from my voice but feeling it creep into my words anyway.

I lift my head from the seat and press the side of my forehead into the passenger window; it's colder than the seat, and the contrast is helping to soothe my headache.

"I'm just really sorry, Nance," Joshua says to me again.

I feel my brow furrow.

"You know, Joshua, it seems like you're always sorry," I say too sharply.

I can feel him stealing looks at me. I look at him; he's trying to balance steering the truck while looking at me.

"Nance, you know it was my idea, and it was a bad one. I am trying to tell you I know that, and I am sorry."

"Yeah, seems like you have a lot of ideas, Joshua," I say, looking at him through the darkness. The only light that reaches his face is from the back glow of the truck's headlights.

"What is that supposed to mean, Nancy?" he says to me, the first time he has been angry with me.

"This," I say spreading my hands. I am mad—mad that I let him talk me into his stupid idea, mad that I am the only one that has visible deceit, mad that there's a siege and standoff between us and the United States government over them fucking us over.

"Hey, Nancy, let's not say things we'll regret and don't mean. It was upsetting seeing George. For all of us." Joshua says this firmly. I look at him; he's being sincere. I study his face in the artificial light, the dark shadows under his eyes, his hair a bit too long, his denim jacket, and I wonder if he is mad about everything, too, coming into a made family, never really starting one of his own.

"Who is Julia?" I ask too quietly, trying not to let the words out of my mouth.

"What? What are you talking about?" he asks me, confusion making his words dance.

"You know exactly what I am saying—who is Julia?" I demand. I can feel my agitation slip up my throat and spit out my mouth.

"Kempler? My student?" he asks, glancing at me like I am nuts.

"That's right," I say, unable to not make my voice hard.

"Nancy, you've got to be kidding me. I come home every day with you—when would I have time to see Julia Kempler?" he asks me. He doesn't mock me like George would have, and I can feel my body soften.

"Why is she always in your office?" I ask him, something I have wanted to know but have been afraid to ask. Having Joshua meet George gave me the courage to air all our dirty laundry.

"Nancy, have you lost your mind?" He looks over at me.

"Joshua!" I feel myself shouting. Through the windshield, I see a massive black bear standing on his back legs in the middle of the road, the yellow-orange headlights lighting him up like he is a monster straight out of hell. I can see that instead of moving, the bear opens his massive mouth—if we could hear him, we would have heard him growl, and he moves his arms as though he could swat us away.

Time freezes. We rapidly get closer, and I can make out the bear's mangled black fur, matted in what looks like blood from a fight, with slashes all over its body. He is missing an eye and has a large open gash on his chest. Joshua swerves wide, just missing the animal. He swings the car back onto the road, causing it to slide on the ice and snow. My head hits the side window so hard it feels like lightning has struck me. I feel a current of pressure rushing to where there is about to be a lot of pain. Joshua slams on the breaks, bringing the truck to a jerking stop. My back and head slam back into my seat.

I feel him put the truck in park and slide over the bench, and then his hands are on my head.

"Nancy, Nancy!" he says, hugging me. I open my eyes, watching the snow pour down in the headlights of the truck. I grab Joshua's arm, which is wrapped around the front of me; one of his hands is checking the baby, pawing at the bump. She kicks at him; I feel both of us relax.

"That was crazy. It's early for them, isn't it?" Joshua is saying to me.

"Bears?" I say confused.

"Christ," he says. "Thank god we're just about home. I thought they didn't leave hibernation till later on in spring."

I feel his forehead resting on my head.

"I love you, Nancy. Remember that is what this whole cursed trip was about. I want to marry you; we're having a baby."

I find myself sobbing. Joshua holds me, cradling me. I know he is going to make a good father. I suppose I've already seen him being a good father to my sons.

"I never would have suggested it if I'd known more. I should have spoken with Eugene first. And Julia—Julia, Nancy, I've asked her to help me with Paul's application to the university. We were going to surprise you for Mother's Day. Paul wants to be a history professor, a professor of Native American history."

I find myself sobbing even harder.

"Hey, Nance, it's all right. Things have been hard, but they'll get easier," Joshua says, trying to wipe my tears away with his rough fingers.

"Before you know it, that baby will be out of you, and I can help more, hold it and stuff."

I find myself laughing through my sobs. Joshua has no idea that right now is actually the easiest part of having a baby. I look at him, his cheeks streaked with his own tears. He kisses me, and I feel myself kissing him back.

"Let's just get back. I think the best thing for both of us is something hot and the boys," he says, wiping away the rest of my tears.

I find myself smiling. I feel the back of Joshua's hand resting on my cheek.

"We'll be just fine, Nance, even if we have a bastard."

I find myself laughing at his bad joke.

"Let's go, then," he says more to himself than me, sliding back over the bench. I watch as he adjusts and checks the rearview mirror, shaking his head. He looks forward and shifts the truck into drive. Joshua drives slower than before, turning us onto the reservation, when the snow starts coming down even harder.

I know this bend as Joshua turns off the road and into our driveway. I look down at my hand. I hadn't realized he was holding it. I see a blue pickup truck, illuminated in the light of our house that is lit up like a Christmas tree. The truck, its headlights have been left on; it's the same one Timothy had come home in that day. I see the Savoy in front of it. Dad's already home.

"I wasn't expecting Timothy," I say, no excitement reaching my voice. Today of all days for him to reappear.

"Does he ever let you know what he's doing?" Joshua says, glancing at me, trying to hide the worry from his voice as he parks the truck.

We hadn't seen or heard from him since that day a few months back. I didn't know for sure, I just had my motherly instincts that he was part of the standoff at Wounded Knee. My hand goes to my stomach as I see Teddy running toward us in his winter coat and pajamas. My stomach flutters, and I open my door and quickly hop out of the truck. Joshua's already out and taking strides toward my youngest son.

"Mom! Dad! It's Timmy, he's got a gun to his head, by the shed. Papa says that it's OK, but I don't think it is!" Teddy runs to me, and I see his eyes are swollen; he's been crying. I take his hand; it is freezing. He tugs me hard toward the shed that Dad and Joshua built. We crunch hurriedly through the snow. The shed's oil lantern is lit, casting a dull light on Timothy, who is standing with a revolver cocked at his temple in front of the lonely tree Dad had taken to stringing his kills up in. I watch Timothy's empty shirt sleeve flapping where his other arm would have been as he shifts on his feet. His long black hair is swirling around him wildly; he's moving jerky, unnaturally. I see Dad standing in front of the shed about ten feet away with his hands in the air as though he is trying to calm him. Behind Dad are Paul and Daniel. The boys glance at us, and I can see some relief flood into their eyes. The light from the shed makes it look as though they are all under a spotlight.

"Timothy, what's going on?" I demand, puffing cold air as I stop next to Dad.

"You're living with the enemy, and you don't even care what they've done to this earth, to this place, to us. They've created a void of nothingness. No god lives here, nothing but junk—shit, they all make us slaves, too!" Timothy screams at me in a voice I don't even recognize.

"The government! They created all these declarations, the Declaration of Independence, the thirteenth, fourteenth, and fifteenth amendments, all these laws. We aren't represented by any of them. They hold us here in these parcels of land, these shitholes, like prisoners. It's like we are in a fucking concentration camp while they run around our mother destroying her! And you know what? We can do nothing to stop them. We all sit around doing nothing!"

I feel my breathing seize in my chest.

"He's been talking like this since he pulled up, Mom," Paul says to me in a way that makes me look at him like an adult for the first time in his life.

"Timothy, have you been taking drugs?" I ask, my mother's intuition telling me he is on something heavier than the dope I used to find in his room. I feel everyone looking at me.

"What if I have, Mom? What then? Don't you realize that everything in this country is for nothing? They tell us it's a democracy, but for whom? I was there, we shot them for nothing!" he screams, not looking at any of us.

I watch as his dark eyes dart around, unable to focus on anything. The snow has wet his hair so much that it is starting to stick to his flannel shirt, which looks like it hasn't been washed since he was living at home six months ago.

"Timothy, put the gun down and come inside. You can have some coffee and stay here," I say, the tiredness creeping over me, as though all the blood has been drained from me. I just want to sit down.

I am sick of his dramatics, everything always had to be such a show and we the unwilling actors. He'd always been like that, just like his father. I step toward him, my boots crunching in the skiff of snow. I hear the shot before I feel anything. I hear screaming and touch my stomach right above the baby. It feels hot. I look at my fingertips; they are red. I touch the spot again and look at my fingers in disbelief. They're red. It looks like blood is pouring out of me through my purple sweater. I hear yelling and hear two more shots fire. I feel myself sink into the snow; my knees hit first, but it's as though I am weightless, I am lighter than a feather. I watch blood dripping onto the white ground in front of me; everything is in shadows, our silhouettes long in the snow.

"Mama!"

I hear Teddy and look up at him. He's holding my head. I see Joshua's face, next to Teddy.

"Call an ambulance!" I hear him screaming.

"Get her in the truck!" I hear Eugene yelling.

I look back to my youngest son and try to raise my hand to touch his soft face. I need to speak. I try to open my mouth, but all I feel is warmth spilling out of me.

"Jesus fucking Christ!" I hear Joshua yell.

I feel him yanking me up from the cold ground and feel Teddy's tiny hand grab mine. I see nothing but darkness. The voices around me fade, and I feel my eyes blink and open to warmth. I close them and take a deep breath, which brings a smile to my face. The air smells delicious, like hot straw and fresh flowers. I open my eyes and notice the sun, which is so bright. Pollen, butterflies, and bugs drift through the air in a lazy, magical dance.

My arms are heavy as I look down at them. There is a golden-haired baby girl in them. She looks up at me with her big blue eyes, her father's eyes. *I will name you Summer, Summer Little Wolf,* I think to myself, smiling as she puts one of her chubby fists to her mouth. She smiles back, beautiful.

"Nancy," a child's small voice calls to me. I look toward it. I don't see who called me, but to my left there are more buffalo than I have ever seen before in my life—thousands of them in the endless sea of prairie grass. I have never seen a living one. One of the generals, Sheridan, I think, killed them all.

"Nancy," the voice calls again to me.

I look in the direction of the voice and see a little boy right in front of me dressed in traditional clothing—buckskin pants and shirt with very fine beading. I find myself smiling at him, and he smiles back at me, making me smile even more broadly. He looks very much like each of my sons did at his age, four or five, black hair and black eyes that dance like shooting stars.

"This way," he says in a language I haven't heard in a very long time. I follow him with my daughter into the light.

CHAPTER 27

▲▲▲▲

I SMILE FROM BENEATH THE RIM OF MY HAT—the sight of my two younger brothers upon their saddles with the sun burning across us—there is no place I would rather be. My eyes draw back to the distance in the barren valley as smoke swirls into the sky from the Indian encampment. I chew at the inside of my cheek, annoyed with the brazenness of their behavior; they're not even trying to conceal their location. *Twilight of the setting sun for them*, I think to myself, pulling Vic to a stop, the death lodge before us. I search for Major Reno. Looking behind me at the sight of so many men mounted never fails to leave me awestruck. I finally spot Reno, and my eyes narrow in on him. Major Reno catches my glare and trots his horse over to me, with Bloody Knife trailing behind him. I signal my men to officially halt.

"Major, this is where we are to part ways. You take your companies across the ford and flank us on the other side of the river. We'll chase the warriors toward Captain Benteen as discussed at the officers' call," I say, searching the man's liquor-stained gaze, praying to god he is in good understanding of my orders.

"Yes, General," Reno says, saluting with one hand, his other folding his reins, looking a bit shaky. I find myself scowling beneath my moustache and nod, forcing him to leave, and I look at Bloody Knife, who edges his horse closer to mine.

"Make certain the major doesn't divert from his orders," I say just barely above my breath.

My Indian nods at me. I watch him urge his horse after Major Reno, who is already ordering a line of soldiers to form alongside the opposing bank of the river. My eyes linger as he waves his men across. I find myself grinning as the men laugh and run their mounts through the water. The horses kick up water every which way, drenching the entire company. I turn my attention back to my own men.

"Captains, we are going to stay on our horses as long as possible. Shoot at anything that moves," I say, looking at the rocky slopes and slender timber ahead of us and wondering who or what is watching us. The brush that grazes the earth is no more than three feet high, so there isn't much to conceal them.

"Yes, General," my men answer. My eyes go back to them, and I watch as they hurry to their companies. I look back at Major Reno. He and his companies have disappeared into the trees with my Indians. I squint into the sunlight. Tom runs his horse over to me and pulls his mount alongside mine. I nod at him, and Tom smiles at me.

"He is very much you," Tom says nodding in Henry Armstrong's— Little Autie's—direction.

I look over at my nephew, my namesake. At only eighteen, he reminds me of a youth I never fully lived. My nephew looks back at us and smiles; he is all bright-blue eyes and golden curls, the mark of a true Custer. Henry brings his horse over to ours. I recall how I spent my entire adulthood fighting wars. Wars of morality, wars of freedom, wars of politics—everyone always seemed to have a reason to be fighting for something.

"All of us Custers carry something they can't teach. Remember that, Henry," I say to Little Autie as he stops his horse next to Tom and me. My head snaps to the left as I hear the first rattling of gunfire.

My heart quickens, and I feel something in my chest that reminds me that I am alive. I find myself grinning as I signal to the bugler. It is time to charge; it is time to remember who I am and what I am truly good at.

I kick Vic in his side, shooting us into the timber. I see the dust cloud as we come over the first slope. I know this game; I pull out my rifle and signal for my men to go up the next ridge, and I hear a flurry of hooves and broken branches behind me. I look back to see the captains have anticipated this and are already making their way up—more firing and screaming in the distance. Not the screaming, shrill tones of a warrior, but that of a frightened man. I glance at my brother Boston, who has ridden up next to me. I see the worry stretched across his face; he looks so out of place in his civilian garments, dark brown trousers and white-collared shirt.

"Should we dismount, Autie?" he yells at me.

I slow my horse down, letting him fall in beside me.

"This is a trick they do. They kick up dust to try to steer us in another direction. You just wait; it will settle down," I call to him; he nods at me with weak uncertainty.

My voice trails off amidst the increasing gunfire echoing over the river, where I had just sent Reno. I look to my other side and notice Tom. Behind him I see Yates, Moylan, Keogh, and my brother-in-law Calhoun riding fast toward me. I bring Vic to a stop at the top of the ridge.

"General, should we try to reach Major Reno and his men?" Captain Keogh yells at me.

The screaming from the other side is starting to unsettle the horses, and even Vic is flaring his nostrils and stomping his hooves. I look at our cavalry; on their uneasy mounts they look as though they are popcorn kernels in a low cast-iron pan. Captain Keogh is still shouting something at me over the screaming. I look at him and recall the many hells that we have lived through together. He has a tone, a look on his face I have never heard or seen in him. Something catches my eye in the dust below us, a glinting.

"Bloody hell, shoot any Indian holding a mirror!" I scream, making the captains all look at me, dumbfounded.

"Get back to your men now! Do not dismount unless I order it, shoot the bastard reflecting the mirror!" I scream in a way that makes me no longer sound human.

There's a shrillness to my voice that forces everyone to scramble. I see before us the silhouette of feathers. They're not screaming like they normally do but are as silent as the rocks. Their ponies move like wind between the leaves. I reach for my rifle and fire. I fire at the storm splitters, the thunder dreamers; I fire at what I admire and hate about them and myself. I kick Vic forward.

My horse moves like water, dancing from their bullets, racing down the ridge. I've made my first hit and watch a feathered man slip from his pony. Before I reach the bottom, I have slain two more and shoot out six horses. I hear my men's bullets tear all around us, their shots echoing through the ridge like a song of war.

I reach into my saddlebag to reload. I see a painted woman on a pony coming straight for me. I pull out one of my revolvers and shoot her in the face. Her face explodes, shards of skull scattering into the dust.

"General!" I hear someone call.

"Hold your position and make your way up the ridge!" I scream back, leading Vic up the ridge away from the river and away from the screaming, away from the violence. I feel myself hitting the ground. I roll from the saddle and look at the hole that has appeared in Vic's neck. He is on his side, blood spraying out of him, like the water that had been kicked up from the mounts charging the river, shooting in every direction. I grab what I can of my ammunition from the flailing horse's saddlebag and run up the ridge into the timber; I hear shots being fired all around me. I glance back and see that most my men have been forced to dismount. Some of the horses are still half alive, shrieking in pain and flailing on the forest's floor. I reach the top of the ridge, emerging out of the dust. My chest is pounding, my legs come to a stop, and I look at who is with me. All of my captains and about half our men. One hundred and fifty lost to the screaming, lost to the trills, lost to the smoke and dust and death.

"General?" comes the voice of Tom.

"Keep going!" I scream, running down the hill away from that hell.

I see another ridge with rocks and race for that. I hear bullets cracking into the pines around me, causing me to duck, bark exploding in my face. I don't stop to fire back but instead run for the rocks. I reach the top, drop to my hands and knees, and crawl behind them. I rest my back against them, my mind racing. I look around the rock and see the dust, the mirror glinting, and Major Reno; I hear the horses shrieking. I see all the blood—blood-soaked bodies everywhere; I have not seen such a sight since the Civil War. I lean back against the boulder and steady my breath as I watch my captains trail in; they join me with their backs against the rocks, struggling to catch their breath. I watch their chests heave, some of them splattered in blood, all of us drenched in a film of dust. My eyes search for my baby brother, Boston, and my nephew Henry, but all I see is Tom, his eyes cold, calculated. He is furious. Slowly, more of our men make their way to us, their faces ghostly white beneath the light-brown coating of dust. I see some have pissed or shit themselves; a couple look like they have vomited down the front of their uniforms. I close my eyes and listen. I still hear firing in the distance, but no one is chasing us; no Indian is slithering up the ridge to ambush us.

"How many do you think there are, General?" Captain Yates asks me. There is a hoarseness in his voice—he's the same age as Tom, and I'd always thought of him like a younger brother. Relief floods over me as I spot Boston and Henry to the far left, plastered against a boulder. I don't bother answering Yates, because we need to move if we want to live till sundown.

"Sergeant Kanipe," I say.

"Yes, General," the young man answers, crawling toward me.

"I need you to make for Captain McDougall and the pack train. You need to tell them to make for here, the Little Bighorn River. Tell them to hurry, because we need relief. Tell them we have found the camp that General Terry has sent us to pursue," I say, trying to clear my throat of dust. It feels raw and dry, as there is nothing to clear it with—my skin full of water is on the dead body of Vic.

"Yes, sir," Sergeant Kanipe says. I watch as he crawls to the edge of the boulders opposite us, glancing down at the side we have yet to see. He peers out, then makes a run for it to the east. I close my eyes and listen. No bullets chase him. I open my eyes and reach into my pocket, pull out a small notebook and pencil, and begin scribing a note.

"Adjutant Lieutenant Cooke?" I call out, finishing my note.

"Yes, General?" the lieutenant calls out. I look across at him; he is two men to the right of me, his chest still heaving from our dash.

"I need you to take this note to Captain Benteen. Tell him to come quickly and to bring packs; tell him to bring the packs," I say, looking the man in the eye. I can see he is frightened but not a coward.

"Yes, General," the lieutenant says, taking the note and tucking it into his breast pocket.

His fingers shake as he fastens the brass button. He looks to the east in the direction that Kanipe went, then to the left where the dull sound of men dying lingers in the air.

"Go east like Kanipe and circle round to the south," I say, making the decision for him.

"Yes, General," Cooke replies, sounding relieved that someone made the choice for him. I watch him stand and quickly disappear over the ridge into the timber and pray that the men make it to where they are supposed to be. I don't have to do a check to know that without our horses and packs, we won't be able to make a stand till sunset.

"General?" I hear Tom's voice and look over at him. His sweat has streaked the dust on his face, making it a muddy mess. A grimace of a smile reaches my mouth.

"What should we do now?" Tom asks, and I see that he is tense, his body is stiff—he wants to kill them.

The dull sound of our men who are still alive but unable to make it up to the ridge reach us like a promise of death. I look at the sunlight pouring through the spruce branches, dancing with the dust.

"We stand until Captain Benteen relieves us coming in from the south. This will create the hammer and anvil we wanted. It is sooner than I thought, but all for the better, right? We will be done with this campaign and able celebrate this country's independence with our wives," I say, trying to be reassuring. The chorus of "Here, here" comes from my men. I look at them; to make it this far means they are not cowards. Crouching, I start going through our weapons, feeling it is safe enough to move about down low.

"What do you think the hostiles are doing, General?" James asks me.

I glance at my brother-in-law as I finish loading my revolvers and rifle. I touch my hunting knife, making sure it is securely tucked into my belt.

"Preparing their counterattack. They know we are here. What they don't know is the number of men we've got left. I will take it as a blessing that they haven't run, as we would have to spend the rest of this campaign chasing them," I say, none too eager to be tiptoeing in moonlight in hostile territory.

"Aye, General," comes the soft voice of Captain Keogh.

He knows what I am talking about. The Indians could be as slippery as fish, teasing us with a fight only to vanish. I look at the men gathered around me and find myself smiling again.

"What's that, then, Autie?" comes the young voice of my nephew.

I look over at him. He looks like a frightened child, his pale smooth face streaked in dust and blood, his blue eyes as large as saucers.

"Just reminds me of the war, the first time in a long time that anything has felt like that," I say.

Momentous, I think, *that feeling that we're on the cusp of history, the cusp of change.* I stand, my men growing more silent than silent, and look down over the boulder down the ridge where we have run from. I see nothing but the settling dust and trees that have been torn apart by bullets. Two shots fire at me, narrowly missing my head. I see some feathers at the bottom, and I raise my rifle, my fingers pulling the trigger twice. Two shots crack through the air, and I hear a man screaming. I sit back down and smile, and I look at my men who are looking at me with anticipation.

"They are there, open fire!" I yell, standing.

Gunfire cracks out like the thunder in a summer storm, but the Indians still don't fully reveal themselves. I know we have to move or be slaughtered where we stand. If we can bide our time for McDougall and Benteen to arrive, we will win, securing this territory. *I wonder what that victory will give*, I think.

"Make for the next ridge!" I scream.

Leaving the safety of the boulders, I run for the ridge behind us. We need more distance; we need to break the grasp they have on us. I dive through the branches, bullets raining around me. I duck into the brush at the top of the ridge and wait for whoever is still standing to join me. I see my brothers and brother-in-law, Captain Keogh, and Captain Yates.

"Armstrong," Boston says to me in a shaky voice.

"Henry?" I say.

My brother nods. Here is where Henry's—Little Autie's—journey ends.

"God save us," I say, looking at the smattering of captains, privates, and sergeants I have left.

"Where is Captain Benteen?" Captain Keogh shouts at me.

"There should be firing from Major Reno's position pushing them to us," Captain Yates says through heavy breathing.

We all grow silent, and nothingness rings back at us. No shots, no trills, no moaning of dying men.

"I'll kill that spineless coward myself if he retreated," Tom spits out.

No need, I think to myself. Any one of us will kill him—maybe we will all take turns.

Without the boulders, I know we have nothing left to conceal us from their bullets. I look around and notice that behind us is a steep ridge. My thoughts are broken by a man running in front of us, an Indian in buckskin, hair the color of raw gold flying behind him and eyes like a darkened sky. He has no weapon but a stone war club. He doesn't wear a headdress as a chief would but has two hawk feathers streaming halfway down his back. I see the white lightning bolt painted down his face and white hail spots.

"Fire!" I scream, standing suddenly. We rain bullets, and the bloody savage with hair the color of the sun dances through them.

There are only about fifty of us left. I see the bodies, all blue, all army blue, the color of freedom, the color of progress, lying on the hill of the ridge we'd just run up. The gunfire rings out, but not one bullet even comes near the Indian with the long golden hair. I waste three more shots as I watch him disappear. I look at Captain Keogh, who is standing next to me, his rifle at his side and the color drained from his face. I hear the war cry before I see what is coming. There are more Indians than I could have imagined. This dream I have, the dream of securing this land they waste, is turning into a nightmare.

"Make for the next ridge!" I find myself screaming. I turn and force my legs to run down the hill, then back up the steep ridge, my boots slipping on the dry earth and loose rock. I fall and scramble back up, bullets tearing into the earth all around me. I hear bullets cut the air around me, snapping into trees, and then I hear trills and screams.

"God save us!" Boston screams.

I look back to see half his head get blown off. For a moment, it is as though time has come to a standstill. A bullet barely misses my own skull, and I force my legs to run harder into the hill. I look beside me and see the blond curls of Tom; next to him is Captain Keogh and about twenty privates. I look ahead of us and see the top of the ridge; relief floods me, and I dig my boots harder into the ground. The ridge is larger and flatter than all the other ones we have just passed over. We reach the top, and I make for the middle, looking around and breathing raggedly.

"Band together!" I scream in a craggy voice I don't recognize.

The men, my men, look at me, confused.

"Band together!" I scream again, praying for the sound of the other infantry's bugle, but silence rings in my ears, not the shrill call of brass.

My men gather close to me, and I close my eyes, thinking of what our best move would be, when the gentle voice of Captain Keogh cuts into my thoughts.

"Our father who art in heaven, hallowed be thy name."

All I can see is their feathers, dancing. I see the pain. I see something in their faces I've never seen in war.

"Your kingdom come, your will be done, on earth as it is in heaven." Captain Keogh pauses as though god may answer back.

I open my eyes, raise my rifle, and return to the edge of the top of the ridge, looking down the slope we have just escaped from. I begin firing at anything that moves, drowning out the captain's words. All I hear is thunder.

CHAPTER 28

▲▲▲▲

I BRUSH AT SOMETHING SOFT TICKLING MY CHEEKS, my eyes fluttering open. I see the long, bright-green tendrils promising something I now know I'll never find.

"Timpsila," Swift Fox says to me; his voice sounds soft in my ears, kind. My eyes find him. He is sitting with his knees pulled up near his chest, the timpsila balanced on the tops of his knees. His black eyes search my face.

"Are you still upset?" he asks me in a voice that makes me sadder.

"I'm not upset," I say, looking up at the clear summer sky, the cool air of the morning that is full of so much promise.

We moved camp, alongside the Rosebud, so I started sleeping beneath the pines by myself. I turn my head fully and look at him; his eyes are so full and black that I feel my own eyes begin to blur with tears.

"I can't stop seeing what I saw."

I let the tears slide down my cheeks, and I look toward the sky, begging her for answers. The past few nights Swift Fox, along with everyone else, has left me alone. This is the first we have spoken since that night. Movement catches my eye, and I turn my head to see him leaning toward me. His mouth softly kisses my tears away, and I close my eyes.

"Think, soon this will all be a memory, a dream. You'll have one of those things the white women wear."

"A dress?" I say, opening my eyes and looking over at him.

He lies down next to me in the grass, adjusting his shoulders and flattening the blades beneath him. I watch a smile spread to his lips, revealing a handsome face. Swift Fox rolls on his side and tickles my cheek with the onions.

"I was thinking of a corset."

I roll on my side to face him, and I find myself smiling. I see his hair is wet, and my hand reaches out and gently touches it.

"I don't even know what that is," I say, thinking of the corset.

"It goes with the dress," he replies, his grin growing wider.

My fingers spread into his hair; it is soft like new grass.

"Everyone is swimming in the river and gathering timpsila—even Crazy Horse is down there," he says to me, still smiling.

I smile, thinking of the chief swimming.

"Laughing?" I ask, my eyebrows raise trying to envision it.

"No, never," Swift Fox says to me through his smile, a smile growing back over my face.

"I need to leave here," I say, rolling back onto my back and gazing once again up at the sky, wishing that it would swallow me up.

"I know, I promised we would. Will you wait for me?" Swift Fox asks me.

I roll back on my side and look at the man I married and try not to think of all the things I saw.

"I am still here," I whisper.

"I know," he says, the smile slipping from his face.

"He is close—Pehin Hanska Kasota, Custer—we can all feel it. I need to watch them bleed, Little Wolf. For your mother, for our ancestors, for our children," he says, his face becoming very still.

He touches my stomach, and I let more tears run down my face.

"I don't know if it's right," I say, closing my eyes.

I had not wanted to admit that feeling even to myself. I didn't want to tell that to Swift Fox, but I can't stop the words from my soul spilling out of my mouth.

"What is right? What is wrong? They have blurred those lines. They call them government," he says to me.

I feel him stroking the tears from my cheek with the backs of his fingers.

"We call our choices from god, and only god can tell us what is right—not some white man in a distant city from a distant place. They have left us no choice. I have to break the bodies, to punish them in the afterlife and their next life. Their pain was mine, and now they must live with it, too." I hear the promise in Swift Fox's voice, full of the certainty that I lack.

I look at the man whose child I am carrying. "You are a chief," I say.

I meant it as a question, but it comes out as a statement.

"All our chiefs are dead. They killed them. They want us dead; they want this land. It makes no difference to them that this land is more to us than just a place to rear cattle and grow crops and strip rocks out of. That wasuns are in the Black Hills carrying the voice of the Wakan Tanka. They care for nothing but the physical," Swift Fox says, gesturing to the forest around us.

"They think that if they control that and kill all the buffalo, they control us. But you can't kill what is in here," Swift Fox says, tapping my forehead and chest. "You can't control what god gives us. All our chiefs are dead, like the camp you came from. I am still willing to fight, Little Wolf. I know this is dead or dying," he says, gesturing again to the forest, "but I can't live with myself knowing that I didn't at least try to fight for her, her rocks, her streams, her magic. I am honored to be your husband, and when we are trapped in a cabin and given government rations, I will look back at this as the happiest time of my life."

I feel the tears now streaming down my face.

"For our son, I fight," he says putting his hand on my stomach.

"How do you know it is a boy?" I say, grappling with the pain of knowing what is being done to us and what we have to do.

"My family has never given birth to a girl," he says, looking at me and smiling. "We only marry them."

I watch as his eyes search my face.

"We'll have a whole bunch of them, sons," he says to me, smiling.

I laugh through my tears.

"We will start our own tribe on the reservation they lock us on." He is looking at my stomach, envisioning what that would look like; I can barely see what he is talking about, but the glimpses I have don't seem so bad. Maybe he is right; it is worse to give up.

The snap of guns firing rings through the air; it is close, and the shots vibrate through my skin. We both sit up. Gunshots answer, firing back.

"They are here," Swift Fox says, hopping to his feet. He holds out his hand for me, the one that is not holding the onions. I take it, and he pulls me to my feet; we both pause and hear an *eyapaha*, a crier, scream, "Custer!"

"This is what we have been waiting for!" Swift Fox shouts, the excitement bubbling out of his voice.

Still holding my hand, he pulls us down the slope toward the river.

"We need to prepare ourselves," he says, weaving us through streams of women and children who are running from the water, some still carrying baskets of the wild onions, their green stems bright in the early sun.

I see Crazy Horse standing among them, yelling at them to go north. He is soaking wet, wearing nothing but his leggings. He looks at us and nods. My husband pulls us to him.

"Custer?" Swift Fox asks.

"Yeah, they are fully armed. They are shooting anything that moves," Crazy Horse answers; his light eyes narrow and grow dark.

More shots ring through the air, making the women and children move quicker. I see feathers and paint heading toward us, the first ready to fight. They see Crazy Horse and let out a trill. He raises his arm to them. "I am going to make sure that the women and children get north, then ready myself," he says, watching the warriors disappear into the brush.

"Hoka hey!" my husband yells, pulling me in the same direction as the women and children, north.

"Hoka hey!" Crazy Horse shouts to our backs.

More fire. I hear the sound of thunder. I see maybe a hundred warriors mounted on the top of the slope, charging in the direction of the firing.

"We need to hurry!" my husband says, pulling me into a light run. I see the tipis, and our pace quickens.

"Brother!"

I feel myself wince at the voice of Coyote Run.

"Brother!" my husband calls to the man falling in beside us.

I look at him. He is already dressed, his face painted half red, half white, and wearing a silver breastplate. We reach our lodge, and my husband lets go of my hand and hugs his cousin.

"Today is a good day to die!" my husband says, ducking into the tent.

I follow him and try not to look at Coyote Run, who has tumbled in after me. My husband tosses the onions into a basket next to the firepit and pulls out his war box. He flints the fire in flames, tosses a handful of white buffalo sage on it, and begins cleansing himself with the smoke.

"We followed them from their camp, and I had the great joy of speaking with Bloody Knife," Coyote Run says, dipping his hands in the smoke.

"No?" my husband says, looking up from his prayer.

His cousin sits cross-legged in front of the fire.

"Yes! I told him I want to make love to Custer the same way he has all these years, and then shots were fired."

My husband looks at me.

"Bloody Knife is like the Grabber, a guide to Custer," Swift Fox says to me. I nod, wondering if Standing Bear is with Custer.

"In hunting us," Coyote Run adds, looking at me with the same disdain I am sure I look at him with.

"Bloody Knife is a mixed Indian. We used to tease him for it. Too much, I guess. He went running to the white men wanting to kill us. But the joke's on him, right? He'll get the same as all of us, a parcel of land, beef, sugar, and death," Coyote Run says, in no hurry to do anything.

I don't say anything, wishing he would leave.

"My wife needs to get dressed," Swift Fox says, glancing at me.

"I thought you two were through?" Coyote Run says, looking at me.

I try not to say anything. I know I can't hide the anger from my face.

"Brother," Swift Fox says firmly.

"I'll see you out there," Coyote Run says, standing. Then, pausing at the tent's flap, he looks back at me.

"Try to fire your gun this time?"

And with that, he is gone. I hear firing and yelling. I look at my things Swift Fox had neatly stored next to the blankets.

"You want us done?" I ask, looking at him.

He looks at me, his face already painted half red, half white. His fingers move quickly, weaving eagle feathers into his braid.

"No, traditionally, though, if someone leaves the lodge, their marriage is finished. I hoped you would come back," he says, nodding at my things.

My rifle is balanced on top of my mukluks and gunstock club.

"Little Wolf," he says to me.

I look at Swift Fox.

"You don't have to come with me; you can go north with the women and children. Help Crazy Horse protect them." His words linger between us.

I think of what I saw that night. The bear, my brother, my mother being raped. I remembered what Frank Grouard had told me, of what the Great White Chief had said: Move to where they want us to move or die. I pull off the soft blue woolen tunic I had been wearing since the Rosebud and pull on the hide vest I was given on the night we wed. I lace up the sides and smile. I feel Swift Fox's fingers in my hair, braiding it for war. I see my wotawe and put it on over my chest and tuck it into my vest. I swivel around to look at Swift Fox, the paint lying in the wooden dish between us. I place my palm into the red and press my hand to my face.

"May god protect me and forgive me, for I know not what is right, only that they want me dead," I say and open my eyes.

Swift Fox is looking at me in a way I've never seen before. He puts his hands out to me; I take them.

"Néá'ese."

"Néá'ese."

I give thanks. I take my carbine. I don't bother with the straps I had made to secure it to my back and instead use the straps for my gunstock club, tying it to my back. I look at my husband who has a revolver holstered to his waist with his war club, quivers, and a bow on his back, and a rifle in his hand.

"Are you going to be able to walk with all of that?"

He grins at me and steps toward me. He grabs me firmly behind the head and pulls me to his lips. We kiss for the first time in days. His mouth is warm and full, and I feel his heat.

"Let us finish this so we can start our life as their prisoners," he says.

I try to smile but feel it dropping from my face. Swift Fox stands, goes to the flap. I have the same feeling as I did at the Rosebud, like I am frozen to the ground.

"This is it," Swift Fox says, his eyes searching my face.

"What you saw with the bear, I saw it too. I dreamt of it before you came with the Grabber. I thought that when I saw you, you were a ghost," he says to me, and I feel the hair on my arms raise as a chill runs down my spine. I touch my medicine bag, my wotawe. *Gray Wolf protects me*, I think to myself silently. My husband is still looking at me. I nod my head, and he smiles and disappears into the sunshine. I feel myself following him; my legs move without my command. Swift Fox sees me and smiles, the sun on his face and glinting in his wet hair like gold. He nods, and we run toward the screams of dying men. The sunshine somehow seems wrong. *It should be a storm*, I think to myself, sweat beading down my back.

I see a dust cloud, and we run for it. On the outskirts, I pause. I see spilled baskets of timpsila, the bright green appearing odd against the dry forest floor of brush, needles, and dried grass. I see small feet. I remember her. She looks lifelessly up to the sky. Her chest has a hole of bright red. I see her two older sisters, and I see his two wives, fragments of bone and flesh scattered among the onions they had been running with. I remember them helping me prepare the night we wed. A hand on my shoulder breaks my thoughts. I feel my tears. I remember my camp, Washita.

"You see, Little Wolf, they are animals, all for gold or a promise from a demon. Land crops, cattle—they kill us haphazardly without any blessings or real reason. They kill because they are told to by some man who doesn't even fight with them or care if they themselves live or die." Swift Fox's words cut through my ears.

I look at my husband, and I think of him ripping the arms off the soldiers he killed. I now know something I wish I had never known. When Sha and I were constantly moving our camp, she had said there wasn't anywhere left for us to move anymore; we were surrounded.

"Why are they doing this to us?" I find myself asking my husband the question I have been running from since my family died.

"Because they are frightened," Swift Fox says, "frightened of themselves. They only want those who submit to their lies, their fake power. They are frightened of who and what we are meant to be; they know we only answer to god, we will never answer to them, we would rather die than be like them. So they know that to keep their power over the people they brought with them, they need to kill us, for there are men who know that the government is an illusion, a lie, and an enslavement of the body, mind, and soul, and if they allied with us, we could defeat them. The men that obey them cannot admit the truth to themselves; they are their slaves; those who deny their power, they try to murder just like us. Evil consumes them, and they will take everything even if they themselves die with it. So, Little Wolf, we have to kill them, because if we simply submit, our children's children's children will never know that we loved them and fought for their freedom." When Swift Fox finishes, I think that for the first time, everything makes sense to me.

"This is Gall's family," I say, looking down at them—the blood, it is everywhere.

"We will mourn them after. I am sure Gall knows he doesn't lie here with them. He is in there, the place we need to go," my husband says to me.

I look to where my husband is pointing. The gunfire is so loud it makes my ears ring, and the dust cloud burns my eyes, making them water.

"Let's go, for them, for your mother, your father, and your brother, for this earth and what is left of our home. Today, Little Wolf, is a good day to die," Swift Fox says to me.

I think of everything I have seen, everything I have survived, and

I hear the words of my father the spring before he died, arguing with my mother. He said it was better to die with the sun on your face and your soul free with god than caged in their poisonous lies.

I feel like I have left my body. I stand there looking at the dead children, and I think of Gray Wolf—and I feel hollow.

"Hoka hey," I find myself saying. I look up and see my horse to the far left, at the edge of the dust. I run for him. He sees me and stomps his feet. I climb on his back, and I see my husband on his pony.

"Let's go!" he screams at me.

I nod my head, and he lets out a war scream that sends something down my back that releases me from stillness. His silver breastplate reflects the sun's light. It is blinding. He charges into the dust, and I follow him, my horse running. I look down at the ground. Gray Wolf is leaping between bodies of dead women and children. I see one of the bodies clutching a dead infant, its lifeless head turned at a strange angle. I look up and see warriors. My husband is charging to the front, and I follow him. I see soldiers screaming as they are picked off with bullets like fishing during a fish run. Warriors leap from their mounts to stab them with their knives or crush their skulls—it is a blur of steel, bullets, and gunstock clubs. I see Sitting Bull and his massive headdress. I see Gall not far from him, shrieking in mourning as he brings his gunstock club to the back of a soldier's skull. I urge Gray Wolf toward my husband. He slides from his horse's back and shoots under the pony's neck at a group of Indians. They are different from the Crow and Shoshoni Indians at the Rosebud, more like us in beads and hide and feathers.

"That is Bloody Knife!"

I hear the excited voice of Coyote Run, who looks at me and gives me a grin that makes me shift. Coyote Run screams and takes off on his horse in the direction of my husband. I urge my horse forward; the bodies on the ground have changed from our women and children to those of white soldiers dressed in blue and gold. The Rosebud wasn't like this; the soldiers had managed to continuously escape us. I look to where they are trying to hold their position. They seem confused—trying to fight, trying to run, horses shot out from under them. I watch as time stops; men are still screaming as their horses die on top of them.

I search for my husband. I see what Coyote Run was so excited about. Bloody Knife stands out from the rest of his people like the Grabber. I watch him raise his rifle and aim at my husband, who is trying to duck behind his pony's head to reload his rifle. I raise my own rifle and pull the trigger, and it slams into my shoulder harder than if I had the stability of the earth beneath me. My horse moves instinctively to the side to compensate. I hit Bloody Knife between the eyes, and the white man beside him is splattered with his skull. I watch as the man's face goes white. His skin is an unnatural red, and he is yelling something. I aim at him and just miss as he moves behind a narrow spruce. The men, the white soldiers, hear what that man is yelling and turn away, running from us.

I feel someone looking at me; it is the black eyes of my husband. He lets out a trill. I am still holding my carbine, pressed hard into my shoulder. I pull the trigger and shoot, and another one of the white man's Indians falls. My horse leaps over him toward the retreating men. I splash through the creek, the water soaking my leggings. I come up next to a soldier on horseback who looks at me, trying to steady his revolver at my face. I do what my husband has shown me to do. Sliding off of Gray Wolf's back, I fire my carbine with one hand under his neck; our hearts beat as one as I hit the soldier in the face. I hear the trill of my husband that creates an echo among our warriors, and I readjust onto Gray Wolf's back. I shoot at everything that moves until I run out of bullets. My finger is still pulling the empty trigger of my carbine when I see my husband shooting his extra revolver. I watch as he pulls empty, then draws his bow and arrow. Like me, he aims at anything that moves, which isn't much. I look through the smoke and dust and see the ridge where the white soldiers have retreated.

"We are going to wait for them to come back." It's Gall, shouting from his pony.

Sitting Bull steers his mount toward us. The three of us stand in silence, myself, Gall, and Sitting Bull. We watch as our warriors dismount and stab the dead and dying men with arrows and knives. Some that are still living moan and begin screaming as the knives reach their flesh.

"I am sorry, Gall," I say.

I look at the small chief, but he doesn't look at me; tears stream down his dirt- and blood-stained face. I look at my husband standing in the middle of the corpses with his hunting knife. I watch as he looks around at the bodies, seemingly satisfied that nothing is moving. He goes to his horse and hops on its back. He sees the three of us, and a huge smile reaches his mouth. Swift Fox trots his horse toward us.

"Your husband is a strong warrior."

I look at Sitting Bull, whose arms are visible. I see that the cuts from the Sun Dance are still raw.

"You are a strong warrior," Gall says, looking at me.

My husband brings his horse in front of us.

"Little Wolf shot Bloody Knife," he says.

I can feel the two chiefs looking at me. I don't look at them. I feel like I am not even here. I feel like I am somewhere else, somewhere where the sun is bright and the buffalo are plenty.

"Little Wolf?" I hear my husband call.

"Is this it?" I ask, looking at death.

"This is just the beginning." We all hear the voice of Crazy Horse, with his two feathers in his hair and a white lightning bolt down the middle of his face, speckled in hail spots.

"Brother, the women and children?" Sitting Bull asks.

"They are safe for now," Crazy Horse answers.

"Custer has split his men," Gall says, his voice raw and shrill. Anger and sadness mixed together make it almost unrecognizable.

"We chased them up onto that ridge," Gall adds, pointing in front of us.

"Who went that way?" Crazy Horse asks, looking back across the water at the base of the ridge where we had been fighting.

"Major Reno and the Indian scouts, Bloody Knife before he fell," Gall says.

"Custer's scouts?" Crazy Horse asks.

"Yeah," Sitting Bull says.

Crazy Horse grunts in what I can only guess is agreement.

"Little Wolf shot Bloody Knife," Sitting Bull says to Crazy Horse.

"She did more than that—she blew his head right off!"

I hear the excited voice of Coyote Run and close my eyes. I wish I could feel the breeze on my face.

"What is this now?" I hear Red Hawk exclaim. I look up to see that she is covered in blood and on foot. She looks up at me and smiles, her teeth looking oddly white against all the red.

"Where is your pony?" American Horse asks, coming up beside us on his horse. With him are two other chiefs I've never met.

"Deader than these poor souls," she says, gesturing to the men that we killed.

"Gall says that Custer has split his men," Red Hawk laughs.

"Custer and his men have been chased off their horses, too. Little Big Man and his lodge are gathering them up, the horses they abandoned, fifty pounds of ammunition in each saddlebag. We chased them up the ridge on that side," American Horse says, pointing the way we came.

"This is your dream, Sitting Bull," Crazy Horse says, his eyes lost in the trees in front of us.

I think of what Sitting Bull had said at the Sun Pole. He had said they were falling from the sky like rain—the white soldiers.

"We reload, then chase Custer up the ridge," Crazy Horse says, not looking at any of us.

"What about Major Reno?" my husband asks.

I know Swift Fox wants to finish them. Crazy Horse looks toward the ridge the Major had scurried behind. "Leave them; they are dead. Pehin Hanska is more important," he says.

I don't have to look at my husband to feel his disappointment.

"The horses are all behind us," Red Hawk says.

I watch her make for the edge of the smoke, and I steer my horse in her direction. I see my husband at my side; we ride in silence. We come out into the grass and sun. There are probably one hundred horses, big like mine and all saddled. Warriors are still rounding them up; some are stripping them of their saddles. I see on the outskirts a collection of guns.

"I need bullets," my husband says, hopping from his horse.

I slide from Gray Wolf, who looks at me and stomps his hooves excitedly.

"Go then," I say, patting my horse's hindquarters.

"How are you holding up?"

I look at Red Hawk. I see the women she fights with checking out the guns; they look newer than anything we have.

"Spencer repeating rifles!" I hear someone yell.

"I am shooting," I say, making Red Hawk laugh.

"Oh well, all this will be over soon," she says.

I look at all the warriors, smiling and laughing. I think of where we will all be soon. I think of the cage they want to put us in.

"All of it will be, won't it? Who will remember us, Red Hawk? When we're gone from our land?" I ask.

She doesn't answer me straightaway. Silence hangs between us, and then someone starts firing one of the new rifles, bringing a round of trills.

"I guess it will be like what Swift Fox says—*we* will have to remember us," she says eventually, as we both watch my husband walking toward us, his arms full of bullets.

"It never gets easier, Little Wolf, shooting," she adds as my husband stops in front of us.

"Little Wolf, for you," he says, dropping a belt of bullets at my feet. Red Hawk smiles at me and makes for her women next to the ammunition. They see her coming and let out a trill, causing a chain of whooping to break out.

I sit down cross-legged and begin reloading my carbine, my fingers shaking as I drop the bullets in the chamber. I glance up and see my husband sitting across from me, smiling and doing the same but with an energy of joy as he finishes and drapes one belt of bullets across his body and passes me the other. I take it and do the same.

"You shoot better than anyone could have thought," he says, beaming at me. I think of all the years I spent by myself in the forest working on my aim, figuring out the quickest and cleanest way to kill. I feel the sadness I'd been fighting since the Rosebud; it is still there, swelling into my stomach and heart.

"Hoka hey!"

I hear the voice of Crazy Horse. He's standing on the edge of the dust cloud with Gall and Sitting Bull. I see American Horse and Little Big Man making their way to them. Crazy Horse nods at them and disappears back into the dust on foot.

"This is it," my husband says, his voice trembling. I watch him stand. He holds his hand out to me, and I take it as he pulls me to my feet. I see Red Hawk disappearing into the dust cloud, her women following her.

"Brother!"

I feel my jaw clench.

"Your wife is as amazing as you swore she was. Are you ready?" Coyote Run asks us.

"I lie anywhere, I fight and die anywhere, on the ground or in the water," my husband says. I watch as my husband's men, the warriors he had fought with for more than ten years, make their way to him and join him in his words.

"I am ready to die anytime, no matter whether I am young or old!" they say in unison. I count twenty of them, and with my husband and myself, that makes twenty-two.

"Hi-es-tzie!"—Custer—my husband calls out, rushing for the dust cloud. I follow, as do the Dog Soldiers; we all enter the pines and the dust. My body feels heavy, and I look at my carbine. The gun, this weapon I have loved so much, now feels strange to me.

"Your husband is one of the bravest men I have ever known."

I don't turn toward the voice of Coyote Run.

"I was there, the day we first saw you, when you came to Crazy Horse's camp with the Grabber," he says.

"I don't remember," I reply.

I hear his laugh. It sounds deep and forced.

"I was at the tent flap. We had just been smoking with Crazy Horse and Horn Chips over the news that the Grabber had with him. We had already heard it from Red Cloud that the Great Chief told us we could move or starve."

I feel him step closer to me. I don't look at him, instead focusing my eyes on the settling dust.

"Swift Fox loved you from that very first meeting. I thought he would have made you his wife that night. I was surprised to find him alone in the morning."

I remembered eating fish with Swift Fox. It seemed like a dream—a memory so distant I wondered if it had actually happened.

"He was right about you."

I feel Coyote Run's hand on my shoulder. Something creeps into me I have never felt before. I shrug out from under his fingers and make my way further through the dust, silence surrounding me. I am grateful I don't hear the footsteps of Coyote Run. I walk light, so light the soles of my mukluks barely touch the soil; no twigs snap beneath my feet. I see the warriors gathered at the bottom of the ridge. The warriors and the chiefs are flat against the earth, silent, as though they are her heartbeat. If you didn't know they were there, you wouldn't even see them. Feathers look like brush, and face paint looks like the earth's floor.

I crouch, disappearing into the brush, and look at the hill leading up to the top of the ridge. It looks empty, the boulders lining the top of the ridge giving the white soldiers a good place to hide.

"Little Wolf," comes my husband's voice, barely louder than the wind.

He is no more than three feet to my left. I lie down on my stomach and look at him.

"Custer is up there," he says to me barely above a whisper.

Something catches his eye, and he glances away, letting out a shrill whistle that sounds exactly like a wren in springtime. I see the flickering of light—one, kill.

I watch as Crazy Horse comes to his feet and runs to the bottom of the ridge between us and the American soldiers. It is as if time stands still as someone at the top stands. He has long, curled, golden hair and a black hat with the fringed buckskin jacket I remember. I watch as he aims at Crazy Horse, but he hesitates. I feel myself stop breathing as I push my rifle to my shoulder and fire at him. I miss his head by less than a foot. I fire again, and then I hear the shots. The bullets dance around Crazy Horse, and he looks back in our direction, a grin plastered across his face.

"Hoka hey!" he screams, running the full length of the clearing.

It is enough that it forces all of us to our feet. We charge the hill, my legs slamming into the steep ground. I see the man firing, under his black hat the golden hair etched into my memory. Just like the day my family died, the sun dances around him.

"That's him!" my husband screams at me.

I raise my carbine to my shoulder and fire, pulling the trigger as one of my feet lands on the earth. I miss Custer by two inches, hitting the boulder instead. I watch as he recoils, the rock chips smattering across his face. I hear trills cut through the air. The shot forces the general to duck back behind the rock, his men following him; all their heads disappear like gophers in autumn.

"Keep going!" I hear Gall yell. I run harder into the earth, my legs burning like my breath. We reach the rocks to see the American soldiers scramble down the back side of the ridge and begin making their way up the next ridge. I kneel and fire into the backs of the white men, one down, two down, three down; my fourth shot is a miss. Custer is now too far out of my range.

I feel someone's eyes on me. I look to see my husband, who smiles at me, the same smile I spent the winter thinking about. The smile that drew me to leave my camp for his. I find myself smiling back.

I hear heavy breathing to the left of me and see Red Hawk crouched over, breathing hard.

"Swift Fox, his men, Custer's men, they are not coming for him," she pants out. I look at my husband; his grin widens. He stands and makes for the chiefs who are gathered talking. I follow him; they pause, looking at us. I hear Red Hawk behind us.

"Red Hawk says Custer's men aren't coming," Swift Fox says.

The chiefs look at my husband as though they hadn't heard him right.

"How do you know?" Sitting Bull asks.

"I caught a scout running from us. He says he was with Bloody Knife and a white man named Reno. They have retreated to a man named Benteen who is Custer's enemy. He is not leaving the safety of their ridge, some distance and on the other side of the river. He also said there are two other great white men, like Custer, who are coming here in two days' time, looking for us," Red Hawk answers, her breath now more even.

"Where is the scout now?" Sitting Bull asks.

"We tied him to a tree," she says.

I watch as Red Hawk unties a pair of moccasins from her belt and throws them to the chief. As they land, I see that they are bloody and that the feet are still in them.

"He won't get far if he gets out of my ties," she says.

The chiefs are all looking at the ridge, watching Custer organize his men. At the top, he is preparing to make a stand.

"What do we do then? I don't think we can defeat all of them, if more like Custer are coming. I don't think we can hide from them and not be brought to the agencies," Gall says, not taking his eyes from the men we are chasing.

I look around; they have lost half of the men that they started with, blue bodies scattering the hills.

"I never thought we would win; I only thought we would die trying," Sitting Bull says, his words sinking into us, something we all know in our hearts. I think of my life. Of wandering in a shrinking forest, game, berries, fish, growing less and less every year, and illnesses, illnesses we have never seen, rotting us from the inside out. I realize for the first time what it is like to live; before I only knew what it was like to try not to die.

"Today is a good day to die," my husband says, watching the white men try to rescue their wounded.

Our warriors fire at them, their blood splattering on the earth before they fall to her.

"Today is a good day to die," I repeat, raising my carbine and shooting one of the men scrambling toward another man screaming.

I watch him fall.

"Today is a good day to die!" Crazy Horse screams.

I watch as he bolts down the hill, his hair flying behind him, fast as lightning. I look at my husband, my carbine lowered.

"I love you," he says to me above the running of the warriors, the trills, and gunshots.

"I loved you from the first time I saw you; I came back to you," I tell him.

He smiles a sad smile at me.

"This is where we all end," he says, looking toward the warriors scaling the ridge.

The white men are trying to form a defensive line against them. I admire Custer; he must know he is going to die. Like us, he is going to fight, a warrior.

"Today is a good day to die," I say, looking at my husband.

"Let's kill Custer," Swift Fox says to me, smiling. He reaches for my hand. I transfer my carbine to my left and take it. It feels as it always does—warm, strong, safe—and we run down the ridge together.

Bullets hit the earth around us as we make our way up the other side. I see a red feather on the ground. I stop and touch her head. She has been shot through the eye. I think of her wife and children. Around me I see bodies of feathers and earth mixed with the blue soldiers. I feel a hand on my shoulder. I look at my husband.

"Look, they are making it through," he says.

I see the chiefs' headdresses and Coyote Run's silver breastplate hopping over a boulder. I hear the crack of rifles and screaming, not of war but of terror. I stand, my husband reaches for my hand, I take it, and we continue running up the hill. We come to the boulders, and my husband lets go and hops over them like a deer over a bush. For me, it is less graceful. I am out of air as I flop on the boulders with my stomach, praying our baby is fine and struggling to get the rest of me to the other side. I land on my feet and look around.

There are bodies everywhere—half are shooting and half are fighting hand to hand, just like the Sun Dance. Dust is being kicked up every which way, making a cloud. The white men try to dance the dance of death with us. Thunder dreamers and storm splitters cut open fast, too fast for them. I see my husband; I see him dancing with a man that makes my body grow cold. He looks like Custer but less rugged, younger, and in a full army uniform. I know his face—it is older, but it is burned into my memory. He had entered my family's tent, he raped my mother, they had called him Tom.

I watch as my husband raises his war club and spins. Tom Custer knows he is going to do this. He lets him and then ducks. Once my husband is facing him again, Tom brings the butt of his rifle up hard into the bottom of his chin. I can see that Swift Fox is stunned, and I raise my carbine to my shoulder. Something bites into my right arm, and the pain is searing. I see it is a cut. A man is getting ready to cut me again. He is beautiful. I have never seen eyes like his, the sadness rimmed in thick black lashes. The knife is on the end of his gun. I pull the trigger, my arm barely able to hold my carbine's weight. His face is gone. I have never killed anything that close before, and I stand there staring at him, his one eye looking up at the blue sky. I feel his blood and face on my face and chest.

I look back to my husband, but he is gone. My eyes search frantically. I feel panic swelling in my chest. I see Coyote Run standing above the body of Tom Custer, smashing his skull in. I feel myself grow full of fear as I scan the chaos for my husband. Through the dust, everything looks the same. I finally see him, his silver breastplate catching what sunlight had made its way through the cloud. I see the black hat and buckskin fringe. They are both fighting each other with war clubs. I hear fewer and fewer gun shots. Bullets must be running out. My legs push toward them. I run through the dust and watch as Custer swings hard at my husband, his hammer catching the left side of Swift Fox's face. My husband staggers from the blow. Custer pulls out a revolver from his side and fires it into my husband's forehead. I feel myself screaming. Custer turns and looks at me as I raise my carbine to my shoulder and pull the trigger. Silence, no bullet leaves my chamber. The general looks amused and raises his club.

I run faster; I run harder. I remember the bear; I remember my brother; I remember where I came from. I hit him hard in the nose with the butt of the carbine, just like what I saw Tom do to Swift Fox. I throw my carbine and pull out my gunstock club from my back. I lock eyes with Custer. They are blue like the sky. The general is ready, and our weapons clash violently, brutally, with force I was never met with during the dance. I swing my gunstock club with an anger I have kept buried in me for a long time, an anger I didn't even know I had.

The general staggers back, blood pouring out of his mouth. I throw my club. Custer's eyes can't focus, and he clumsily feels for his revolver tucked in at his waist. I get there first. I see two of them, and I pull both guns out. I can feel one is light and drop it; I cock the other one and shoot him in the heart. He stops, reaching for his chest, confused. His fingers clutch the buckskin on his chest. The blood doesn't pour out right away. He falls to his knees, and I shoot him in the forehead.

I close my eyes, silence surrounds me. I breath in dust and hear the sound of wood cracking on bone. I open my eyes and see that General Custer is on his back, his eyes wide open to the sky. I feel something to my right and look. Crazy Horse's hand drops from my shoulder; he is standing looking at me, his war club at his side, blood splattered across his lightning bolt. *Thunder dreamers*, I think.

He slowly raises the arm holding his club and lets out a trill that sounds like a growl, like thunder rolling over the plains. I look away and around me. The white men, the soldiers of blue—none of them are left standing. I watch as they are stripped. I hear the chant of women and children; I am surprised to hear their voices and look behind me. They are making their way up the hill, singing the song of death, ripping limbs, smashing skulls, piercing ears. They won't be able to take them into their next life, that's what Swift Fox told me. I look at my husband who, like Custer, lies on the ground, fading back to the earth we once all came from. I see Coyote Run ripping off one of Tom Custer's arms. I close my eyes. My time here is done.

CHAPTER 29

▲▲▲▲

I RUN MY FINGERS THOUGH HIS HAIR; it is soft, like black feathers. His small body moves up and down on my chest and stomach with each of my breaths. *With his fists in balls and his eyes squeezed shut, he reminds me of a chipmunk, or more like a fox,* I think to myself. The dead of night surrounds us, and it is totally silent; we are together alone in the darkness. I gently sit up, cradling him in my arms. The fire has burned down enough so I don't have to worry about sparks burning him, but not so low that we are cold. Swift Fox, that is what I named him, after his father. I carefully put him into the nest of furs I made for him. I watch him squirm a little, then relax. I smile, watching him suck at his fist in his sleep. Even at just a week old, he looks like a perfect blend of the two of us.

I pull on my hide tunic and reach for the gray wolf hide my husband had given me to keep a year ago. *It seems like a lifetime ago,* I think to myself, wrapping the fur around my shoulders. The winter has been milder than some, but the cold is still bitter. I close my eyes, trying not to think of him. It is the only thing I've thought about for the past ten months. I think back to that day, the Sun Dance before, then Hi-es-tzie, Custer. I close my eyes, and I see everything. I open my eyes and look at our son. I wonder if I ever truly understood love until now.

I feel myself standing. I look at the lodge I have made for us. I had found Sha at Red Cloud's Agency. She had already registered all of us. As Sioux, we were to be settled in what they call now South Dakota. Will we remember what it used to be, or will their lies coat us like a rock buried beneath water? Now we were the Great White Chief's Indians, and he wanted us to drink coffee and eat beef that only he could give us. Grow a crop, that is what the man running the agency said. I feel a tear run down my face. I close my eyes and step blindly into the night, our tent's flap caressing my face as the cold hits me. I feel small snowflakes landing on my cheeks. I open my eyes to the late night and listen to the snow crunching beneath the mukluks Red Hawk and Shadows Fall gave me. Shadows Fall said she was going with Sitting Bull to Canada. She had wanted me to go with her, but I couldn't. This was my home, even if I was to be a prisoner in it. The earth still sang her song to me, and I wanted to hear it. I hear a wolf howl as I make my way through the lodges, most of which are in darkness. Some still have the warm glow of a fire. I bend my head back and howl. I howl for my son; I howl for my dead husband; I howl for my lost people. I hear the wolves cry with me.

I find myself weaving through the frozen trees. There is a river nearby. A deep part I had seen in the daylight had thin ice. They had been ice fishing on it earlier in the week. I see it where I had left it, a rock the size of my head at the base of a spruce that reminded me of my brother and the games we used to play. I think of my mother sitting in the tall grass weaving baskets, her fingers so slender, deft, and quick, and my father smiling and sharpening his axe. I walk toward the rock and find myself singing a song the women who had been there, who had seen what I had seen, brought back to the agency with them.

"Long Hair, Long Hair,

I was short of guns, and you brought me many,
Long Hair, Long Hair,
I was short of horses, and you brought me many."

I stop singing and feel someone looking at me. I look behind me; under the first glow of the rising sun, I see Sha some distance from me. I pause, waiting for her to come to me, to tell me I am foolish. I feel the words come from my mouth in a scream.

"Today is a good day to die!" I call to her.

The words are carried to her on the wind. She looks at me and raises her hand. I raise my hand. Somehow she knows, and I know she knows. I feel myself bending and picking up the rock, straining under the weight. I make my way down the gentle slope to the river, carrying the rock, pressing it to my body to keep hold of it. At the river's edge, I pause and take a deep gasp of air and let it go in an icy breath. I step onto the ice. I go to the middle where it is transparent, and I see where the holes have been made. I see something out of the corner of my eye, the flicker of a small person, my brother, I think. A sad smile reaches my lips.

I toss my rock onto the thin ice that has formed over the fishing hole, and it crashes through with a crack, splashing icy water to my feet. I look ahead of me to the other side of the river, to the sparse trees and the grasslands I know are beyond that and try to imagine what it is going to look like now that it is not ours. I think of Deadwood, the mud, the death. This earth is no longer mine. I have become a stranger to it. I only want to hear the forest talk and follow animal footprints. I've become something I don't recognize, and I want to kill them for taking him from me, for taking all of this from me, my family, my land, myself.

I step into the hole; the cold shoots up my legs. I close my eyes to it all. For all I see is violence, all I feel is pain and suffering, and all I hear is hate.

CHAPTER 30

▲▲▲▲

THE UNITED STATES GOVERNMENT STOLE THE BLACK Hills from the
Sioux, as they stole land from every tribe across North America,
through treaties and revised treaties, lies and outright military force,
or starvation. They forcibly relocated the Sioux in 1877. In 1980, the
United States Supreme Court agreed that the Black Hills were wrong-
fully taken, but instead of offering the land back, they gave the Sioux
$104 million, set aside as compensation for their loss.

The nine tribes of the Great Sioux Nation have refused the money,
stating that the land was never for sale. The money is now valued at
1.3 billion dollars, and the nine tribes offered this financial compen-
sation for such a grave spiritual loss have yet to withdraw a dollar.

Hoka hey.

ABOUT THE AUTHOR

▲▲▲▲

ANGIE ELITA NEWELL belongs to the Liidlii Kue First Nations from the Dehcho, the place where two rivers meet. Trained as a historian and holding degrees in English literature, creative writing, and history, a mother to daughters as they wander the world, always listening to stories, honoring the ancestors, revering the truth that we are all connected, every plant, being, and creature; the only thing that will ever matter is love.